FALLEN

Fiona McCready

Published by New Generation Publishing in 2015

Copyright © Fiona McCready 2015

First Edition

The author asserts the moral right under the Copyright, Designs and Patents Act 1988 to be identified as the author of this work.

All Rights reserved. No part of this publication may be reproduced, stored in a retrieval system or transmitted, in any form or by any means without the prior consent of the author, nor be otherwise circulated in any form of binding or cover other than that which it is published and without a similar condition being imposed on the subsequent purchaser.

www.newgeneration-publishing.com

All my thanks

Muchas gracias to Eva for the peace and quiet she gave me to write. Thank you to Lesley for her excellent suggestions and proofreading, and her patience in correcting the same errors I make time and time again! One day I might learn how to use a comma. A huge thanks to Crystal for the cover design that is, once again, a piece of art.

Thank you to pilots Tim and Chris for helping to make my plane crash an authentic one. Thanks to all my friends for their encouragement and the common question: "when's the book ready?"

And lastly, a mammoth-sized THANK YOU to Simon who read, re-read, and helped hugely with this book.

For Simon,
Just the way you are

Today - Friday July 12th, 2013

07:29
On board the AS636, Aeropuerto Barajas, Madrid

The two women sitting at the emergency exit are very different from one another: one wears flip-flops, the other stilettos; one lives in a crumbling bedsit in Madrid, the other in a peppermint mews in London; one is deep in love, and the other once was. Despite their differences, they have one thing very much in common – they are about to die.

Like these two strangers sitting together on a flight from Madrid to London, there will be two moments in all of our lives that sit together, but could not be more different from one another. One of these moments is full of all the things you treasure; lying on summer grass, that joke that always makes you laugh, rain on your skin, the taste of a ripe berry, the sea on your toes, the touch of a lover, the crackle of fire, a deep breath on a tall hill, autumn leaves, a child's giggle, the sun on your face, a full heart, everything that makes your life full and your face smile. This is your last moment. The next moment contains nothing. Emptiness. These two moments will sit next to each other as two strangers.

If you are lucky, life will disappear without warning, smashed like a dropped glass of water. If you are unlucky, life will trickle slowly away, and you will have time to consider all the things you love and are losing. All the fullness that is emptying. But whether your disappearance is instantaneous or dawdling, whether you are black, white, old, young, economy or first-class, there will always be these two moments perched next to each other; one full and one empty. It is at this transition for all the passengers on the AS636 that the story starts.

07:35
Flight deck of AS636, Aeropuerto Barajas, Madrid

"Normally I'd flip a coin, but with the fog we have today…" says Philip.

"That's fine, you fly." Dave takes the right hand seat next to the Captain. He looks at the whiteness out of his side window. "You think we've got enough visibility?"

Philip rolls his head from side to side. "Difficult to tell."

Dave performs a series of checks, clicks and adjustments, and Philip speaks into the public address.

"Good morning, this is your Captain, Philip Bollo, speaking. On behalf of the entire crew it's my pleasure to welcome you onto this AS636 flight to London Heathrow. Up here in the flight deck with me I have First Officer Dave Harris. Your purser for today's flight is Janette, and she is joined by colleagues Wendy and Brianne in economy, and by Kevin and Shelly in business class. Once out of this morning's fog we anticipate a smooth flight as we pass over the Pyrenees, central France, and the English Channel to finally make our approach over the city of London, where you'll get some great views. Flight time approximately two hours twenty. Janette will shortly be showing you a safety video which I ask you to pay careful attention to. If there is anything you require on today's flight, please don't hesitate to ask your nearest member of cabin crew. I wish you all a comfortable flight today and I'll update you on our progress once in the air."

Dave speaks into the APC. "AS636, with information Echo, request pushback."

A female voice with a strong Spanish accent crackles into the flight deck. "AS636. Push approved. Face north."

The two pilots make final checks before Philip taxis the aircraft out onto the runway and awaits clearance.

"You watch *El Clasico* last night Dave?"

Dave beams. "Saw it live."

"Really?" Philip turns from the foggy morning to look at his co-pilot. It's the first time he's looked at him properly and he's surprised by how young he looks, or maybe Philip is just getting old. "You were at Camp Nou?"

Dave nods. "One of the stewardesses from my flight yesterday is going out with a guy at the Embassy. Got us all tickets, in a corporate box."

"Looks like I flew with the wrong crew," laughs Philip. "I saw the game from my hotel bed with room service on my lap."

The two men talk the universal male language of near misses, blind linesmen, and unjust goals for a few minutes, while preparing the plane for take off.

Philip squints into the oblivion on the other side of the windscreen and side windows. "What do you think we have? 300?"

"Let's find out," says Dave as he keys his radio. "AS636, request RVRs."

"AS636 request for RVRs. 250, 250, 250."

Philip nods. "I'm happy with that." The crackling voice has made something about the fog clear for him. She continues.

"Cleared line-up, runway 14 right."

Philip manoeuvres the plane onto the runway. Dave stretches his back and conceals a yawn. He tries to remember whether Karen and Eliza have a play date that afternoon. He hopes so, he could do with a nap.

"AS636 clear for take off," comes the voice through the radio.

Philip grips the thrust lever, looks at all the engine instruments and begins to put pressure on the lever and the engines. The AS636, five crew, two pilots and 160 passengers accelerate along the tarmac.

"80 knots," says Dave.

Philip checks his air speed indicator and looks out the window. "Check."

The aircraft gathers speed and the engines roar.

"V1," says Dave when they reach 125 knots, Philip takes his hand off the thrust lever.

The plane, and everyone in it, is now committed to take off, no going back.

"Rotate," says Dave.

"Rotate," repeats Philip. The nose of the plane lifts like a hound catching a scent and the aircraft rises into the fog.

"Positive climb," says Philip and, after a few moments, "Gear up." Dave raises the landing gear and the plane continues to rise through the fog. Beyond the windscreen the world is bleached, and Dave sits slightly forward in his chair, as though the extra centimetres will give him an advantage against the curtain of white in front of him. "We should be clear of this very soon," says Philip and, as his last word emerges from his mouth, they emerge from the fog. Before Dave even opens his mouth to respond, a flash of black appears, at the same time as a thud on the windscreen.

The plane is flying at 160 miles per hour and the flock of geese is flying towards them at 40 miles per hour. The moment that the plane sees the birds and the birds see the plane lasts an instant, an instant that decides all their futures.

Both men in the flight deck are sitting a few inches taller. Philip's view is obscured now not by fog, but by the remnants of a large bird.

"Damn. Did the engines take a hit?" asks Philip. Dave is looking intently at the instruments in front of him, but before he can speak the plane itself answers the question. It swings steeply down to the right and Philip clutches the controls and pushes his foot on the left pedal.

"Engine failure in the right engine," says Dave. His lethargy has left him and his eyes are scanning the flight deck. The control panel is buzzing and flashing; every gauge and monitor screaming its displeasure.

"OK standby." Philip reaches for the red button to his right and the autopilot kicks in to counteract the yaw. The plane rights itself and takes the pressure from Philip's hands and feet. "Is it severe failure?" He speaks loudly to be heard over the din of the alarms.

"I think so. Yes, we've lost the right engine and vibration rates are up in the left."

Philip has started to sweat, droplets are forming on his hairline and his white shirt sticks to his back and stomach. "Radio it in."

Dave speaks to the anonymous woman, "Madrid tower, Mayday, Mayday, Mayday, AS636 engine failure on take off."

A loud crackle precedes the response. "AS636 Mayday acknowledged at time zero seven, forty one. Identify your failure."

Dave and Philip ignore the radio and focus on their immediate situation. The plane continues to climb on one engine.

"What's happening in the surviving engine?" asks Philip.

Dave checks. "Vibrations increasing."

"OK, we'll land back in Madrid. Get the radar vector for downwind."

The radio has been tediously repeating its request to 'identify your failure' and now Dave speaks to it.

"AS636. Right engine has failed, left engine is vibrating. We're coming back to land. Request radar vector for longest runway into wind."

A crackling moment passes.

"AS636. Turn left now heading 320."

Dave sets the autopilot, heading to 320, the left wing dips and the plane begins to turn in a wide curve.

Philip takes a deep breath and gets onto the PA system.

"Hello, this is Captain Bollo speaking. As I'm sure you've noticed, we haven't made the best of starts today. You will have felt the aircraft sway to the right and the reason for this is that we hit a flock of birds. The right engine was damaged and has been shut down as a safety precaution, but the plane is running well on the left engine and we are going to be returning to Madrid airport to land, it will be about five minutes to landing. Please pay close attention to the cabin crew and keep your safety belts fastened."

As the plane continues through its gentle arc to the left, it lurches sharply into its turn and the nose of the plane drops.

"Shit!" Say both pilots in unison. "We've lost them both," shouts Dave over the sudden cacophony of alerts that is ringing out from the controls. The plane judders, its wings unsure of what they are supposed to be doing.

Philip instinctively grabs the controls. His hands have no effect with the autopilot engaged, but they need to do something.

"Try and get them started again," says Philip, his voice full of tension.

Dave reaches for the fuel control switch, he cuts off the fuel and then pushes it back to run. "Nothing's happening, they're not starting."

"Keep trying. I'm going to fly this myself," shouts Philip. He takes the autopilot out and uses the controls to dip the nose. Some airflow returns to the wings, reducing the shaking, but still to a level worse than anything either pilot has felt in simulated emergencies. Screaming can be heard from behind the doors. "I'm going to fly away from the city. We need to land as soon as possible. We're heading west. I think the city ends in a few km. Can you remember? Is it flat here? Is it flat?"

Dave has only flown this route once and that was yesterday, coming in to Madrid. He wishes he'd paid more attention, but he was too excited at the prospect of corporate tickets to the football.

"I don't know."

The plane shudders back into the fog and the two pilots are blind to their futures.

"Keep trying the engines," demands Philip. "And get on the radio."

Philip swallows hard. His teeth are pushed together, his heart is racing and a large vein in his neck throbs with blood. Every cell in his body is invested in its own individual future, trying to help Philip make the right decisions at the right time.

Dave wipes some sweat from his hairline and again flicks the fuel control switch off. His finger rests on the switch for a few moments and trembles against it.

"Come on, come on," he mutters. Then he switches it back on and curses the engine that gives him no response.

"AS636, we've lost both engines. Intention to land as soon as possible," he says into the radio.

The robotic female voice confirms this action as though it were an announcement of a shopping list. "AS636, intention to land as soon as possible. Confirm your position. Confirm your position." The controlled voice seems out of place in the flight deck of a falling plane. The control panel is a catastrophic disco of flashing lights and buzzing alarms, and both pilots are trying to stay calm.

Philip grips the control column, attempting to ignore the impulse to pull the plane up from its downward fall. Keeping air molecules moving over the aluminium of the wings means keeping hopes and people alive.

"The fog may clear at a few hundred feet," he shouts over the noise. "We won't have time to change course. One last try on the engines, then do the call."

They are speeding towards land they can't see and the screaming from behind the cockpit door is getting louder. Dave is repeating "Oh God, Oh God," under his breath. He makes one last-ditch attempt to start the engines. Please start. Please start. It fails. The plane itself begins to panic as an alert sounds, "Too low gear. Too low gear. Pull

13

up. Pull up." The Air Traffic Controller repeats herself over and over, "AS636 do you read? AS636 do you read?" The ears of the two pilots are saturated with sounds of imminent disaster, but for a few more seconds their eyes are shielded from the corresponding view. Then the blindfold of fog is removed and the earth presents itself. Fields, open fields are below them, and the pilots are so close to them that they can see the smudges of red poppies at the field edges. The glimpse of open land is a glimpse of possibility.

"This is an emergency, this is an emergency, BRACE, BRACE, BRACE," Dave shouts through the PA into the cabin. Philip begins to lift the nose of the plane and the two pilots see the beginnings of blue sky on the horizon.

They are about 100 feet above a yellow field. It is strangely cheerful in colour as though the sun were reaching it through the fog. Beyond the field is a collection of barns and a large farmhouse.

"Ahead! Ahead!" shouts Dave. "Will we clear them?"

"Yes, yes," says Philip, his voice desperate.

Behind the pilots, 32 rows with 160 passengers are braced for their lives to end or to be renewed by a miraculous escape. Their lives hang in the balance, and it is this balance that is tipped, with less than a second to spare, by the decrepit roof of a barn. The farmer had thought about destroying the barn a few years ago, but there didn't seem to be any point in doing so; it would come down on its own in time.

*

Above the field the fog is clearing and, if anyone could see through the flames and plumes of black smoke, they would see a glimpse of colour. There will always be blue sky if you look high enough.

08:23
7 The Stables, South Kensington, London

Tom is trying not to burn toast at the same time as trying to plait his daughter's hair. Katy keeps turning her head to gaze at the blue sky out the window and, as a result, her two plaits are far from symmetrical.

"Do you have your PE kit Miles?" Tom shouts above the television.

Miles looks around, his mouth full of Cheerios. "No."

"Well, go and get it. As soon as Katy's had her toast, we're out of here."

Miles switches off the television. "Where is it?"

"For goodness sake Miles, you know where your PE kit's kept, it's in the… oh shit!"

Two sets of wide eyes glare at Tom. "Daddy!"

Tom finishes tying one of Katy's wonky plaits and rubs his knotted forehead.

"It's still in the washing machine Miles. Sorry buddy, I forgot to put it in the dryer."

"Daddy! I have athletics today."

"Can't you wear Katy's kit?"

Both children glare at him again and shout in unison, "No!"

Miles brings his empty bowl to the kitchen and stands on tiptoes to place it into the farmhouse sink muttering, "I can't wear a girl's PE kit. Yuck."

The phone rings and Tom exhales loudly, just when he thinks things can't get any worse, a voice on the end of the line tells him that they can.

09:23
14 Carrer Lleo, Al Raval, Barcelona

Angelo opens the window and squints at the sun. He lifts papers, tissues, clothes that could be rags and rags that could be clothes. He is searching for a vessel, any vessel. His head is pounding and his eyes hurt. He is considering emptying one of the jam jars filled with yellow water and paintbrushes, when he spies his wine glass from the night before. He pours the dregs away, before filling the glass with coffee. Angelo sits on the floor, the only clear space, with his flute of black medicine, and breathes deeply. The fresh air from the open window and caffeine begin to revive him. He is deep in thought about the colour yellow and why he is using so much of it, when there is a knock at the door.

Señora Carmen, his landlady, who never makes it past the second floor, stands in front of him. She is not out of breath, which means she must have stood there for some time. He tries to shield her, with his oversized shirt, from the hovel behind him, but she shakes her head. The mess doesn't matter.

"Angelo," she says, her voice even croakier than usual. "Let's go inside."

08:28
7 The Stables, South Kensington, London

"Steph, I can't really talk right now. I've got to get the kids to school, and then I'm picking up Beth from the airport. One minute." He holds the receiver to his chest. "Katy, go grab your school bag and get your shoes on. Miles take your PE kit out of the washer, it'll be dry by the time you have class this afternoon. We can ask Miss Bridgeman to hang it by the windows."

"But Dad…"

"Just do it." He gets back on the phone. "So, if you called for Beth, she'll be back here at about 10.30, can you call back then? I've got to go…"

"Tom. Tom, listen to me." Steph's voice is slow and calculated. "Beth won't be back at 10.30."

"Is she delayed?" Tom is confused.

There are a few moments of silence, and Tom wonders whether Steph is still there.

"Tom, sweetheart." Her voice cracks. "There's been an accident. Beth's dead."

09:31
14 Carrer Lleo, Al Raval, Barcelona

Angelo knows he's in trouble, he owes her three months rent. He reluctantly stands aside for her to come in and then clears some space on the sofa. He gestures for her to sit down but she swiftly shakes her head. God he's in serious trouble, is she going to evict him?

"Señora Carmen, sit down, let me make you a coffee." Charm doesn't come easy with a hangover, but Angelo forces a smile.

She shakes her head. "You sit down."

Angelo obeys, unsure of what's going on.

She looks down at her tights, which have formed rings above her woollen slippers. The sun is shining on her, highlighting all the lines and wrinkles that usually hide in the darkness of the hallway. Angelo thinks she would make a great painting and tries to commit the details to memory.

"Your girlfriend," she says, still keeping her eyes on her wrinkled tights. "Maria."

"What did you say?" Angelo pulls himself out of the mental painting and back into his studio.

"Maria. She was flying to London this morning – yes?"

"Yes, I told you yesterday." He wonders what his batty landlady wants with Maria.

"From Barcelona?"

Angelo sighs. "No, from Madrid. Señora, listen, I know you think she spends too much time here, but she lives in Madrid, she has a place there, you can't charge us extra rent just because she spends the odd night."

The old woman looks at Angelo with watery eyes and then looks away.

"The AirStar flight from Madrid to London this morning?" she says.

"Yes."

There is angry shouting from outside in the street. They both look to the window then back at each other.

"It crashed. No one survived."

How Tom and Beth ended

5 days ago
08:17, Sunday July 7th, 2013
7 The Stables, South Kensington, London

Beth had been awake a while already, savouring the rare silence, and gazing out the bedroom window. Over the last few weeks she'd insisted on sleeping with the curtains open - "it makes for a more natural awakening," she told Tom. Like most things she suggested, he yielded easily, despite the fact that he was a sensitive sleeper whose sleep was conditional on strict factors, complete darkness being one of them. He now slept in a Virgin Atlantic eye mask, together with his Marks and Spencer Boxers, a SpongeBob T-shirt the kids had given him, and his trademark socks, marked with each day of the week.

Beth turned over to look at her husband, but with the Virgin Atlantic logo sitting at a jaunty angle across his face, and a line of saliva forming a dark well on the pillow, she turned back to the window for a better vista. It still wasn't much of a view; the pristine tiled roof of the house opposite, topped by sky, but it was still a view.

Tom woke to the familiar rumblings of footsteps along the corridor. Before their tumultuous entrance he lifted his eye mask, located his wife in the mist of a new day and kissed her shoulder.

"Morning sweetheart," he said.

"Good morning."

The gap between 'good' and 'morning' was broken by the door hitting the chest of drawers, and Miles and Katy bounding into the room and onto the bed. Tom sat up in mock surprise.

"Beth, we've been invaded by monkeys. What shall we do?"

Beth took one last look into the blue, before turning over with a smile.

"Well, I don't know. How on earth do we get rid of monkeys in the bedroom?"

"By taking them to the zoo?" suggested Miles, an answer that was both very astute and also top of his list of things to do.

Tom smiled at his wife. "Well, that's always an option. But, well, I always think that monkeys are better off in the wild. I think we should release these two… out of the window!"

The children squealed and Tom reached out and grabbed a leg.

"I've got one," he yelled in triumph. "It's a wild one, just look at those ferocious teeth."

Miles bore his teeth in what he hoped was a fierce snarl, revealing a gap at the front.

"Shit!" said Beth. Three sets of eyes looked at her in surprise.

"Mummy!" said Katy.

"What's wrong?" asked Tom.

"Nothing, nothing," said Beth, slipping out of bed and leaving the room.

Tom attacked his two monkeys until Beth returned. She stood at the door, her dark hair forming an unlucky horseshoe round her face.

"Miles, did the tooth fairy visit?" she asked.

Miles stopped mid-scream, his eyes dropped and he prodded his gummy gap with his finger. "No, she didn't come mummy."

"Are you sure? Maybe you should check again? Sometimes she hides her gifts very well."

Miles ran off down the corridor with his older sister trailing after him. Screams of excitement were heard from the next room. "She came! She came!"

Tom looked at Beth. "You forgot?"

She nodded her head, trying to appear nonchalant.

"But you went in last night specifically to put the money there." Tom was confused.

Beth went through to the en-suite bathroom and let the water run. The noise meant she could ignore Tom. She couldn't tell him that the tooth fairy had forgotten her duties because she was busy crying in the corner, listening to the gentle snores of Miles and Katy.

*

All of Tom's attentions, his time and his love, were devoted to his family and ensuring they lived in a happy home. His mathematical mind was reputed to be the best in London when it came to risk analysis and, as a result, he'd moved from company to company over the years, each move giving him more money for fewer hours. Now he was able to take the kids to school and pick them up every day while still earning an easy six figures from home.

Beth didn't need to work, but she chose to and, unlike Tom, it kept her away from the home all day, most evenings and some weekends. As New Business Director for a top international advertising agency, she worked at least double the hours of her husband and spent chunks of time at the agency's international offices, mostly Paris, Madrid, Berlin and New York. From Tom's point of view, he couldn't understand why she persevered at the job. For the last few months she had been downright miserable about it, returning from each business trip in a guilty slump as she listened to what Tom and the kids had been up to.

Two months ago Miles had won first place in the 100m sprint at his sports day, while Beth was on a weeklong trip to Berlin for a global pitch. As she walked through the door, Miles threw himself and his plastic medal at her.

"Mummy! Mummy! Look what I've got!" he yelled into the folds of her hair.

While Miles was busy salivating on her neck, admiring his own medal and rambling about his triumph, Tom came out of the kitchen and saw his wife's face, crumpled in sadness and gripping her son tightly. Tom approached her, gave her a kiss on the cheek and rubbed her back.

"Welcome home," he said with a smile.

Later that evening when the kids had been tucked in, he put his arm around her, as she read her book on the sofa.

"There'll be plenty more," he said to her.

"Sorry?" she said.

"Sports days. There'll be plenty more, and more medals I'm sure. He's a winner like his mum." He smiled at her and she leant into him.

"I know," she said. "But this was his first. I should have been here."

"You had business sweetheart. You're great at your job and you're great at being a mum. It's difficult being that great."

She mustered a smile. It quickly disappeared and she looked up at him. "And what about being your wife? You think I'm great at that?"

In all honesty, she was pretty poor at that; his wife had become an occasional shadow to him. Work had meant she was hardly around and, when she was, she was so exhausted that she seemed to trail along after the family, not adding anything, just being there.

"Of course. You're a great wife. You're my great wife." Tom hated conflict.

Since that conversation things had improved, or at least shown the promise of improvement. He had no idea why, or what provoked her decision, but Beth had decided to quit her job.

"It's just too much," she told him. "All this travelling, these long hours, it's not worth it. I don't need to do it." Her words were resolute but her tone had been the opposite, unsure.

"No, sweetheart. You don't. But it's your decision, I know your work means a lot to you."

Once again, Beth wondered where the man she first met had disappeared to, when had he been replaced by this diplomat?

"My family means more," she said, looking out the window. She couldn't look him in the eye and her voice was full of sadness.

He squeezed her shoulder.

"Well, I can't wait to have you at home more."

She looked at him with gloomy eyes. He felt for her, he knew it was a big decision, a huge change for her, she had always worked, always been driven, always been a success. He pulled her into his arms. Beth smelled the lavender of their washing powder in his cashmere chest. He always smelled so clean.

"The kids are going to be over the moon," he said.

She nodded into his jumper and he held her tighter.

*

She showered, dried her hair, and spent a few minutes painting a happy face in lipstick and eyeliner.

Downstairs Tom was cooking breakfast; always a grand affair on Sundays, and the kids were watching cartoons. She squeezed his shoulder, poured herself a glass of water and sipped it slowly, looking out the window.

Beth spent a lot of time recently staring out of windows, but Tom mistook it today for a desire to go out.

"How about we go to the seaside?" he asked her. He meant to put the proposal to her quietly, but Katy whipped around on the sofa, like a puppy at the sound of its lead.

"The seaside? Yippee! Miles, we're going to the seaside!"

Miles jumped up, the adventures of Ben Ten instantly forgotten. He started jogging on the spot frantically, a habit he had acquired recently when his excitement was too much to express in his limited vocabulary. The behavior always made Beth and Tom laugh, and for a moment the scene was that of the perfect family; Miles convulsing in anticipation, Katy giggling at her brother's antics, and Tom and Beth wrapped in each other's arms and smiles.

*

As Tom helped Miles out of his pyjamas, and struggled to get his wiggling limbs into T-shirt and shorts, Beth searched for the kids' sunhats.

"We can't be too late back this evening," she said over her shoulder.

"Huh?" said Tom, distracted.

"I need to prepare for this week's meetings. Francois wants a status report tomorrow and we're going over finances Tuesday. And I'm taking the first flight in the morning."

Tom left Miles to struggle with his own socks and came to stand behind Beth. He squeezed her tense shoulders.

"It's your last trip sweetheart, I think you can relax a little."

Her shoulders remained taut. "That's *exactly* why I can't relax. I want to leave everything in a good place, so the new BD can pick things up easily."

"What was his name again?"

Beth thought a moment. Good question, what was his name again? "Erm, the new BD? Pete, Pete Wheeler from CPG."

"Well, if Pete's half as talented as you, he'll be just fine."

"A-ha! Found them." Beth turned around with two little sunhats in her hand, she placed the one patterned with sailing boats onto Miles' head, squeezing it into place. "Gosh Miles, you've grown. What a big head you have."

"All the better for thinking with," he said. "That's not my sunhat." He shook his head and pulled off the hat, dropping it on the floor.

"Yes it is darling, the one with cherries is Katy's."

"No," he said stubbornly, crossing his arms.

Tom turned around from packing a beach bag. "He's right Beth. I bought him a new one when that one got too small."

"You did?" said Beth quietly.

"Yeah, a few months back, I've got it here." He raised a navy blue Lacoste sunhat from the bag. "Ready troops?"

"Ready!" squealed Miles, jumping from the bed and sprinting out of the room.

*

Brighton was a treat for everyone. The sun shone on them all day. They made sandcastles, paddled in the sea, chased mummy with seaweed, ate fish and chips, lost bagfuls of pennies in the arcade, listened to daddy screaming on the rollercoaster, ate melting ice creams, watched hippies on a tightrope, wandered through the lanes, bartered with an artist for a painting of beach huts, and watched a young student playing guitar under one of the arches.

Katy danced in front of the student's empty guitar case and Miles, never one to be outdone by his sister, jumped around like a little maniac. The busker was lanky and the skin was so stretched over his long fingers that it looked like a set of bones strumming the guitar strings. It seemed odd for such tuneful music to come from such awkward fingers. He sang through his greasy hair and ignored Miles and Katy.

"Do you remember when you had a gig in Brighton?" Beth's eyes shone as she looked up at Tom.

"A gig?" His eyes misted over in thought. Looking back to their early days together was like looking at two different people, two strangers. "God, that was a lifetime ago."

"But you remember?" Beth asked urgently.

"Yes, it was at some dive, oh what was it called, Cats or something like that."

"Alley Cats," she said and her eyes glowed.

"That was it, Alley Cats! We went along during the day to do a sound check, and there was that drunk in the corner who kept telling us he knew the secret of a happy life."

Beth laughed. "Simon the drunk with his big secret. But he wouldn't tell us what it was!"

"By the looks of it, it was whiskey."

Beth put her hand into his and squeezed. The memory of a sticky, dark bar was filling her with happiness. "I thought I was in love with you before then, but that night confirmed it for me."

"Really?" Tom looked away from the busker, and down at his wife. "Was it 'Love Light' that did it for you?"

Beth's eyes glowed as they looked back into his, and Tom's heart pumped faster. His wife hadn't looked at him that way for a long time, he'd forgotten how special her eyes could make him feel. She had beautiful wide eyes, a souvenir from Columbia that was passed from every mother to every daughter in the Franco family. Beth held his stare and Tom had a flash of memory. He remembered how deeply and quickly they had fallen in love all those years ago, how her brown eyes would stare into his as he sang to *her* alone, in a crowded room.

"You remembered," she whispered. "Where's your guitar now?"

Tom looked to the sky to try and locate his guitar, his long-lost friend, but was interrupted by Miles.

"Daddy! Mummy! He's playing the Peppa Pig song!"

The guitarist didn't look too happy that his original composition was being compared to a cartoon pig, and he glowered at Miles who was bouncing from foot to foot. His frown soon lifted as Tom dropped a fiver into his guitar case, "Keep on playing mate," he said. "You've got a talent. OK kids, let's go."

Miles and Katy howled their annoyance at having to leave, and the student pocketed the money. Of course he'd keep on playing. Music was his life. There was nothing that would take priority over his guitar.

On the ride home, Miles slept. He nodded off before Beth even finished buckling his safety belt. Katy watched the big wide world zoom past her window and cupped her hands around her nose and mouth.

Beth turned around in her seat. "What are you doing Katy?"

"My hands smell of sun cream, vinegar, and pennies," she said. "And I'm never going to wash them again."

"Why not?" Beth laughed. "That doesn't sound like a very nice smell."

"It isn't. But I don't want to forget today."

Beth beamed at her daughter, then looked to little Miles, open mouthed with the remnants of ice cream revealed beneath the folds of his neck. Then she turned to Tom. He had caught the sun, his nose was red and a deepened tan line peeped out from his T-shirt, exposed by his 'ten-to-two' grip on the steering wheel. She didn't need to look up at the sky on the journey home, she kept looking from one happy face to the next and, when she looked at herself in the tiny mirror, she realized that her face matched the others.

Two days ago
18:52, Wednesday July 10th, 2013
7 The Stables, London and an anonymous hotel somewhere in Paris

Beth Skyped with the family before the kids went to bed. She saw the fluff of Miles' freshly washed hair just peeping into the screen, she saw Katy's rosy-cheeked face and pink princess pyjamas, and Tom sitting between the two, his T-shirt dusted in talcum powder. She could almost smell the post-bath cleanliness.

Tom saw a miniature version of his wife in a small rectangle. She wore a simple white shirt and sat in front of an unremarkable cream wall. When he double clicked her nose, she filled the screen. Immediately, he noticed dark circles around her eyes and a paleness to her skin. Her last week on the job and she was clearly working herself too hard.

"Mummy!" shouted Miles and Katy in unison.

"Hello," she said. "Miles, I can't see you. Tom can you move the camera...OK, now I can't see daddy... OK that's better."

Miles was lifted onto Tom's lap, his feathery crown just tickling his daddy's chin.

"Mummy, at ballet class today we got our outfits for the show. Mine is pink with a white tutu, it's the same as Lola's, and Kitty's, and I have a matching scrunchie, but the tutu is too tight and Miss Huggins says it needs adjusting."

Miles was bored by the ballet chat, he leant back into his father and started picking his nose.

"Daddy says he's useless with a needle and thread, so can you do it for me?"

"Of course I can," said Beth with a smile, glad to be needed.

"Because it needs to be done before the dress rehearsal, which is next Tuesday, and…"

Tom interrupted, looking at the image of his wife with concern.

"Sweetheart, are you OK? You look tired."

Beth nodded too many times. "Yes, yes I'm fine. A little tired yes, but well, it's my last week, they've got to get their money's worth out of me haven't they? And Miles, what have you been doing at school? Miles! Stop picking your nose."

Miles had forgotten he was being watched. He snapped to attention and took his finger out of his nose.

"What?"

"I asked what did you do at school?" said the image of mummy.

"Erm," he concentrated hard on remembering. "We had music class, and I got the cymbal. We had to act like a storm and Mrs Pitman said I was very good to save my cymbal until right at the end when I made a big crash. She said it must have been difficult to have it in my hands and to wait until right at the end. I said it was like having a wee-wee, you have to wait until the right time to do it."

Everyone laughed but Miles, who remained very serious.

"Well, that's a good way of explaining it," said Beth. "You obviously have great patience and great musical talent, like your daddy."

Miles turned to his dad and asked him something. Beth listened with a smile as Tom explained what being patient meant. When he finished, both kids were nodding up at him. They were besotted with their father, they hung on his every word, like Beth had once done. Could she get back to that?

"Hey Tom," she said loudly at her laptop. He looked at her. "Do you think you can find your guitar?"

He looked doubtful.

"I'm sure the kids would love to see what a great musician you are."

"We would daddy," said Katy.

"I was never a great musician," he said looking at Katy. "It was just a stupid hobby."

"Can you play *Twinkle Twinkle* daddy?" asked Miles.

Tom laughed. "I've never played it before, but I'm sure I can learn."

"We can wait," said Miles. "We will be patient."

"But for tonight, daddy will just have to sing it for you," said Beth.

"And you mummy and you!" shouted Miles.

"I'm sorry Pickle. But I can't sing it tonight, I'm in a different country remember?"

"That doesn't matter," said Katy. "Please sing it for us."

"But I'm in the middle of a hotel lobby," said Beth looking around.

Miles turned to his daddy, who held the answers to all the world's questions. Before he was able to ask what a lobby was, Tom picked him up and put him on the floor. Beth got a close-up of her son's button nose, then the laptop was lifted beyond Miles and to a view of Tom's powdered shirt.

"OK kids, let's get you and the laptop upstairs and then mummy and daddy can sing *Twinkle Twinkle* for you."

Shouts of glee exploded from the laptop and various people in the lobby stared at Beth and her screaming computer. She muted the shrieking and watched the screen as it juddered down the hallway and followed Miles' Thomas the Tank Engine slippers up the stairs. In the kids' room the curtains were already drawn and Katy's ladybird nightlight shone between the two beds. The beds were rapidly filled with the forms of her two children. Tom moved a miniature chair to the end of the beds and positioned the laptop on it, his face looming into shot to check the angle. He was so close she could see he hadn't shaved that day. He then took his place, seated on the floor, between the two beds.

"OK, are we ready?" asked Tom.

"Yes!" screamed Miles and Katy.

Beth turned the sound up.

"Ready mummy?" asked Tom.

"Ready daddy," said Beth with a smile.

As Tom started singing, Beth joined in, quietly at first but then with more volume when she saw Katy's smile glittering in the darkness. As the camera adjusted to the dim lighting she then made out the twinkles of Miles' eyes, and sang even louder. Suited men and women in shoulder pads and silk scarves looked at Beth, either in bewilderment or in annoyance, but Beth didn't care, she was singing a lullaby with her husband to her two children, who meant the world to her. And as soon as she got back from this last trip, she was going to show them what they meant to her, make up for lost time, show them that they were the twinkling stars in her life. She had been stupid ever to think otherwise.

When Tom and Beth had repeated their duet three times over, Tom stopped singing and winked at his wife.

"OK kids, time to say goodnight." He switched off the nightlight and Beth could just make out his dark figure leaning over Katy and Miles in turn.

"Night night Katy," he whispered.

"Night daddy."

"Night night Miles."

"Night daddy."

"Good night Miles, good night Katy," Beth said into the darkness of the screen.

"Good night mummy," came Katy's voice, "I love you."

"Me too," said a sleepy Miles.

Beth was about to respond, but Tom reached over and switched off Skype. The last words from Katy and Miles rang in her head, like the last notes of a melody she didn't want to end. The last notes of a melody she'd never hear again.

How Angelo and Maria ended

21 days ago
11:53, Friday June 21ˢᵗ, 2013
14 Carrer Lleo, Al Raval, Barcelona

"Why the fuck not?" demanded Angelo. "You agreed to move here, you said you just needed some time, you've had some fucking time. Maria, we hardly see each other, you spend half your time in Madrid; it makes for half a fucking relationship. And there's nothing to keep you there, you said so yourself. If you loved me, you'd come." He slammed his fist onto the loosely nailed set of planks that made a ramshackle table between two crates.

Maria leant over to touch his hand, but he pushed her away, his eyes narrowed, and stared at the floor.

"I do love you Angelo. God I love you so much. I love you like I can't remember loving anyone else, but I need time away from you."

He looked straight at her. "Why?"

"Because, *mi amor*, when I'm with you, it's, well, it's so intense. Neither of us gets anything done. You haven't painted all week, we only leave the apartment when we run out of wine. Our lives stop when we're together, everything stops."

"*Es amor*," he said.

She smiled sadly. "It is, but we can't function when we're together, don't you see?" Maria ran her fingers through her long hair.

He sighed. "The reason life stops when you're here is because I hardly see you. When you're in Madrid, you may as well be on the other side of the world for all I hear from you. And when I do see you, I need to show you how much I love you, to make up for the time we're apart. If you lived here, we'd function, it would be less intense, you could write and I could paint, and we could start our future together." He paused, his eyes wide and almost hazy with the dream. A moment passed. "Or I could come to Madrid."

Maria looked up with a start. "You can't come to Madrid."

"Why not?"

"Because, because it would suck the creativity out of you. Madrid wouldn't work for you. It's capitalism, it's concrete and glass, it's the centre of the economy, the centre of a failing economy, it's Velasquez and Goya, it's *Las Meninas* and endless paintings of kings on horseback.

It's not got the fluidity of Barcelona, the curves of Picasso, the melting walls of Gaudi, the optimism of Miro. Madrid is heavy and relentless, it's about making money, not about making art."

Angelo was impressed by her knowledge of art, but not convinced by it.

"But it *is* art, it has some of the best galleries in the world."

"You don't take your inspiration from other artists, you take it from people." Maria was raising her voice. "*Madrileños* won't inspire you."

"You inspire me!" he shouted back, "and you're in Madrid. Why won't you let me into your life? I'm ready, I'm fucking ready to let you into mine. Come in! Come the fuck in, close the door and live with me, live our lives together."

He stood up, grabbed a bunch of paintbrushes and snapped them. It was a bad habit of his when he became angry, and remnants of his anger littered the apartment like a forest cut down. Angelo stood by the window, and pushed the broken shards of brushes into his palm.

Maria approached him from behind, and tentatively put her hands on his slim waist. He allowed her to do so, she leant her head into his shirt and breathed in cigarettes and coffee.

"It's only been six months Angelo, six fantastic months. I didn't think I could feel this strongly about a person, but it scares me, do you understand? What we have scares me. It excites me and it scares me. Just give me a little more time. Please. Be patient with me."

Angelo eased the force with which he jammed the splintered wood into his palm.

"Don't be scared," he said, his voice gentle. "This is the most natural feeling in the world."

"Just give me some time," she whispered into the threadbare material.

"OK."

She moved her hands beneath the fabric of his shirt and moved them round to his stomach, feeling the heat of the sun on his skin. She held him tightly, burying her face into his smell and inhaling him. She kissed him through the paint and stains of his shirt, and moved her hands up through the hair of his chest. She felt every contour and every one was all hers. She felt his skin rise and fall, in shallow movements at first, becoming deeper as her hands moved down his chest and past his stomach. She slipped a hand past his waistband and sunk her teeth into his back as her hand gripped hold of him. Angelo's head rolled back as he indulged himself in his two favourite sensations, the feeling of the hot sun and Maria's hands. When he had had enough of both, he turned around, grabbed Maria and pushed her up against the window frame. He undid his trousers, let them fall to the floor and lifted Maria's dress.

Maria smiled at him. She was glad they had stopped talking about their feelings, much better to just feel them.

10 days ago
09:21, Tuesday July 2nd, 2013,
Apartamentos Buenavista, Calle de los tres peces, Madrid

Maria's heart and world stopped at the edge of a blue cross. She dropped the test on the tiles of the bathroom. It rolled over once and then settled itself, looking up at her with its mean blue eyes. Her head fell into her hands. She hated herself. How could she have been so stupid?

He'd want it. She knew he'd want it. This was the news to make all of his dreams come true. She'd move to Barcelona, live with him in the studio and they'd bring up their little Angelito together, immersed in colour, sunshine and poverty. A family made of a whole load of love and nothing else.

There was no way it could happen.

4 days ago
15:43, Monday July 8th, 2013
14 Carrer Lleo, Al Raval, Barcelona

There was something not right about Maria. In everything about her there was a reluctance, an anxiety, the way her arms hung, her fingers twitched, her eyes darted. Angelo looked into her eyes and their edges crinkled into a plastic smile.

"*Hola*," she said brightly. She walked immediately into the apartment and into his arms, avoiding his stare. "How are you?"

"All good," he said into the crown of her hair. She stayed in his arms longer than normal, but when he pulled away to kiss her, she just smiled and walked to the window.

"How's the masterpiece?" she asked, turning to the canvas.

"*Mierda*," he said. "A piece of shit."

She looked at the painting and silently agreed. He was experimenting with landscapes and this one was a dreamy collection of cork and olive trees, languishing in a yellow meadow.

"It's a very happy picture," she offered.

"Happy are postcards, not masterpieces," he said. He went into the kitchen to make some coffee.

"Maybe you need some anguish in your life?" she said quietly, addressing the canvas rather than the man.

She stared into the distance of the painted horizon, and lightly touched the meadow flowers, yellow paint came off on her fingers. Yellow was far from the way she was feeling.

Angelo came back into the studio with a coffee pot and two cups, one without a handle.

"Perhaps I need some tragedy in my life," he said as he filled the cups with black coffee. "Like Van Gogh, or Lautrec." Maria smiled. They often thought exactly the same thing, it was like they shared a mind. And, in truth, when she was with him about half of her mind went unused. It was the half she didn't need, the half that worries, analyses and doubts. It was the half that thinks rather than feels. But today with Angelo she wasn't feeling, she was thinking, and the worry of what lay before her was revolving in her head, like a pinball rolling and bouncing around the inside of her skull.

She shouldn't have come to Barcelona with his life still growing inside her. She should have dealt with it, immediately. Then she could have stood in front of him without the secret in her belly and the little mass of worry in her head. She'd have a lighter conscience, or perhaps it would have been heavier, who knows? Angelo stood behind Maria, looked at the painting and sighed, then he wrapped his arms around her waist and kissed her neck.

"I've been using a lot more cadmium since meeting you," he said.

"Sorry?"

"Yellow," he said. "Have I made *your* life yellow?"

She said nothing. His hands moved beneath her shirt and came to rest on her belly, she held it in, worried it would betray her.

"What's wrong my sweet?" he asked.

"Nothing, nothing at all," she said.

"Tell me. You can tell me anything."

No, I can't, she thought. *I can't tell you anything.*

"I'm just feeling a little unwell," she lied. "It must have been the bus journey."

"Let me make you feel better," he said, moving one hand up to her breast and caressing it through her bra. Maria concentrated on the meadow, the cork trees and the blue sky in front of her. The meadow. The cork trees. The blue sky in front of her. She took deep breaths, focusing on the imaginary scene, rather than the one she was in. Angelo sighed in her ear and moved his other hand past the waistband of her skirt and inside her knickers.

Maria felt her stomach contract, and a sudden wave of nausea rose inside her. As if to affirm the lie she had just told, Maria ran to the bathroom and vomited into the toilet. She felt physically and emotionally disgusting. She wanted to vomit so hard that the seed of the baby in her would swim out her mouth and be flushed away. Gone, no longer her problem. Her eyes filled with tears, and the mess she'd made in the toilet bowl blurred over. She heard Angelo's approaching footsteps and quickly locked the door.

"Maria? Maria, are you ok?" he called from outside.

She bit her lip. "I will be," she said from the floor.

"What's wrong? Was it something you ate? Can I get you anything?"

She just wanted him to leave her alone, leave her to cough up her guilt and spit out their baby.

"Erm, maybe some paracetamol?" She had never seen any legal drugs in Angelo's apartment, and she hoped they would take him a long time to locate, perhaps he'd even have to go to a pharmacist.

"Ok, ok. Give me a minute." Angelo looked back into the studio, scratching the back of his head. Did he own such a thing as paracetamol? He went into the kitchen and searched the back of his cupboards, past the coffee, wine and whiskey. This would be a sensible place for painkillers, he thought, beyond the items that cause the pain.

But of course there was nothing, he'd never had the need for medications before, pain was part of life and there was no need to diminish it. Maria suffered frequent headaches but she always had pills with her. Of course – she always had pills with her.

Angelo found her satchel by the easel, he opened it and riffled through its contents. At the base, among the hairclips and coins he found a small white box of paracetamol.

"Got some!" he shouted.

Just as he was about to close the bag, something on a piece of paper caught his eye. It was the AirStar logo. He unfolded the piece of paper and saw an e-ticket, for a flight from Madrid to Heathrow at 07:35 on Friday. He was confused. What was Maria doing going to London?

He stood outside the bathroom door. "Maria, Maria? Why are you flying to London?"

Maria panicked. What could she tell him? Why was she going to London? She stalled for time.

"What? Sorry I can't hear you through the door?" The door was paper-thin and they both knew it.

"I said, why are you flying to London?" His voice was louder and edged with anger.

She stalled for more time by retching into the toilet. She had nothing left inside her to cough up, just some blatant lies.

"One minute," she called. "I'm coming out." She stood up and flushed the toilet, still formulating the lie. She gargled some tap water, it clarified the lie, and then she splashed water on her face, making it as clean and believable as possible. She took a deep breath and opened the door.

Angelo stood, puzzled, outside the door, holding her packet of paracetamol and the e-ticket. Her heart throbbed when she saw it. She grabbed the paper from him before he could scrutinize it any further.

"I was about to tell you," she hesitated, and gestured back into the bathroom, "but then…"

"Well?"

"It's great news actually, the magazine have asked me to cover an exhibition at the Tate in London. Hyperrealism. It opens this weekend." She looked him straight in the eye. "Can I have that paracetamol?"

He passed her the packet and she went into the kitchen to pour some water. Her heart was beating so loudly, it was as if it wanted Angelo to know she was lying. Her hands shook as she filled a glass.

Angelo poked his head round the door. "Really?"

"Really."

"I didn't know the magazine covered foreign exhibitions."

She swallowed two tablets, slowly. "It's their first one, and they asked me to do it."

"Wow," he said. "That's great, that's really great! London hey? You ever been before?"

Her heart began to slow and she shook her head. "No, first time."

"We should celebrate." He reached into the cupboard above her head and pulled out a bottle of red, checking the label. "This one's been waiting for a special occasion. And now we have it. Oh actually… maybe you shouldn't." He looked with doubt at her stomach.

"What?" she said panicked.

"I mean, you've just been sick." He looked concerned.

"No, no. I'm feeling a lot better now, really. Let's celebrate." Maria desperately needed a drink, she needed it to celebrate her successful lie, she needed it to forget her situation, to forget why she was really taking that flight on Friday, and she needed it to get through the night with Angelo lying alongside his own baby.

3 days ago
10:42, Tuesday July 9th, 2013
Café Contrabandista, Barcelona

She couldn't stand another night with Angelo. It was too much. She had made up her mind, and any more time with him would just loosen her resolve. She lied and told him that the magazine had requested a meeting with her the day before her flight to London. She also insisted that they go out of the apartment that morning. She couldn't bear to spend more time in Angelo's studio, surrounded by all the things she loved about him, and alone with him, vulnerable to his hands and body. She was safer outside, where her love for him and his for her were diluted by people, voices, traffic, other lives. Over a breakfast of churros and coffee, Angelo asked her about the exhibition. She was glad to be talking about something solid and practical.

"It's hyperrealism," she said. "The idea is for the art to look as real as possible, more like a high-res photo than a painting. The detail the artists achieve is amazing, however close you get to the work it still appears to be photographic."

Angelo wasn't impressed.

"I think a painting has to do *more* than a photograph."

"What do you mean?"

"Well, there is a skill in painting like you say, hyperrealism, but it's just copying. Real art should tell you more than a photograph ever could. It should give you an insight, it should show you how the artist felt, show you how the model felt in the case of a portrait. A painting is not just a copy, you may as well take a photograph."

"Well I guess some art is more about the skill of the artist than anything they are trying to communicate."

"They should always be trying to communicate something," he said.

Maria loved it when Angelo spoke about art. She wondered if a child of his would have the same passion. She wondered if she was robbing the world of a great and passionate artist.

"You look sad," he said.

She looked at him and brushed some sugar from his lips. "Just to be leaving you so soon."

*

After breakfast, they wandered through Parc Guell, stopping to watch a flamenco dancer practising in the shade. She danced on a wooden board that her heels had polished to marble. Her hands twirled and twisted happily above her stern face. Maria and Angelo watched for a few minutes and, for Maria, every stamp on the board was a reminder of time passing, a reminder of a time that had passed for them. When they left the dancer, she felt like crying. They headed to Metro Lesseps where they were to part.

"So I'll see you when you get back from London?" he said.

She couldn't speak and just nodded her head and made the shape of a smile. They kissed, embraced and parted.

"*Hasta luego, mi amor*," he called after her.

"*Adios*," she shouted back, taking one last look at him, before descending into the darkness of the Metro station. She fished into her bag and pulled out her sunglasses.

How Tom and Beth began

14 years ago
21:17, Saturday February 6th, 1999
The Winchester Arms, London

Tom was doing an open mic night at the Winchester Arms when he first saw Beth. He was seventh on the line-up and he'd already had to endure three Oasis covers, one Burt Bacharach classic sung in the style of Oasis, and three unknown songs that the crowd went mad for. He could only guess that they were current hits. It all sounded like shit to him, but the audience were clearly not so discerning in their tastes. He groaned into his beer, already apprehensive of the response he was going to get.

He got comfortable on the chair, adjusted the mic and tuned his guitar with a few chords.

"Woo-hoo, sounds fucking great! Fucking great!" shouted his mate Chris from the bar.

Tom rolled his eyes, cleared his throat and talked into the microphone.

"Hey. My name's Tom Turner and I'm going to sing one of my own tracks." Just these few words had many people racing to the bar or the toilets, wanting to fill their glasses or empty their bladders before the next *real* act came on. "It's called *Paper Lover*."

It was during the second verse that he spotted her. Tom remembered that he was really bad at looking at the audience while he sang and so consciously looked up to find himself staring straight into her face. It was a beautiful face, tanned and fresh, with big brown eyes. He looked straight back down into his guitar where he felt safer. Only when he'd finished the song did he look up. Chris was whooping from the bar and the beautiful face hovered above hands that were clapping wildly. An angel with frantic wings. He let his curls hang over his face and tried not to smile as he packed his guitar away and left the microphone to suffer the next rendition of *Wonderwall*.

Attraction can make women bold and men shy, and this is exactly what happened with Beth and Tom. She didn't lose a moment in walking over to him at the bar.

"Hi," she said. "That was great, really, really great." Her voice was crisp and slightly clipped, not the type of voice he expected to hear in a dive like the Winchester. "God I really, really..." Beth stopped, realizing how really, really gushing she sounded, and changed tack. "Can I get you a drink?"

"Erm, yeah, thanks," said Tom.

She smiled at him and he smiled back.

"So what would you like?"

"I'll have a pint of lager."

"And me," said Chris, craning his head between the two of them. "I'm with the band."

She smiled politely. "Sure."

Tom couldn't believe that such a beautiful, well-spoken girl was buying him a drink. As she leaned over the bar he took the chance to look her over and, when he realized that the whole of her matched up to the face and smile, he became more nervous. Beth knew he would be looking her over, she could feel his eyes on her. She leant over, sticking her rear out, just more than was needed for the barman to hear her order. The mating display began.

"What about Stacy?" whispered Chris to Tom.

"Fuck Stacy!"

"You wouldn't mind? Coz I'd love to."

"Chris, shut the fuck up. All that's happening is that this girl is buying me, *us*, a drink."

"So you won't be taking her home?"

At that point, Beth turned around.

"What was that?" she asked.

"Chris, my friend here, was just saying – he needs to go home soon, after this pint."

Chris looked dejectedly into his full beer.

"Well, it was good to meet you Chris. I'm Beth by the way, and if you're with the band, I hope to see you again very soon."

Fuck, she was smooth. Tom was supposed to be the cool one, the one with all the lines, but this girl made him nervous. He drank his pint way too quickly, made small talk, and tripped over his words. He began to wish he hadn't planned Chris' early exit, he needed the moral support. When his mate turned to leave, he felt like begging him to stay, to help, to act the fool, to make Tom look better, but even Chris was one step ahead of Tom.

"So I'm off now mate. Said I'd meet up with Stacy – right? You remember?"

Tom's face twitched, an almost imperceptible movement, a swelling of a tiny muscle next to his eye that betrayed his gritted teeth.

"Sure mate. Thanks for coming along. Really appreciate the support."

Chris slapped his friend on the shoulder and disappeared with a smile, leaving Tom and Beth alone at the bar. He bought them both another drink and, while Beth popped to the loo, he slipped a shot of vodka into his lager. She returned with a swagger and a smile that almost had him downing the whole thing.

"So," she said. "Tell me about you."

"What do you want to know?"

"Well, let's start with your music."

Tom's nerves, his twisted words, his awkward stance, all evaporated as he began telling her about his music. He became animated and natural. He told her about his first ever guitar teacher, who had a constant runny nose and would let it drip on Tom's guitar whenever he demonstrated something that Tom had done wrong. Mr. Henberry and his dripping nostrils made Tom a perfectionist, as he couldn't bear to see his beloved instrument splattered with shining drops of mucus. He told her about the first song he ever wrote for a girl at his primary school who went out of her way to ignore him, he called it 'Don't be foreign Lauren.' At one point he almost forgot who he was talking to and had to completely change the track of a story so that it didn't end with a threesome.

Beth was captivated. It almost didn't matter what he was saying, it was the way he was saying it that gripped her. His blue eyes sparkled, his eyebrows and hands danced with his voice, it was as though something was tickling him from the inside. He was so passionate about his music, she felt she could listen to him all night and, when the bell for last orders rang, she wanted to smash it into the landlord's head.

Tom bit his lip. "Sorry, I haven't stopped talking have I?" He kicked himself for barely asking her one question. If his limited experience had taught him anything, it was that girls liked being asked questions. You scored bonus points if you looked interested in the answers.

"How about we go back to yours?" she asked, looking him straight in the eye.

"Erm, well." Tom was firstly shocked, and secondly was trying to recollect what level of mess he'd left his flat in – burglary or bomb blast?

"It's fine if you'd rather not." Although her face told a different story. "It's just that you were in the middle of telling me…" Her voice trailed off as she realized she had no idea what he had been telling her.

"How about we go back to yours?" he asked, with hope.

"I'm a student. And my room is disgusting to say the least."

This made him feel a little better. Not only did being a student mean that she would find his flat at the very least 'grown-up', at most bohemian, it also meant that he knew something about her, without even asking a direct question.

"Sure, let's go back to mine."

*

She sat cross-legged on the carpet. A brave position to take in his studio, since he hadn't vacuumed since signing the contract five months ago. She sipped at a tumbler of red wine that was more suitable for guzzling, and he played guitar. He had felt awkward when she first asked him to. He had strummed the odd chord while trying to maintain a conversation with her, but quickly his fingers became carried away with what lay beneath them.

She was happy to be forgotten. She couldn't take her eyes from his hands. He had beautiful careful hands, that were contoured with defined veins and muscles, and she watched his fingers as they skipped around the strings; at times gentle and caressing, at others aggressive and determined. Without words, his hands were telling a story, a story of love and passion. As he moved from one song to the next, she looked up at him. He was gorgeous; from his scruffy blonde curls down to his torn Converse All Stars, she was attracted to every part of him but it was his hands she loved the most. They weren't large or small but they were agile, they were rhythmic, they were creative. Her pulse quickened. As much as watching his hands captivated her, she wanted to take them away from the guitar. She wanted to be the strings beneath his fingers.

Beth put down her glass, got up from the floor and moved to stand behind his chair, lightly touching his golden curls. His playing slowed to a gentle pace, and she saw his shoulders rise and fall in slow deep breaths. She pulled a curl to its full length and let it spring back. She ran her fingertips unhurried down his neck. The heat of his body filled the gap between them, and over the quiet strum of his guitar she could hear him breathing. Her eyes never drifted from his hand on the neck of the guitar, his fingers moving adeptly from shape to shape. She ran her fingers around the neckline of his T-shirt and under the cotton. His skin was soft and clammy. Beth bent her head down to smell his hair, a mixture of smoke and something nutty. Tom stopped playing.

"No, don't stop," she whispered in his ear.

Tom resumed playing, but this time only a few basic chords with his left, and the gentle picking of a lullaby with his right. He didn't have the focus for anything else.

Beth kissed the side of his neck and he could feel her cool breath penetrate his whole body. She ran her hands across his broad shoulders and down his arms. His forearms were thick and defined and her fingers lingered around them, feeling the tiny movements beneath the skin as his hands moved on the guitar. Her fingers trickled past his wrists and came to lie on his knuckles, where she could feel the beginnings of each note he played. She closed her eyes and felt the music through his hands.

Tom loved his guitar more than anything in the world, but at that moment he would happily have thrown it out the window. Since first laying eyes on Beth, he had wanted her.

He played a quick riff from a Rolling Stones track that made them both laugh, then put the guitar on the floor. It knocked over Beth's glass and a red shadow crept across the carpet. He took her hand and guided her around to stand in front of him. He had been nervous of her earlier, of her beauty, of her confidence. But now his mind had emptied all of its responsibility into his body, and his body was more than ready.

"You're beautiful," he said.

She smiled at him. Now that the moment had arrived, she felt nervous. He pulled her towards him. She knelt on the floor in front of him, and looked into his eyes. They stared at her with intensity. Tom pulled Beth's hands towards him and, since she was still not close enough, he pulled them behind him. The two of them were just at the point where a beautiful face becomes contorted and ugly, the point in all great romances where the eyes are closed. But however close they got to each other, Tom and Beth remained beautiful, and they looked into each other's eyes as his lips first touched hers. The sealing of the lips is like the sealing of a promise; I want you and you want me, and as soon as their lips touched all obstacles and worries disappeared.

He closed his eyes and kissed her gently. He released her hands and took a hold of her head. Her short dark bob was as soft as silk under his fingers. He pulled away and looked at her one last time to appreciate her beauty before he took it for himself. He kissed her roughly, pulling her face towards him. His hands moved through her hair to her neck. She felt small and fragile but his body didn't want to be gentle with her. He was breathing faster with the exertion of holding himself back. He needed to be closer to this girl.

Beth loved the way he kissed her. She wished he had indulged her for longer with his gentle kisses, but when his force increased, her body responded and she found her lips pushing against his, like a fight. Her hands explored his chest through his T-shirt and ran down towards his belt. He groaned in anticipation and lifted up her shirt to transfer his kisses from her pretty face, down her throat and into her cleavage.

She lifted his shirt, and the moment he had to take his mouth from her skin, to peel his T-shirt over his head, felt like forever. He rushed his mouth back to her breast, unfastened her bra and moved his lips to her nipple. Beth inhaled sharply and let the air out slowly in a delicious sigh.

She pulled back from Tom and saw the want in his eyes. He couldn't bear to not be touching her and his fingers slid up her slim waist, felt the curve of her breasts and moved up to the softness of her neck.

In Beth's head she could still see the way his fingers danced around the guitar, and it gave her a thrill to feel those same fingers moving over her skin. She took his right hand and brought it to her lips, closing her eyes to remember the way it took control of the guitar. She kissed his knuckles lightly, and then moved her mouth down each of his fingers, thanking each of them with her kisses, for the way they stroked the strings of his guitar.

Beth was so absorbed by his fingers that she didn't even notice his other hand undoing the buttons of her jeans, and slipping inside her knickers. She nibbled and licked his fingers with more intensity as his left hand explored her.

Tom couldn't wait any longer. The way she kissed him and the way her body responded to his touch told him that she was ready. He stood and pulled her up, bending to kiss her, his lips pushing against hers urgently. He grabbed her by the shoulders and, while still kissing her, pushed her onto the bed. It was covered in notes and lyrics for a new song, but as she lay on top of his crumpled pages, all he saw was her beautiful body and the way her eyes shined at him. She wiggled out of her jeans and knickers and stared up at him. Tom pulled off his jeans and boxers and moved on top of her, his eyes locked with hers. Both of their breathing shallowed as he positioned himself. Only the gentle scrunch of paper beneath them and their quiet breathing broke the silence.

Slowly, Tom pushed himself into Beth. He moved slowly back and forward inside her and she arched her back and gasped as his hand found her breast and squeezed her hard. She moved her hips with his rhythm and felt him deep inside her. She reached up and grabbed his head, full of curls, pulling it towards hers and kissing him, again and again. Her hands were all over him, in his hair, down his torso, along his broad back, she wanted to feel every inch of him. Tom's movement and breathing became faster, urgent. Beth opened her eyes and saw him staring down at her, his eyes shining and wide. The intensity of his stare was enough, she took a deep breath, grabbed his hips and pulled him deep inside her, pushing against him, moving her hips quickly, once, twice, three times. She abandoned herself to Tom and he to her.

07:46, Sunday February 7th, 1999
Flat 5, 62 York Road, London

Beth woke up with the sun. Tom had his back to her and was gently snoring, it sounded vaguely musical and made her smile. As her eyes lost their night mist she took in her surroundings. There was a sheet draped across the window next to her, held in place with clothes pegs, it did nothing to darken the room. She glanced around the tiny studio that had last night been romantically shrouded in darkness. Dirty plates, cutlery and glasses glinted in the early morning glow, like dirty stars dotted around the flat. Two guitars were propped up by the other window and a third, the one he had played last night, lay on the floor next to a lightning bolt of red wine. The carpet was mostly covered with papers dotted with chords but, even where it was exposed, its colour was disguised by stains. The corner that served as a kitchen was only discernible as such by the existence of an overflowing swing bin and a large white fridge, rusting at the corners. She daren't imagine what was festering inside. Night had been very flattering to Tom's flat and she realized the same could probably be said of her.

She ran her fingers through her hair and tried to mould it into shape, but a couple of side kinks fought against her efforts. She ran both index fingers under her eyes, removing the sleep and mascara she assumed had gathered there. She pinched her cheeks to give them a glow and arranged her face and hair on the pillow, creating a pretty picture for him to turn over to see. Then she waited, listening to his slow raspy breathing and watching his naked shoulder rise and fall. She waited, then she coughed, then she put her hand on his waist, then she fell asleep.

When Tom finally woke up, it took him a few moments to realize the hand on his waist wasn't his own, then a few more moments to remember who it belonged to. He lifted the hand from his skin and turned over in bed. She was more beautiful than he remembered, more beautiful than anyone he had ever woken up next to. Her short dark hair bent and hung in every direction around her face and her skin looked exotically dark against the pillow. Her mouth was slightly open but her breathing was completely silent. He watched her serenity for a few minutes and wondered what was going to happen between them. A one-night stand? A short fling? At the age of twenty, Tom didn't factor in any other possibilities.

When his bladder overpowered his thinking, he slipped out of bed and padded to the bathroom. Beth woke and watched him go, with a big smile on her face. His blond curls had been pushed into a messy mohican and she longed to put her fingers through them again.

"Good morning," she said when he came out.

"Morning," he said, suddenly feeling self-conscious of his naked body. He tried to act cool, as though he was completely used to having his penis aired in front of an audience, a beautiful audience, but he found himself creeping back into bed and covering himself with the sheet. He propped himself up on his elbow and smiled at Beth who smiled back.

"How long have you lived here?" she asked him. "Oh, and sorry if I asked you that last night. My memory fails when I have too much to drink."

"Did you have too much to drink?" he asked, suddenly worried that it was only alcohol that had got this stunning woman into his bed.

"No, well, yes. At least more than I'm used to."

Tom felt a pang of disappointment.

"I've been here five months," he said looking around his space. "I had to be in London. There's not much opportunity for musicians in Hartlepool, in fact there's not much opportunity for anyone."

She laughed. "Apart from kids with aspirations of working in a chicken factory. I remember you telling me."

He smiled, happy that the night's conversation had not been a complete waste of words. "Exactly, if you want to be a chicken plucker, it's the place to be."

"Who'd want to be a chicken plucker!" she said.

"My dad," Tom said, putting an end to her giggles. "Well, I'm not sure he ever *wanted* to work in the factory, but he does. From seven till four every day, or the nightshift if he needs to earn more money."

"And your mother?" Beth was shocked. She never would have guessed Tom was from such humble beginnings.

"She works in a café, in a garden centre. How about your parents?"

Beth shifted in the bed, she suddenly felt coy.

"My dad works in the foreign service." She reached out and pulled one of Tom's curls, which sprang out of her fingers as though it didn't like her answer.

"What does that mean? Is he a spy?"

"No, nothing that exciting." She paused. "He's a diplomat."

"Wow." Tom was impressed and also a little intimidated. "What does that involve?"

She shrugged. "Working in different countries, building relationships, endless parties with endless polite conversations."

"And when he works in different countries – you get to visit him?" Tom was excited by anything outside of Hartlepool, let alone anything outside of England.

She smiled at him, realizing just how different their upbringings must have been. "He would work in different countries for years at a time. We would live with him."

"In different countries?" He was stunned. "What countries have you lived in?"

"I was born in Columbia. That's where my mum's from. My dad met her while he was stationed there."

Tom made a mental note to find out where the hell Columbia was.

"Then we moved to Paris when I was about three. After that we came back to London and then to Madrid. That was dad's last foreign assignment."

Tom didn't know what to say. Her life was like something out of a film, a strange film he couldn't understand. He knew London was a cosmopolitan city, but he didn't realize his bed would be.

"You speak different languages?" he asked.

She nodded. "Do you have tea? Shall we have a cup of tea?" She got out of bed, pulling his T-shirt past her naked bottom, feeling self-conscious about everything she was. He got out of bed, stark naked. He forgot his previous embarrassment, and trotted to the kitchen, his penis swaying confidently between his legs.

"What languages do you speak?" he asked, while sifting through the kitchen clutter.

"Spanish and French," she said, leaving out Italian and German.

"Wow." He couldn't help but be impressed. In all situations he tried to maintain his cool, nonchalant exterior, but this girl had knocked that aside. He found a box of tea and pulled out two bags. "And your mum? What does she do?"

"Being my dad's wife is a full time job," she said. She found two mugs and took them to the sink to wash them but, finding no implements to do so, they just got a cursory rinse. "She spends her time organizing events, hosting parties and fundraisers, that sort of thing."

"Sounds like a busy life," he said.

"It is. Do you have milk?"

"I doubt it."

He put the kettle on and the tea bags into the mugs. They stood side by side and watched the kettle in silence. After a few moments of watching the cheap plastic kettle do nothing, she ran her hand up his arm, his skin warm against her cold fingers. Her hand trailed onto his shoulder and then down his side. She watched as his penis began to grow. Tom turned to her, forgetting their conversation, forgetting how different she was from him. Bodies don't care how many languages another body speaks, or the number of countries that body has lived in. He kissed her, running his hands all over her firm body. By the time the kettle boiled he was already inside her.

10:32, Friday April 2nd, 1999
University of London Intercollegiate Halls, Russell Square

Tom's cool, relaxed attitude towards girls disappeared after his night with Beth. He couldn't get enough of her. Hearing her voice on the phone wasn't enough, seeing her eyes shining at him at one of his gigs wasn't enough, he craved time alone with her. Time when he shared her with no one. Unfortunately, Beth's lecture timetable was packed and, since she was studying History of Art, she also had to spend a fair amount of time in galleries. Tom had tried joining her on a few visits, but she had told him, in the nicest possible way – she had diplomatic blood after all – that he was too much of a distraction. When he couldn't be with her, he was playing guitar and writing songs. His feelings for her had made him a prolific poet, and his flat was covered with a fine layer of scribbled lyrics, like a romantic mist that had settled. To pay his rent Tom worked in a local pub, and under the bar he kept a notebook and pen that he darted to fill between pints. It quickly became sticky with beer and sweet sentiments. Every word he wrote was inspired by Beth. He realized that, before her, all his words of love were based on lust alone, now there was some real feeling behind the word; every time he wrote it, every time he sang it. He was completely and utterly in love for the first time in his life.

"I've got a gig coming up in Brighton," he said to her as they lay together on her single student bed. "You want to come with me?"

"Yes please!" She said, sitting up. "You know? I've never been to Brighton."

He frowned at her. "You've been all over the world, but you've never been to Brighton."

She shook her head. "Nope, never, and I'd love to go. You've been?"

"Yeah, I have a cousin and a few mates down there. I've been a couple of times." Tom felt a buzz of excitement at the prospect of showing her around the town; around the secret haunts his cousin had introduced him to, showing his local expertise. She might have the inside track on the rest of the world, but he could at least show her a good time in Brighton.

"When's the gig?"

"A week next Saturday," he said.

"I can't wait. I'll book us some train tickets. Can we stay over?"

"Of course. My cousin fixed the gig for me, and he says they'll pay me fifty quid if I keep the crowd happy. We can stay in a hotel."

"Can we get a hotel room for fifty pounds?" she looked puzzled.

"Of course we can," he laughed. "It won't be The Grand, but we can get a room."

She rubbed her hands together. "A dirty weekend in Brighton in a cheap hotel, how exciting!"

He smiled, but felt a little pang of hurt from her words. Fifty quid was a lot of money to spend on a hotel. He looked into her Columbian eyes and wondered about all the luxury they had seen in their life.

11:37, Saturday April 17th, 1999
South Eastern train from London Victoria to Brighton

They took an early morning train from Victoria station, well, early from the perspective of a student and an aspiring musician. The sun shone through the scratched train window and they watched the green peaks of the South Downs meet with the blue sky of a cloudless spring day. They were enlivened by the prospect of a whole weekend together, and various people choosing seats on the train avoided those in eyeline of

Beth and Tom. There are few things that can make you feel more alone or more old than a young couple in love.

When they arrived at Brighton station, they meandered down to the beach, taking up the whole pavement with their chain of guitar, man, woman and overnight bag.

"The sea!" shouted Beth. "I can see the sea!" The green horizon twinkled at them in the sunshine and they sped up their lover's amble, even releasing their vice-like grip on each other to navigate past the hoards of people. At the promenade, they leant over the railings and watched the tranquil sea bordered by a chaotic beach full of people, making the most of an unseasonably hot April. The sea lapped gently at the stones.

"I love watching people," said Beth.

"I love watching you, watching them," he said, turning to her.

She smiled at him but cast her eyes back to the scene in front of her. "There are much more interesting things to watch than me. Look at everyone out there, in their own little individual lives, all with problems, all with worries, but all here, on this beach in the sunshine." She talked as though to herself. "I love the seaside. I love the fact that it's the same the world over - a universal pleasure.

"In Columbia my mother's family has a beach house in Cartagena. It's on a private resort with 24-hour security. The beach is in a large bay bordered by two rocky hills that stretch out into the sea. It's easy to forget how poor Columbia is, particularly the north, when you're there.

"One day my brother and I went to play in the sea, there was only us there with a few rich ladies under parasols on the beach, we were really bored. When the wind blew in a certain direction we could hear the screams and shouts of children, so we decided to go find them. The lifeguard on the beach had fallen asleep on his high chair, so we snuck past and climbed up the rocky hill. It was really hard work getting to the top but when we got there we practically ran down the other side. It looked like paradise! There were children everywhere, splashing and screaming and the beach seemed to go on forever. We forgot all about our little playpen on the other side and raced down the rocks and into the water. We made lots of friends that day, scrawny dark children without a care in the world. Even their parents befriended us, letting us share their watermelon and fizzy drinks.

"They only had a few plastic cups and so they filled them up with this pink drink that tasted of bubblegum, and then they passed them round. My brother and I had never drunk out of plastic before. It was the best afternoon, all I remember doing is laughing. It was only when the sun started to set that we remembered where we'd come from, and that we needed to get back. We said goodbye to all our new friends, and promised to come back the following weekend to play with them, then we clambered up the hill."

Tom watched Beth. She was staring out to the horizon and a puzzle seemed to have gathered her eyebrows together.

"We were so confused when we got to the top of the hill. The beach was full of people, adults, and there were boats in the sea with big lights on. As we climbed down we noticed that some of the adults were policemen. We really had no idea what was going on."

She laughed and shook her head. "As we got to the base of the hill, someone shouted, and then everyone was running to us. My dad got to us first, his eyes were red but he looked so happy to see us. I jumped into his arms and my brother climbed up him and we held onto him like little monkeys. He was looking at the sky and he kept saying 'Thank God, Thank God' over and over. A crowd gathered around us and everyone was talking at the same time, I remember feeling scared. Then my dad walked through the crowd and I caught sight of my mum, she was kneeling in the sand and she was bent over. My brother shouted 'She's making a sand castle!' but it was only him and I that laughed. It was only when we got right up close to her that she looked up at us. I still have no idea what the look on her face meant, I'd never seen it before and I've never seen it again.

"My dad put us down in the sand in front of her. The sky was turning pink and all the boats were coming in. We stood awkwardly in front of her, biting our lips and looking at each other. After a few moments she grabbed us and pulled us into the sand. She held us there as the sun went down, and as all the other people went home. Her skin went from hot and clammy to cold as the stars came out. I wondered if we'd be there all night." Beth was silent a moment and her eyes glazed over. "Finally my dad said "*Ven adentro mi querida*, come inside my darling." She picked us both up, and walked up the beach to the house. She's a tiny woman, and normally had trouble picking one of us up. In the house, she took us to her bedroom and got straight into bed, still holding us, and that's how we spent the night. We were covered in sand and still in our damp swimsuits, but we were so tired from our day on the beach that we fell asleep straight away. Michael weed himself in the night and so we all woke up in a wet sandy mess. And it was that day that we got our mother's wrath!"

Beth looked at Tom for the first time since she had started her story. Her eyes lit up at the memory of that distant morning.

"There is no anger like a Latina anger," she laughed. "And there is no Latina anger like my mother's! At first we thought we were in trouble because Michael had wet the bed, so I kept saying 'It was him' and he kept saying 'It was her.'"

She stopped laughing and looked out to the sea again.

"But then we listened to what she was saying. She kept saying that she thought we were dead, that we had drowned. She yelled at us that she had punched the lifeguard because he'd fallen asleep, she yelled at us that dad had called in the best divers he could find, she yelled that wandering off into the hills was dangerous, she yelled and yelled. We sat in our sandy mess until she stopped yelling, and then we tried to explain. We told her we were perfectly safe, that we'd found some new friends on the other side of the rocks, that their mothers had looked after us, and even given us melon and fizzy drinks. We thought we'd done a good job of explaining the situation to her, and that she would be happy someone else's mummy had been looking after us. But it was at that point that she got even more angry. She yelled so loud and started shaking us. I began to cry and I could tell Michael wanted to. Dad ran in and tried to get her hands off us, but she was digging in her fingers so tightly, he couldn't get them off. "*Diablitos! Diablitos!*" she kept shouting at us. "They've been with the *campesinos*," she shouted at dad, "sharing their dirty food and drink!" We had no idea what she was talking about, our friends were just kids like us, they weren't dirty, and they had the whitest teeth I had ever seen. I wanted to tell her that but I never got the chance.

"Eventually dad got us out of the bedroom and locked mum in there, where she continued shouting. He called one of his friends, a doctor, who was also at the beach resort, and he came round and visited mum. He must have sedated her because the bedroom became very quiet. Dad gave us both a hot bath and while we were in it, we asked whether we had been very naughty. He told us we had, but he said it in a nice way. He said we shouldn't have gone off on our own, and that we shouldn't play with children whose family didn't have a house on the resort. Michael asked why not, and dad told us that those children were different from us. I think I told him that the only difference was that they had darker skin and drank out of plastic, but he said there were lots of differences. When I asked what they were, he wouldn't tell me, he just said there were lots of differences and that we were never to play with them again. And so we never went back. We didn't keep our promise. The next weekend I wondered whether our little friends were on the other side of the rocks, in the same sea as us, playing the same games, and looking up at the rocks to watch for their new friends." She looked at Tom and smiled. "There really is no difference between people when it comes to the sea and the sand."

Tom liked her story. He liked hearing about her past, the exotic life she had led. She didn't speak about it often, perhaps she was trying to lessen the differences between them, by not talking about them. This story definitely made him think about their different upbringings. He was one of the kids on the other side of the rocks, he knew that.

"Want to get your feet wet?" he asked her.

"Definitely."

They took the stairs down to the lower promenade and asked one of the café owners under the arches to look after his guitar and her bag. Then they walked hand in hand across the pebbles to the sea where they spent two happy hours splashing, jumping, skimming stones and paddling like children. Children from two different worlds. When hunger got the better of Tom, they headed back to the café and ate greasy donuts washed down with icy bottles of beer.

"You owe me a couple of songs," said the café owner, nodding to Tom's guitar. "For looking after your things."

Tom shook his head. "We'll just leave a good tip."

"Go on," said Beth. "He's really good," she assured the café owner. "He's got a gig tonight at Alley Cats."

"Well this can be his rehearsal," said the man, passing Tom his guitar case. He reluctantly took the case and removed his guitar, playing a few chords and tuning up.

"What do you want?"

"Know any *Stones?*"

Tom smiled. "I can do that." He played the riff from his first night with Beth, and then played the whole of *Satisfaction*, at first with his guitar alone, but then as the music caught him, he sang along. A small crowd gathered on the promenade outside the café terrace, and a few people ventured in and took tables. Feet tapped, heads nodded and mouths sang along. As the song ended, a ripple of applause took over, and the café owner whispered in Tom's ear "A few more songs and the beers are on the house." Tom played some crowd-pleasers; *Love me do*, *Brown-eyed girl* and *Mrs Robinson*, while Beth sipped free beer, and listened to the compliments whispered around her about the musician. He ended his set with a flurry of finger work and the small crowd whooped as he put his guitar away.

"You can enjoy more of that at Alley Cats tonight," shouted the café owner at his full terrace. "And for now stay for Happy Hour!" It was far too early for Happy Hour but he was a businessman with an eye for opportunity and a fridge full of old beer that needed to be drunk or ditched. He patted Tom on the back as he went to the bar to brief his greasy bartender to look happy.

"That was great," said Beth. "Play like that tonight and you'll go down a storm."

He sipped his beer. "I'm thinking of trying out a new song tonight."

"Yeah?"

He nodded. "I hope you like it." He looked through his blonde curls at Beth and hoped he had the courage to sing it for her.

*

They checked into their guesthouse and Beth entertained herself and Tom by walking laps of their tiny room and musing over every tiny detail.

"Look, look. A picture of the old pier… A kettle! Tom look, there's a kettle in our room, I don't think I have ever seen a kettle so small… And biscuits, we even have biscuits." She opened the window and craned her head out. "And look Tom – we have a view of the sea."

She pulled him up from the bed where he lay and dragged him to the window. All he could see was a backstreet full of large bins and a mangy cat. "Where?" he asked.

"There, there look. Wait, I'll get out of the way… now stick your head out further and look over that white roof."

He stretched and saw a small green sliver of sea, a fragment of the view from the window, but the only thing she seemed to see. "Oh yes, I see sea!" He turned to her and smiled. "A room with a sea view, for one person at a time anyway."

She hugged him tight. "It's perfect. I love it. It has everything a big hotel would have, but in miniature, and with more character. But wait." She pulled away from him and looked around the room, assessing every wall. "Where's the bathroom?"

He laughed. "Along the hallway."

She pulled back from him further, her smile mixed with suspicious eyes. "You're joking, right?"

He took her hand and led her out of the room, round a corner and pushed open a door. They stood on the threshold of a salmon pink bathroom, him with a big smile on his face and her with a look of astonishment, as though the door had opened onto another world.

She shook her head, in complete disbelief. "Well I never."

He loved her so much at that moment; the girl who had travelled the world, who spoke three languages and was astounded by a shared hotel bathroom. Her head was still shaking in bewilderment when he took it into his hands and kissed her. He then led her into the bathroom, locked the door behind them and made love to her on the salmon pink bathmat. Afterwards they shared a bath with his feet either side of her head.

"I hope other guests don't use the shared bathroom like we have," she said.

"I couldn't help myself. The romance of the pink was too much for me."

They laughed. "We'd better get out soon," she said. "You have to be at the venue early right? And you don't want to be all wrinkly." She looked at his waterlogged toes.

"Just five more minutes," he said, laying his head back and breathing in the steam from the bathwater.

A knock on the door made him raise his head. "You gonna be much longer in there? I'm dying for a slash," came a man's voice from outside.

"Just coming out mate!" shouted Tom. They looked at each other sheepishly and giggled, before raising themselves out of the water and looking for towels.

"Shit! They're in the room," said Tom.

Beth opened her mouth and scanned the little bathroom in sheer panic. She grabbed a towel that hung by the sink, but it was tiny. She held it against herself, it covered the bare essentials at the front but nothing more.

"I'm putting my clothes back on," she whispered.

"But you're soaking."

"I don't care," she said. "I'm not going out there naked."

Tom considered putting his clothes back on too, but he hadn't brought another pair of jeans. Fuck it, he thought, what would Keith Richards do? As soon as Beth was dressed, soaked but dressed, he gathered up his clothes into a bundle and held them in front of him, covering himself, but as nonchalantly as possible. He opened the door.

A red-faced man in a football shirt stood outside, hopping from one leg to another.

"All yours mate," said Tom. The man stopped hopping and raised his eyebrows as they left him to the steamy salmon oasis.

"So that's why it's called a shared bathroom," he called after them, watching Tom's wet behind wobble around the corner. He looked after them for a few minutes, forgetting his urgency. "Lucky bugger," he muttered.

*

They arrived at Alley Cats around six after fish and chips on the beach. The bar was tucked away behind and below a hotel on the seafront. It was reached by rickety iron stairs, and only made itself known by a small neon sign at the base of the stairs. Inside was dark and cool even though the sun still shone bright outside. As their eyes adjusted they took in the deep red interior walls that seemed to have two tones of the same colour, perhaps damp or mould. A pew-like bench stretched along two walls, a bar filled the other and the fourth wall was what they had just entered through. Small metal tables were dotted around and a few mushroom-like stools stood or lay on their sides. The place was tiny, dark and depressing, and Tom loved it.

"This is great," he said to Beth. "Wow, this is really great. The acoustics will be amazing."

There were only two other people in the bar, an enormous barman who should have picked a place with higher ceilings to work, and a middle-aged man in a creased suit jacket hanging over the bar. Tom introduced himself to the barman, and in doing so made himself known to the drunk.

"I have the secret!" yelled the drunk, raising his face, which was pockmarked and red. "I tell you I have the secret!"

"Ignore Simon," said the barman. "Want a drink?"

Tom ordered two beers and attempted to ignore the drunk, as the barman went off to change the barrels. He positioned himself between Simon and Beth, hoping to deflect the drunken slurs so they didn't reach Beth with such force.

"I have the secret!" yelled Simon, spitting saliva over the bar in front of him.

"We all have a secret," said Tom.

"But I have *the* secret. The secret to a happy life," confided Simon.

Tom and Beth smiled at each other. "Whiskey I'm guessing," whispered Tom.

"You can mock me," said Simon, one eye fully closed, the other searching for some light. "But very few people know the secret, and the people that do don't pass it on easy. I may never pass it on." He shrugged his shoulders in his oversized creased jacket. "I may keep it to myself, maybe it will die with me."

"I'm curious," said Beth to Tom. "What do you think he thinks he knows?"

"What he thinks he knows and what he actually knows are two different things."

The barman came back, poured two pints, and talked to Tom about the set-up of the evening. Then Tom got his guitar out and played a few tunes, experimenting with different locations in the bar, not that there was much choice. Beth chatted with the giant barman who, despite his size and rugged appearance, was a softly spoken man with a love for plants. He was very excited to find out that Beth was from Columbia and quizzed her on all the flora she had grown up amongst. While she described the avocado tree that had grown in their courtyard, Simon screamed out, as though seized by a spiritual power.

"The plants know! The plants know! Those avocados you grew, and the lemons, they all knew! They all know the secret!"

The barman smiled at Beth and shook his head. "I hear about this secret every day."

Just then a group of men entered the bar, and made the collective noise that men, the world over, make when they see an old friend; the macho way of saying 'We've missed you.' One of them, a squat man with curly brown hair approached Tom, his arms outstretched.

"Tommy!" Beth watched as Tom's face lit up and he embraced the man.

"Chappers! It's been a long time."

"It's been too long cuz, you get taller every time."

"And you get fatter," said Tom, shaking his cousin's stomach.

Beth heard the same soft twang in the new man's voice. It was strange to hear, for some reason she had thought Tom's accent was unique.

"You remember Steve, Damo and Luke." They all shook hands, exchanging memories of their last meeting. Tom beckoned them over to the bar where Beth watched on. He put his arm around her.

"This is Beth," he said. "This is my cousin Pete, and this is Steve, Damo and Luke." He pointed to the three friends in the wrong order, and they rearranged themselves in a comedy fashion until they were in the right order from left to right.

"You're going to need to stand in that order all night," laughed Tom. "I'm shit with names."

"Good to meet you all," said Beth, shaking hands with them, and giving each a smile that Tom knew they would not forget in a hurry.

They sat around and drank beer, as the bar gradually filled up and drunk Simon told more people about his secret. Tom had never been with Beth in a group before, and he was impressed with the way she handled herself in a herd of men, paid each of them individual attention, asked questions, made them laugh and remembered the smallest thing they had mentioned in earlier conversation. Tom could tell that everyone round the table was completely charmed by her, and he swelled with pride, knowing that this enchanting girl was all his. He almost forgot what he was there for, and had trouble leaving her when it was his turn on the microphone. He realized with guilt that his group had paid no attention whatsoever to the first act; a hippy girl whose folk music had been a background noise to the laughs and banter from his table. She didn't return his smile when they passed each other.

There were whoops and cheers from his table as he made himself comfortable on a high chair, and adjusted the microphone. He looked out into the bar, it was throbbing with people now. The sticky floor was littered with Converse All-Stars and flip-flops, and the rare heat that radiates from sunburnt English limbs filled the room. Tom recognized a few faces from the café earlier and greeted them with a nod of his head.

"Hey. My name's Tom and I'm going to sing a couple of songs you might know." He looked into the crowd. "And perhaps one of my own," he muttered.

He played a couple of chords, cleared his throat and launched into his first song, an unusual version of a Tracy Chapman classic, barely recognizable by the energetic fingerwork and beats he drummed into the song. The noisy crowd gradually became quiet as parts of their brains latched onto something familiar in the music, like an old friend tapping them on the shoulder, 'remember me?' Moments of enlightenment dawned around the room, and shoes began to tap the sticky floor. Tom kept his eyes on his fingers but was glad to hear a decent round of applause as his first song ended. He retained the energy of the crowd by playing three more covers, a Kinks classic, a Pink Floyd favourite and a little-known Beatles track that had the music aficionados in the room foaming at the mouth as they shared their knowledge with anyone around them.

He got a massive cheer when he stopped for a sip of beer. He looked into the audience, past all the clapping hands and pint glasses he saw Beth. She was looking straight at him, her eyes shining, like the first time he had seen her. He smiled.

"I hope you don't mind," he said into the microphone. "But I'm gonna play one of my own now." He stretched his fingers, and took a deep breath. He could hear his heart beating a rhythm too fast. "Have mercy on me please, it's a ballad."

The crowd cheered and made themselves comfortable.

"They love him," whispered Pete to Beth. "There's something special about his music." She nodded in agreement.

Tom began to play, so quietly at first that people had to strain to hear the melody. Gradually he played louder, finger picking a six-note bar over and over, until it seemed like an old favourite to the crowd. Heads nodded, fingers tapped and mouths hummed along. Even drunk Simon at the bar seemed to be listening when Tom started singing.

In a crowd,
Or just us two
All is dark,
Apart from you

In my arms
Or in my mind
You give me light
Thought I'd never find

Hope you feel for me what I feel for you

Love Light
A sparkle and glow
Never believed in first sight
Now I know

In and out
You shine so bright
With you it's day
Never night

Your eyes my stars
Your heart my sun
Stay with me
When all is done

Hope you feel for me what I feel for you

Love Light
A sparkle and glow
Never believed in first sight
Now I know
Now I know

He repeated the chorus a couple of times to finish and was amazed to hear voices joining his. He cast his eyes past his curls into the audience and saw mouths he didn't know singing the words he had written. He looked past everyone, and sang the final chorus, with very little guitar, straight at Beth. She was in the middle of a swaying chain of singers, their arms around each other, wailing the lyrics, *his* lyrics. Once he had located her, he saw nothing else, just Beth, sweet sweet Beth. When he stopped playing the crowd erupted, but he barely noticed. She smiled at him and he was the happiest man in the world.

*

That night, beneath the stars, on the pebble beach, she made him play it again for her. This time his eyes didn't touch the guitar. Afterwards, she took his hand and kissed it.
"I love you Tom," she said.
"I love you too."
They had both known it from the very start.

15:17, Friday August 6th, 1999
Train from King's Cross to Hartlepool

Beth was confident in every social situation, could converse with people from all walks of life, could work a room like no one Tom had ever met, but here she sat on the train pulling in to Hartlepool, fidgeting and nervous.
"You're gonna be fine," he said. "They're just normal people, well normal for where I'm from." He smiled, but inside he was just as

nervous, and had bitten his already short fingernails down until they hurt. He pulled down their overnight bag from the luggage rack and squeezed her hand.

"OK, let's do this," she said.

They got off the train and through the ticket barrier. Tom spied his parents by the ticket office and was glad to see his mum had been able to get his dad out of a tracksuit for the day. He stood awkwardly in a pair of jeans and his favourite sweater, a souvenir his sister had bought him from her trip to the Guinness factory in Dublin over ten years ago. His mum was wearing a flowery blouse, which he assumed was a new purchase from the charity shop, and a pair of beige trousers. Her hair was a new shade of yellow blonde, it was different every time he visited.

He guided Beth over to them.

"Hey mam, hey dad," he said, as casually as his heart would allow.

"Ello sweetheart," said his mum, pulling him down a foot to give her a hug.

His father nodded at him "Alright son."

"This is Beth," said Tom, his voice leaping higher at her name.

Beth offered the bunch of yellow roses to Tom's mother, hoping she wouldn't notice how hot and damp the plastic had become in her hands. "Hello, it's lovely to meet you both."

Tom's mother took the flowers and gave Beth a tight hug. "Ello Beth, so nice to finally meet you. Call me Carol. Ooh, I love yer 'air," she said, stroking Beth like a puppy. "I tried that colour once, but it went 'orribly wrong, do you remember sweetheart? I looked like somethin' out of a circus. T'was your auntie Barbara that 'elped me with it, I'm sure she did it on purpose, we 'ad your cousin's wedding coming up and…"

"I remember mam," said Tom. "Dad, this is Beth."

"Alright pet," he said, keeping his hands firmly in his pockets, and his eyes down. A moment passed, and the two women smiled at each other. Beth liked the way Tom's dad had unruly grey curls and the same introverted posture as his son.

"OK, let's go," said Tom. They all walked to the family car, a battered Sierra. Tom squeezed Beth's hand and gave her a wink.

Tom's mum babbled nonsense for the ten-minute car journey, and for once Tom was glad of it. As she talked about the comings and goings in the village and the various problems of his extended family, his heart began to slow, maybe this weekend would be OK after all.

At the house, Tom's mum put on a pot of tea before she had even changed from her comfy lace-ups into her slippers. She then took great pride in showing Beth around the two-up two-down. The lounge had so many floral patterns it looked like a garden in bloom, among the flowers sat Carol's pride and joy: a commemorative cushion of Charles and Diana's wedding. After putting this gingerly into Beth's hands she also showed her a little clay fish Tom had made at school, and then a set of framed images of him as a child. Beth oohed and aahed over the pictures as she was introduced to Tom at every age from a baby up.

"That's Tom on his first day at school… cried like a baby when I left 'im. That's when he decided e'd 'ad enough of curls and he shaved his whole 'ead, look at the state of him Beth, you'd cross the road to avoid a thug like that wouldn't yer? And that's 'im picking up 'is high school prize, we were so proud of 'im." She reached up and ruffled Tom's hair.

"What was the prize for?" asked Beth.

"Maths. He were an absolute whizz at maths. Top of 'is school. Teacher said he could go to a top university. But he were more interested in guitar."

"Fat lot of use that's gonna do us," muttered his dad from behind the Racing Post.

"Yer know Beth, lots of musicians are real good at maths," she continued, paying no attention to her husband. "Yer know, Brian May from Simon and Garfunkel has a degree in Maths."

Tom rolled his eyes, "Mam, why would a man called Brian May be in a band called Simon and Garfunkel?"

Carol shrugged her shoulders, "Don't ask me sweetheart, but I'm sure he 'ad good reason, he were a very clever man." She turned her attention to Beth, "Now let me show yer upstairs and yer room." Tom's dad looked over his paper at his wife and slightly raised his eyebrows, there had obviously been words spoken about the sleeping arrangements.

As Tom and Beth followed Carol's pink fluffy slippers up the stairs, her talking continued.

"Now, Philip and I, oh, I sound like the Queen don't I! Well anyway, me and Philip like to think of ourselves as modern people, modern parents."

Tom put his hand to his curls and shook his head, dreading her next words.

"And we know that yer both adults, who will be doing what adults do, with each other, and most likely, I don't know, but most likely sharing a bed from time to time. But in this house, yer dad's house…" she said turning to Tom.

"Please mam," he pleaded. "We really don't care where we sleep, we're here to spend time with you, not time in bed."

Carol cocked her head to the side and her face glowed with adoration for her only son. Beth noticed that they shared the same blue eyes.

"Sweetheart, yer such a … sweetheart. Well, I'm glad yer said that, coz as yer know we have only the two bedrooms and so we've put a blow-up bed on the floor in yer room, for yer to sleep on and Beth can have the bed." She pushed open a door and Beth peeped inside. The room was small and the blow-up bed was butted up right next to the single bed, as though half a double bed had collapsed to the floor. Tom's bed was made up in stripes of grey and blue. There were framed pictures around the room of Jimmi Hendrix, Slash and other guitarists Beth didn't recognize. On closer inspection later that evening she saw the pictures had been cut out of magazines, some even ripped out by hasty teenage fingers. A chest of drawers was topped with a lace doily and a bowl of pot-pourri, obviously later additions to the room. Next to the drawers sat a large bottle half-filled with pennies.

"Saving your pennies for a rainy day?" asked Beth with a smile.

Tom shrugged, and Carol spoke up. "Take a closer look luv."

Beth went over to the bottle and noticed a messy scrawl across it in fat black pen. She squinted at it trying to make out the words.

"For my… 1960 Gibson Les Paul, not to be broken till filled up, and ONLY for this purrpuss," she read, laughing.

Carol shook her head. "He were never any good at spelling. Like his father. Philip is no use to me when it comes to the crossword, can just about spell 'is own name."

"When did you start collecting pennies?" Beth asked Tom.

"When I was twelve."

"You knew at twelve that you wanted that guitar?"

"I knew before then, but I only started collecting at twelve."

"And there's not just pennies in there, luv," said Carol. "He puts 'is birthday and Christmas money in there too. That's probably the most valuable thing in the whole 'ouse." She laughed.

"Where's that tea?" came a shout from downstairs.

"Just comin' luv," Carol shouted back. "Come down for a brew when yer settled," she said, leaving the room.

Tom squeezed Beth's hand and smiled.

"You still put money in there?" she asked.

"Every time I come back." He reached into his pocket, pulled out a handful of change and let it clink into the bottle. Beth took her purse from her bag and did the same.

"Ready for your first of many cups of tea?" he asked.

"Yes," she laughed. "Let's go."

*

The weekend passed quickly, lubricated with an ongoing flow of tea and chatter from Tom's mum. They had a roast chicken with all the trimmings on Sunday, and afterwards Tom walked Beth around the neighbourhood. He showed her his school, the park where he'd had his first kiss, the fish and chip shop where you could still buy scraps for 20 pence, and the garden centre his mum worked in. They climbed up to the local viewpoint, to survey the whole town and Tom pointed out the smoke rising from the distant chicken factory.

"Wow, it's almost bigger than the town itself," said Beth.

"And employs almost everyone," said Tom. "About half of my class ended up there."

"Did you think you'd end up working there?"

"Never," he said. "I always knew I wanted to get out of town, and from the age of ten I was set."

"On what?" said Beth with a smile.

"On being a rock star."

They both laughed. "Well, I'm pretty sure you're going to make it as one," she said, turning to him. "I've never met anyone with the talent and drive that you have. I find it completely inspiring. You just need to stick at it and you'll be discovered. Then you'll be rich and famous, and I'll never need to work."

She bit her lip and looked back at the chicken smoke. She had made the assumption in her head that they would be together forever, but she hadn't meant to make it out loud. Tom tried to hide his smile by looking in the opposite direction.

"Fancy a pint in the local?" he asked.

She nodded, glad of the change of subject.

"We'd better go now, before the chicken pluckers clock off for the day."

They walked hand in hand to the Crooked Billet and bought two pints for the price of one in London. The landlord, a friend of Tom's dad, chatted with Tom, in a strong accent Beth couldn't decipher. She nodded and smiled at the appropriate times and amused herself by listening to Tom's changing accent and vocabulary.

"You're becoming a true northerner again," she said as they took their seats.

"I am?"

"Yes, your accent's coming back."

He laughed. "Well it's a good job we're leaving tomorrow. So how've you enjoyed the weekend?"

She nestled in beside him as he put his arm round her, not caring that the landlord and a few other familiar faces were looking on.

"I've had a *really* good time. Honestly, I have. Your mum is lovely, so genuine and chatty. And your dad, well, he's a good pair of ears for your mum. And in his own abrupt way, he's been very sweet to me. He even filled me up a hot water bottle last night and gave it to me, without a word."

"Did he? He must be getting soft in his old age. They like you Beth. I can tell."

"I'm glad."

"So perhaps soon, I can meet the famous Willowmans?"

"Maybe," said Beth, taking a big slurp of beer.

10:12, Tuesday December 21st, 1999
Euston Station, London

Beth went to her parents' place in the Surrey countryside for Christmas, and Tom went home to Hartlepool. His mum had invited Beth to spend a few days with them, to experience a Turner Christmas, but she'd declined saying she needed to spend Christmas with her family. She sent Tom home with a hamper of cheese for his parents. "I know exactly what my dad will say about that one," he laughed, pointing at the Stilton. He put on a deep Yorkshire accent "Am not eating that rubbish, it's full o' mould."

Beth went with Tom to Euston to catch his train. They had not spent more than two days apart in almost a year, and both of them felt nervous about a week. Tom had no idea how he was going to make it through a week without her, he clutched his guitar case tightly, perhaps the other love of his life would help him through. Beneath the departures board, they held each other until the last announcement was made for his train.

"I'll miss you," she said.

"Me too."

"You'd better go, or you'll miss your train."

He squeezed her tight and then used all his strength to wrench his arms from her. He felt a huge distance parted them already. He jostled his rucksack into position, picked up his guitar case and the hamper, and took one last look at Beth before running for his train. She stood watching his figure get smaller and smaller, and then she watched his train get smaller and smaller, and then she had nothing left to watch but the space he had occupied.

10:12, Friday December 24th, 1999
Surrey and Yorkshire

Time apart from your love is hard enough; time apart from your first love is torture.

Separated from one another with lonely days full of family made them both miserable. Both sets of parents noted a slower gait, a distractedness, and an expression of melancholy on the faces of their children. Christmas did little to change their demeanour. The only thing that brightened their days was their 6pm telephone call, but even as this drew to a close their misery would seep back in.

"I miss you so much," whispered Beth on their third phone call. "I knew it would be difficult but I had no idea how much."

"I know, let's never do this again."

"Unfortunately Christmas comes round every year," she joked.

"I don't mean Christmas, I mean time apart. Let's not do it again."

"Deal," she said.

03:56, Christmas Day, 1999
Willowman Grange, Surrey

Beth woke in the dark like an excited child. She put on her reading light and reached to the end of her bed where she had put Tom's present. She tore through the glitzy snowflakes and gasped when she realized what she held in her hand. It was a framed piece of lined A4 paper. Dancing down the page with no correlation to where the lines sat was Tom's messy scrawl, crossed out and rewritten in places. At the top in neater handwriting, she read, *Love Light for Beth*.

11:46, Wednesday December 29th, 1999
Waterloo Station, London

Even when minutes pass like hours, and hours like days, they still pass and eventually Tom and Beth's ordeal was over. He met her at Waterloo, and once again they held each other tight, the only stillness visible within the throng of people rushing to get somewhere. After a few minutes they were jostled out of position by a rush for the 12.52 to Strawberry Hill. Tom slung her bag over his shoulder and his arm around her waist. They walked across Waterloo Bridge to Embankment, stopping twice on the way over the bridge to appreciate the view and each other. It was a freezing cold day, where the peaks and domes of London rose like snowy mountains into the sapphire sky. Beth loved blue skies; she had grown up beneath them in hotter climates and always stopped to appreciate them.

At his flat, they dumped all the paraphernalia that was getting in the way of holding each other truly close. Bags, hats, scarves and coats were thrown on the sofa and Tom wrapped himself around Beth.

"Every single part of me missed every single part of you," he said into the crown of her head, inhaling her familiar shampoo.

"Me too. God it's so nice to be in your arms again." She buried her face into his thick jumper. After a moment, she lifted her head from the warmth of his embrace. "But there's still too many layers between us." He returned her cheeky smile and soon the sofa was piled even higher with the troublesome layers that get in the way of lovers.

*

Later that evening, due to the coldness of Tom's flat that always seemed to have a draught passing through, they had their clothes back on and were huddled together on the sofa.

"So tell me about the Turner Christmas feast?" asked Beth.

"Well, we only had my Auntie Babs and her new man round for lunch, but you'd have thought we were cooking for the entire Royal Family. Auntie Babs had told mam that her new man was some flash businessman and so mum was fussing with the house for days beforehand. She removed every single cushion cover, every tablecloth and every doily…"

"That's a lot," laughed Beth.

"That *is* a lot, and she washed, dried and ironed them! All because she thought Newcastle's answer to Richard Branson was coming for lunch. Dad kept saying 'stop fussing woman, Babs'll be shot of him in a week.' But she wouldn't listen."

Beth was really laughing, she could just imagine the scene, and she loved hearing Tom tell the story. His week up north had left his voice heavily accented and he didn't have to try hard to impersonate his father.

"We had two chickens in the oven, a mountain of tatties, every vegetable you can think of boiling soft on the stove, and a bottle of Cava in the fridge, then the doorbell rang. Mum jumped out of her skin, anyone would think she wasn't expecting them. She checked her new hair in the mirror, took off her slippers and apron and went to welcome the *entrepreneur*. You should have seen her face…"

Now Tom was laughing so hard he had to stop talking.

"What? What was he like? What was your Auntie Babs' new man like?" Beth couldn't wait to find out and found herself laughing at the answer before she'd even heard it.

"A drunk! Just like Simon in Brighton, but in worse clothes. He couldn't walk straight. When mum opened the door he had one foot in the flowerbed, one foot on the path and Babs was pulling him to the house. Mum's face was a picture. She pulled herself together and opened her mouth to say something, but Babs shook her head and said 'don't bother Carol, he's completely out of it. He'll sleep all afternoon.' And that's exactly what he did. We put him on the sofa, on top of mum's beautifully ironed cushions and he passed out."

"That's awful! Your poor mum!"

"I know. And he snored so loudly that mum had to put Bing Crosby on full blast to disguise the sound."

"Did your mum see the funny side?"

"Only after we'd all drunk the Cava and some beers, before that she kept looking over at him, sadly, seeing him dribbling all over Princess Di."

"So was he a businessman?"

"Nah. That's what he told Babs, but turns out he's a professional gambler. Had won big on the horses that morning. While he was passed out Babs took some money from his pockets, gave fifty quid to mum for the food and fifty quid to me for my guitar bottle. Said if he couldn't contribute his company to the afternoon, he could contribute some money. So it all turned out pretty well."

"So is your Auntie going to stay with him?"

"No. Dad was right. He was gone by the next morning."

"I wish I could have been there, but it's probably for the best, I couldn't have kept a straight face."

"You wouldn't have been the only one. Dad laughed all afternoon, I've never seen him laugh so hard and for so long."

They sipped the cheap wine that had formed part of Carol's gift to Beth. It had sat inside a floral bag next to a bottle of unknown perfume.

"Did you say you had chicken for Christmas Day?"

"Uh-huh."

"What, no turkey?"

"No, we always have chicken."

Beth pondered this, then laughed. "But you must have chicken all the time at home."

"Yes," his voice tightened slightly, "and we have it for Christmas too."

An awkward moment passed before Beth changed the subject. "What are you doing for new year?"

"Oh, yes, I meant to talk to you about that." He hesitated. "I know we hadn't made any plans so I told Nigel I'd work at the pub. It's triple time coz of the millennium and the punters will be feeling generous."

Beth was relieved. She could ask her mother's question and be assured of the answer she was hoping for.

"That's a shame. My parents are holding a new year party and they asked me to invite you."

"Really?" This was the first time that Tom had been in the same sentence as her parents, let alone invited to a party. He didn't relish the idea of meeting them in such an imposing circumstance as a party celebrating a new millennium, but he knew he had to do it sooner or later. After all, he was planning on spending forever with their daughter. He made up his mind.

"I'll tell Nigel I can't work the shift. He gave me first option coz he knew I needed the money, but there's plenty of others to work that night."

"No, really Tom. It's fine. You can meet them another time. You'd miss out on good money if you came."

"It's only money," he shrugged.

"You really don't have to come. It will be full of my dad's family, boring diplomats and their pretentious families. You'd probably have more fun in the pub."

Tom considered this. He probably would have more fun in the pub. But this felt more important than fun, it was like a duty he had to perform. He couldn't imagine life without Beth, and he couldn't ignore what else might be included in that deal.

"I want to spend it with you. We can see in the new year together, and I can meet your family."

"OK," said Beth. "As long as you're sure."

"I'm sure," he said. She wasn't.

*

"Do you have a suit?" asked Beth.

Tom looked at her as though she'd asked whether he owned a nuclear weapon.

"God, no. Not unless you count my old school uniform which mum treasures like the Holy Grail."

"OK, well how about a smart shirt?"

He raised his eyebrows. "What kind of party is this?"

"Listen Tom. I know you're not going to believe me, but I really think you're going to feel more comfortable at this party if we get you some smart clothes. Hey, maybe you can borrow something of Michael's?"

"Isn't your brother a diplomat in training?"

"Yes."

"Well, I don't want to look like a diplomat in training. People will expect me to be bloody diplomatic."

She suppressed a giggle. "Please. I won't make you look like a diplomat. I won't make you look like an idiot. Just a teeny bit smarter, on this one evening only, so you don't feel out of place."

"Beth, we both know I'm going to feel out of place."

"Well, yes. But we can at least try."

"Bloody hell. The things I do for you!"

14:07, Friday December 31st, 1999
Waterloo Station, London

They met at Waterloo station, ready to take the train together. Beth hardly recognized him at first. His most unruly curls that normally hung over his eyes were gone, he wore a navy wool jumper she had not seen before, and jeans. And on his feet, she couldn't quite believe, were a pair of brown suede boots. They were scuffed, and made him look like a boy experimenting in his dad's shoes, but they were not his trademark shabby

Converse. She was so happy with his effort that she held him as tightly as she had after their week apart. Waterloo was fast becoming their brief encounter station for cinches.

"Oh Tom." Eventually she let go of him and stood back to look again at him, still not sure she had just embraced the right man.

He shrugged. "Wanted to make a good impression." He looked down at his shoes. "But don't expect this again."

"I won't. And I don't want to see it again. The new Tom is just perfect for this weekend, but I don't want to see him again."

"Thank God, coz these shoes are killing me."

She laughed. "Where did you get them from?"

"Borrowed them from Chris, but his feet are three sizes bigger than mine, so we improvised."

"What did you do?"

"I'm wearing my Converse inside them."

She bent over laughing. "You're joking me?"

He shook his head. "No. It worked fine to begin with but now I can hardly walk."

"Well, you only have to walk to the train now. Come on, let's go."

*

When they arrived at Windlesham station Beth hailed a cab. Tom had been glad to know her parents wouldn't be meeting them at the station, it gave him a little longer, but it was only prolonging the agony. He wasn't great at meeting new people at the best of times, and this was probably the worst of times. When Beth told the cabbie the address of her parents, he turned around in his seat.

"You know the people that live there?" he asked.

"Yes," she said.

"Lucky girl."

Tom had assumed that Beth's parents had a nice place, but this little exchange and the size of the houses they were passing made him question *how* nice. And the further they went the better the houses became. Both of them sat quietly in the back of the cab, hoping the other couldn't hear their nervous heart beating. The cab slowed and turned off the road and stopped in front of a huge set of wooden gates, surrounded by trees. A sign in swirling writing announced that they had arrived at Willowman Grange.

"Shall I let you out here love?" asked the cabbie.

"No, just wait please."

Beth got out of the car, approached the gate and typed a code into a little box. The wooden gates parted slowly, so slowly that Tom wanted to charge at them, 'enough of the big fucking reveal!' he wanted to shout, 'just let me in there.' Beth got back into the car and squeezed Tom's hand. They drove along a road surrounded by forest, and they drove and they drove. Finally they emerged into the sunshine and Tom and the cabbie got their first look at the Willowman residence.

"Fuck!" they both exclaimed in unison.

The forest opened out onto a huge green space, and the house sat slightly uphill at the back. The road wound past large metallic sculptures that bore some resemblance to fat women.

"Mum collects art," said Beth. "Mostly from South America."

The house itself was huge and imposing, you could say it resembled something from a Jane Austen novel, but Tom had no idea who Jane Austen was, and had nothing to say. He counted sixteen windows along the front, ten at the top and six at the bottom. A grand columned entrance sat in the middle and was alive with ivy. Two tiny figures, one half the size of the other, stood between the columns.

"Just your parents live here?" asked Tom.

"And Michael, and Tia Lolli."

"Who the hell's Talaly?"

Beth laughed. It felt good to laugh.

"Ti-a Lo-li, like a lollypop. She's my second mother."

"Second mother? What the…?"

"Don't worry, I'll explain when you meet her. She doesn't speak a word of English."

As the car got closer, Tom saw that the two figures were waving. Beth's father was either a very tall man, or her mum was a very small woman. The car stopped outside and Tom realized that both were true. Beth paid the taxi and flew out of the car, and up the stairs, to embrace her father, then mother. Tom, feeling more than a little awkward, took the bags from the cabbie.

"You've done well there, mate," muttered the man.

"And this most be Tom!" came a booming voice from the top of the steps. Tom attempted a smile and staggered up to meet the voice. He had never been to a house that had so many steps just to get to the front door, it was hard work with two pairs of shoes on. If they had so much money, why not just make the road reach the door? Tom reached the face of Beth's mum at least three steps before reaching her dad. Beth's mum was petite, with jet-black hair swept onto her head like a Mr. Whippy ice cream, possibly an attempt to look taller. Her face was the type of face that needed no make-up but was smothered in it. She wore a pale pink trouser suit and scarf. She was very beautiful.

Beth's dad looked as though he had just ran a Gilette razor across his chiseled jaw and was now smiling at camera. He had grey hair, every single strand of which was disciplined into a gentle wave towards the back of his head. He had a broad smile and crinkly eyes, all of which was directed at Tom. He was only one step above Tom, but it felt like a mountain of difference.

"Let me help with those bags my man," he said, reaching for the bag in Tom's right hand with his own left. He then extended his right to Tom.

"It's great to meet you at last. I'm Jim, Beth's father."

"Good to meet you too." He paused. "Jim." Tom had never shaken the hand of a diplomat, had never much thought about handshakes before, but felt intimidated by, in awe of, and inspired by this man simply by the way he grabbed and shook his hand with his winning smile. Tom had no idea you could communicate so much in a hand.

"And this is my wife, Veronica."

Tom extended his hand but Veronica ignored it, put both her hands on his shoulders and kissed him on each cheek.

"Is nice to 'ave meet you," she said in a strong accent.

"Great to meet you," said Tom. "And thanks for inviting me to your party."

"No is problema. We want very much for you to be 'ere."

Veronica then launched into Spanish, the language she was clearly more comfortable in, and chatted with Beth, pulling her inside. Jim stood to one side and gestured for Tom to enter. There were too many things going on for Tom to concentrate on one. Beth was speaking in a foreign language, Jim was saying something about the weather, and Tom was entering the biggest hallway he had ever seen, TV programmes included. He tried to keep track of Jim's animated chatter.

"So, we've had all four fires burning for the first time in seven years, it really has been an exceptionally cold winter. But I guess you're used to the cold weather Tom, being a northern boy."

"Oh yes, it can get very cold up there. But we only have one fireplace to worry about," he joked.

"Well, it would be nice to have fewer of them here to keep an eye on, but at least we get some use out of the forest. We'll have to take you for a walk round later, you look like a good size for chopping wood." He patted Tom's broad shoulder.

"Never done it before, but happy to try," said Tom.

"Good man. Now Beth, maybe you can show Tom up to his room, he's in the red room at the back."

"Which one?" she looked puzzled. Tom couldn't believe there were enough bedrooms to confuse Beth in her own family home.

"The one we usually put the *campesinos* in when they visit."

Veronica punched her husband in the arm, with surprising force for a little lady. "*Madre mia*. The same yoke every time. 'e thinks 'e's funny Tom, but you no need laugh. I only laughed before 'e married me."

This made them all laugh. Jim bent down and kissed his tiny wife on the top of her head, in a similar way that Tom often did with Beth. "Luckily I didn't just marry you because you laughed at my jokes." Veronica gave a little smile to her husband and her eyes shone. Tom wasn't used to seeing old people still very much in love and it made him feel a little awkward. He picked up their bags in order to look elsewhere.

"OK, we'll get freshened up and come down," said Beth heading to the curved staircase.

"We'll be in the drawing room," said Jim, putting his arm around Veronica and heading into the darkness behind the stairway. Tom was baffled by how the family orientated themselves in the house, telling each other where to go and where they would be. In Hartlepool you could shout from any room in the house and be heard in any other, in fact you probably didn't need to shout, unless the telly was on. Tom carried the bags up the never-ending staircase behind Beth. At the top she turned around and smiled at him. He stopped a step below.

"Congratulations, you've passed," she whispered with a beaming smile. He had no idea why she was whispering, but he found himself doing the same.

"You think they like me?"

"I know they like you. Dad asked you to chop wood with him – that's a sure sign."

"Well, I haven't said two words yet, it could all fall apart when I actually say something."

She chuckled. "Then don't say anything." There was a tiny element of seriousness in her eyes, but she turned around and it was gone. "Let's get you to your room," she said, turning right along a wood-panelled corridor. "Oh and sorry, mum's a strict catholic, we're pretty much at opposite ends of the house."

Tom trailed after her, turning his head from side to side to take in the abstract paintings they passed. Angular faces with ferocious eyes stared at him in anger or shock, it was hard to know. Maybe they'd never encountered a northern man before. The hallway was lit up as Beth pushed a door open at the end.

"Here's your room," she said, standing to the side to let him enter.

"Bloody hell." The bags fell from his shoulder. He looked around, open-mouthed. "This is bigger than my whole house put together." He walked from the door to the four-poster bed, and then to the first set of bay windows, and was amazed by how many steps he'd taken. The window overlooked the back of the house, a picturesque arrangement of lawns, gazebos, trees and more sculptures. In the trees at the end he spied a yellow flag in a clearing.

"What's that?" he said, pointing.

Beth came to stand next to him. "A golf course."

He nodded. "You get lots of stray golfers walking into your garden?"

"Only my dad," she said. She didn't want to explain that it was their own private course. "Let me show you your bathroom." She walked through a door that was easily missed, seamlessly part of the wooden panels. He followed her. He was running out of wonder now, it had been exhausted on the driveway, great hall and bedroom.

"Why are there two sinks?" he asked, genuinely puzzled.

She put her arms around him and stared into his confused face. "For two people, his and hers." Her answer did nothing to ease his confusion and he looked from one marble sink to the other and back again.

"Hey," she said. "Hey!" He looked down at her, as though noticing for the first time that she stood before him.

"I know it's difficult, but try to ignore all this." She gestured with her eyes to the double sinks. "It's just things. It means nothing. It means nothing to me." She stroked the side of his face, missing the curl that hung there the day before.

"Sure. I know. It's just things." He repeated her words. He had none of his own that he could add with any conviction.

She kissed him. Partly because she wanted to, and partly because she wanted him to stop looking at all the superfluous things that surrounded them. He kissed her distractedly to begin, but then he remembered how much he loved kissing her and soon he forgot where he was, only knowing he was with Beth. His hands began to move up and down her body and were only stopped by a strange voice coming from the bedroom. Beth pulled away from him and ran back through the door.

"Lolli, Lolli!" She shouted.

Tom looked tentatively back into the room and saw Beth embracing a diminutive grey-haired lady with a stoop. Beth's embrace was pushing the woman's back into a straight position and he could see the pain in her closed eyes that rested just above Beth's shoulder. They held each other, in this painful position, for much longer than Beth had held either of her parents. Finally Beth let the woman return to her stooped angle, and a flurry of Spanish passed between the two of them. Lolli had a gruff voice more likely to emerge from a big man than a little woman. She had downturned eyes and grey skin that hung from the bones of her face, she reminded Tom of the anguished paintings in the hallway. She wore layer upon layer of black, a large silver cross and tights gathered around her comfortable shoes. Her man's voice interrupted Beth's excited gabble with the odd word or question. Tom was just wondering how long he should stay hidden with the twin sinks when Beth remembered him.

"Tom, come and meet Lolli!"

He sidled out of the bathroom, not quite sure how to greet an elderly woman, let alone a foreign one.

"Hello Lolli, it's nice to meet you." He stuck out his hand, and she looked at it with an angry pout.

"She doesn't speak any English, give her two kisses and I'll translate for you."

Tom bent down almost to a right angle and kissed the woman on both cheeks, she peered at him with suspicion as he did so, then she looked him up and down and then up and down again. She said something in Spanish and Beth laughed.

"What did she say?" asked Tom.

"She said you have big feet."

"Well, yes. This weekend I do." He paused and smiled at Lolli, who didn't return the gesture. "So how are you related?" he asked Beth.

"We're not. At least not by blood. She was my nanny, still is my nanny. But she's more than that, I spent more time with her as a child than I did either my parents." Beth squeezed Lolli's hand and the woman's face creased into a big smile, not that she understood a word of what Beth had said. "She was also my mum's nanny when she was little."

"Wow, she's been with your family all that time? In the different countries."

Beth nodded. "She left Madrid when she was a teenager to work for mum's family."

"And she never learnt any English?"

Beth said something to Lolli, who turned to Tom and said in a tentative voice, "Feesh an cheeps."

They all laughed and Tom gave a little round of applause. It was more than he knew in her language.

Lolli spoke a few gruff words to Beth and then left the room.

"She said these are fresh towels for you." Beth patted the pile on the bed. "And tea is ready downstairs. You ready for round two?"

Tom took a deep breath. "Let's do it."

*

The afternoon passed relatively smoothly. Jim was a great conversationalist and was able to input and give opinions on pretty much every subject, including contemporary music and guitar. Tom was relieved to find that they shared an admiration for the talents of Jeff Buckley, Jarvis Cocker and Paul Weller, and a disdain for Oasis. He wasn't sure what he'd have done had Jim's opinions been reversed. There is a fine line to walk between keeping your girlfriend's father happy and pursuing your own opinion, but luckily this was a line he didn't have to walk, at least not this day. Veronica was an astute host, catering to Tom's every whim, even before the whim had struck him. She was caring and tactile with him, touching, squeezing and hugging Tom like one of the family. She also had a quick, brutal sense of humour, most often directed at her husband, but also reserved for her absent son.

"Miguel is late, always late. Is a true Latino. Lazy and late. But always 'as the best excuses, that's why 'e will be a great diplomat."

Michael, or Miguel as his mother called him, was over two hours late already, but Tom was doing just fine with the rest of the family. After tea, the four of them wrapped up warm and took a stroll around the garden. Jim showed Tom how to chop wood and the two women stood arm in arm, stamping the ground and puffing little clouds into the air, as Tom demonstrated a surprising talent for it.

"You're a natural Tom!" exclaimed Jim. "If you weren't our guest I'd be keen to put you to work on the whole darn forest."

"Maybe next time," said Tom with a coy smile. He really couldn't believe how well his visit was going, how well he was getting along with these people from a different world, whilst in their world.

Around 5pm, after an extended walk around the grounds, they headed back to the house.

"Is time we prepare for party," said Veronica. "Get on our dancing shoes." She winked and nudged Tom, who sincerely hoped there would be no dancing.

As they walked back they stopped at a sculpture that very loosely resembled a male form.

"You know who this is?" said Veronica to Tom.

He stood back and cocked his head to take in all its angles. He averted his eyes from the impressive triangle that sought the sun from the middle of the figure.

"I really have no idea," said Tom.

"Oh, come on," said Jim. "Look at its strength and virility, it's clear who it is."

Veronica and Beth both laughed, in a tired way that suggested they'd heard the line before.

"Is 'im," said Veronica.

"Who?" said Tom.

"'im" repeated Veronica.

Tom was baffled. "Him, but who is him?"

Beth and her father both stifled laughs.

"'Im, 'im," said Veronica, an edge of anger in her voice.

Tom said nothing, his blush said it all. He had no idea who she was talking about.

"Is 'im, my husband, 'im," she waved her arms frantically in the direction of Jim.

"Oh." Tom suddenly realized that part of Veronica's accent meant that she couldn't pronounce her husbands name.

"Yes, 'im, 'im!" she was shouting now. Beth and her father were almost bent double from laughing. "is not funny you two," she said, directing her anger at her family now. "'e needs his ears clean out."

Slowly they made their way back to the house, Jim stopping now and again to resume his laughing fit.

*

The family and Tom were dressed and ready for guests when Michael finally arrived. They made a splendid sight for him to encounter as he entered the drawing room. His mother was resplendent in a cream lace cocktail dress, pink pearls and matching heels. Jim wore his traditional Savile Row charcoal suit with striped shirt, open by three buttons. Three buttons for parties, two buttons for lunch and buttoned up with a tie for work. A silk handkerchief, matching his wife's pearls and shoes, poked flirtatiously from Jim's breast pocket. Beth was her usual dissident self, wearing trousers rather than a dress, with a silk backless blouse and heels. And her new boyfriend, the man Michael had heard so little about, was very well turned out. He wore a navy suit, the exact cut Michael approved of, a crisp white shirt and brown brogues, very familiar brogues.

"Miguel!" shouted Veronica. "Why so late? Every time, so late." She embraced her son.

"You wouldn't believe the London traffic," said Michael in a deep clipped voice, so different from his mother's. "*Everyone* must be heading to a new year party."

Veronica rolled her eyes at Tom as Michael shook his father's hand and nodded at his sister.

"Hey Beth. Going to introduce me?"

There were nerves in her voice as she spoke. "Michael, this is Tom."

They shook hands, and Tom paid special attention to exerting force and direction. Michael did the same and the battle of the hands would have been declared a draw. Michael had of course realized the suit was his own but, in line with his training, when the penny dropped – it dropped in his head quietly. The two men were well matched in height and proportion, and without a word spoken by Tom they could have been peas from the same rich pod.

"Good to meet you mate," said Tom. And the pods were split.

"Great to meet you Tom. I've been very much looking forward to seeing you in person, and you exceed expectations in the flesh." He looked down at Tom's attire.

"Oh, yeah. Thanks," said Tom. "For this."

"You're very welcome," said Michael, "mate." The word sounded foreign in his noble accent. There was a moment's silence, and then the diplomat intervened.

"Drinks!" said Jim. "Everyone, this is the start of a party, and I suggest we start as we mean to go on." He beckoned to one of the waiting staff on duty for the evening. "Champagne for four."

Tom hated Champagne, it tasted like vomit, but he sipped it and smiled.

*

The first guests were Beth's hugely pompous godfather and his wife. His lips and neck were so full and his face so red that he resembled someone in anaphylactic shock. His wide wife dripped jewels like a willow tree drips leaves, and both of them walked with steps that were more to the side than they were forwards. After the tact of Beth's family, their directness came as something of a shock.

"With that voice, I'd guess you're from north of the border," said Roger.

"What border's that?" asked Tom.

"The class border," said Roger, bursting into snorting laughter that soon engulfed his wife also.

Tom was struck dumb, Michael stifled a smile and Jim jumped in with his usual poise.

"This good man is from Hartlepool, an industrious town in the north, and without towns like that, I don't think you'd have got to this happy stature in life." He patted Roger's burgeoning stomach and they all laughed, not entirely sure of what Jim was inferring, but laughing all the same. Fortunately the next guests arrived at that point, and from then onwards, a steady stream of aged nobility traipsed up the many steps, out of breath, and out of any genuine interest in Beth and Tom. All eyes were on the hosts Jim and Veronica, and the couple was drowned in pearls and platitudes all night. Michael was the stepping-stone to reach the golden couple and was equally engaged in chat of the most banal kind, most of which seemed to comprise eager talk of a certain bottle of Champagne. Beth and Tom mostly entertained each other at the periphery of the room.

"Your parents are lovely," said Tom. "But do they really choose to hang out with these people?"

Beth giggled. "It's all part of dad's job. Some of them are OK, honestly, but a lot of them just suck up to dad, and think he's impressed by their bigoted attitudes."

"And is he?" asked Tom.

"No, not at all. But he needs to entertain them. Needs to maintain this circle around him. One false word and his circle would collapse, and his circle is his power."

Jim and Veronica introduced Tom, and re-introduced Beth, to top bankers, politicians, two representatives of the House of Lords, numerous diplomats, a historical author whose name was familiar from bestseller lists, and various senior businessmen whose roles and companies were a string of acronyms that meant nothing to Tom. Luckily Jim got into the habit of introducing Beth and Tom to the guests as they first arrived and after less than a minute would direct the new guests towards the makeshift bar. From here they could begin their descent to drunkenness and their ascent of the social levels within the room, happily dispensing with Beth and her unintelligible northern boyfriend. Eventually they would finish their social climb by looping back round to Jim and Veronica, where they would attempt to engage in meaningful conversation and stay at the summit of the room long enough for others to notice.

The only people that Beth and Tom spent time with, other than each other, were Jim's secretary and her fiancée Sam. Bella was in her mid-twenties, cocky and pristine, with a marginal accent that erred towards cockney after a few glasses of Champagne. Sam was a strapping farmer from Cambridge who had wanted to see in the new year at his rugby club but had been overruled by Bella. He didn't seem fazed by his surroundings and, despite Bella's protests, he drank as though he were with his rugby mates.

"You been to many of these types of parties before?" Tom asked them.

"No," said Bella. "I've only been working for Jim seven months. Wasn't even expecting to come to this one, but I bit his hand off when he invited us."

"And told Tim…" Sam started.

"It's Jim," said Bella, rolling her eyes.

"And told Jim I was keen as mustard to come along. While the truth was I'd already paid twenty quid for the rugby club party. Non-refundable."

Bella rolled her eyes again, she seemed to spend more time rolling her eyes than using them to look at her fiancée. "Well, it looks like you've drunk more than twenty quid's worth already, you'll have made a profit from beer in no time."

Tom was glad to have come across Bella and Sam. They were an island in shark-infested water and he clung to them all night. Beth left them a couple of times to chat to familiar faces and to keep up her status as diplomat's daughter, but she always had a half smile aimed at Tom from wherever she was in the room. Bella also made attempts to dip her toe in, she made progress with a few lecherous men but mostly sidled back to the protection of the island. The two couples spent a fun evening drinking, mocking the guests and taking bets on who Jim would choose to share his *Belle Epoque 1969* with at midnight.

"Every new year he opens a special bottle from his collection," explained Beth. "Mum gets a small glass – she's not really a drinker, Michael and I get one, dad of course, and then he has enough for two more people. The last two years the PM was here so, naturally, he and his wife got a glass. Some years it's a sure thing, like Terry Waite or Jeremy Irons after he won his Oscar, but this year's anyone's game."

"My money's on the blonde model who turned up with that old banker, if I was your dad I'd definitely want to share some liquids with her," said Sam.

Bella gave him a shove. "I'll go for the heiress in the wheel chair, it looks like she might not live to see 2000 and there's still time for her to change her will, not that your dad needs it of course," she added looking to Beth.

*

A few minutes before midnight, the drunken din that had reached a crescendo suddenly hushed. The string quartet on the raised portion of the drawing room by the mantelpiece, fell quiet and Jim mounted the step in front of them. He was taller than most in the room, except for the leggy model in six-inch heels, and now he towered over them, the king of kings.

"Good evening everyone, I hope you've all had a cheery evening full of good company and good Champagne, and I hope the same can be said of the past year for each and every one of you. A lot has changed in this little year of 1999 for the UK and for Europe, and with new currencies, new parliaments and new technologies, who knows what the new millennium has in store for us. There will be change, that we can be sure of, but throughout change there is one thing we should all hold true to, and that is: our values." He paused. "And I'm not talking about sterling value Dickie." He nodded at a skinny man with coiffed hair and everyone laughed. "I'm talking about traditional values; the importance of family and friends and caring for one another, caring for the common man." A few sets of eyes looked to Tom's group. "So in welcoming in the new millennium I'd like to invite a few people to join me for a special drink."

The crowd held a collective breath as Veronica climbed the step to stand next to her husband, a bottle of Champagne clutched in her hands.

"We all in for a fiver each?" whispered Sam, and his compatriots nodded.

Jim took the bottle from his wife and rocked it in his arms. "I've been nursing this baby here for over twenty years. In fact it was given to me by the British Ambassador in Argentina in 1979, he himself had been nursing it for ten years. So this baby's been well weaned!"

This caused a wave of titters around the room. "Jose-Luis gave it to me on a very special occasion, it was the birth of my daughter, light of my life."

Veronica reached up and gave him a hard elbow.

"Second light of my life, after my wife of course." He corrected himself and the crowd chuckled once more. Tom looked at Beth. Beneath her dark skin and in the low light it was hard to tell, but there was definitely more pink in her cheeks. He held her hand and she gripped it tightly.

"And so, this old festering bottle was presented to me at a time when I was blessed with the greatest gift of all, my daughter Elizabeth, and it is only right that in drinking it I celebrate those who have helped make her the intelligent, strong, caring woman that she is today."

Shoulders around the drawing room, that were raised in tense anticipation, dropped, and the drinks waitresses were nodded at vigorously by men that realized their next drink was not coming from Jim.

"The first four glasses, as is customary, go to my family, to Veronica, Michael, Beth and myself. The fifth glass is going to a woman who is not actually here with us, she is most likely downstairs watching dreadful Spanish soap operas."

Beth and her mother both laughed out loud.

"It is going to a woman who has dedicated 60 years of her life to this family. Orphaned at the tender age of seventeen, she left Madrid to live with distant relatives in Columbia and here she began her career, firstly as nanny to baby Veronica," he touched his wife's shoulders. "Then years later to Michael, and finally to Beth. She is never far from our thoughts and our hearts and her commitment to this family has never waivered. Her only flaws are that she hates parties and doesn't speak a word of English, so all this is lost on her." He paused for the laughter to settle. "But Beth will make sure the Champagne makes its way with my heartfelt sentiments to our lovable Lolli Lobato. Tia Lolli. Second and last to receive my new year's honours is someone who has had a profound effect on Beth, for the better. Take a look at my daughter tonight and you will doubtless see that her eyes shine bright, her hair gleams, her skin… in fact her every cell exudes happiness."

Beth's grip tightened on Tom's hand and he wondered why she was so on edge. Surely she was used to these kinds of exultations from her father.

"And there is one man to thank for this profound happiness that has entered my daughter's life. Tom, I thank you."

Tom's heart lifted a few inches in his chest and seemed to interfere with his breathing which momentarily stopped. Jim was looking right at him, and had said his name, surely there was no other Tom he was referring to.

"You're up mate," said Sam from behind.

"There is Champagne for everyone of course," continued Jim, gesturing to the waitresses who were fluted, primed and ready. "But for a celebration of Beth's happy life, past, present and future, I invite Tom to join the family to crack open this special bottle. Happy new millennium! everyone"

Beth dragged Tom to the front and the next few minutes passed in a blur of countdowns, Champagne pops, clinking glasses, a barely recognizable strings version of *Auld Lang Syne*, back-patting, handshaking and kisses. Despite the three glasses he'd already drank that evening he still hated Champagne, and this was the worst of the lot. He tried to sip it and convert his groans into appreciative noises. He gave Beth a respectable kiss on the lips.

"Let's get out of here," she whispered to him.

"How?" he asked.

She turned her attention to Jim. "Dad, we'll take a glass down to Lolli, make sure she has some company to see in the new year."

"Alright darling," he said, emptying the remains of the bottle into a glass and handing it to Beth. "You're dismissed." He gave her a wink.

Tom followed Beth out of the room, into the darkness at the back of the grand staircase, along a hallway and down a far less salubrious set of stairs. The walls and ceiling narrowed in on him and as he emerged at the base of the stairs he felt like a cat squeezing through a mouse hole. And there was the mouse, watching television in her little cave.

Beth spouted out a flurry of excited Spanish. Tom was beginning to realize that either Beth was very excited at every opportunity to speak Spanish, or else it was the language itself that had an energy bursting to get out of its every word. As she spoke, Tom took in his surroundings. He stood in a mid-sized room with a low ceiling, it was of dolls' house proportions compared with the rest of the house. A single bed against the wall had its bed covers pulled tight and perfectly folded into the corners like an envelope. A wooden chest of drawers faced the bed and at the far end of the room, past a low arch, sat two armchairs angled toward a flickering television. Beth stood in the arch and beckoned him.

"I was just explaining to Lolli, about dad's big speech and his thanks to her."

Lolli didn't look too impressed by the news. In fact, from Tom's perspective, she looked like she wanted to be left in peace with her television, but they persisted anyway. Beth spoke a few more words and handed Lolli the Champagne flute. She looked at it as though she'd never seen one before and like it was the ugliest thing her eyes had ever encountered.

"Sit down Tom," said Beth, patting the armchair. He squeezed himself into the armchair and Lolli looked at him like he was uglier than the Champagne flute. Beth perched on the arm of Lolli's chair, proposed a toast that only confused Lolli and they all took a sip of Champagne. Lolli practically spat hers out and shouted something that made Beth laugh.

"She thinks it's poison," said Beth. "She wants to know if ours tastes like shit too."

Tom nodded emphatically at Lolli. "Tell her I agree."

It was ironic that the only two people honoured to drink the famous Champagne were the only two who would have described it as tasting like shit.

Lolli put her glass on the floor and hushed Beth and Tom into silence. An important twist in her television show had commenced. For the next twenty minutes the three of them watched a melodramatic Spanish soap opera in which two affairs and one murder were exposed. After all the pomp and pretension of upstairs, Tom found himself relaxing and enjoying himself. Beth and Lolli muttered to each other quietly in Spanish, probably trifling things like "who's that?" "the husband" "Why's she going in?" "to collect her daughter" "What's she doing with that child?" "She's the babysitter." At the end of the show, Tom noticed that Lolli and Beth were holding hands. It looked like the most natural thing in the world.

11:32, Saturday January 1st, 2000
Willowman Grange, Surrey

"Well, Tom. It was a pleasure to have you spend New Year with us, and next time you must bring your guitar." Jim shook his hand, in the same powerful way that made Tom swoon the previous day. This time though, it was accompanied by a manly pat on the shoulder.

"I will Jim. I'll learn that Jeff Buckley song for you."

"Good man."

Veronica kissed Tom goodbye in the same way she had hello. Although outwardly friendly and tactile, she was more difficult to read than her husband and Tom wondered what she was thinking. Beth embraced them both and whispered something in her father's ear. Then she reached for Tom's hand and they descended the too-many steps to their waiting taxi. It was the same cabbie as the day before and he gave Tom a thumbs-up when he got into the car.

"Happy new year mate, looks like it's going to be a good one."

*

For days into 2000, Tom was reeling over his time at Willowman Grange. Not only had the house and party astounded him, but so had Beth's family. Her reluctance to introduce him to them any earlier in their relationship, despite three or four visits to Tom's family home, had made him question how welcoming they were going to be, but they couldn't have been more hospitable. He was part of the family as soon as he climbed the steps to the grand entrance and said his first hello. He had felt so welcomed, and so special, the whole time he was there, especially in the presence of Jim. Tom couldn't help himself, he was totally in awe of the man, the way he handled himself, the way he handled others and made everyone feel unique and appreciated. He had a power over people and was the kind of man that other men like to find fault with, but Tom had no such desire, he was happy with the perfection of Beth's father. And now that he had met Jim, he could identify pieces of him in Beth; the way she listened and got along with people, how comfortable she was meeting new people, how charming she was.

He also saw how Beth had inherited the best parts of Veronica's Latino looks and character. They had the same petite, perfectly formed bodies and dark eyes, almost black. Like Beth, it was difficult to assess what her mother was thinking behind those dark shutters. Beth also had her mother's tactility, the two women rarely had a conversation with someone without touching their arm, holding their hand or patting their knee. At first, this kind of intimacy with near strangers had made Tom jealous whenever Beth exhibited it, but he soon realized she used it regardless of who she was talking to, male, female, old, young, even drunk Simon in Brighton was not immune to her touch. Breaking into the personal space of someone, especially a British someone, was rarely done, but Veronica and Beth did it so innocently and with such tenderness, that it only added to their charm. Veronica was witty and, despite her thick accent that might suggest otherwise, she had a razor sharp intelligence that kept her one step ahead of everyone else, even her husband. At the party, it had been Veronica who kept her arm linked with her husband's and steered him around the room, encouraging time spent with the right people, and avoiding it with others.

Tom liked Veronica very much, but there was something guarded about the way she spoke with him, and it was the same with Michael.

This was normal behaviour he supposed, and, as Beth kept saying. "They loved you, all of them. Even Lolli." Tom wasn't so sure. Like Jim, Lolli was completely genuine with her feelings and letting them show, but hers appeared the exact opposite to her employer's. As it turned out he didn't have to worry about Lolli.

15:42, Tuesday March 14th, 2000
Flat 5, 62 York Road, London

With the new millennium off to a positive start in Tom's mood, and a negative start in weather, he spent the first few months of 2000 in his flat, writing, playing and seeing Beth. He felt as though his love for her had been legitimized by both families and he was now free to celebrate it; to write and sing about it as much as he pleased. He made sporadic money from shifts at the pub, and he also picked up some bar work at the Astoria on Tottenham Court Road. The work was frantic, with punters desperately trying to load up on pints before the headliners came on, and then racing for a drink when their least favourite song was played. Despite the chaos, Tom loved being there. The smoky air was alive with heavy guitar, the roar of the crowd and an amplified voice from the stage that controlled the room. Through the haze of smoke, Tom could see hundreds of bobbing heads, moving together like life buoys on a rough sea. Strobe lights darted across the sea in search of something, and as a song reached its crescendo they would find the lead singer and cast him in a heavenly glow. At these seminal points, Tom would happily tell a punter to fuck off, but luckily his colleagues liked him and his passion for music, and would step in before Tom even noticed the ill-timed approach.

Tom was a likeable guy, approachable and down to earth with no pretensions and he made lots of friends at the venue. He became known as 'Curly' and, much to his annoyance, everyone liked to ruffle his hair as they said it. A couple of guys who worked the door agreed to let Beth in when the head of security, a little man with a big self-image, wasn't around. She'd hang around the front entrance pretending to wait for a friend, until one of the giants on the door gave her a nod. He'd then accompany her past the ticket checks and deposit her at the bar. Tom loved Beth being there, but mostly ignored her, partly on purpose so the bosses wouldn't suspect, but mostly because he was completely absorbed in the music. He was just happy to have her there, breathing in the same smoke, hearing the same melodies, having the same bass pulse through her ears. It meant he could relive it all later with her, when they were lying under the sheets and he couldn't sleep for excitement.

After most gigs at the Astoria Tom would be more interested in getting his hands on his guitar than getting them on Beth. But she didn't mind, his passion for music and his guitar were a huge part of what attracted her to him, and during those first few creative months of 2000 she loved him more than ever. The more he played and the more he wrote, the more she wanted him. The more excited he became about a new melody, the more she wanted to move the guitar and replace it with her body, but she was patient with him during those months. And it paid off, when he had perfected a melody, written a verse he was happy with, or simply managed to replicate a difficult riff he'd heard at a gig, he loved her with more passion and focus than at any other time. Tom was hitting creative and physical highs he had not reached before.

While Tom was absorbed in his music Beth attempted to follow his lead and throw herself into her degree. Piles of art books were stacked in a corner of Tom's flat and Beth would select a number of them to encircle herself with, while Tom strummed, sung and noted his melodies. Her books were supposed to act as a moat, a defense against the distraction of love, but it was futile. The more Tom played his guitar, the more Beth wanted him and the less she wanted to read about the Renaissance. She normally watched silently in awe, but that afternoon as he put together a melody she would be humming for weeks after, she told him how she felt.

"I love how gifted you are with a guitar."

He looked up at her, as though shocked he was sharing the room with someone.

"How just your fingers and a few strings make beautiful music. And I love how you never tire of it and how you're always true to it. The passion and drive you have for creating music, it takes my breath away, I can't describe it. You wouldn't be you without music. Please, promise me, you'll never stop."

He grinned. "Well, I'll just stop for a moment." He put down his guitar, crossed the moat and sat cross-legged on top of her textbook.

"I'll never stop loving my guitar, and I'll never stop loving you." He smoothed a piece of hair behind her ear. "I promise."

"And I'll never stop loving you," she said.

Tom had never been happier in his life.

18:21, Friday April 21st, 2000
London Astoria

Gig season was coming to an end and Tom's shifts at the Astoria were thinning out. He was talking to one of the sound technicians, Luke, about what he intended to do in the summer, and about the amplifiers needed for the various festivals Luke had lined up to work at.

"You sound like you know about amps. Do you play?" he asked Tom.

"Yeah, I do. I love to play."

"What kind of stuff?"

"Acoustic, and mostly my own songs, but I'll stretch to the Stones or Kinks if a crowd needs it."

"A crowd? You've played some gigs?"

Tom nodded. He didn't like talking about himself and he hadn't meant to insinuate he drew a crowd. "Well, yeah, mostly just open mic, and the odd pub gig."

"Hey Curly, tell you what. After tonight's gig, there's nothing doing for over a week. Bring your guitar one afternoon and we can connect you up."

Tom was stunned. "You mean here? Play here?"

The guy laughed. "Yes, here. The famous London Astoria, with a crowd of one!"

"Can I bring my girlfriend?"

"OK, a crowd of two."

15:52, Monday April 24th, 2000
London Astoria

Tom didn't normally get nervous in front of a packed pub, but today, in front of Beth and Luke, and enough empty space for 2000 more, he was in pieces. Luke had heard massive names play there; The Stone Roses, The Charlatans, Suede, and even Oasis, though Tom thought they were crap, and now he was about to hear Tom Turner – a one man show, just Tom and his eight year old Fender Strat. Tom warmed his fingers up on some arpeggios and the circle of fifths, while thinking about what to play, he'd been thinking about it non-stop for 76 hours but now he was on stage, he thought some more.

Luke was showing Beth how to control the spotlights, and Tom could hear her laughing at something he said. The sound booth was so far away he couldn't make out any of their words. He gulped and drank some water.

"OK Curly," Luke's voice boomed into the open space. "Let's get the levels right. Just give me a couple of bars on the guitar, something I'll know. And no Spice Girls or I'm walking."

Tom played some Leonard Cohen and The Clash. It was a good warm up for his fingers and, although playing other men's notes, it sent a buzz through him to be playing iconic songs in an iconic venue.

"OK, that's good. Keep playing." Luke hummed along to the tune and sang a couple of wrong words, while adjusting the levels. He had an awful voice and it made Tom feel better.

"Right, now for some vocals. Feel free to sing the right words."

Tom sang the words, quietly at first, and stopping when feedback screamed through the empty space, but louder as the feedback stopped and as he got accustomed to his magnified voice. Beth trained the lights onto him and he no longer saw anything but the guitar in his hands.

"Sounding good Curly," boomed Luke's voice. "We're set to go."

Tom stretched his fingers and took a sip more water.

"Now live on stage," this time it was Beth's voice ringing through his ears. "Britain's newest star, no! The world's newest star! The man you've all been waiting for. Put your hands together for the gorgeous, the talented, the only, Tom Turner!"

Two sets of hands clapped at first, and then Luke located a soundtrack of an audience going wild. Tom laughed and as the soundtrack faded, he started playing his own songs, some for the first time in front of an audience. And what a great place to showcase them – the London Astoria.

An hour and a half passed without his acknowledgement and it took three attempts for Luke to interrupt his singing.

"Hey Curly! Curly! You're sounding great, truly great, no joke, but we need to get out of here before the cleaners come in."

Tom had trouble leaving the stage, he dearly hoped he would be back there one day. He took a deep breath before descending from glory down eight steps onto the sticky floor, the place where thousands, millions of people stood every year to hear their favourite singer. He didn't want to be one of those millions, he wanted to be their favourite singer.

Beth raced up to him as he walked into the darkness at the back of the room. Her eyes were glinting, and he thought they had tears in them.

"That was amazing," she said. "You were amazing. You were made for this." She flung her arms round him, and he gripped her with his arm. One hand on his guitar, one on his girl.

"It's all I want to do Beth. It's all I want to do."

16:21, Saturday May 13th, 2000
Willowman Grange, Surrey

"So let's hear it my man," said Jim. "I've been looking forward to this."

Veronica and Jim sat next to each other on the sofa, both nursing gin and tonics. Jim leant forward in anticipation, while Veronica kicked off her shoes and tucked her legs into the many cushions. Beth sat on the floor in front of her parents, she had a smug look on her face. She knew they were going to love it.

Tom tuned up. "Well, obviously Buckley was a complete perfectionist, can't really be improved on, but I've played around with some of the timing, added a bit more interest around the verses, but left the chorus as it stands. Of course, I can play it straight if you like."

"No, no, let's hear the Tom Turner version. We're all ears."

Tom started. His left hand flitted from fret to fret and his right strummed out a rhythm more energetic than the original. He didn't look up, but if he had, he'd have seen Jim's eyebrows rise and his body straighten up. He was impressed, very impressed. And then Tom started singing and Jim's eyebrows had nowhere left to go.

By halfway through the song, Tom's peripheral vision caught Jim's foot tapping next to Beth, and as a result he belted out the rest of the song, filling the drawing room, and possibly most of the huge garden with his voice. He finished with a flurry of fingerwork and then the room was silent. For a split second in the silence, Tom thought maybe he'd taken it too far, maybe his voice had broken on some of the higher notes, maybe he should have kept it simple. But then the applause began. Like the rest of him, Jim's hands clapped in a way that would make other men jealous, causing more volume than three normal men put together.

"Outstanding! Amazing! Seriously Tom, you have quite a talent there. Veronica, wasn't that amazing?"

Veronica was smiling, possibly more at her husband's animation than by the music itself. "Yes, Tom. I like very much your song. Possibly more than the original itself, but I never much liked thees 'eff Buckley."

Jim was shaking his head in disbelief. "And even Lolli liked it!" He gestured to the door and Tom turned around to see Lolli leaning against the doorframe. She said something in Spanish and Beth shook her head sadly.

"What did she say?" asked Tom.

"She asked if you knew anything in Spanish and I said no."

Tom cast his mind back to all the dreadful crooners his mother listened to, and had forced him to learn on guitar. Julio Iglesias had been one of her favourites.

"Well, I might know something." Now it was Veronica's turn to lean forwards.

Tom played the first few bars of *Besame Mucho*, and Lolli and Veronica both shrieked in excitement. "*Si, si!*" they both shouted. It was strange to see Veronica lose her self-control over a couple of chords.

"I don't know the words," said Tom, still playing, but aware he would make a fool of himself if he attempted singing anything in Spanish.

"No matter, no matter. We help." Veronica beckoned Lolli from the doorway and put her arms around her on the sofa. Lolli's face creased up into a smile, the first one aimed at Tom. The family facing Tom made a pretty picture and he looked to them to guide his playing. They swayed and nodded and when he played the bars of the opening verse, every single one of them sang out the words. Amazingly, the blend of Lolli's toad-like croak, Veronica's high squeal, Jim's operatic tenor, and Beth's half decent voice was almost a harmony. As the second chorus approached, Tom played some extravagant fingerwork akin to flamenco and the whole family wooped. Then Jim stood up and offered his hand to Lolli, she thought about it a few seconds and then accepted the dance. Tom slowed the guitar and Jim and Lolli danced a careful rhumba. Jim moved Lolli and her old legs, wrinkled in tights, elegantly around the room, and at the open French doors, Tom saw Lolli's face lit up by sunlight. Every crease and every line was illuminated by a wide smile.

And that was Tom's last memory of Lolli.

13:37, Wednesday June 28th, 2000
York Road and Willowman Grange

"Slow down Beth, I can't hear what you're saying." Tom's heart was racing, he had no idea what she was saying, just that she was saying it through tears. He held the phone closer and concentrated on her jumbled words.

"She's dead. She's dead."

"Who's dead?"

"Lolli! Lolli's dead." Beth's words were desperate and angry, although Tom had no idea who she was angry with.

"Bloody hell. What happened?"

"They... they found her in her armchair. Yesterday morning. Her heart, her heart just stopped. Oh poor, poor Lolli." Beth was crying frantically like the women in Lolli's soap opera. He had to get to her.

"Where are you? Beth, where are you?"

"I'm at mum and dads."

"I'll come," said Tom. "I'll be there as soon as I can."

"No! No. Don't come. It's too much. Mum hasn't spoken since she found her and dad's busy making arrangements for the, for the... We're flying to Spain tomorrow, that's why I called."

"OK, well. What should I do? God, I wish I could see you."

Beth cried harder. "I wish that too, but it has to wait. Mum needs me here. Oh poor, poor Lolli."

"When can I see you? When will you be back?" Tom was beginning to feel tearful himself. Crying, like laughter, is contagious among those you love the most.

"I don't know. I don't know. I'll call you."

"I love you Beth."

"I know," said Beth. "I love you too."

*

Tom had never had to deal with anything as serious as death before, and he had no idea what to do with it. He didn't even know how to handle the word, what sentences to put it in, what words of comfort to fit around it, he felt utterly useless at the time when Beth needed him the most. It was probably a good thing he hadn't seen her before she left for Spain, he'd only have messed up the chance to make her feel better, and that was now what he was doing every day when she called; messing up. He tried instigating the type of conversation they might usually have had, but the circumstances were far from usual and talk of Wimbledon, Euro 2000 and the weather got him nowhere. Beth wanted to talk about Lolli, what had happened to her and Tom hadn't the faintest idea how to contribute.

"I still can't believe it's happened. You know, one day she was fine, mum said she'd cooked *Bandeja Paisa* as a special treat the day before, and then the next day she had a headache, went downstairs to watch TV, and never came back up again." Beth started crying.

Tom considered saying something like 'it's how she would have wanted to go,' but that didn't sound right, he thought about 'at least there was no pain,' but perhaps there had been. He couldn't work out what to say, so he said nothing.

The daily call normally ended with Beth lamenting "Poor, poor Lolli," over and over again, until finally she'd run out of tears, or perhaps patience, and hang up. It was bad to feel this way but Tom was glad when the call ended, it was a relief. It also became something of a blessing for him when the daily calls dwindled to alternate days. She told him that the funeral was approaching and there was lots to be done, but Tom knew the real reason she wasn't calling so often – he was useless when it came to death.

**13:37, Sunday July 9th, 2000
Waterloo Station, London**

Tom was nervous and paced back and forth beneath the huge Waterloo clock. Anyone observing him would have presumed he was awaiting a first date, but he had been on countless dates with the girl he was meeting. Tom had shared everything he was and everything he had with Beth and now he had to try and share death, something he knew nothing about. Chris had given him some advice over a couple of pints the night before, "When she looks like she wants you to say something, just give her a hug. But don't expect anything more than a hug! Not for at least a few weeks. If you really do need to say something, look sincere and say "I'm sorry."" Tom had misgivings about any advice Chris gave on women, but with no other perspectives on offer, he was willing to give him the benefit of the doubt.

Just as he was mulling Chris' words over, someone tapped him on the shoulder. He turned around and at the sight of Beth his nerves vanished and were replaced by concern. He grabbed her, there was much less of her, and he held her bony body against him. How could ten days make this difference to a person? He didn't want to look at her, not until she was healthy, happy and beautiful again, but after a minute or so she pulled away from him. Her big brown eyes looked even larger in her shrunken face, like Veronica's anguished portraits in the Willowman hallway.

"I'm so unhappy," she said.

His throat was so constricted he couldn't even reach for the two words he'd rehearsed. He took her bag, put his arm around her shoulder and led her out of the station. He couldn't subject this fragile being to the turmoil of public transport. He bundled her into a black cab and spent his week's food budget sitting in silence, holding the cold hand of the girl normally so warm, until they got to his flat.

*

Beth had missed the last two weeks of term and an important exam but the Dean, a close friend of Jim's, had words with her tutor and the Willowmans were assured their daughter could retake the exam in autumn. This left three months of summer sprawling at her feet, with nothing to fill the time but grief. Tom and Beth had made exciting plans, including a holiday somewhere sunny, salty and simple, but Beth was in no mood for a break and was in no mood for summer. He tried everything to cheer her up; he cooked for her, took her to exhibitions he thought she might like, he sang to her. When all this failed, he became more practical about the condition she was struggling to get out of. He took books out from the library with titles like *Moving forward after loss* and *How to deal with the loss of a loved one*, and he also found some information from his local GPs about bereavement counselling. The pamphlets and books were well rifled through, but only by his own fingers, and the advice they gave him was beyond his capability. It wasn't in his nature to console, he'd never had to.

11:53, Wednesday August 2nd, 2000
Intercollegiate Halls, London

Fortunately for both Tom and Beth, help arrived in the unlikely form of fellow student, Steph. Beth had referred to Steph a couple of times in the past. They shared a kitchen, among about twelve other students, and Steph had endeared herself to almost everyone in the hall by bringing home free burgers after her shifts at McDonalds. She was a bubbly girl studying law at the London School of Economics, but without the pretensions of most students on her course.

One month into the summer break, the college contacted Beth and asked that she clear out her room; they were offering study programmes to foreign students over the holiday and needed to free up the halls. Tom offered to help and Beth agreed that she would pack up her things, then give Tom a call to help her carry them back to his. She left him with the posture he had grown to associate with her, shoulders slightly stooped as though she didn't have the energy to lift them, head hanging low and hair covering her face. He expected to hear from her within two hours, but as the third hour ticked past, a layer of panic settled inside him and after three hours and seven minutes he was on his way to Tavistock Square and the intercollegiate halls.

He passed security by immersing himself into a geeky group of Chinese students. He couldn't have been more out of place but, stooped down, keeping his blonde locks out of view, he snuck in. He made his way up to Beth's room and as he pushed open the door that led onto her corridor he was shocked to hear the sound of laughter; Beth's laughter. It had been so long since he heard it that he stopped in the doorway, not wanting to do anything that might hinder the noise. He heard speaking, but couldn't make out the words, then another burst of laughter. He was confused but overjoyed. He stayed in the doorway, until he was forced out of it by another student. He moved down the corridor and stuck his head round Beth's door. She was sitting on the bed with another girl and noticed him immediately.

"Hey," she said. Her eyes were red, her cheeks wet and she held a tissue in her lap, but the tone of her voice was lifted, spirited, it didn't seem to match.

"Hi," said Tom. A few seconds passed before anyone moved. Then Beth came to Tom and wove her fingers into his.

"I'd like to introduce you to my friend Steph."

Steph smiled at Tom. She was pretty in a more obvious way than Beth. She had the blonde hair, blue eyes and button nose that made her an instant looker, she was the kind of girl that men won't approach, and the kind of girl you're surprised to find is a nice person. But she clearly was.

"Hi Tom, how are you?"

"I'm good, I'm good." He paused. "Thanks." He turned to Beth. "Want me to come back later?"

Steph answered for her. "No, no, I've gotten in the way for too long already."

Steph got off the bed, she was barefooted and extremely tall for a girl. She bent down and hugged Beth, for a long time. "So, I'll see you tomorrow? At the café on the Serpentine?"

"Eleven o'clock, I'll be there," said Beth. Steph smiled at her friend, and left the room, almost forgetting Tom. "Oh, bye Tom! Nice to meet you," she turned around in the corridor. He couldn't help but notice what a great behind she had.

"And you," he called after it.

And that was how Steph entered their lives. She was set to stay.

*

That night Beth ate a good meal, she talked with optimism about the summer and she made love to Tom for the first time since Lolli's death. Afterwards, Beth slept like a baby for eleven hours in Tom's arms. For months she'd slept fitfully and Tom was so glad to have her serene little face gently snoring, that he didn't move the whole night for fear of waking her. He had no idea what had happened that afternoon, he was just glad to be seeing recognizable pieces of his girlfriend again, and he was extremely grateful to Steph.

*

Over the next few weeks, Beth saw Steph nearly every day, and she slept over in her room on occasions. In any other set of circumstances, this amount of new contact with someone might have made Tom suspicious, or jealous, but he soon realized that Steph was offering what he couldn't; she knew how to deal with death.

Steph was staying in halls over the whole summer, basically because she had few other options. Three years ago both her parents had died in a car accident on a wet road in Edinburgh. They had been celebrating their 25th wedding anniversary. Not wanting to live with her grandparents or her overly sympathetic and unstable aunt, she had moved in with her older sister Laura, and Laura's boyfriend. The two sisters had grown closer, had worked through their grief together and had come out the other side with a rational philosophy about death that made them both feel better about what had happened.

"They're not religious," Beth told Tom. "But what made them feel better about their loss was the fact that wherever their parents are now, their bodies, their souls, whatever the hell is left of us when we die, they are together. And one day Laura and Steph will be there also. Maybe it's in the ground, getting eaten by worms, but even if that's the case, Laura and Steph will be with their family. And it's the same with Lolli. Maybe she's looking down on me from heaven, like mum says, maybe she's decaying in the ground like dad thinks, I won't know, until I'm in the same place as her. And that's one thing I can say for sure, that one day I'll be in the same place as Lolli."

Tom thought this sounded very depressing, but was happy that Beth could take comfort from it, and he reminded her of it in her down times. The past few months had shown him very clearly that he hated thinking about death, let alone talking about it. Fortunately Beth seemed to be getting all her talking done with Steph, wandering around the Royal Parks, sipping coffee in Covent Garden, or meandering through Camden or Portobello market. The combination of London's diversions together with Steph's understanding were proving to be the perfect therapy. Within a month, Beth was able to talk about Lolli without tears.

"You know, Lolli left me some lovely jewellery. It's at mum and dad's, I thought it would make me too sad to wear it, but I think it might actually have the opposite effect. There's a pretty emerald ring she wore every day, and I think I'd like to wear it every day now too."

"You want to go down to your parents?" asked Tom. This was another great step in Beth's recovery. Up to that point she had been reluctant to go to the house, full of memories, full of souvenirs of Lolli, and full of her mother's grief.

"Maybe at the end of summer."

Of course there were days when Beth's progress faltered. Days when she didn't get out of bed, didn't eat, hardly spoke and didn't seem to notice Tom's presence or feel his touch. But these days were becoming rare.

11:24, Sunday November 12th, 2000
Flat 5, 62 York Road, London

After a slow start to the academic year, Beth's studies were back on track and her tutor told her she was in with a chance of getting a first class degree. The prospect thrilled and scared her.

"I wish she hadn't told me. Now if I don't get a first it's going to be a massive disappointment, and I'll know I could have done better. But if I do get a first... well, it would certainly open a lot of doors."

Tom had a feeling that lots of doors were going to be open to Beth anyway.

"Well, you have half a year, six months of hard graft, and if you work as hard as you can then, no matter what, you can't be disappointed in yourself. Right?"

"Tom Turner. You make a good point. And what's six months of hard work in a whole lifetime?"

"Exactly, then you can put your feet up and drink tea for the next 60 years."

She laughed, but the theory was one she adopted in all seriousness. Tom had never seen her, nor anybody for that matter, work as hard as she did in those last months of her degree. Her time was devoted to reading, lectures, tutorials and galleries. Tom's flat became as much a shrine to the history of art as it was to his music. Huge library books were propped up against spare walls, or lay open to display highlights from five centuries of art, from Botticelli's *Primavera*, past Monet's *Soleil Levant* to end in Tracy Emin's messy bed, which much resembled his own. The small studio was a chaotic homage to music and art. It was as though a giant fan of art and music had overindulged in the two and then spewed up his messy guts over the tiny space. Beth's work ethic rubbed off on Tom, or maybe it was just that he had more time on his hands with Beth out so often. That autumn he took on more bar work, did more gigs, and contacted a list of promoters he had been compiling for over a year. His Gibson Les Paul bottle at his mum and dad's house showed the rewards of his efforts, and he calculated that by Christmas he should be able to afford the guitar of his dreams. As an incentive to save the money and buy the guitar, he booked some studio time with Luke and one of his technician mates in January. With all their hard work,

Beth would be a first class graduate and Tom would be a recording artist in no time.

Between Beth's studying and Tom's music and bar work, their time together became precious, but also more gratifying in its rarity. Their busy lives apart meant they had more to talk about when together. Tom tested Beth on her studies, read her essays and made suggestions for improvements. In doing so, Beth came to realize just how intelligent her boyfriend was. Tom may have devoted his life to music, the one thing he was most passionate about, but it was clear to her he was clever enough to be successful in all any number of different careers. He picked up on details in articles and essays that would have escaped her, and he helped train her mind into a sharp toothcomb that allowed no minor details to slip past it. She began to feel more confident about gaining a first.

Likewise, Tom's future in music was looking more and more promising. With Beth's ability and confidence in meeting new people, she helped him approach a number of promoters. A few of these made the effort to hear Tom's music at various open mic sessions, and two had approached him afterwards and shown real interest in getting him on their line-ups.

As well as their current pursuits in art and music, there was another subject that filled their minds and their conversations; their future together.

"Maybe your mum is more liberal than you give her credit for," said Tom. "She might be fine with us living together."

Beth laughed. "There is no way my mum would agree to it. She's a strict catholic and, since Lolli died, she's become even more devoted. She didn't even sleep with dad until after they were married."

"Bloody hell. Well, I'm glad you don't share her beliefs."

"We're just going to have to work on some sort of pretence. Maybe I could say I was sharing a room with Steph after graduation, but you and I could move in together."

Tom really didn't like the idea of lying to Beth's family. "That's a great big lie to live in," he said.

"I know." She held his hand. "But I know my mother, and this is really the only way. If it makes your conscience feel any better, I can keep some things at Steph's and spend the occasional night there."

Beth's suggestion didn't make Tom feel any better, but he had one of his own, one he had been thinking about for a long time, one that would make everyone happy, including Veronica. He just needed to check with Beth's dad first.

Back to today - Friday July 12th, 2013

08:30
7 The Stables, South Kensington, London

Tom's life stops. It stops in his bespoke, high-gloss kitchen, while he leans on the marble work surface, phone in hand. It stops despite the fact his son creeps out of the utility room and offers his arms full of wet PE kit to Tom. It stops despite the fact his daughter skips back into the kitchen, schoolbag in hand, turning pirouettes. Life stops.

"Tom, can you hear me?" Steph's voice is trying to reach him from somewhere. "Tom, listen I'm coming round. I'll take the kids to school. They don't need to know yet. I'll be five minutes."

09:42
14 Carrer Lleo, Al Raval, Barcelona

After a moment, Angelo laughs. Although the sentence hit him like a punch to the chest, he catches his breath, and realizes it's his batty old landlady talking.

"What are you talking about? There's been no plane crash. I'd have heard."

She cranes her head into the room behind him. "How?"

She has a point. Without a radio or television, his world revolves without news of what happens outside his window. But his phone; someone would have called, someone of authority, surely.

Señora Carmen's bottom lip is trembling. "Come with me."

He follows her down the stairs and with every step his throat tightens and his heart falls a little lower in his chest. A plane crash? Everyone dead? Are these slow steps down the staircase the last he will take knowing Maria to be alive?

She pushes her apartment door open, smoke and the familiar noise of her TV fills the hallway. He follows her in, walking through a dark smoky corridor. He hears the news before he sees it. "No survivors. Passenger list still to be confirmed but the flight was full." He sits less than a metre from the blaring TV, in the armchair moulded to fit his landlady, and he watches the carnage of an AirStar plane wrecked in a field, the AS636 which left Madrid for London at 07.35 that morning.

The plane is scattered in fragments, pieces of meaningless metal smoking in the fields. Angelo sits in the threadbare armchair in a room that hasn't changed for twenty years, he leans forwards and puts his head in his hands. A plaque of Maria Magdalena, yellowed from cigarette smoke, looks down on him in pity from above the television.

08:32
7 The Stables, South Kensington, London

After Steph hangs up, Tom holds the phone to his ear a few moments longer. Telephones can be such enemies. If its chirpy ring hadn't interrupted his morning routine, if its myriad of cables hadn't connected him with Steph, his life would still be intact; he'd still have a wife and the two children standing in front of him would still have a mother.

He puts the phone down. Without words, he puts Miles' PE kit into a plastic bag, helps him with his school tie and laces, and manages to assemble his two children in the hallway. Katy continues to spin pirouettes, practicing for her big performance only days away.

There is a knocking at the front door and Katy stops prancing around.

"Who's that daddy?"

He opens the door and Steph walks in, all smiles and breezy, casting only a fleeting glance in Tom's direction.

"Auntie Steph!" Katy and Miles cry out in shocked happy unison.

"Hello Katy, hello my little pickle," she says ruffling Mile's fluffy hair into a static halo. "I'm taking you to school today, and I can see you're all ready."

"Can I show you my dance routine Auntie Steph," pleads Katy.

"Maybe later sweetie. We've got to get you off to school. Say goodbye to daddy."

Katy's big brown eyes look up at her father. "Bye bye daddy." He stares into her pretty Latino eyes, thinking how much they look like Beth's. She waits for him to lean down for his morning kiss and frowns at him for making her wait. He kisses both children and they skip out the door with Steph.

"I'll come straight back," she says, squeezing his arm.

The door slams shut behind them and silence rings through Tom's ears. He stands for a few moments on the doormat. Then suddenly his knees give way and he collapses onto the floor. He rests his head on the cool wood of the door, the door he carried Beth through over ten years ago. And in all that time, in this house, he hasn't shed a tear. Now he weeps like never before, tears streaming down his cheeks onto the doormat, loud sobs filling the hallway and the house. Sadness streaming out of his eyes, his lungs, his mouth and his hands that pound the mat, sadness trying to find an outlet, but not finding enough, and getting strangled in his throat. He weeps his despair for forty minutes until Steph returns. Miles' wet PE kit sits next to him the whole time.

09:51
14 Carrer Lleo, Al Raval, Barcelona

Señora Carmen makes some coffee, sniffing as she does so. Angelo is one of her least favourite tenants; always late with rent and covering her attic room with paint and squalor. However, she had liked Maria, she was sweet and attentive, and this made her revise her opinion of Angelo somewhat. Now poor Maria was gone, smashed into the ground with 166 other people, and Señora Carmen has to deal with the aftermath that sits in her lounge.

She takes a sweet coffee in to Angelo and places it in front of him. The blonde newsreader talks excitedly at Angelo's bowed head. She speaks about the crash with relish, and keeps repeating words like 'horrific' 'ghastly' 'remains' and 'tragedy.' It is probably the highlight of her career. Señora Carmen turns off the television, and petty everyday noise from the street take its space. She sits on one of the dining room chairs and watches Angelo. Just as she is wondering what to do with this miserable soul, and looking to Maria Magdalena for help, a ringing noise trills from the miserable soul, making her jump. *Nuestra Señora* certainly works quickly. Angelo doesn't flinch or move to answer it, so she locates the mobile phone in his shirt pocket and answers it. The familiar voice of Angelo's cocky friend, Xavier, speaks.

"Hello? Angelo? I heard about the crash. Was it Maria's flight? Man, are you there?"

"He is here," she says. "In my lounge, hasn't moved since he heard the news."

"I'll be right there." Xavier hangs up. She is glad to be handing this tragedy over to someone else, and crosses herself in recognition of Our Lady's speedy work.

Twenty minutes later, Xavier moves Angelo's body back to his apartment, where it adopts the same position on his sofa; stooped forward with head in hands. Xavier puts a large whiskey in front of him. It sits on the floor two hours, before it's drunk by Xavier.

"Man, talk to me. Say something. Please." Xavier paces around the studio, filling and emptying his glass of whiskey. "Listen. What can I do? You want me to get someone?" Xavier quickly realizes that is a stupid question, without family and without Maria, Angelo only has one person left in his life, and that is him; the man asking the stupid questions. "Listen. You sure she took that flight? I mean there's a chance she missed it?"

Angelo's head turns to his friend, his eyes wild and wide. "You think? Maybe she's alive?"

Xavier is glad to see life in the body of his friend, but immediately regrets his suggestion. "Well, it's a possibility, a slim one. You tried calling?"

Angelo stands up and searches for his phone. He is frantic, a whirlwind of energy spinning around in search of life, the last traces of life which his phone might reveal. He lifts and throws clothes, pushes canvases from their perches, kicks a chair out of his way.

"Where's my fucking phone?"

Xavier scans the studio, turning a full circle.

"Angelo, it's here!" The device sits tight in the corner of the sofa, like a naughty child trying to disappear from view. Xavier picks up the phone and lets out a loud sigh of relief.

"You've got a text from Maria! Man, she's alive, you've got a message."

Angelo races into the apartment and grabs his phone. His face is alight with hope. He opens the text message and a split second later all hope drains from him. Enough of these fucking last hopes, now he has the proof, in writing. The death certificate is signed by Maria herself.

Xavier picks up the phone from where it has dropped to the floor, and reads.

Falling. Love you always. Never stop painting. M

Xavier offers Angelo the whiskey glass. He takes the bottle instead.

09:16
7 The Stables, South Kensington, London

Steph hears Tom sobbing behind the door and takes a few deep breaths before knocking. She has to be strong for Tom, but she isn't sure how long her strength can last. He opens the door and looks at Steph in complete bewilderment. He doesn't know what he is doing, doesn't know how he is going to get through his first day as a widower, doesn't understand how life is going to continue. For the first time in a very long time, he has more questions than he has answers. Unflappable, reliable and confident Tom is lost, the platform that held him and every part of him securely in place, has collapsed. He doesn't understand a thing and, when he looks at Steph, his eyes beg her for the answers to all these questions, he needs answers, but she has none to give. A tear rolls down her face.
"I'm so sorry Tom," she stammers. "I'm so sorry."
They stagger into each other's arms and weep for the wife and friend they've lost, for the mother who won't see Katy's ballet production, for the mother who Miles will all but forget, for the daughter who'd made her parents so proud, and for the woman Tom thinks he knows better than any other.

13:38
14 Carrer Lleo, Al Raval, Barcelona

Xavier tries to stop him but he is pushed aside with a strength that belies Angelo's wiry frame.

"Get the fuck off me!" Angelo shouts. He grabs the next picture in the stack and slices it open with the knife, a serene landscape of rolling hills and puffy clouds is divided into two, then three, then shredded. There'll be no more blue skies in his studio, no more pointless oranges and apples, no more vibrant flowers. Xavier watches helplessly from the floor where he landed. Angelo flies around the studio wielding the knife like a madman and butchering one painting after another, he yells sounds rather than words, primeval noises of pain. He slays his agent Teresa's favourite still-life; a somewhat phallic arrangement of chess pieces and grapes, and throws its remains at the window, before turning to his next victim. And there sits Maria; her long plait falling to the petite hands that have caressed him time after time, her over-sized shirt covering the body he knows and loves every inch of, her delicate mouth that kisses with such tenderness, and her twinkling eyes. They gleam at him and tell him that, beneath the clothes and skin and beauty, her heart is his, was his.

Angelo falls silent, the knife drops to the floor and his body sags. He lets out a tiny whimper, "Maria, my Maria," and he tries to get his arms around the canvas. Xavier looks away, averting his eyes from the lovers in the corner.

14:59
7 The Stables, South Kensington, London

Tom can't remember ever drinking so much tea, even at his mum and dad's house, but the familiar procedure gives him some comfort, something to hold onto, one thing that hasn't changed that day. He's just had an awful conversation with his brother-in-law; two grown men trying not to cry down the phone at each other, and mostly failing. Michael is a strong man like his father had been, and to hear the tremble in his voice as he skirted around any words that put Beth into the category of dead, made Tom's heart crumble. Michael's diplomatic contacts were going to see what they could do about bringing Beth back to the UK.

"We'll bring her back Tom," said Michael. Then his voice gave way, "We'll bring back my little sister." He hung up.

Steph only leaves him alone for twenty minutes, to dash home and pick up some clothes, as she will stay with the family a few days. During those twenty minutes Tom reconnects the television that Steph unplugged and watches blankly the smoky field where his wife's life ended. He thinks about her last moments, did she know she was dying? Who was she sat with? Did someone hold her hand as they plunged to their shared death? Did she scream? Did she suffer?

He isn't quick enough to turn the television off when Steph returns to the house. She puts her arm on his shoulder.

"It won't help; reliving it, watching it. There was an awful accident and Beth died. She's gone sweetheart, she's at peace."

Tom nods to the empty words.

"And that's what you're going to have to tell the kids," says Steph.

"What?" Tom looks at her in panic.

"You have to tell the kids what happened. When they get home from school."

Tom shakes his head, over and over. "I can't. Steph, I really can't. I can't do this, I just can't."

She holds his hand and swallows. "You have to. Tom, they have to know. There's nothing wrong with showing that you're sad to Miles and Katy, there's nothing wrong with showing your feelings." She swallows again, trying not to show hers. "I'll pick them up from school, and bring them back. They'll be expecting to see Beth. You have to tell them."

He continues to shake his head while Steph puts the kettle on.

16:32
14 Carrer Lleo, Al Raval, Barcelona

Xavier smokes one cigarette after another while Angelo whispers in the corner, his head is pushed against the acrylic face and his hands caress the painted hands. Xavier only stops smoking when he reaches the end of the packet. He stands up from the floor and begins to pick up the shreds of canvases that lie scattered around the apartment, like sad autumn leaves. Angelo continues nursing his one remaining picture, oblivious to the destruction that Xavier is clearing.

Xavier finds a couple of dustbin bags and fills three with the scraps of Angelo's life's work. He isn't sure what do with the bags, their contents are useless, unrecognizable as art, but they seem too precious to throw into the communal bins outside. Angelo's brushstrokes, his imagination and talent, shouldn't be left to rot among yesterday's dinners and the flies. He stacks them by the door, and goes to raid the kitchen for food. He finds that the fridge is full, a souvenir of Maria's last visit, and helps himself to some bread and ham.

"Want something to eat?" he shouts into the studio. With no response, he tucks into his late lunch and tries to remember how Angelo came out of his catatonic state when his mother died. The truth was that he had been a changed man for years after, he had only really become himself again since meeting Maria. And now she had fallen out of the sky. Xavier shakes his head as he fills his belly, Angelo must have done something really shitty in a past life to deserve all this.

15:45
7 The Stables, South Kensington, London

Katy and Miles run into the house, two mini whirlwinds, making a gleeful noise and throwing off their school accessories into the hall. The ties, blazers, shoes and bags have held them captive for long enough today. The noise frightens Tom. It means that the moment has arrived. He's not ready, but then he'll probably never be ready. His heart thuds in his chest, his palms are wet and his feet bounce on the floor. Given the choice of fight or flight he knows which he'd take right now, but he needs to stay, needs to be strong. Katy dances into the room, she is too little just yet to be graceful, but she isn't far off. Tom watches her as she bounces around the sofa in her socks, arms outstretched and her little belly protruding from her white shirt. She is so excited about Tuesday's dance production – will they still go?

Miles wanders in, he is still trying to get his tie off and his face and fingers are screwed up by the effort. He has managed to make it into a tight little knot, high up near his neck. He spots Tom and walks over to him, tripping over the corner of the rug as he does so. He stands in front of his father and watches Tom's fingers at work, they are as useless as his own, they are shaking. Miles looks up at his father.

"Daddy, what's wrong with your fingers?"

Katy stops spinning and comes to see what Miles is talking about.

"Daddy, your fingers are wobbling," she says.

Finally Tom releases his son from the stranglehold of his school tie. He looks up into the eyes of his two children. They look concerned.

"I'm fine," he says. "Daddy's fine." They don't seem to believe him. Steph enters the room and stands by the door. He has no escape now.

He pushes his hands into the sofa at his side, in an attempt to stop them shaking.

"Kids, something happened today. Something bad." He swallows, all the words he had rehearsed in his head, all the euphemisms for death have disappeared at the sight of his motherless children.

They wait for more. Tom wants to leave them not knowing, wants to leave Katy prancing around the room, wants to leave Miles to go get his train set and animals, to build a new farm railway the same as yesterday. But it's not to be.

Katy screws up her face in confusion.

"Where's mummy? Is she upstairs?"

"Mummy Mummy!" Miles squeals, remembering that Beth is due home. His eyes light up and he looks around, expecting her to spring from behind the curtain or the kitchen island.

"Mummy's not home," says Tom. "Mummy's not coming home." Steph comes to stand behind the sofa, she squeezes his shoulder, as though trying to transfer her strength into him.

"Mummy was in a plane this morning." He takes a deep breath and digs his fingers into the leather beneath them. "The plane crashed. And everyone on the plane." He pauses. "Everyone on the plane... died."

The two pairs of eyes continue to look at him, not flinching.

Tom takes their little hands in his. "Miles, Katy. Mummy's dead."

Katy's forehead knots in confusion and Miles continues to look at his father, his expression blank.

"So when is mummy coming back?" asks Katy.

"Where's mummy?" asks Miles.

"Mummy isn't coming back," says Tom. His eyes fill with tears. "She's never coming back. She's in heaven, in the sky." Katy's eyes well up at the mention of heaven, she doesn't remember much of her Grandpa dying, but she remembers he went to heaven and she hasn't seen him since. Miles lets go of Tom's hand and wanders over to the window, he looks up at the sky.

"And when will she be back?" For little Miles, heaven sounds like one of the faraway cities that Beth spends time in, like Paris or Madrid.

Katy starts crying, quietly. "What about my ballet production? She promised to change my tutu. What about my tutu?"

"I'll change that for you darling," says Steph.

"But I want mummy to do it!" Katy says. "I want my mummy to do it!" She is shouting now, and crying at the same time. "I want my mummy to do it! I want my mummy!"

Miles meanders over to the sofa, confused by his sister's outburst. He stands a safe distance from her wailing, and watches her in surprise. Tom is crying now, he can't stop, and this further confuses little Miles. Katy continues howling for her mummy and Tom wants to shout along with her "I want my wife! I want my wife!" But he manages to part with different words when his sobbing allows it. "Sweetheart, she's not coming back. Katy, mummy's gone, she's in heaven now."

Finally Miles' confusion is converted into something else. It's the sight of his father crying that acts as the catalyst. He doesn't mind seeing his sister crying, she does that all the time, but his father has never cried. Miles didn't know that adult eyes had the mechanism for tears. His little face screws up into a ball and he starts wailing like the rest of his family. Tom leans over, grabs Miles and pulls him into his arms. He does the same with Katy, and soon they become a throbbing ball of wailing and tears, the noise rising and dipping in volume as they feed off each other's misery. Steph leaves the room and sits on the stairs, her head in her hands. It's too much for her to witness.

After several minutes, the crying of the group lulls and Miles and Katy rest their wet faces on Tom's shirt, sniffing occasionally.

"So, when is mummy coming home?" asks Miles.

18:00
14 Carrer Lleo, Al Raval, Barcelona

The fridge lies empty in the kitchen and Xavier lies full on the sofa. He is sprawled and snoring, a line of saliva dripping from his open mouth reflects the sunlight that streams through the window. His is a scene of peace and contentment. Not far away, Angelo kneels on the wooden floor facing all that remains of Maria, her painting. He rocks back and forward, his weight transferring from the bones of his ankles to those of his knees. The movement has become painful, and this makes him feel a little better, well perhaps not better, but it makes him feel something, something closer to Maria. His thoughts run round and round in circles, Maria in the sky, falling from the sky, knowing she will die, in pain, no longer in pain, and Maria in the sky again. Her eyes glint at him, as though they are challenging him. 'Come on Angelo. You love me don't you?' His mind is awash with grief and whiskey, but it shows a clear path to how he can be with her again, the only way.

For the first time in hours he lifts himself from the floor. His legs don't work at first, his joints refuse to budge, and his body appears to be against his idea. He rubs his knees and ankles, urging them to wake up. Slowly they respond, they'll go along with him, they're up for it. Xavier doesn't even stir as his friend casts a shadow over him. Angelo looks out the window, firstly at the blue sky, the sky that Maria fell from, the sky that she was returned to, and then down to the ground four storeys below.

"Fuck! Fuck!" he says loudly.

Xavier moves, wipes the saliva from his chin and changes position, before falling asleep again.

Angelo is annoyed with the height of his apartment. The ground is too close, too fucking close. He could climb up onto the roof. It might work, but it might not. He grabs the bottle of whiskey next to Xavier and finishes the dregs. He grabs a handful of paintbrushes from next to the window, and breaks them over his knee in anger. He studies them, sticks them into his palm and goes through them one by one, disregarding the bluntest, before returning to Maria on the floor.

"I'm coming *mi amor*, I'm coming," he whispers to her. He stares into her painted eyes and for a few moments is lost in them. Then he grips the broken brushes until his knuckles whiten and his veins swell. He touches the jagged edges to the white of his wrist, and presses hard until his arm runs red, then he drags the broken shards across his wrist, pulling and tearing the skin. Pain burns through him, but the relief is immaculate. Maria is still holding his stare, urging him on. He goes back over the bloody line these brushes have painted, pressing harder still, feeling the resistance of veins and carving through them. He is feeling light-headed as he transfers the broken brushes to his other hand, but this hand is stubbornly refusing to help, unwilling to grip the bloody handles which have done it so much damage. The hand dangles from his sliced wrist and the fingers reach to grasp the brushes, but fail, like the claw of a fairground game that tries but fails at every attempt to find a grip.

'Come on Angelo, that's a half-hearted attempt,' says Maria, 'I want your whole heart.'

He places the brushes, bristle side down, between his legs and crosses them, so that the gruesome jagged ends are wedged into place, sticking up from just above his knees. His lifeless left arm hangs by his side in a growing puddle of deep red. His painting arm must paint its own destiny. He places the inside of his wrist over the jagged edges. He lifts and lowers his arm slowly and methodically, each time higher and each time coming to rest on top of the broken ends. His breathing is shallower with each movement. After repeating the motion over thirty times he whispers to Maria, "I love you," before plunging his arm down onto the spiked brushes, with the same force he had used to throw Xavier across the room. Three brushes pierce the skin, two pierce the artery and one slides past the bone and out the other side. Angelo's body lets out a booming scream, his mind and heart might want to be left to die but his other organs are still fighting to survive, and screaming for help could be their last chance.

Xavier jolts awake and his eyes open to the most gruesome scene they have ever encountered. Angelo lies in a pool of blood on the floor, next to the knowing smile of Maria's canvas.

"Angelo! Angelo! Fuck, Angelo!" Xavier kneels in the blood next to his friend. The colour has drained completely from his face, and lies around them in a growing halo of deep red. Blood pumps from his severed left wrist, and bubbles out from beneath his right which is impaled on top of something.

"Fuck! Fuck! Angelo, hombre, hombre, can you hear me?" Xavier shouts, swears and stammers at his friend. He looks around the studio and races to a pile of clothes. He ties a shirt around Angelo's left wrist to curb the bleeding, but it immediately turns red, before he has even finished the knot.

"Shit, Shit! What the fuck, Angelo, what've you done? What've you done? A tourniquet, that's it a tourniquet."

He ties another shirt tightly around Angelo's left bicep and before he even thinks about what to do with the right arm, he grabs his phone and with sticky red fingers dials 112.

"Ambulance, ambulance quick! My friend, my friend's cut himself up. Sliced his wrists open."

The operator sends an ambulance and talks Xavier through some basic first aid while he waits. By the time the ambulance arrives, Xavier is a mess of tears and blood, and Angelo lies like an angel on the wooden floor, two red wings have formed beneath him, and a slight smile seems to have emerged on his bleached face.

20:00
7 The Stables, South Kensington, London

Miles really doesn't understand that Beth is gone forever, which makes it both easier and harder for Tom to spend time with him that evening. Easier because Miles follows his evening ritual without interruption; play, tea, bath, story and bed. For seconds at a time Tom is able to forget that anything is wrong. Harder because now and again Miles cocks his head to one side, screws up his little face in confusion and asks "When is mummy coming home?" or "Why is Katy so sad?" Explaining what has happened to a four year old is going to take a lot of patience and repetition, Tom realizes. Repeating the same conversation over and over might be tiresome at other times, but now it is heart wrenching.

Steph spends time with Katy that evening. The many years that lay between first meeting Steph and today, made Tom forget that she has been through loss herself, and helped Beth through her own. She is something of an expert on death. She treats Katy as an adult, although only eight years old and tells her the same things that made Beth feel better when Lolli died. Before Tom enters the kids' bedroom to read Katy a story, he hears Steph talking.

"So you understand that, although you may not be able to see mummy anymore, she is always going to be with you." Steph talks quietly, so as not to wake Miles, but Tom can still hear her.

"Yes… but I'd like to see her," says Katy in a tiny voice, verging on more tears.

"Well, you can still see her. If I close my eyes," there is a pause. "I can see your mummy. She has her hair tied up in a ponytail, wearing one of the scrunchies you made for her. She has a big smile on her face and is waving, like she does at the school gates. Can you see her Katy?"

"Yes, yes I can. She is wearing the pink top that I helped daddy pick for her for Mother's day. She looks very pretty."

Tom cups his hands around his mouth, he feels an unbearable wave of sadness, and it wants to come crashing out.

"So you can always see her," continues Steph. "When you close your eyes, she'll be there. And you can see her in your dreams of course, maybe you'll see her tonight."

There is the ruffling of bedclothes as Katy gets into bed.

"Auntie Steph. What will daddy do without mummy?" asks Katy.

"What do you mean sweetie?"

"Well, all daddies need mummies."

Steph pauses for a moment. "Don't you worry about your daddy. He's going to be just fine, I promise you."

Tom tiptoes down the stairs, story time would have to wait a little longer. Daddy really doesn't believe he is going to be just fine.

23:00
Hospital de Barcelona

"You are here with Angelo Octavez?" asks the doctor.

Xavier leaps to his feet, kicking over his plastic cup of coffee, but not caring.

"Yes, yes. Is he going to be OK?"

The doctor looks weary and grey, and from his expression it's impossible to tell whether he has good or bad news to share. He nods and Xavier sinks back into his seat with a loud sigh.

"Thank God."

"He's had a transfusion, three litres." He says this with an edge of anger in his voice, as though he begrudges Angelo the blood. "He'll be monitored for 24 hours and then transferred to B ward. In these cases, a psychiatrist is always assigned. He or she will be along tomorrow to talk to him."

Xavier dislikes this doctor and the way he talks about Angelo like just another unhinged patient the world would be better off without.

"His girlfriend was killed this morning," says Xavier. "She was on the AS636 to London."

The doctor barely acknowledges that Xavier has spoken. "You need to go to the nurses' station and fill in some paperwork for Angel."

Xavier stands and heads to the much more appealing faces at the nearby desk. "His name's Angelo," he says as he leaves. "Prick," he says under his breath.

23:34
7 The Stables, South Kensington, London

"I know it's hard to believe Tom, but you and the kids will get through this." Steph separates his fingers from the glass of untouched red wine and puts the glass onto the coffee table, next to Miles' toy train. She holds his hand and squeezes it, trying to wake him from his trance. "You will all get stronger through this, you will bond tighter, and in the future you will only have happy memories of Beth."

He sighs and looks at Steph. "I just can't stop thinking, thinking about…"

"I know. I know." She strokes his hand. "But she's at peace now. And it would have been quick, almost instant." Steph doubts this but knows it is what he needs to think right now. "And in that instant, she would have been thinking about you three." She also doubts this.

After a few moments silence, Tom speaks.

"Steph, I don't think I can do this on my own. It's beyond me. It's beyond anything I ever thought I'd have to deal with."

"You don't have to do it on your own sweetheart." She talks like she does with the little ones and it immediately soothes Tom. "I'll be here at every step."

"She always said you were the sister she never had."

To stop Tom seeing her tears, she draws him to her and he rests his head on her shoulder. Her short hair feels foreign against his cheek, and it has a fragrance he doesn't recognize, but she wears the same perfume as Beth and so he nuzzles closer to her neck and closes his eyes.

And in this position, breathing in the aroma of Beth on her best friend's neck, Tom falls asleep, and his first day as a widower comes to an end.

23:59
Hospital de Barcelona

Angelo lies in a white room, under white sheets that lend a colour to his pallid skin. Lines are attached to his chest and also to a weak vein that peeps out from under bandaging on his right hand. His eyes haven't opened since they closed forever lying on the floorboards of his studio. Behind the refuge of his eyelids, he is with Maria, they are making love and are free to celebrate their love forever together. He knows he did the right thing in joining her, and this way they will never be apart again, his heart that was broken earlier that day, swells with happiness.

Life goes on

10:41, Friday August 2nd, 2013
Outside Madrid

AirStar and the Spanish Aviation Authority have organized a memorial service to remember those who perished on the AS636. Contrary to the stereotype of Spanish efficiency, this has come about very quickly due to the government's desire to clean up the disaster as quickly and cheaply as possible. After a huge clear-up effort and negotiations with the landowner, the blackened field has been converted into a garden of remembrance. The bulk of the human remains were considered too damaged for DNA identification and have been placed in a mass grave, on which an eternal flame will be lit by the Spanish president at midday. 167 trees of different origins to represent the nationalities of the deceased will be planted, with the help of the next of kin. The eyes of the world media will be on the event and the Spanish government is keen to put on a good show, and demonstrate that a financial crisis does not devalue or lessen the honour they bestow on the dead. Due to the number of British fatalities, the Prime Minister, along with his wife, will be in attendance and, with so many officials present, security is paramount.

  Although an act of terrorism as the cause of the tragedy was ruled out, it was done so, in true Spanish style, a little late and nerves are still frayed. As Tom's taxi pulls up at the gates, the taxista has to open the boot and show his identity documents while the police radio through his ID number to verify his status. Miles and Katy shuffle closer to Tom as the policemen circle the car and ask the windows to be opened. A sweaty policemen with his hair stuck down onto his bulging forehead, says something cheerful to the kids, but their Spanish is still elemental and they just frown at him. He taps the bonnet of the car and they drive past the security unit and down a lane.

  Tom spots a throng of people milling around up ahead, in their black clothing, it looks like an ant's nest. Adrenalin has been coursing through his veins ever since they landed in Madrid yesterday, he's nervous as hell and hasn't slept in days. He has no idea how Miles and Katy are feeling, how they are going to react to the memorial, whether it was a good idea to bring them or not. He looks down at each of them in turn. Katy is pretty in pink. She refused to wear a more sombre colour.

Her dark hair is tied in two perfect plaits, courtesy of Veronica, and she has white lacy socks and pink sandals. She is staring at the blue sky, like Beth used to do. When they first left the hotel that morning, she had stopped on the pavement and gawped at the sky.

"Daddy, look how blue the sky is here. It's much bluer than at home."

They had all looked up and agreed with her observation. Before Veronica and Michael got into their taxi, Veronica had bent down next to Katy.

"Is so blue today because mummy is shining down from 'eaven," she whispered. "Shining especially bright today, because all the other mummies and daddies from the plane are shining too."

Katy had nodded, she seemed to like Veronica's explanation, while it had made Tom feel uncomfortable.

On the other side of Tom sits Miles and his halo of blonde curls. There are little beads of sweat gathered next to his ears and he looks most uncomfortable in his shirt and tie. Unlike Katy, Miles and his English skin are not friends with Spanish heat.

Tom leans over to take off Miles' tie. Veronica had insisted he wear one.

"I think we can take this off buddy," says Tom. "What do you think?"

Miles' big blue eyes look up at him. "Yes please daddy."

Tom removes the tie and undoes the top button of his white shirt. "Better?"

Miles nods gratefully. Katy leans across her father. "You can borrow my fan if you like Miles," she says, offering him the floral souvenir she bought from the hotel gift shop. She wafts it in front of her brother's face and his curls rise and fall. He takes the fan, holds it with both hands and attempts to cool himself down. It is not quite the elegant movement of a native Spaniard, but it works, and Katy and Tom both smile at him.

The car stops and, looking out of the windows, they realize they are in the centre of the ant's nest. There are lots of police, security guards, suited men and women on walkie-talkies, and rows of photographers behind a barricade. The taxista checks his coiffed moustache in the mirror before getting out of the car, ready for his moment in front of the camera. The photographers train their lenses onto the taxi door as it is opened.

"OK kids, let's get out," says Tom. "You first Katy."

Katy emerges, pretty as a flower, from the car. The precious image of her, an English rose with Latino heritage, emerging from the car to say adios to her mother, will be in many of the British papers the following day. Her well-to-do lineage will be documented, alongside a smaller image of diplomat Jim Willowman who died of pancreatic cancer just last year. Much will be made of his Columbian widow, Veronica, who has buried her husband and daughter in less than eighteen months, with stoicism and elegance.

Tom gets out of the car and his hand is instantly grabbed by Katy. Then follows little Miles. His angelic looks also capture the attention of the media and, in years to come, the family will be able to laugh at the picture of the sweaty little boy that emerged from the taxi clutching a pink floral fan.

For a few moments Tom and his children stand in the baking sun, not knowing what to do, or where to go. They are rescued by Michael, pristine in a charcoal suit and black tie, who is never lost, even at the memorial service for his sister.

"This way Tom," he says, beckoning towards a white marquee. The family approach the shade, they make a striking image. Michael slows his walk to accompany his mother across the dry grass. Her black hair, sunglasses, dress and heels make a beautiful silhouette of mourning and she is by far the most elegant woman at the memorial, outshining all the other wives, mothers and dignitaries. Tom, tall and fair, walks tentatively behind, holding the hands of his children and trying to keep Miles focused on walking forwards.

In the shade and safety of the marquee, the family are joined by countless other families, all of them missing one, maybe two, perhaps more, of their own clan. Motherless and fatherless children, widows and widowers, parents who have outlived their children, and lovers with no one to love, wander around, sipping orange juice and acting as though their hearts are still whole. Small, sad smiles are shared between them, and without words they ask each other 'how will we get through this?'

Michael, his father's son, approaches and chats with the highest ranking people in the room. Veronica walks her own path, but never far from Michael, and she occasionally returns to her son, swimming back to the boat to remind herself she is safe in this stormy sea. She has done this all before, she knows the routine. She keeps her dark glasses on and offers smiles and words of comfort to those trying to keep their heads above water.

Tom gets cool drinks for his little threesome and finds a quiet corner to sit in.

"Does Uncle Mike know all those people?" asks Katy.

"No, not all of them," says Tom. "But he is very good at meeting people."

Miles is still fanning himself in a clumsy two-handed way, but between the fan and his apple juice, he is kept busy.

"He looks happy. Why is he happy today daddy?"

"He's not happy sweetie. He's very sad. But I learnt a long time ago that Michael, like Grandpa, is a great actor."

"But I thought Uncle Mike was a diplomat, not an actor."

Tom smiles. "He is both, but above all he's a great actor. He's able to make you think one thing, whereas in reality the very opposite is true." Tom eyes Michael with something that could be awe or resentment. A moment passes.

"I think mummy was like that," says Katy looking into the folds of her pretty dress.

Tom looks at his daughter strangely. "Why do you think that?"

She doesn't look up at him, just shrugs her shoulders.

12:14, Friday August 2nd, 2013
14 Carrer Lleo, Al Raval, Barcelona

Angelo is lying in a different room, but still in white sheets and bandages, and almost in the same catatonic state. He has been at home now for nineteen days, although the state of his flat would suggest its inhabitant never returned. Without his pictures, paints, jars of discoloured water and piles of brushes, the apartment looks desolate, lacking purpose and life. Without the decorations of his relationship with Maria; the wine glasses, the coffee cups, the bedclothes forever tangled, a scattering of her clothes entwined with his, the apartment appears lonely. And, like his apartment, Angelo lies desolate, lonely and without purpose.

He knows the memorial ceremony is happening today, now even. He wouldn't have gone, even if he'd received an invite. He's not capable, physically or mentally. He looks at his wrists, even with the layers of wadding and bandages they appear thinner than he ever remembers. He moves his hands around in circles. There is still a faint pain that he likes to feel.

12:30, Friday August 2nd, 2013
Outside Madrid

The trees are planted simultaneously. It would take far too long if it were done individually. Beth has been given a British Ash tree and Veronica has brought along a tiny Columbian flag to tie on one of its branches. The family has been assigned an assistant to aid with the planting. Pablo looks about 22 and, with more tattoos than skin, as if he comes from the wrong side of the tracks, but he is very sensitive to the situation and stands somberly next to the hole, holding the sapling that will become Beth's tree. He speaks with a thick Spanish accent.

"Een your awn time, you may plant thees tree, and feel thee 'ole with saul." He gestures at the spade and pile of soil next to him. Having spotted the flag clutched in Veronica's hand, he repeats himself in Spanish, and Veronica smiles her thanks.

"Tom, do you want to start?" asks Michael.

"Sure," says Tom. It's actually a nice feeling to have something to do, some use for his restless hands. He takes the tree from Pablo and leans it towards Veronica. She ties the flag to one of the highest branches, ties another knot and one more for luck. She clutches the flag around the branch and bows her head in prayer. Miles opens his mouth to speak, but Tom hushes him into silence. Veronica spends a few minutes in prayer and, by the end, tears are streaming from under her Chanel sunglasses. Michael puts his arm around his mother and, although he is trying extremely hard to maintain his control, his jaw begins to wobble.

Tom places the tree into the hole and holds it upright, while Michael takes up the spade and begins to shovel the soil. Busy hands and minds help divert the tears, and Tom's diplomatic brother-in-law is soon back in control. Spade after spade, the hole gets shallower and shallower.

Katy looks down at her pretty pink dress, lace socks and spotless sandals. She considers them for a moment and then kneels down next to the heap of soil. She scoops up little handfuls of earth and throws them into the hole. Miles needs no further encouragement to get his hands dirty and immediately joins his sister. He is less coordinated, however, and manages to get as much soil over him and Katy as he does in the hole.

Veronica laughs. "Cheeldren! You looked so preety and now you are covered in mud!"

They both smile up at her. "It will wash off Granny," says Katy. "Don't worry."

Michael and Tom change places, so that Beth's husband and children finish the job between them. They are almost finished when Miles picks up his plastic cup and fills it with soil. It still has enough juice in it to act as an adhesive and, with some help from Pablo, he makes a perfect little mud castle next to the tree. The whole family stand back to appreciate their work.

"A beautiful tree for your beautiful mother," says Michael, looking at his niece and nephew.

They all look up into the young green leaves of the tree, they contrast beautifully with the bright blue cloudless sky. One by one they remember what Veronica had said about the blue sky that morning.

17:07, Saturday August 17th, 2013
14 Carrer Lleo, Al Raval, Barcelona

There is a knocking at the door that Angelo is trying hard to ignore. He hates noise at the moment, anything that brings him out of his stupor is a curse to him, he just wants to stay submerged in the deep darkness of his misery and his painkillers; sinking deeper and deeper, away from life on the surface. But this awful din is bringing him back to the surface and, when he hears a key turn in the lock, he is forced to break through.

Señora Carmen stands in the doorway surveying the apartment. She used to hate the way it looked, the squalor, the souvenirs of his bohemian life scattered across every surface, but she hates it more now. The emptiness worries her, and every time she climbs the stairs she thinks she will find a body. She crosses herself outside the door every time.

"Angelo," she says.

He doesn't look at her but raises his head slightly.

"Angelo, I was hoping you could help me with something."

He hardly stirs.

"I need to get my winter blankets washed at the launderette." She looks at the sun searing through the window and knows her statement sounds ridiculous, but he wouldn't know. "Can you go for me?"

Angelo hears the words, but doesn't really comprehend them. He stares blankly at the floor.

She walks towards him. "Come on Angelo, come help. It would be a big favour for me. My old legs can't walk all that way." *Although they have had more exercise in the last few weeks, climbing these stairs, than the last few years*, she thinks to herself. She grabs his shoulder and pushes him in the direction of the door, as you would a stubborn toddler. He stumbles ahead of her.

She gives him two laundry bags of blankets and some money and sends him off in the direction of the launderette. When he picks up the bags and struggles down the road with them she realizes just how weak he's become, stopping every few paces to drop the bags and breathe deeply. She watches him from the front steps and sighs. He needs to get out more and get over her. It's never going to happen stuck in the attic room like a decaying piece of furniture, and the last thing she needs is a depressive tenant who leaves her wondering if he is upstairs living or upstairs dying. She goes back into her apartment, smokes a cigarette and thinks about other chores that could get him out of the building.

Angelo walks to the launderette. He has not been outside for over a week, in fact he has hardly moved for over a week, and his body struggles to make the adjustment. He walks robotically a few steps before he stops, drops the bags to the pavement and takes deep breaths.

He then picks up the bags and starts over. He is a wind up toy losing its mechanism.

At the launderette, the wrinkled old Chinese woman, who looks as though she has been put through a washing machine too many times, eyes him suspiciously. As he sluggishly pulls the blankets from the bags and gets himself wrapped up in them, she tuts, shakes her head at him and goes to help. Young people are so useless, especially men, especially men with long hair. Angelo sits on the bench and watches blankly as she loads two machines. Next to him on the bench sits the bedraggled centrefold of a newspaper. The rest of *El País* is nowhere in sight. The double page is a montage of small photographs, all of them faces. Faces that smile, some that stare, faces in monotone and faces in colour, young faces, old faces, black, white and pink faces. Every image butts up against the next, a crowd of anonymous people without names. These are the nameless strangers you might pass in the street and pay no attention to. Angelo's eyes drift from one to the next with no reason to linger. But then he spies the headline and his heart leaps for every person: *MEMORIAL SPECIAL – MEET THE FALLEN.*

18:33, Thursday August 29th, 2013
7 The Stables, South Kensington, London

Tom is trying to catch up on emails, but a month of messages about timber share prices in Brazil are struggling to hold his focus. Miles and Katy are giggling at Peppa Pig, but when the theme music rings out, Miles toddles over to Tom.

"Daddy, can we sky call mummy?"

Tom sighs and looks into the big blue eyes of his son. "Miles, it is a Skype call, not a sky call, and we can't Skype call mummy, no."

Miles looks down at his bare feet and mumbles.

"But mummy is in the sky. Everyone says so. Why can't we sky call her?"

Tom rubs his forehead and looks to Katy for help or distraction. She is sucking her thumb, a habit she has recently adopted.

"For goodness sake Katy, will you stop sucking your thumb," he says. "You're not a baby anymore."

This is distraction enough for Miles. "Baby! Baby!" he screams at his sister, in fits of giggles. "Katy's a baby!" He hops from foot to foot in front of Katy.

She removes her thumb and her mouth sets into an angry scowl. "You're the baby," she says to Miles. "You're the baby!" she screams, getting up off the sofa. "You don't understand anything. You don't even understand that mummy's dead. She's dead. You don't have a mummy anymore! You're a baby without a mummy."

"Katy!" Tom shouts into the noise of her screaming voice, trying to silence her and her nasty words. But it's too late. Miles' face crumples in on itself and he is sobbing loudly. Tom picks him up and cuddles him as Miles tries to form a sentence through his tears. "I'm not… I'm not… a baby, a baby, without a mummy." Katy bites her lip. She feels bad that she made her brother cry but she was only telling the truth. Perhaps sometimes it is better to tell a lie.

19:56, Sunday August 25th, 2013
14 Carrer Lleo, Al Raval, Barcelona

It's been a over a week since Xavier's last visit and he's scared about what he might find behind the door, but Señora Carmen has kept an eye on Angelo, and even mentioned that he'd been painting again, which is hard to believe. He knocks on the door and shouts for a few minutes before going to get the key from Señora Carmen. This is not a promising start to the visit. Will his friend be drunk and slurring in a pool of whiskey and saliva, or worse, dead in a pool of blood? The sight that meets him on the other side of the door is a whole world away from what he is expecting, it's a world he recognizes. Xavier feels as though he has stepped through a magic door that has taken him to another dimension, a past dimension.

"Angelo?"

The man at the window pays no attention.

"Angelo! Man, it's me. What're you doing?" He walks past the piles of canvases, and past the easel. Only when his shadow darkens the painting in front of Angelo does he turn.

"Oh," says Angelo. He squints at his friend a moment. "Xavier!" He says it as though he has only just remembered the name of his oldest acquaintance. "What're you doing here?"

"I have exactly the same question for you," he says patting him on the back. Xavier's face is one big smile.

Angelo shrugs. "Painting."

For the first time since walking in, Xavier looks at the canvases. He finds himself surrounded by faces. Men, women, and children stare at him relentlessly. They all share the same expression, they are not happy, not sad, not scared, not surprised, they are blank. Their cheeks, mouths, eyebrows, chins reveal nothing, but there is something in the eyes. There is a glow behind all of the eyes, a light that seems to be coming from deep within each of them, as though they all know something, share something that Xavier is not part of. They look at him with a confidence, a knowledge, that disturbs him. Taped onto the bottom corner of each of the paintings is a small photograph. He looks closely at them and realizes they have been cut out of a newspaper.

"Angelo, who are these people?"

"They're dead," says Angelo simply. He points to the cut-up centrefold that is lying on the floor next to his palette of paints.

"Memorial special," reads Xavier. "Memorial of what?"

And then Xavier answers his own question in his head. "Oh."

Xavier wants to ask Angelo why he is painting the dead; the strangers that fell out of the sky with Maria, but he is happy to see his friend doing something familiar, and he doesn't want to spoil it.

"You want a drink man?" he asks.

"Sure."

Xavier goes into the kitchen and is amazed to see that the fridge has some basic supplies in it, including a bottle of wine that hasn't been touched. Things are really looking up. Back in the studio, Xavier drinks, and Angelo mostly ignores his wine and his friend, while he continues to paint. It is the most content scene the apartment has witnessed since July 12th.

20:51, Tuesday September 24th, 2013
7 The Stables and Willowman Grange

Despite all of Michael's efforts and those of his many Spanish contacts, none of Beth's remains have made it back to England in time for her funeral.

"I'm sorry, but it doesn't look as though it's going to happen," he tells Tom over the phone.

"But it was over two months ago, they promised to return the bodies... what was left, to the families as soon as possible. It was in all the press." Tom can't believe his wife won't be making her own funeral.

Michael sighs down the line. "I know Tom, but what the Spanish authorities say and what they do are entirely different. There's been some cock-up with the DNA samples."

"But, but, there must be something we can do. I mean... you're a diplomat. You're a Willowman."

He sighs. "I'm sorry Tom. No one and nothing can bring her back for next Friday."

"So we need to rearrange the ceremony?"

"No," said Michael. "I have no idea when the remains will be returned, if they even will. Everyone is committed to the date, and it would break mum's heart to know the truth."

"Then what?" asked Tom, baffled.

"We're going to have to... well... improvise."

11:47, Monday September 30th, 2013
Willowman Grange

Less than a week later and the two men find themselves in the furthest corner of the Willowman Grange estate with Barry, head florist from Zelda's Flowers, and his van. Veronica has taken the kids to terrorize animals on a local farm. Barry looks at the two men with something between alarm and sorrow as his beautiful flowers are thrown into a huge steel bin. When the order for 60 bouquets of white roses had been phoned through he had been overjoyed, and when the address was given as Willowman Grange he was over-overjoyed. Now that the order is being fulfilled he has his doubts; a bumpy drive through the woods followed by the decimation of his beautiful creations was not what he had in mind.

Barry watches in shocked silence as Tom and Michael unwrap the cellophane and ribbons from the last of the bouquets and throw the few dozen roses into the bin.

"Thanks so much Barry for your service today," says Michael, shaking Barry's limp hand and slipping him a fifty-pound note. Michael throws clumps of cellophane and ribbons into the back of the van. "If you could just dispose of all this paraphernalia that would be great. As stated on the phone, we really appreciate your discretion, and would be most grateful if news of this transaction could go no further." Barry seems engrossed by Michael's voice and hand rather than his words, and Tom remembers what an imposing man his brother-in-law can be. Michael was always like his father but, since Jim's death, he seems to have become him in entirety.

"Please don't tell anyone about this," says Tom, clarifying Michael's words. "Not a soul." Barry looks at the ground and begins to count the number of people he has told about the order. Tom pats him on the back and directs him towards the cab of his van.

Barry sits in the cab for a moment, trying to work out where he is, who he is with and why 720 roses have been thrown into a bin by such charming people.

"Cheerio Barry," calls Michael, pounding on the back of the van.

"Bye-bye," mutters Barry to himself. He starts the engine and rolls off into the trees. He manages to get himself lost trying to escape, he crosses a fairway and narrowly misses a phallic sculpture before he finds the main drive. He is contemplating just how strange rich people are as his van curls between trees and then out through the gates. He would have been even more confounded by their behaviour had he glanced into the rear-view mirror. A thin tendril of white smoke winds into the sky behind him.

15:32, Tuesday October 1st, 2013
14 Carrer Lleo, Al Raval, Barcelona

Angelo stands back and squints at the newest face that stares back at him from still-wet eyes. It is a young boy, maybe eight or nine. His eyes are magnified behind round green-rimmed glasses and his hair stands spiky above his chubby face. Angelo nods his approval of the picture and scrutinizes it from a few different angles. He takes some fresh tape and attaches the young boy to the wall adjoining the kitchen. The boy sits between a smartly dressed middle-aged man with a receding hairline and a freckled woman in her early twenties. Beneath him, a dark beauty with shining skin, and above him an old man with a weary face. The boy seems happy in his new position and stares out serenely. Angelo stands captivated by the boy for a few moments, was it this boy who sat with Maria?

    Angelo's catatonia has been replaced by a frantic obsession, an energy that needs no rest. He can't sleep, he can't concentrate on anything else, he needs to paint. But it is not the process of painting he's obsessed with. It is the dead. He doesn't care about their names, their backgrounds, their families. Whether they are a Phoebe or a Fernando, a sister or a son, a lawyer or a layabout, all of that is trivial, meaningless. These 167 strangers all shared something, they shared death, and they shared death with Maria, his Maria. They all fell from the sky together, their bodies burned together, and somewhere between the two events they died together. Maybe they clutched at each other, these nameless strangers that sat in the same rows and smiled at the same airhostesses. Perhaps they held hands. Maybe they prayed together, prayed for life to win against death. Maybe they screamed together, maybe they sat in resigned silence together. And one of these anonymous faces sat with Maria, perhaps he or she chatted with her, perhaps they had foreign tongues and just smiled politely at one another until the first signs of danger arose. Then maybe they gasped, hugged, screamed, prayed together, like all the other passengers forced into the most intimate of relationships with strangers.

    Since the day at the launderette, Angelo has been painting, almost nonstop. He forgot about Señora Carmen's blankets turning circles in front of him, he left without them, and did not hear the Chinese woman shout after him. All he took back with him were the images of 167 people, and as soon as he got home he cut them out into a pile of faces. He didn't look at the front or back of the centerfold; the article that spoke of their traumatic ending. He isn't interested in the ghastly words some fame-hungry journalist might have used to raise sympathy and eyebrows. He is interested in Maria, and with whom she journeyed from life to death.

The painting of Maria sits on the wall now, the wall from where his father's portrait once stared. She looks at Angelo every second of every minute, and her eyes glow with love. He doesn't need to look at her all the time, although he often does, he knows she loves him, that they shared the closest of relationships, but now there is someone else who shared something even more intimate with her, they shared death and they now share what is beyond death. Angelo wants to do justice to that unknown person. Every single one of the plane's passengers has possessed him and he must do what he can to honour them.

Angelo turns away from the young boy with the thick glasses. He takes a roll of canvas, measures and cuts out a piece that he takes to his easel. He tapes it to the wood and reaches for his pile of cuttings on the table. He picks up a scrap of paper that could be *the* face, the face that was the last one Maria saw. The woman is in her thirties and attractive. She has dark, almost black eyes and hair pulled back from her oval face. Although the image only shows her head and shoulders, she looks petite, a neat little bundle. She is smiling and Angelo smiles back at her. He likes the idea that this is the face.

10:02, Friday October 4th, 2013
Willowman Grange

Two urns of cremated roses, masquerading as Beth, sit on the mantel of the drawing room. It's obvious that Veronica is trying not to look at them but her eyes keep glancing at them, as though to ensure they are still there, her daughter remains in the room. It is the only sign of vulnerability that Veronica exhibits, and Tom cannot believe her resilience. She buried her husband less than eighteen months ago, and here she sits, preened and polished, about to bury her daughter. The family Tom married into is made of strong stuff, statues made of a stone that will never crack, no matter what the pressure. Michael stands and approaches the middle bay window.

"People will start arriving soon," says Michael.

"Aye," says Philip. It's not the first time he has visited the Willowmans' house, but he still sits in it as though in an uncomfortable museum. As if the surroundings were not awkward enough for him, he always seems to be here for funerals.

"I'm sure there'll be a good turnout," says Carol. "She were a lovely girl."

"Aye," says Philip again. Carol has made him promise to be more communicative on this visit than the last, and he is trying his utmost. Philip never particularly liked Jim, but he appreciated the way he filled all the gaps in conversation with the right-sounding words, and he wishes someone would do that now.

There is silence for a few moments. Carol pulls her navy blue skirt down over her knee, wishing she had gone for something longer. Philip drinks his beer. Veronica alternates between smiling at the family and glancing at Beth, and Michael nods at everyone in turn.

"Well the vicar seems very nice," says Carol breaking the silence.

Everyone murmurs their agreement. "Aye," says Philip.

Two hours later and the first of Beth's urns is about to be lowered into the ground next to her father, in the rose garden at Willowman Grange. As she sits peacefully on the ground, Michael reads a section from *The Little Prince*, Beth's favourite story, while a string quartet plays *Adagio for Strings*. Tom has no idea whether this is how Beth would want to be buried, they never talked about the words and music that would accompany her into the ground. They only ever talked about living; their jobs, their children, their home, they never talked about dying. Michael is reciting without reference or notes.

"In one of the stars I shall be living. In one of them I shall be laughing. And so it will be as if all the stars were laughing, when you look at the sky at night..."

But they did once. They did talk about dying, at least they tried. His mind grabs at a distant memory.

"And when your sorrow is comforted, for time soothes all sorrows, you will be content that you have known me."

He thinks back to a time many years ago, a family ago, a marriage ago, when Lolli died, Tia Lolli. Michael's voice trails off into the distance, like a ticking clock as you fall asleep. Tom knows he should be paying attention to these pertinent words read at his wife's funeral, but something is bugging him.

He concentrates hard so as not to lose his train of thought. He focuses on when Lolli died. He remembers how the young and vibrant girl he fell in love with changed, how she became shrunken and hollow in a matter of days, how her eyes dimmed, her voice muted and her personality all but disappeared. And then Steph came along. He glances at Steph, their resident expert on death, the strongest ship in the stormiest of seas. She stands tall behind dark glasses that she probably doesn't need. They exchange a small smile.

The string quartet is building to a crescendo and trying to distract him. He pushes his eyelids shut to concentrate. Tom thinks about Beth as she was recently, the way she looked, walked, spoke, smiled. And there it is, when he thinks about her smile it comes to him, the realization that was just out of reach a few moments ago, now firmly in his grasp. It's there for him to play with, to turn over, and to inspect. The Beth he knew in the last months, maybe year, of her life was not the vibrant, charismatic person he met and fell in love with all those years ago. And it wasn't just the inevitable passing of time that separated his recent wife from the woman he first met, it was something else. The contrast took his breath away. The woman he'd shared his life with recently was more like the Beth he had known in mourning.

Was she still in mourning over her father? He had died nearly eighteen months ago, and his death, unlike Lolli's was predicted, planned and implemented perfectly, in true Willowman style. The best doctors and anaesthesiologists had kept him pain free and lucid in his own home, until the pancreatic cancer that had crept from the very insides to the very outsides of his body took him away. All the family were at the Grange when he died, and each of them had had their own time with him to say goodbye. Beth never told Tom about her goodbye, and now he wonders whether she never quite got over it. He tries to remember back to the time of Jim's death, but all he remembers are calls in the night, endless trips out to the Grange, walks with the kids around the estate, and plenty of brave faces. He remembers Beth being devastated at his diagnosis but pragmatic about his death and the plans.

"It comes to us all Tom," he remembers her saying. "Dad will be with Lolli, and wherever they are, I'll join them one day." He remembers that sentence and bites his lip firmly, as he watches his wife's make-believe ashes being lowered into the ground next to her father's real remains. He knows that she never meant it in the literal sense, but it pains him that he couldn't add weight to her theory by planting her ashes next to Jim's.

After Jim's death, Beth hadn't demonstrated the intense period of mourning that she felt when Lolli died, but something more subtle was there, a dimming of her eyes, a dimming of herself. She didn't smile like before, she didn't shine like before. And now Tom realizes, it never came back. The sadness, weariness that appeared in Beth around her father's death, never subsided. Maybe he noticed it at first, and expected it to fade, but with time he must have grown accustomed to it, or plain ignored it. Either way, when she herself died, she was still in mourning over her father, or something else was keeping her sad.

He can't believe he hadn't noticed this before, but with all of life's distractions he never thought about their beginnings together, and the woman his wife once was. It was now, standing over her grave, that he thought about the Beth he first fell in love with. And the difference between then and now was happiness. She had it then, all those years ago, but recently it had gone. When did it go?

Tom weeps like he hasn't wept in a long time. He doesn't care who's watching open-mouthed as his body heaves out great loud sobs, and tears run down his red cheeks. He's crying so loudly in his own little world of despair that he doesn't notice Katy screaming for her daddy, he doesn't feel Miles' little hands clawing at his trouser leg. He doesn't feel his father patting him on the back urging him to pull himself together.

He isn't crying because his wife is dead, he is crying because she wasn't happy alive. She had been unhappy, for years maybe, and now she was dead and there was no way of ever, ever making her happy again. When did it start? When did he begin paying so little attention to the woman he loved? Did she still love him? Is she happier dead? He knows these questions will plague him forever and he cries harder for the answers he will never get.

This is a funeral and everyone expects tears, but Tom's outburst is so out of character and so volcanic that everyone else is stunned into silence, their tears drying rather than flowing on their cheeks. The service is over and people walk past the grave, leaving flowers and words of goodbye with Beth. They walk rather hurriedly, keen to leave the widower alone in his gloom. Lastly, Philip peels Miles from his father's legs and carries him away and Veronica leads Katy by the shoulders. The only people left are Tom and Steph.

Steph walks over to Tom and puts her arm around his heaving shoulders. He cries for another twenty minutes before he feels the weight on his shoulder, and realizes it's Steph. He tries to form words but getting them out in the open is like an admission of guilt, and he struggles to find his voice between the sobbing.

"She, she…"

Steph removes her glasses to look at Tom. In her black high heels they are eye to eye. Tom had been right, the sunglasses were only protection from the sun not for concealing tears, her blue eyes are as clear as ever.

"She… wasn't… she… wasn't…"

"Wasn't what?" asks Steph.

He takes a deep breath. "She wasn't happy."

Steph looks away from Tom, to the fresh heap of soil. She opens her mouth to say something, but then closes it.

13:54, Friday October 4th, 2013
Willowman Grange

Tom didn't want to, but his sense of duty kicked in, and now he is circling the drawing room exchanging useless small talk with people who knew his wife in some small or big way. Some faces have names, but a great many not, and he wonders how Beth touched these people's lives. It's bizarre to think that his wife, his soul mate, knew so many people who are strangers to him.

"I'm so sorry for your loss," says the painted face in front of him. He tries to place the woman, have they met before? She has smart cropped hair and red lipstick, looks like an advertising type.

"She was a great woman. I used to love working with her." He was right.

"You worked closely?" he asks.

"Yes, we worked on the Mars and Land Rover accounts together."

Tom nods. These sound familiar to him. "And you worked together until, well, until recently?"

She cocks her head and looks at him strangely with narrowed eyes. She opens her mouth to speak but Michael fills the space where her words would have floated.

"The great Angie Harman! How are you?"

They kiss on both cheeks and Angie's puzzlement is whisked away by Michael's charm.

15:12, Monday October 7th, 2013
14 Carrer Lleo, Al Raval, Barcelona

His brush is assembling portrait 42, a handsome face; a wide jaw, healthy tan skin bordered by short fair hair at the top and the beginnings of a white shirt at the base. It's the type of face that hasn't been damaged by smoke, drugs, drink and loss, although of course now it has been damaged beyond recognition. Maria, like all other women, would have been attracted to him, and Angelo is sure he would have been attracted to Maria. Did they sit together? Was he her final companion? Her fellow passenger who flew into death with her?

Angelo is mixing some magenta into his complexion when the buzzer rings. He ignores it for a few minutes, but this person is persistent, probably Xavier in need of a drink. Angelo speaks into the intercom.

"Yes," he says.

"Angelo. *Mi tresor.* Let me in."

Angelo sighs and buzzes her in. He hasn't heard from Teresa in months, he forgot she existed. She has an amazing talent for staying away in times of difficulty and arriving at his door when she sniffs the faintest whiff of sellable acrylics. He looks around his studio. It is swathed in paintings, more than it has ever witnessed. There is more paint than there is white space but there is nothing his agent can do for him, he's not selling these, it's his own private collection. He hears the sound of slow heels on the stairs and leaves the handsome face on canvas to open the door.

Teresa, engulfed in blue silk, climbs the final few steps as though reaching the peak of a mountain. At the top she stands in triumph and takes a minute or so to catch her breath, only the sound of her lungs fills the gap between them.

"Angelo, *mi tresor*, how are you?" She kisses him on both cheeks and a blue cloud swathed in expensive perfume enters his apartment.

She only takes a few steps inside. Her head seems to turn 360 degrees as she takes in her surroundings.

"Well Angelo. You never fail to surprise me, so I don't know why, but I am mighty surprised."

He walks back to his easel and number 42. He picks up his brush, but it sits limply in his hand. He can't continue with Teresa in the room. Her heels tap around the wooden floor and she looks at every face in turn, finishing at the portrait of Maria. She talks to Maria rather than to Angelo.

"I never thought you'd be able to replicate the quality of this painting, of Maria, but you have done it, over and over. How many are here?"

"41."

"Angelo, I'm astounded." He knows what she's astounded by - the calculation of potential commission she could make.

"I'm not selling," he says. "None of them."

She turns to him. "You have to, Angelo, these will make you a fortune."

He shakes his head. "They're staying here."

She paces around the room, considering her next move like a fox circling its prey.

"Who are they all anyway? People off the street?"

He doesn't answer, but when she turns to him he gestures to the newspaper headline that lies torn on the table. She picks it up and her eyes literally glow with the potential riches she can see reflected in the print. Teresa's heart is beating fast, she's thinking about the exhibition, what a media stir it would create, how the families of the dead would pay extortionate prices for these beautiful memorials to their loved ones, and

149

how she would get 15% for them. An exhibition of the dead, *'Meet the Fallen'*. She looks around, once again, at the dead faces surrounding her and starts to concoct the marketing spiel. *A heartwarming tribute to all those who perished in the AS636 tragedy, by an artist who lost the love of his life to the same catastrophe.* And there is the sticking point; the artist himself. She needs to work with Angelo carefully, he is fragile she knows, still grieving. Teresa has never been in love with anyone before, she had a brief infatuation with a gold trader who was a collector of art. She visited him on his yacht in Marina Port Vell and became obsessed with him as soon as a servant showed her through to the gold-trimmed cabin that housed his collection. He was fat, bald and sweating, but by the time he entered the cabin her infatuation had taken root. It was never love, though, never had been. Still, she would have been upset had he died, especially if it had happened before she'd sold him the Scott and the Pedrosa sketch. She tries to transfer these thoughts to Angelo's situation, and tries to empathize.

She smiles at Angelo. Her lipstick looks fresh and moist, or perhaps she is salivating. Everything about her face looks sickly sweet, from the pink lips to the blue eyeshadow umbrellas above her eyes. Her face is like a collection of ice cream flavours.

"How many are you going to paint *mi tresor*?" she asks.

"All of them," he says.

"And how many is that?"

"167."

Her eyes flash beneath their blue umbrellas. She has time, plenty of time. She can plan the exhibition, think about the venue, get the word out, and she can work on Angelo. She will need to make use of all of her charm and cunning to make this come off, she may also need to invest in some skills unknown to her, sympathy and compassion. She likes a challenge and she likes making money, so she is already beginning to relish what she has ahead of her.

She touches Angelo's arm. "Well, I only came to check that you are alright *mi tresor*. I am truly sorry for your loss and I completely respect what you are doing here." She whisks a theatrical hand around the studio. "Honouring the dead."

She kisses him on both cheeks and heads for the door. With one hand on the handle she turns to him.

"I will come again soon," she says. "Just to check how you're doing." With her spare hand she blows an extra kiss in his direction. The gesture is so insincere that Angelo thinks he can hear the kiss land with a wet thud by her feet.

"Close the door after you," he says. "And next time you come, the answer will still be no."

She screws up her eyes and cocks her head, as though puzzled by what he is referring to.

"*Ciao ciao mi tresor.*" She walks tentatively down the four flights to the street, and by the time she enters the sunshine she has already made a shortlist of potential exhibition venues.

11:34, Tuesday October 8th, 2013
7 The Stables, South Kensington, London

As soon as Tom has deposited his parents on the train back to Hartlepool he races home. He hasn't felt this sense of purpose for months. His heart is beating fast, not from the exertion of scurrying across London, but at the prospect of what he is going to find at home. He breaks the house rules and doesn't remove his shoes before sprinting up the stairs two at a time. Firstly he goes to the kids' room. He grabs the princess frame from Katy's bedside. Beneath the beaming face of a Disney Princess is a photo of Katy, Miles and Beth in the garden. It was taken just after their Easter egg hunt that year, and Miles' face is already smeared in chocolate, and he's licking his fingers. Katy wears a wide smile and looks directly at the camera, as does Beth. It is Beth's smile Tom is interested in. He takes the picture to the window to let the sunshine light up her expression. And there he sees it. The teeth and mouth are arranged into the form of a smile; they have the right shape, but there is nothing real about it. Beth's eyes look lost and distant in this happy family photo, and that's because, Tom realizes, this wasn't a happy family.

He goes to his office and turns on his computer. It beeps a cheery hello to him and lets him know how many people have sent him messages. He ignores them all and goes to his pictures folder. He picks randomly from the last twelve months. At first he scrutinizes every shot;

the family squeezed around his parents' dinner table for a Sunday roast, Miles and Beth paddling on a grey weekend in Dartmouth, Beth and Michael in their finery at one of Veronica's fundraising dinners, Beth on the sofa in the background as Katy turns pirouettes in a white tutu, but soon he is flashing through images, scanning each for signs of Beth, signs of her happiness. Scenes of holidays, school sports days, birthdays replace each other on screen, a growing pile of days in which Beth's smile remains the same. Maybe he is imagining it? After all she is smiling in all these pictures, and they're only photographs, they can't truly capture someone's happiness. He goes to his calendar and clicks back through the months, trying to locate Jim's death. At 2pm June 21 2012 he finds the funeral.

Back in his pictures folder, he finds a gap of several months either side of Jim's death. Planning for death and recovering from it have few photo opportunities. He looks back further and finds a folder, 'Bluebell Wood,' dated March 2012. He smiles. Just the name of the folder brings back happy memories, and he finds them all inside. Playing hide and seek in the pine forest, running through the bluebells, Beth and Katy hanging from a tree like monkeys, a picnic in the sunshine, a stranger's cheeky dog stealing a sausage roll. Every image is colourful and vibrant, they could be used to sell washing detergent, and Beth is also colourful and vibrant. Beth is happy. On this bright day eighteen months ago she was happy. A wave of relief washes over him. She had been happy. It was Jim's death that brought about a change in her, a change she never got over.

He flicks through more recent images of their life together. The only flash of his wife's happiness that appears is in a photo that Katy took about four months ago. Veronica had given her granddaughter a camera for her birthday and, for about a month, it went everywhere with her. In this image, Beth is at the security gates of Heathrow airport. She wears a crisp white shirt with a large bow at the neck and her hair is swept neatly behind her head, her big laptop case hangs over her petite shoulder. She looks beautifully professional and her red painted lips are parted as they shout something at the camera. She is surrounded by flying commuters and holidaymakers but she doesn't notice them. Her eyes shine at the camera. She is happy, happy to be going on this work trip? Happy to be leaving the family? He tries to remember where she was going, what business she was doing at that time, perhaps a pitch, perhaps a new client meeting.

Tom stares into the shining eyes of his wife. Can it really be that only work ignited her joy recently?

11:47, Monday October 14th, 2013
14 Carrer Lleo, Al Raval, Barcelona

Angelo has been neglecting this face, trying to ignore it, but it hasn't ignored him. It calls to him from the table, from the bottom of the pile of paper faces where it lies buried. It craves attention, preys on Angelo as he paints and even as he sleeps. The media say this face isn't to blame, that this isn't the face that killed 167 people, but Angelo doesn't watch or read news and so hates this face. This is the man that held Maria in the air, and this is the man that plunged her into the ground. Angelo stands at the window face to face with the man. He wears a white shirt with golden epaulettes, a hat emblazoned with gold wings, the crown of a sky king, a man that can hold 70 tonnes of metal and hundreds of lives in the air, with just his hands.

Angelo tapes the newspaper cutting into the corner of a freshly cut canvas. He is not sure why he is painting this man, he doesn't want to do him justice, doesn't want to honour his memory, but he wants to silence the face that keeps tormenting him, and maybe painting him will do this. He begins the painting as ever with a wide brush and fat yellow lines mapping out his features, the layout of the land. He surprises himself with what a good job he does of this, the captain begins to rise out of the canvas. Angelo then mixes some paints, tones of skin and hair to bring the dead man to life. After applying a layer of base colour to the lines in front of him he stands back to check his work against the photo.

"Way too light," he says to himself. He begins to mix new shades, adding more hues and black to correct the colours sitting on his palette. He applies a second layer over the man, but once again is unhappy with his colours. After four layers of base paint he is finally content, and begins sweeping more detail into the portrait; highlights of dark and shade, hair texture and the ornaments of a pilot. The process swallows

Angelo whole and he finds himself unable to stop, unable to rest, unable to even take his eyes from the picture.

It is not until late in the afternoon that Angelo finishes his 45th portrait; that of Captain Philip Bollo. The sun has dipped over the other side of the apartment block and so the light cast by the window is grey, not the brilliant white of the morning. Angelo needs some time apart from the picture, he feels exhausted by it, as though it has stripped him of all energy and all capacity to judge it. He leaves the apartment and takes a walk around the block, allowing his pulse to slow and his thoughts to spread beyond the face. On his way back into the building, Señora Carmen's door opens.

"Angelo, this package came for you." She hands him a brown paper package, about the size of a shoebox. He takes it without a word, heads up the stairs and leaves it in the corner of his studio, before approaching the newest canvas. The fresh air and environment outside of this shrine has allowed him to forget the detail of what he's painted, he just has a vague recollection of the original lines he forged. When he looks at the picture he nods solemnly. The image is perfect, it captures the person completely. The two men stare at each other for seconds that grow into minutes. Finally Angelo removes the canvas from the easel and looks for a space to settle him.

He uses fresh tape to secure the man on the wall next to Maria, and steps back to check the position. Captain Philip Bollo and Maria sit side by side. The gleam of her eyes and the healthy glow of her skin make a shocking contrast to the man next to her. His portrait is shrouded in darkness, eerie blues and greys define the shadows of his face, and his epaulettes and hat are pure black shadows. The portrait is almost a silhouette and its background is made up of dark and foreboding clouds. The eyes are grey and glassy and barely defined from the rest of his features.

Angelo surveys his whole studio and smiles as his gaze returns to the pilot. Among all the images in the room, Captain Philip Bollo's is the only one of death.

19:37, Wednesday October 16th, 2013
7 The Stables, South Kensington, London

"Katy's autumn production is coming up," says Tom. He twiddles his thumbs and sips the wine he really doesn't want to be drinking.

"Oh really? Does she have a big part?" asks Steph.

"No, not at all. She didn't go to ballet class for two months after... well since July. But she is getting back into it, and she has a small part, I think she's a pumpkin."

Steph laughs. "A pumpkin? Doesn't sound particularly elegant."

Tom forces a chuckle and drinks more wine. "No, no it doesn't. But I have to go."

Steph remains quiet. It's clear Tom has something else to say.

"And I need to ask you a favour."

"You want me to babysit for Miles?"

He shakes his head.

"Oh shit, you want me to make a pumpkin outfit! Listen, I have to tell you I am fucking awful at sewing, it was the only subject I ever failed. There must be someone else you can ask. Honestly, she'll look more like a rotten carrot than..."

"Come with me," says Tom quietly.

She pauses. "Sorry?"

He gulps. "Come with me Steph. I need you there." He can't look at her and keeps his eyes down.

She takes the sweaty hand that rests on his tense knee. "Of course Tom. I'm there."

"I can't do it on my own," he whispers. His lips begin to tremble and he uses every muscle in his body to try and stop them.

"You won't," she says.

20:42, Friday November 1st, 2013
7 The Stables, South Kensington, London

"You were so good tonight Katy," says Tom stroking her hair. "You were the best ballerina on stage."

Katy is nestling into her Princess covers, exhausted after her big night, but she turns to her father, her eyes wide.

"Do you think mummy was watching?"

He hates lying to his children, but death seems so much more palatable from a liar's point of view. "Yes, I'm sure she was. And she'd have been very proud."

"I think she'd have made a better pumpkin outfit than Nanny did."

Tom laughs. His mother had never been much good at sewing and some of Katy's outfit had remained on the stage after she had left it.

"I think you're right sweetie, but no one was paying attention to the outfit, only to your dancing, and it was tip-top. You were the prima ballerina." Katy bites her lip to stop her beaming smile extending off the side of her face.

He kisses her on the forehead. "Goodnight prima ballerina." He switches off the light and can still see her teeth smiling in the dark.

"Goodnight daddy."

Tom goes downstairs and joins Steph on the sofa. She has already poured him a glass of red wine. He sinks into the sofa, exhales a breath that he feels he has been holding all night, and takes a few slugs of wine. He closes his eyes and lets his head fall back onto the sofa.

"I'm glad that's over."

"You did great Tom." She pats him on the knee. "Really great."

He opens his eyes and tilts his head towards her. "Thanks so much for coming Steph. I couldn't have done it on my own."

"Yes, you could."

He shakes his head. "I couldn't. All those people, the parents, the ballet teachers, not knowing whether to come say hi, come say sorry, or just to pretend they hadn't seen me. And did you notice – the place was packed, but I still had two seats free next to me. Bereavement's made me a leper."

"People are nervous about death Tom, they don't know how to approach the subject, they don't know how you might react. You remember when Lolli died?"

He sits upright and turns his body to Steph, nodding.

"You didn't know what to do, what to say, remember?"

"I was clueless."

"That's how everyone feels around you now. They all want to help." She holds his hand. "Everyone can see how sad you are Tom, and they just want to say the right thing, do the right thing, but they have no idea what the right thing is."

Tom narrows his eyes, blocking out some of the peripheral distractions, he wants to focus all his attention on Steph's reaction. "You know what makes me saddest Steph?"

She shakes her head. She's probably expecting to hear him lament over the kids' future without a mother, or perhaps his doubt that Miles will ever remember his mother.

"The fact that Beth wasn't happy when she died."

She looks at him, puzzled.

"I mean for the last few months, years even. I don't think she was happy. I think it might have had something to do with Jim's death. Something she never got over."

Steph keeps quiet, but Tom thinks there is a glint of recognition in her eye. She knows, she knows Beth and she knows why she wasn't happy. Now it is his time to keep quiet. He hopes Steph will fill the gap between them.

A moment passes and a practiced glaze falls across Steph's eyes, like curtains concealing the truth. "Well, Jim was a huge piece of Beth's life. He held a massive influence on the whole family, of course it affected her a lot. But she was happy." She smiled. "Of course she was happy, she had you and the kids, a fantastic home, the best fucking shoe collection in West London." She laughs. "What more could she have wanted? What more could anyone want?"

"I was hoping you could tell me."

"Tom, listen. All Beth ever wanted was you. You were her world. And then you gave her Katy and Miles and things just got better. You were the perfect fucking family, I should have hated you guys!" She chuckles, but once again the laugh is an empty one.

Tom knows there was something inside of Beth that kept her subdued and dimmed before her death, and Tom is sure the woman in front of him knows what it was.

"Was it me Steph? Did her feelings for me change when Jim died? Did he say something to her?"

Steph's usual composure shows a tiny crack, there is a just perceptible drop of her shoulders and she exhales louder than she means to. Her body seems to be saying 'Fucking wake up Tom! There was a problem and it was right in front of you,' but her mouth says, "She loved you Tom, just like she loved the kids, and her life here." She finishes her glass of red, although it was still half full. "She had everything Tom." There is a harshness in her voice. "She had fucking everything."

Steph stands up and Tom does the same to look her in the eye. He always forgets how tall she is. Her height makes her a force to be reckoned with for strangers, but Tom is no stranger. She is looking at him defiantly.

"I've got to go Tom, I've got a big day at work tomorrow." She heads for the lounge door and trips over the rug that has been there since they bought the house.

"But it's Saturday tomorrow," Tom calls to her retreating figure.

She doesn't even try to correct herself as she slams the front door behind her.

14:32, Sunday November 3rd, 2013
14 Carrer Lleo, Al Raval, Barcelona

There's a nervous energy about Angelo that makes Xavier uneasy. It's preferable to the catatonic state he sunk into after the crash, but Xavier doesn't know how this energy will be diverted when the portraits are complete, when Angelo is surrounded floor to ceiling by faces of the dead.

Today Angelo is working on a little old lady, who looks closer to death than to life in her photograph. Wrinkles pull all of her features down, as though age is already dragging her into the ground. Her eyes are tiny slits in her layers of skin and her lips are barely distinct from the other lines. A cross hangs from her loose skinned neck. Did this ancient body sit next to Maria? Would this woman have been scared of death, scared of plummeting from the sky? Or would she welcome it, feel relieved that it was all over at last, the aches and pains and loneliness of age coming to an end.

"What's that?" asks Xavier, pointing into the corner.

Angelo looks away from the old lady and follows Xavier's finger.

"Oh, a package," he says, before continuing his painting.

"You're not going to open it?" says Xavier picking it up and turning it over. "Post mark Madrid."

Angelo's' eyes don't part from those of the painting in front of him. "Go ahead."

Xavier tears off the brown paper and unwraps layers of newspaper. Finally a set of eyes is revealed and Xavier stares blankly into them. He is confused, surprised and intrigued by what sits in the paper, his mind struggles to grasp how this portrait has come to be here.

"Angelo, who bought the portrait of your father in Madrid?"

Angelo is engrossed in a silent dialogue with the old woman in front of him.

"Angelo man! Angelo!"

He looks up at Xavier, who repeats his question. "Who bought the portrait of your father when you were in Madrid."

Now it is Angelo's turn to look confused. He wanders past the easel, side steps the table and comes to stand with Xavier. His eyes meet those of his father.

"Maria," he whispers. "Maria bought it."

Angelo picks up the portrait and both men are surprised further to see that another picture sits beneath. The same sad eyes stare out at them, but in a younger face.

"My... my self-portrait," says Angelo. His head is flooded with questions, memories and thoughts he can't quite map together.

"Maria bought that too?" asks Xavier.

Angelo shakes his head. "No, no. She didn't go to the exhibition, it went to an unknown buyer. She bought my father's picture from a café where it was hanging. That's how we met."

"You think she was the unknown buyer?"

Angelo is shaking his head, his face screwed up in puzzlement. "It doesn't make any sense."

Xavier removes the second portrait from the paper and finds a folded piece of paper beneath. He hands it to Angelo. "Maybe this will help." Angelo reads the elegant writing aloud.

"Hello. Firstly, I just want to say how sorry I am for your loss. Maria was a lovely woman, and a fantastic tenant when she was at the apartment. Secondly, I apologise for the delay in getting this to you. Maria left these with my husband to post to you the evening before she left, but my husband, who would forget his head if it wasn't screwed on, put them in a cupboard and forgot all about them. I found them yesterday when I was tidying up." Angelo lifts his eyes to Xavier, shakes his head and then returns to the letter. "Apologies again for your loss and I hope these arrive safely. Blanca Casares."

"She *was* your buyer," says Xavier. Angelo is staring deep into the letter, as though somewhere between the lines he will find some answers. She must have been the unknown buyer, and he's beginning to wonder whether she was unknown in other ways.

**19:22, Tuesday November 5th, 2013
Willowman Grange**

It is fireworks night. Despite losing Jim, the head proponent of the event, the Willowmans continue to put on an extravaganza worthy of a new millennium and the whole family, including Tom's parents, have come along. Carol loves visiting her son's in-laws, as a royalist who had mourned for three months after Diana died she loves visiting stately homes, and a trip to the Willowman's is as close to royalty as she's going to get. Her husband on the other hand couldn't care less and would much rather be sat at home drinking from the never-ending teapot and watching snooker. However, he relented, mostly for the sake of seeing his grandchildren, and he finds himself oohing and aahing with the rest of them as Michael's spectacular fills the sky. Tom remembers last year, that Miles was scared stiff at the first whizz bang and had spent the duration of the display in Beth's arms. Tom remembers standing beside his wife, holding Katie's hand and hearing broken snippets of Beth's words.

"They are just little stars sweetheart... when they get high enough in the air they are so pleased that they burst with happiness... and then they make lots of little happy stars."

Tonight, Tom wonders whether Miles remembers any of what Beth told him that night. They are watching the stars burst with happiness over Windlesham and Miles is clinging to the neck of another woman, a taller blonde woman: Steph. He watches as Steph holds him on her hip and cradles him to her chest when the loudest rockets launch.

Suddenly a new thought enters Tom's head – maybe Miles will take Steph to be his new mummy. The thought makes Tom want to cry and smile at the same time. He feels hugely sad at the notion that won't leave him alone – the notion that Miles will completely forget his mother. But he feels a tiny warmth in his heart when he thinks about Steph. She is the woman who made sense of death for Beth fourteen years ago, she is the woman who took Beth to hospital as Tom desperately tried to get home from New York for the premature birth of Katy, she is the friend who will drop everything to help Tom and his family, and she is the friend who has become a surrogate mother for his two children these last few months. And it is only now, that Tom realizes this is exactly what Beth would have wanted.

16:13, Saturday December 21st, 2013
14 Carrer Lleo, Al Raval, Barcelona

Christmas in Barcelona, the city of transients, is a quiet time. Even the vagrants, who appear to have no home and no family, seem to find somewhere to go and someone to go with at Christmas. Xavier had been concerned about leaving Angelo alone in his studio of death.

"Come back to Sabadell with me," he said. "You would make Christmas a lot more bearable. My sister and her three little shits will be there. You could stop me from killing them, it's a big job and my mum's not up to it anymore, so this year those kids are gonna get it. Come on man. We can raid the old man's drinks cabinet and get s on *Ratafia*."

"No," was all Angelo said. When Xavier pressed him further, he expanded by three words. "No, I have plans."

Xavier sincerely hoped these plans didn't involve a wristful of split paintbrushes.

*

Angelo has barely left his flat in five months and he feels out of place and awkward standing at Barcelona Nord bus station. At his studio he is surrounded by the silent familiar faces of his portraits. Here, he is surrounded by strangers drenched in festive cheer. They scuttle around shepherding their young and calling to one another like a flock of raucous birds. He has never liked crowds.

Finally his bus pulls in and he joins the line of noisy passengers with their flapping arms and tickets. He finds a seat at the back and stretches himself across the entire length with a glare that will ensure that seats 52 to 56 remain his. As the bus pulls away he hopes the noise level will drop as the journey progresses, but the festive spirit keeps energy levels high, and he endures eight hours of frivolity.

At Madrid he follows the instructions he noted down on the phone call with Blanca and finds himself outside Maria's home for the first time. He crosses the street to assess it. Apartamentos Buenavista is an anonymous, crumbling building and, like all the others in Calle de los tres Peces, it offers anything but a good view. A faded Spanish flag hangs from a first floor balcony, and some hopeful lines of washing droop in the winter chill. He expects to see something, smell something, anything that connects him to Maria, but there is nothing. He looks from window to window, hoping for a connection with one of the homes within, but gets nothing.

It's early, too early to wake Blanca and so he wanders the streets of Maria's neighbourhood. He stops for an espresso in a tiny sliver of a coffee bar and wonders whether Maria came here. Perhaps her lips drank from this very same cup. It looks dirty enough for her kiss to still be upon the rim. He drinks another and as the street comes to life, his heart is beating fast, perhaps due to the caffeine, perhaps due to his proximity to Maria's home and the prospect of seeing it. Life on Maria's street starts with the sound of a single shutter opening but, like the first bird that heralds a new day, there is soon a cacophony of sound. Delivery vans roll up the street, the newspaper kiosk opens and racks of news are positioned on the pavement, voices shout to one another, and the day begins. Another day on this street without Maria. Does anyone miss her? Has anyone noticed she is gone?

At 08:49 Angelo rings on Blanca's buzzer. He couldn't wait for 9am, the time he told himself was respectful.

"Hello," says a female voice almost immediately.

"Blanca?"

"Yes."

"It's Angelo."

"Come on in Angelo. First floor."

The door clicks a welcome to Angelo and he pushes it open. The hallway is dark and it takes a few moments for his eyes to adjust from the bright sunlight outside. Wooden panels, scuffed at the base, reach halfway up the walls that are painted a deep red. A concrete staircase rises on the right side of the corridor and behind it Angelo spots a set of metal mailboxes. He approaches it and reads the names of Maria's 24 neighbours. There are three blank labels on mailboxes 12, 17 and 23. Was Maria always a blank label or has Blanca removed her name?

He climbs the stairs to the first floor. A bulb pops on as he nears the top and a fat belly appears in the light, making him gasp. Above the belly sits a narrow chest and a head that mirrors the size and shape of his stomach, giving the man an hourglass figure in all the wrong places. He looks less than happy to see Angelo.

"Hello," says Angelo.

"Hello," says the fat man.

A moment passes and the two men look each other up and down, both somewhat disgusted by the appearance of the other.

"I'm here to see Blanca Casares," says Angelo.

"I know."

"Can you tell me where she lives?" asks Angelo, craning his head around the tiered belly to gesture at the row of doors behind.

The man looks at Angelo a few moments longer.

"Blanca! Come here woman!" he shouts suddenly, making Angelo jump once again.

A door opens at the far end of the corridor and a lady, as skinny as this man is fat, comes out. The man nods at her, as though giving her permission to approach.

"Hello Angelo dear," she says. "I'm Blanca, come on up." Angelo clears the final few steps and she looks at him intensely. "Gosh, you do look just like the portrait," she says before turning down the corridor.

He follows her into her apartment. Blanca is twig-like, with a perfectly coiffed grey perm that could be a wig, and she wears a dark woollen dress about three sizes too large for her. The fat man that Angelo presumes is her husband scuffles along behind. The apartment is full of plastic flowers and more dark wood panelling. It has the sense of a foreboding forest tricking you into its false spring. Blanca leads Angelo into a tiny sitting room where, thankfully, there are only two chairs. She takes one and beckons Angelo into the other. Her husband snorts as he shuffles past and into the darkness of another room.

"It's lovely to meet you Angelo," she says. "I wish it was under nicer circumstances."

Angelo offers her the tiny smile he has cultivated since July. "It's good to meet you too."

She pours him some tea from a steel pot. "I have to admit, I was quite surprised to hear that Maria had a boyfriend."

"She never mentioned me?" asks Angelo. It's strange, but he already knows the answer to this question, and he knows it is unlikely that Maria ever mentioned him to anyone, though he doesn't know why.

"Never." She hands him a cup of tea. "She was ever such a lovely girl, but very quiet about herself. She was always asking me questions about me, Manuel, my family, but she never talked about herself. Not many people are interested in my little life. It made a nice change." Angelo is like most people and is not interested in her little life, he's interested in Maria's. He wants to see her apartment, to find out whether it will help answer any of his questions, but he realizes good manners will keep him here till the tea is drunk.

"I guess that's how writers are," says Angelo. "Always observing others."

"She was a writer?" asks Blanca. "Well, I never!"

"What did you think she did?"

"Well, to be honest. I didn't think she had a job. She seemed to be a girl from money, if you know what I mean."

"Maria?" Angelo is thinking about her sandalled feet, her gypsy skirts and her handmade jewellery.

"Well, yes. I mean, she never appeared to go to work and she spent most of her time away from the apartment. I assumed she was a woman of means."

He smiles. "She worked freelance." Blanca looks blank. "And she visited me in Barcelona a lot."

She nods her head, but her face isn't convinced.

"Did she have any friends here? In the building?" asks Angelo.

"Oh no dear. She was happiest in her own company. Sometimes I would see her out and about on the street or in a café, but she was always alone, in her own little world."

Manuel's belly appears at the door. "When's breakfast?" it asks.

"In half an hour or so."

"I'm hungry now," he says, and as if to confirm this fact, his stomach lets out a loud rumble.

She opens her mouth to appease him but Angelo speaks first. "I'd like to spend some time alone in Maria's apartment if that's OK."

Blanca looks at him, her perm cocked to the side. "You know it's completely empty of Maria's stuff."

"Sure, I assumed that, but still…"

In answer to Angelo, she addresses the stomach. "I'll be back in five minutes to prepare breakfast." She sips her tea and then stands and leaves the room. Angelo follows the neat little perm out of the door and up a second set of dark stairs. Light floods the second floor only once Angelo reaches it, as though Blanca's tiny frame was not enough to wake the motion sensor.

"Here it is," she says, gesturing to number 12. She sifts through a large chain of keys, straining to make out the faded numbers on them. Angelo scrutinizes door 12, the scuffed wood at the base which Maria's sandals may have pushed at, the bronze doorknob, polished to a high finish perhaps by her hands.

Finally Blanca locates the key and fights with the lock for a moment or two. Angelo's heart is beating fast, really fast, he feels like pushing Blanca out the way and kicking the door down. He is expecting so much from this door, he is expecting it to reveal a room full of Maria, a room full of answers.

"There you go my dear," says Blanca, pushing the door open. It swings open quickly, in a way that shows the door is not old and sturdy, but imitation and cheap. And there it is. A basic, tired studio room presents itself to Angelo with a whiff of mustiness, and disappointment slows his heart. Blanca steps back and he enters. As soon as he crosses the threshold he is in the bedroom, the kitchen and the dining room. A small window opposite casts a dull light into the room and he turns on the single bulb to illuminate the scene. Did Maria really live here? He cannot picture his exuberant, beautiful Maria in this weary, ugly setting; it would be a hummingbird in a hen coop.

A single mattress on a rusty frame butts up against the left hand wall and a set of four beige threadbare cushions are lined up, attempting to create the effect of a sofa. A faded Persian rug separates the bedroom from the kitchen on the opposite wall. A two-ring hob, a sink, a microwave and a fridge with rusting corners comprise the kitchen. Beneath the window, facing Angelo, is a small table with a yellowing cloth and two dining chairs, and either side of the window sit two picture hooks.

Angelo turns to Blanca. "Did you see the apartment much when Maria was here?"

"A few times, yes. There were some problems with the boiler and there is a certain knack to the hob that she never seemed to grasp." She laughs. "She really was rather clueless when it came to things like that."

"And how was the apartment? How did she have it? Just like this?"

"Yes, dear. This same arrangement with a few things of her own."

"Like what? What things?" Angelo wants to see the apartment as it was, with Maria at home here, with trinkets and colour and touches that lessen the bleakness and desperation of the place.

"Oh, she didn't have much at all. The two portraits of course. The one of you hung there in front of the bed, and sometimes it was propped up on the chair at the table. The other one never moved. It was a real miserable face that stared at you as soon as you entered. I never liked that one – gave me the creeps. Then she had a few basic bits and bobs for the kitchen, her computer, and her bedspread, oh, and always a suitcase in the corner. But very few possessions. As I say, she was always coming and going."

None of this sounds like Maria and, if Angelo hadn't received the package of portraits labelled with this address, he wouldn't believe that Blanca was talking about the woman he loved.

"And where did you put all her stuff?"

Blanca looks at him with a curious smile. "There was nothing left. Other than the two pictures she asked Manuel to post, she took everything with her or threw it away."

Now it is Angelo's turn to look curious. "What do you mean? She was taking everything to London?"

Her eyes screw up beneath her perfect perm.

"Yes, she was leaving the apartment, she hadn't finished her contract but she paid in cash what was remaining, and then she left on that flight. She said she had some work to do in London and after that she was moving in with somebody, I guess that was you, yes?"

Angelo nods. He guesses so.

20:34, Tuesday December 24th, 2013
7 The Stables, South Kensington, London

"Listen, if you two don't go to bed soon, then Santa won't have a chance to visit and bring presents," says Tom.

"Your dad's right," says Steph. "Santa is on a very strict schedule. He has to get round all the children in the whole world, you don't want to delay him do you?"

Miles looks very concerned at this possibility, while Katy smiles slyly.

"I want Santa to see all the kids," says Miles, his eyes wide.

"Then we had better get you both to bed hadn't we?" says Tom. "Is everything ready for him?"

Miles approaches the fire tentatively, he doesn't like to show cowardice but every lick and pop from the dying flames make him jump. "Carrots for the reindeer, mince pie and sherry for Santa, and two stockings," he confirms. "And you are sure the fire will be out by the time Santa comes?"

"I'm positive buddy," says Tom. "Now let's get you to bed."

*

"You want to see something heartbreaking?" Tom asks. He has wanted to share this with someone for so long.

"Well, that sounds like a tempting offer for Christmas Eve, I can't wait to see what you'll pull out for the big day itself."

He smiles. "Is that a yes?"

"Sure."

Steph tops up both their glasses of wine as Tom roots through a kitchen drawer. He returns and passes a ripped red envelope to Steph. She turns it over and reads the address aloud.

"Santa Claus, North Poole, I had no idea he lived in Poole?" She laughs. Tom's mouth only twitches.

She pulls out a piece of folded A5 paper and opens it. The border is decorated with felt tip Christmas trees, stars and something that might be angels or reindeers. The handwriting is in alternating colours of green, yellow and red and slopes down into the corner. Steph can just imagine Katy, her tongue out, face set in concentration as she composes her letter. She reads aloud, squinting at the letters that don't seem to make words she knows.

"Dear Santa. Me and my brother Miles were very very good this year, in a very very sad station." Steph looks puzzled.

"She means situation," says Tom. "It's a word they keep hearing."

Steph continues. "We don't want toys for Christmas. Daddy thinks we want toys, but we only said that to him so he doesn't get sad. We would really really like mummy back for Christmas. Can you please help? Everyone in our family will be so happy with mummy back. We are leaving stockings out, but don't worry about filling them." Steph takes a deep breath. "We just want mummy. Love from Katy and Miles."

The writing and decorations took up so much space on the paper that there was hardly any space for Miles' name, but he had scrawled it as neatly and as small as he could in the bottom corner.

"They wrote it together," she says.

"Yes, and they're expecting mummy back tomorrow." Tom puts his head in his hands. "Did you see how excited they were tonight?"

"I thought that was normal for Christmas Eve."

"This was a new level of excitement. Steph, I'm dreading tomorrow, almost more than the funeral."

She runs her hand down the back of Tom's head. It's a gesture that Miles finds comforting at bedtime or when he has got too worked up, and Tom finds it working for him too.

"Tom sweetheart. Remember when all this first happened? When you thought you didn't have the strength to tell the kids. Well, you did that and then you did everything else you needed to, you talked to

Veronica, went to the memorial, the funeral, back to work. You are so strong Tom, and you're doing perfectly, and you'll be perfect tomorrow."

"I'm not strong Steph, I'm not strong at all. I'm a collection of bones that wants to crumble in a heap." He sighs. "Every day when I wake up and remember my wife is gone, I just want to cry. And then I remember her face, her most recent face, and it wasn't happy, hadn't been for a long time, and I didn't even notice. What kind of husband was I?" He clenches his fists. "And when I remember what a shit husband I was, then I want to scream and kick and shout." His voice is getting louder. "And fuck everything! Fuck the religion that Veronica bangs on about, fuck the stories about Beth in the sky, fuck all the stupid lies I tell to keep the shitty truth of death from the kids." Tears pierce his eyes and he takes deep breaths to try and make them retreat. "This is not how my life was supposed to be Steph."

A few moments pass.

"You know I was fifteen when both my parents died." Tom turns to Steph, his mouth all out of anger. She has never mentioned this to Tom before, never talked about her personal experience with death. She makes it very easy to believe she's had no negativity in her life. "I was an orphan. I thought that was only a word that happened to black kids in Africa or skeletal babies in Eastern Europe, not someone like me. I was smart, pretty, popular, I was going places, and then everything stopped. And I thought, what is the fucking point in being any of those things when death can just creep up on you and take your foundations away, take away your family. What was the point in GCSEs, college applications, boyfriends, homes, building a future for yourself?"

This question hangs in the air and Tom looks forward to the answer, it sounds like the answer he is searching for. Steph takes a sip of her wine.

"And what is the point Steph?"

She looks at him. She has a weary look on her face, one that Tom hasn't noticed before. "Life is distraction enough for death," she says.

"What?"

"There is no point Tom." She shakes her head sadly, as though she wishes she had the answer he craves. "One day we'll all be dead. It's just that some: my parents... Beth, get there quicker. In the meantime, we have life to distract us. We have ballet productions, birthdays, shit TV, jobs, holidays, family, or at least what fucking remains of it. All of this keeps life ticking on, and when the ticking stops we'll join Beth and my mum and dad and all the other dead fuckers that you care or don't care about."

Tom's mouth has fallen open. He can't believe that this is Steph's attitude, her philosophy on death. He knows her to be cynical and straight-talking but he was at least hoping for *something* positive, a ledge to try and get his fingernails to clutch onto. But she offers no ledge.

"And this, this is what you told Beth when Lolli died?"

She smiles and Tom is glad to see the weariness of her expression subside for a moment. "You're always thinking of Beth aren't you?"

He feels bad now. Steph has shared her death philosophy with him, has spoken of her dead parents for the first time ever, and all he can think about is his wife.

"I'm sorry, I mean. It's just, I'm a little surprised by your thoughts, and I was wondering if you'd shared them with her."

"Not in such a frank way Tom. You're strong, an adult, a father. Beth was still young when Lolli died, I couldn't tell her what I just told you. And anyway, my ideas on death were still young, still forming. I told her what she wanted to hear, the optimistic side of death, and I listened to her, and asked the right questions. That's what the bereaved need. That's what I have done for you too, and the kids. I have listened, let you talk, been witness to your sadness, every emotion needs sharing Tom, whether it is positive or negative."

"But you never show any negative emotion Steph. You are always completely happy." Her eyes meet his and they are sharing an emotion with him, an emotion he hasn't seen for a long time. His heart races.

"I'm not always completely happy, but I am always completely happy… when I'm with you," she says. "And the kids," she adds quickly. But it is too late. Steph has shared something with Tom, something that she has kept hidden for over a decade.

23:24, Tuesday December 24th, 2013
Apartamentos Buenavista, Calle de los tres peces, Madrid

Angelo sits at the small table, his hands resting on the thin cotton of the tablecloth. There is a dark stain that slides off the edge of the cloth by the wall, and he wonders whether it was Maria who made the mark, a clumsy glass of red perhaps. He sips his wine and tries to imagine her opposite him. But try as he might, he can't bring Maria into this dingy little place, he can't get her past the threshold and into the room, it's not for her. Even in his studio, which is palatial by comparison, he felt she deserved more and was accustomed to better. He had always secretly wondered whether the state of his apartment was the reason she was reluctant to move in but, looking around him, he sadly realizes that it was something entirely different, and he realizes that Maria was someone entirely different also.

    He drinks the last of the wine and wishes he had bought a second bottle to see in Christmas Day. A plate of food kindly donated by Blanca sits in front of him untouched, and he pushes it to the other side of the table. He stands, has nowhere to go, and lies down on the hard single bed. He lies on his side for a few moments before standing to switch off the light and returning to the bed. In the darkness, blind to his surroundings, he feels slightly better, and he wonders whether Maria felt the same. Darkness can be a blessing when surrounded by sadness, but it can also be a shield from the happiest moments. Angelo used to hate turning out the light in his studio when Maria lay next to him. He remembers a conversation they had in the early days of their relationship.

    "Angelo, I'm sleepy, please turn off the light." She lay naked next to him, the white sheet up to her waist and her long hair flowing to meet it.

    "But then I can't see you, and if I can't see you then maybe you don't exist."

    She laughed. "I promise I exist, in and out of the dark."

    He hears her gentle voice speak these words now and, lying in her cramped single bed in her cramped apartment, he feels a tiny warmth within him, for the first time since arriving in Madrid.

    "Now my darling," he whispers, "you only exist in the dark."

He lies awake all night, trying to find answers in the darkness to the new questions rolling through his head. How did you come to live here Maria? Why was your life so transient? What were you hiding from everyone? Were you leaving me or joining me? As the dawn casts a dull grey light onto Maria's box room, he still has no answers.

06:14, Wednesday December 25th, 2013
7 The Stables, South Kensington, London

He hears the stampede of tiny feet before he hears the voices, "Daddy, Daddy! It's Christmas!" The noise doesn't wake him, he's been awake all of Christmas Day so far. They bound into his room and bounce onto the bed.

"Daddy, daddy, can we go and see what Santa has brought us?" asks Miles, his hair a bouncy crown of golden curls.

Katy stands in the doorway hopping from foot to foot. She is a little time bomb of excitement ready to explode when she sees her mum downstairs. Tom thinks he might cry.

"Katy, why don't you go and wake Auntie Steph." At least then there will be one stable adult in the room.

Katy turns to race down the hall and bumps right into Steph who appears like Christmas magic. She is wearing red tartan pyjamas, her hair kinks in a myriad of directions and her cheeks are rosy. Tom has never seen her without make-up. From the first day Beth introduced him to her friend at university, the glamour of Steph has been impermeable. The glossy nails, crafted blonde bob, and cover girl make-up have always given Steph the perfect exterior. Along with her brash language and constant demeanour, she has built something of a castle wall around herself, physically and emotionally, and it is only now on Christmas Day that she seems to have let her defences down. He is surprised by how beautiful she is and for a moment he forgets the traumas of the day that lay ahead.

"Auntie Steph!" cries Miles. "You're still in your pyjamas."

Miles and Katy find this hilarious and skip around giggling. Steph looks abashed, again a weakness Tom has never seen before.

"Well, it is quarter past six on Christmas morning," says Tom, smiling at Steph. "Sleep well?"

"Yes," she says. She is the only one in the house who did.

"Can we go see our presents daddy?" screams Miles.

"Can we see what Santa Claus brought us?" says Katy, giving her brother a sly little grin. They both hop onto the bed and start bouncing around, like fleas on a hot plate.

Tom raises himself and sits on the side of the bed, putting on his slippers slowly. He is dreading going downstairs and trying to explain to his two children that not even the magic of Christmas can bring their mummy home. He stands up, and Miles and Katy race off down the stairs, a clamour of screams and heavy feet. He follows them wearily and Steph trails behind.

"Happy Christmas Tom," she whispers as they descend the stairs.

As Tom reaches the bottom of the stairs the screams and whoops of his children end. They raced into the lounge like little formula one cars, but halted as though they hit a crash barrier. Tom rounds the corner and sees his children as two statues, in front of the mantelpiece. They stare at their stockings, full and bulging. It is a few moments before Katy turns to look at the Christmas tree, and then she turns a full circle, slowly, taking in every inch of the room. Every inch is full of presents but empty of mummy, and as she rotates her eyes fill with tears and her bottom lip protrudes.

Miles remains standing, confused, in front of the mantelpiece.

"Where's mummy?" he asks no one in particular. "Where's mummy?" He turns to Tom, his little face screwed up in puzzlement. "Did Santa come?"

Katy stands in the middle of the room, surrounded by her family, but looking completely alone. She begins to cry. Tom crouches and puts his hands on her shoulders.

"Katy sweetheart. Santa Claus can't bring mummy back."

"Why not? Why not? We sent him a letter and we've been really, really good." Her tears are flowing fast.

Miles realizes that mummy won't be joining them for Christmas and he starts howling. The noise is a catalyst for Katy and her crying becomes loud and uncontrolled. Tom gathers both children together and sits on the sofa, holding them close to him. He wants to be brave today, wants to show the children that Christmas still exists without mummy, but his throat is full of tears and he can't say a word. The children sob in his arms, a picture of misery surrounded by presents and Christmas surprises.

"What's that on the mantelpiece?" asks Steph, loud enough to be heard over the weeping.

Miles and Katy look up at her, snotty and red faced. They follow her pointing finger, and their crying subsides slightly.

"An envelope," says Katy surprised. She stands up and approaches the mantelpiece. "It says Miles and Katy on it." She wipes her hand and forearm past her running nose.

"Maybe you should open it," says Steph.

Katy looks at Tom, warily. He shrugs his shoulders, he has no idea where the envelope came from.

Katy approaches the mantelpiece and, on tiptoes, reaches for the envelope. She stands for a few moments looking at it, before tearing it open.

"What is it?" asks Miles. "Read it. Is it from mummy?"

She shakes her head, her long hair swaying in front of her wet face. She begins to read aloud, pausing for the difficult words, and squinting in concentration.

"Dear Miles and Katy. Thank you so much for your letter. I have to say it was some of the best hand…writing I have seen this year, and the pictures were, were, erm, mar-vel-ous. Every year we select our favourite letters and hang them in the workshop to en-cour-age the elves, and this year, yours took… pride… of place. The elves loved it.

Now, I have to tell you some news. I spoke with your mother and she told me there is nothing she would like more than to come home for Christmas, to see you both and daddy, but un…un…fort-un-ately she is un-able to. She says that you have been such good children, and you have been really helping daddy, and she watches you every day, but she can't come back from where she is. Like me and Mrs Claus, your mummy now lives in a very far away place and she can't come back, but one day you will see her. And she says she will come visit you in your dreams and give you plenty of kisses and hugs.

Al...though you didn't ask for any toys in your letter to me, I asked your mummy what you might like and she told me, so I hope you are happy with what she chose for you.

Remember Miles and Katy, your mummy loves you very much, but until you see her one day, you must give all your love to daddy, because he needs it most.

I wish you a very, very Happy Christmas. The elves say hi, and Rudolph says thanks for the carrot. Yours always, Santa Claus."

Miles climbs out of his father's arms and goes to stand next to his sister, looking at the letter. He can't read any of it, but he touches it, tentatively, as though it might disappear in a puff of smoke.

"Santa wrote us a letter daddy," he says. Then he turns to his sister. "And he liked my drawings, he said they were mar-well-us. Read it again Katy."

As Katy reads over the letter once more, and Miles follows her finger that traces the words, Tom looks at Steph. Her eyes haven't left Tom since Katy started reading, she appears nervous, like perhaps she did something wrong. Tom stares into her fresh morning face and his eyes soften into a smile. "Happy Christmas," he mouths to her.

22:51, Tuesday December 31st, 2013
14 Carrer Lleo, Al Raval, Barcelona

"You want to get twatted and head down to Albundi's," asks Xavier. "Jesus and Enric are down there."

Angelo doesn't respond. He is standing in front of Maria's portrait, a glass of whiskey dangling in his limp hand.

"Listen man, you're not going to find any answers in that portrait, or in any of these." He gestures to the 88 faces that surround them. "And I, for one, do not want to see the new year in with a roomful of dead people."

"I can't believe the way she lived. In that cramped dark space. And where was she going? Why did she leave?"

"Maybe because it was a shithole, like you say. And what you really can't believe, my friend, is that she preferred to live in that cramped dark space, than here with you."

Angelo shrugs. Xavier is right.

"And anyway, what does it matter how she lived? You're no snob, you don't care about that stuff. It wouldn't have changed how you felt about her."

Angelo turns from Maria to look at Xavier. He shakes his head.

"It just felt so transient. It made me think I really knew nothing about her. I know nothing about how she lived, I know nothing about where she was going, and I know nothing about how she died. There are too many things I didn't know about her, about the woman I loved. I need to know something. The least I can know is how she died."

Xavier is bored with this same conversation and has already had too much to drink. "In a fucking plane, in a fucking fireball of a plane, that's how she died. What more do you wanna know?"

His words are strong but they leave no imprint on Angelo. He wanders the length of the two walls covered in portraits, his eyes connecting with every painted pair. Every face, every pair of eyes, every mouth, is beautiful, all deserving to accompany Maria to her death. Did this pair of eyes look into Maria's as they fell out of the sky together? Did this mouth whisper words of comfort into Maria's ear? Did those broad shoulders embrace his little Maria? Every portrait feels like a friend to Angelo. He has spent more time with them since the crash than with anyone else and they have been his therapy, his roomful of nurses.

"Go," says Angelo to Xavier.

Through his drunken mist, Xavier is feeling a little sheepish about his talk of fireballs. "No man. I'll stay here with you. We can see the new year in together. Smoke some weed, finish the whiskey, start the year as we mean to go on." He pats Angelo on the back.

"No Xavi. You go out. I'll stay here. I'd prefer that." He looks from painted eyes to half-closed ones. His best friend stands before him in the shadows. It is new year's eve and Xavier has chosen to welcome in 2014 with dark Angelo in his tomblike apartment. Angelo realizes that Xavier has been standing in the shadows with him for six months now, waiting for some light to emerge.

"Xavi. Thanks for everything this year. It means a lot to me." He returns the gesture and pats his friend on the shoulder, holding his hand in place. "Next year will be better."

"I hope so," says Xavier, trying to focus and failing.

Angelo leads him to the door. "Wish the guys a happy new year from me and I'll see you soon." He opens the door and deposits his friend behind it.

"But man, I can stay. I'd like to…"

"Happy new year Xavi," says Angelo closing the door on his face.

The two men stand either side of the closed door, both of them unsure of whether Xavier will leave. A few moments pass, and then Angelo hears heavy footsteps stumbling down the stairwell.

Angelo retreats to his default position, standing in front of Maria. He recently lowered the position of the portrait so it replicates her height.

"Next year will be better," he says. *Because I will find out the truth*, he thinks.

He strokes the waves of hair that hang down over Maria's shoulder. His fingers are beginning to wear away the paint in that spot.

He sits on the window ledge and the first moon of 2014 casts a bright light across his studio, illuminating the hopeful eyes of all his companions. He is happy to be spending midnight with his new friends.

10:53, Friday January 17th, 2014
BDB Head Office, London

He sits on the hard leather sofa and tries to concentrate on the pictures and words that *Campaign*, the magazine for advertising professionals, is trying to instill in him. But they are not trying hard enough and his mind is elsewhere. It has taken two months to get here. Two months of missed calls, vague emails, and cancelled meetings. Tom wonders whether Angie Harman is this elusive with her clients. He guesses meetings about toothpaste and coffee beans are easier to get through than meetings about dead colleagues.

His fingers flick back and forth over the same magazine pages, but his eyes hardly leave the huge station clock that hangs behind the reception desk. It ticks loudly past ten o' clock, as though taunting him with how unimportant he is in Angie's schedule. It is sixteen minutes, or 960 ticks, before Angie's red shiny heels come into view in the glass lift.

They are followed by a simple but smart black dress, topped by her trademark dark bob and red lipstick. She seems to be biting her acrylic nails but immediately stops when Tom comes into view. In true advertising style, she straightens her back, widens her lipstick smile, and marches her heels at Tom. Perception is reality, and she wants Tom to believe she is the assertive, poised professional he has heard her to be.

"Tom, my love," she says, louder than necessary, and kisses him on both cheeks. "How are you?"

"Fine," says Tom. "You're looking very well."

"And you," she lies. He has grown too slender for his broad shoulders, his eyes are barely holding up against the bags that weigh them down and his skin has a grey tinge to it. These are the remnants of the man she once met and immediately desired.

"Shall we go out and take a coffee?" she suggests.

"Actually, I'd quite like to stay here. Your office maybe?" Tom wants to see Beth's workplace, to find out what it was that made her so happy here.

"You sure? There's a fantastic macchiato waiting for you around the corner."

"Maybe we can bring it back here?"

Angie relents and calls over to the receptionist. "Send someone to get two coffees from Clara-Clara, and have them brought up to my office."

Tom follows her to the lift, up 22 floors, past rows of trendy media types in torn clothing and thick-rimmed glasses, and into her glass office. Her window has a view of the Shard, and when she sits behind her desk it seems to emerge from the crown of her neat bob, giving the impression of a neat little elf. The little elf speaks.

"How are the kids?"

"They're getting along OK thanks." There is so much he could say about the children, and they are normally his favourite subject, but today he doesn't want to dally. He doesn't want to make small talk about the family. He doesn't want to ask Angie about her new supermarket campaign that's all over the billboards and people's lips, and he doesn't want that red lipstick to bullshit him. When he speaks, he feels strangely like the Tom of decades ago, the Tom whose only charm lay in his bluntness.

"Angie, I came here to talk to you about Beth." There is a stiffening in her face, but she nods her compliance.

"Beth wasn't happy, for some time I believe, maybe the last year or so."

Now Angie is shaking her head, her eyes confused, but she doesn't speak.

"Don't try to convince me otherwise, because I know she wasn't. But one thing I do think, actually I know, is that she was happy at work. When she went on business trips, did pitches, brought in new business, I think she was truly happy. She seemed most happy when she was leaving the family to go to work."

Now Angie is looking more confused.

"So I came here to get a feel for her workplace. To try and find out what it was that made her so happy here, but so unhappy at home. And you are the only person from work that came to the funeral, so I thought I'd talk to you. You worked closely right?"

Angie runs a hand through her bob and dislodges a chunk of hair, it sticks out at a tangent, ruining the perception of perfection.

"Tom," she hesitates. "We did work closely, but that was a long time ago."

"Then who else did she work with? And why didn't they come to the funeral?"

She takes a deep breath and looks at a silver award on her desk glinting in the sunlight. She is considering whether to tell him the truth or the award-winning, highly paid fabrications she is famous for.

"Angie? I'd appreciate the truth," he says.

She smooths her hair back into place. "Tom, honey. When Beth died, she hadn't worked here for nearly a year."

Her words are clear but they hang in the air like a mist that needs time to settle before Tom can see clearly. But he sees nothing clearly even after a minute of silence.

"I don't understand. She went to another agency without telling me?"

Angie looks at her desk and shakes her head. Just then a twig-like girl in a miniskirt knocks on the door and brings in two coffees. She has the appearance of someone who doesn't let food, drink or even air pass her lips. She closes the door behind her and Tom asks.

"What happened?"

"I'm not sure any of this is going to help you Tom. What's done is done. Sleeping dogs and all that, I think it's…"

"Angie. Tell me," he says flatly.

She looks at her vintage Omega. "I have a meeting in five minutes."

"Then you'd better tell me quick."

She looks at her award, and the framed adverts that surround her. Perceptions are so much nicer than reality. She takes a deep breath.

"Beth was a great worker, conscientious, intuitive, and a generally nice person, which isn't that common in this industry. She could have gone a long way, all the way." She gestures to the ceiling and the three more floors above her. "But about the same time that darling Jim died, her work started to slip, just little things at first, being late for conference calls, forgetting to send out reports. Obviously I assumed she was going through some kind of grieving process." She shrugs, obviously unable to get her head around that kind of human weakness. "I got HR onto it and they offered her counselling but she refused it, said she didn't need it. But something was very definitely wrong. When her mistakes continued, I thought perhaps she was pregnant, these kind of silly mistakes are often the first signs." She speaks about pregnancy as though that too is a weakness. "I was expecting her to come and tell me the news, I was ready to congratulate her," although her tone would suggest otherwise. "But instead, things got worse. She went away to Paris for a big global pitch, and completely missed the rehearsal, was nowhere to be found. She turned up for the pitch presentation but wasn't engaged at all. And then an existing client in Berlin contacted me to complain about a workshop she had run. He told me it was badly prepared and that she delivered it in a completely disinterested way. So I called her in. I expected her to be massively apologetic, you know how Beth was – always keen to please others, but in all honesty Tom, it seemed like she didn't give a flying fuck. She sat there, where you are now and just shrugged whenever I asked for a response. Now, I'm not the heartless bitch everyone has me down for, and I wanted to give her the benefit of the doubt, so I gave her three months to turn things around."

"And what happened?" asks Tom.

"She didn't."

He is speechless and the room is silent until a knock on the door breaks the silence. The twig girl sticks her head around the door.

"Your next meeting is ready Ms. Harman."

She nods and the stick head retreats.

"She left the company before the three months was up, in October last year. I asked her to leave."

Tom is shaking his head in disbelief, cluttered thoughts bounce around inside, but he can't make them line up in any sense of order.

"She didn't tell me anything. I didn't know anything was wrong. So where did she go after here? I mean, she went to another agency right?" Some cluttered thoughts were struggling into alignment, like unruly army cadets forming a line. Beth had lost her job, was too ashamed to tell her family and had found something else.

"No dear. She didn't find another position." Tom's army cadets scatter. "In fact she wouldn't have found another position after here. Word travels fast in this industry and a firing from BDB will keep your CV off everyone's desks. And, as far as I heard, she didn't even try to get another job."

"What *did* you hear?"

Angie shrugs. "That she was concentrating on her family life, spending time with the kids. That sort of thing." Angie is the kind of woman who doesn't understand what that sort of thing entails, but holds a marked disdain for it anyway.

Tom is scouring his memory over the last year of Beth's work, Beth's fictitious work. "But what about the big Mars pitch in Brussels, or the filming of the new VW ad?"

"All mine," says Angie, her red lips full of pride. "Did Beth tell you she was working on them?" The words 'cheeky bitch' are on the tip of her tongue.

Tom scours for more. "What about Pete Wheeler, her replacement?"

"Well, that's not a complete lie, he started shortly after Beth left. All mouth and no trousers if you ask me, but he plays squash with JJ so, as long as he keeps losing on the squash court, he'll keep winning here. Prick."

Tom's baffled mouth is trying to form another question when there is a knock on the door and stick girl pokes her head into the office once more. Even her head is stick-like, she could have stuck it through without opening the door.

Angie cuts the girl off before she speaks. "Yes, I know Catrina," she shouts. "I'm on my way." Angie stands up, heralding the end of the meeting. She walks around the end of her desk, which is littered with awards making a miniature skyline of glass and silver, and kisses Tom on both cheeks. She keeps hold of his upper arm a moment longer, not as strong as she had hoped.

"I'm sorry I couldn't give you more answers darling. But to be honest, I have no idea what happened to Beth."

Before Angie leaves the room, Tom pulls something from his pocket and thrusts it in front of her. It is the image of Beth at the airport.

Angie looks at the image and smiles, her watertight veneer of bitch just cracking,

"She really was very beautiful when she smiled wasn't she? This is an old photo right? A few years back."

Tom shakes his head, but he is shaking it to himself. Angie turns in the doorway.

"Feel free to finish your coffee up here. Enjoy the view."

Tom is left with an incredible postcard view of London city, glittering in the rare winter sun. After inspecting the awards on Angie's desk, many of which Beth had claimed to win, he sits down and looks at the image of his mysterious happy wife in front of him.

"What happened Beth?" he asks her. She smiles at him from the airport. She took her secret onto that flight with her, and took it to her death.

15:10, Sunday February 2nd, 2014
14 Carrer Lleo, Al Raval, Barcelona

The new year has given Angelo fresh momentum for his death project. Perhaps it is the bitter weather that has arrived in Barcelona, a biting wind that blows dark clouds around the sky and litter around the streets.

In Barcelona, residents prefer to stay indoors and lament the lost sunshine, while hardy northern European tourists on tight schedules get propelled from gallery to restaurant. The wind wants the city all to herself and Angelo is happy for her to have it. The glass of his large studio window shakes and rumbles and, rather than sunshine, his apartment is shrouded in darkness. He doesn't like to paint in artificial light, and so his recent portraits have been painted in the winter gloom. They hang on the third wall of his studio, the first of his new friends to grace this position. A businessman in his late thirties with early baldness sits next to a teenage girl with pink streaks in her hair. Beneath them another odd couple stare out into the shadows. A well turned out lady with an Alice band and pearls hides a tiny smile, that could be smugness. Next to her a huge black man with hanging jowls and flyaway hair conceals his expression within folds of skin.

The physical differences between Angelo's people are blatant, but at the same time they all have a similarity, that shared look in the eye. Teresa stands in the middle of the room and, even from her dispassionate point of view, she feels something that makes her shiver under her cashmere. All those eyes, those knowing eyes staring at her from beyond the grave. For dead people they seem strangely alive, and even the child faces look at her with an intelligence she doesn't understand, or like. She is spooked, and for the first time in a long time loses a little of her composure.

"Can we, erm, can we put a light on in here Angelo? It's awfully dark."

"The light won't make a difference," says Angelo.

Teresa seeks a chair that will face away from the myriad of faces, but finds none, so she stands facing the window.

"How many now?" she asks.

"112."

"Gosh *mi tresor*, you have been busy." Teresa soon forgets the eyes bearing down on the back of her head, and thinks about the numbers circulating at the front.

He doesn't answer. He knows what she's here for, she comes every few weeks to check up on him. He shouldn't have agreed to it, but he was three months behind on rent and owed Xavier almost 500 euros. Of course, he has no intention of going ahead with it, but Teresa offered him an advance on sales. He took the advance but will skirt the exhibition. These portraits are going nowhere.

"We will be ready well in advance of the anniversary date," she continues. "And did I tell you? AirStar are interested in sponsoring the event. They are funding various things across Madrid in tribute to the crash; some godawful children's choir, a modern dance performance, that sort of thing. They are still working on damage limitation of their reputation and they feel these types of events, handled carefully, could be good for them. You know, it would show their ethical, caring side. Or something like that." She shakes her head, baffled. "But whatever, they are offering a large sum. Of course," she smiles, "I will make sure they double that sum. You know sweetie, we…" she changes course quickly, "*you* are set to make a lot of money from this exhibition, more than you know." She looks at him, but his expression is vacant. "You can move out of this place." She waves her jewelled hand vaguely around the space, still unwilling to let her eyes wander.

"I don't want to move," he says.

She laughs, assuming this to be a joke. "And perhaps you can buy some more crockery," she cups her hands around the broken cup and takes a sip, "so that your hugely successful agent can have a coffee cup with a handle."

Angelo stares at the cup in Teresa's hands. He doesn't like it there, surrounded by perfect varnished nails and jewels.

"Maria loved that cup," he says.

"I find that hard to believe sweetie. I think it was just that she loved you."

Angelo takes the cup from Teresa, it's nearly finished anyway. He looks into it, as though it holds all his answers. Teresa can see one of his moments coming on.

"Well, I had better be off. I'll be back next week." She kisses him on both cheeks and heads for the door, keeping her eyes to the wooden boards. "Bye everyone," she calls without thinking. Outside the apartment she shakes her head, berating herself. "Teresa what are you doing? Talking to a bunch of paintings!"

Inside the apartment, Angelo looks up from the cup to the 112 faces. "Don't worry, she's gone now."

19:37, Tuesday February 18th, 2014
7 The Stables, South Kensington, London

"Thanks for bringing her home Steph. I'm not sure how I'm going to get this to work, what with Miles' football on a Tuesday now as well."

Katy prances into the hall and goes through her ballet positions on the wooden floorboards, giving each its name in perfect French.

"*Croisé Devant, Quatrième Devant...*"

"Tom, you know I really don't mind helping out." She pulls on Katy's ponytail, lovingly.

"I know Steph, but I can't call on you every week. You have your own life to lead."

She shrugs her shoulders. "It's fine really. And anyway, there's not much going on in my life right now." She is concentrating on Katy's hair, rather than looking at Tom and quickly changes tack. "Your French accent is really good Katy, in fact it's *parfait!*"

Katy doesn't hear Steph but continues manoeuvring her body into new positions and rolling her tongue around their names. "*Effacé Devant, à la Seconde...*"

"She gets that from Beth," says Tom. "She was great at languages." Tom is itching to ask Steph what she knows about Beth's work at BDB, but he can't ask in front of the kids, and something is telling him that she might not be all that honest with him. He cocks his head to look at Steph and wonders whether her loyalty is to her dead friend or to the people that friend left behind. His thoughts are interrupted by Katy tapping on his belly.

"We did a Valentine special tonight daddy," says Katy. "We learnt some moves from Romeo and Juliet. That's a play by Jack Spear."

Tom smiles. It had been easy for him to forget Valentine's Day, he forgot it every year anyway and this was no different, but now he remembers some plans that Steph had mentioned.

"Hey, didn't you go away for the weekend with your new man?"

Steph nods, then smiles, and rolls her eyes, her gestures saying "yes I did, what a joke, why did I bother?" Tom feels a tiny pang of unexpected happiness.

"Not great?" asks Tom.

"Fucking awful," says Steph. Katy stops at *Quatrième Derrière* and looks open mouthed at her father, waiting for Steph to be told off.

"Why don't you go and practice your ballet in the lounge sweetie where you have more room?" says Tom.

Katy's open mouth leads her ballet shoes down the hall and out of sight. She expects that Steph is going to get a *big* telling off.

"What happened?" asks Tom. "I thought this one had a chance."

"So did I, he had everything going for him. Seriously, he was husband material on paper. But you know what they say, if something seems too good to be true…"

"It probably is," finishes Tom. "So what was wrong with him?"

"He chose this weekend, when I was a captive audience, to tell me about his mental health issues. About his child abuse as a kid, about the addictions he suffered, the self-harm episode, the suicide attempt, and the way he spirals out of control at the first sign of rejection."

"Wow, what did you do?"

She shrugs. "What the fuck could I do? I rejected him. And got the first train back to London."

Tom bites his lip in an attempt not to laugh. Despite looking all-woman, sometimes Steph was such a bloke. She had little patience for sensitive types, in fact she had little patience whatsoever, and was just waiting for the perfect man to walk into her life and fit into the little gaps she had reserved for him.

"You weren't worried about what he might do?" asks Tom.

"Not my problem now," she says. Tom raises his eyebrows and she softens slightly. "Although I did call the hotel to check they hadn't found a body hanging from the chandelier that night. Supposedly he spent the rest of the weekend chewing the ear off the barman with his 99 problems."

"But a bitch ain't one," laughs Tom. She laughs too. Firstly just a chuckle, but then they look at each other and crack with laughter again and again. They aren't just laughing at what he said, now they are laughing at all the episodes in Steph's dismal love life. It feels good to laugh, and he doesn't want to ruin the moment by bringing up Beth.

"My love life's a mess," says Steph, laughing so hard she can barely get the words out.

"You're not the only one, my love life's dead," says Tom. He doesn't mean the pun, and when the word comes out he stops laughing for a moment, as does Steph. But then they both giggle.

"A widower and a woman who can't keep a man for longer than four weeks," smiles Steph. "What losers we are!"

"Steph, I really have no idea why you can't hold onto a man for longer than a month." He means this to sound like a genuine mystery to him, but it comes out like a strange mix of a compliment and insult, and she looks at him with uncertainty.

"I just haven't *dated* the right guy yet," she says. There is a perceptible emphasis on the word 'dated', as though Steph may have met the man but just not dated him yet. Now Tom feels a little uncomfortable, but not in a bad way.

He smiles. "I think we should celebrate. An anti-Valentine night for losers in love."

"I'm in," says Steph, her eyes shining. "Can we get shitfaced?"

Tom laughs. Steph has a real teenage mentality when it comes to alcohol, perhaps because she had to be such a grown-up when she was a teenager.

"Sure. How about Friday?"

"You're taking the kids to see Veronica on Saturday morning," says Steph.

"Oh yeah. I need to be on top form for that. How about Thursday?"

"A school night?" Steph's eyes shine again, she likes mischief. "Let's do it. OK I'd better go. I'll say goodbye to Katy."

Steph passes Tom and heads into the lounge. He follows and can't help but notice her perfect bottom. It was one of the things he remembers about his first meeting with Steph, and in fifteen years it doesn't seem to have aged at all. In fact, Steph doesn't seem to have aged at all. He can't quite decide whether she was an old teenager or a young adult when they met. After Steph leaves, and Tom has put Katy to bed, he spends the evening thinking about his wife's best friend at 18 and at 34. Unlike his wife, she has remained constant, always chirpy, always swearing, always helpful, always there. She has been a constant in his life. He then starts to think about himself at 20 and himself now. It's much easier to assess *other* people, easier to see the changes, the improvements, the faults that emerge in them over time, but casting your assessment inwards is far more difficult and Tom feels uncomfortable looking at himself back then. He's not sure why he feels awkward looking back at himself, is he embarrassed by the man he was? What would he think now if he were to meet the grubby singer-songwriter that he once was? Would he look down on him? These questions begin to trouble him, rolling around inside his head like pinballs knocking loudly on the edges. He tries to think about Steph again, good steady Steph, but the pinballs keep bouncing around, demanding attention. What happened to the other thoughts that used to bounce around in this head? The thoughts of lyrics and stories, melodies and music, the thought that nothing meant anything without music in his life. Is Steph really the *only* thing that has remained the same in all that time?

17:34, Wednesday February 19th, 2014
14 Carrer Lleo, Al Raval, Barcelona

Portrait 124 is a blind man. He has a high forehead and spiked fair hair, and his eyes are bulging but closed. Angelo looks around the room and wonders whether any of his death friends acted as this man's carer, or perhaps he had a wife or girlfriend, a pair of seeing eyes for him. Angelo paints this man's round cheeks, his full forehead and short hair, his mouth slightly parted, as though asking a question. When it comes to the eyes, he paints them shut. The likeness to the photo is good, but Angelo is not happy. Everyone else looks at each other across the studio with a quiet understanding, a sparkle in their eyes, a hidden knowledge. Angelo contemplates the blind man. Just like everyone else on the plane, he knew he was falling, knew he was dying, he may not have seen the terror; the fear in his companions' eyes, but he would have felt it, and possibly more than anyone else. And now this man sees, he sees what happens after your body ceases to exist.

An hour later, and the blind man hangs on the third wall, the top painting of a new column. Although his eyes are closed, a glow surrounds them. A light shines out from their edges and appears to seep through the fine layer of skin that covers his eyes, like a star wrapped in cotton. Angelo smiles at the man and he seems to smile back. Perhaps Maria shared her last moments with him.

Angelo looks at Maria on the far wall, and in the greyness of the falling sun she appears unreal, just a canvas covered in paint. He approaches her, but she remains dull and lifeless. He looks at her from different angles but can't find the life in her. His heart is beating fast and he has a sudden desire to talk to someone about her, to have proof she existed, that she is not just a dangerous figment of his imagination, not just a heap of paints on a piece of canvas. He considers going down to see Señora Carmen, but he owes her three months' rent and he knows she will not be ready to chat about a dead person, when there is a real life debt in the room. He calls Xavier, but he gets his voicemail. Blanca! He ransacks his apartment looking for the letter with her number. He finds it under a pile of newspaper images and quickly dials the number. The phone rings and rings and Angelo panics, will no one confirm that Maria existed?

"Hello?" Angelo sighs in relief at the sound of a voice, despite it not being Blanca.

"Hello Manuel. It's Angelo, can I speak with Blanca?"

There is no response. "Can I speak with Blanca?"

"No," says Manuel. "Goodbye."

"Wait, wait!" shouts Angelo into the phone. "Please Manuel."

Angelo hears Manuel's breathing. He can imagine him, standing in the kitchen, phone in hand and huge belly resting on the work surface.

"Is Blanca out? Can I call back later?"

All Angelo can hear is Manuel's breathing. It sounds as though he has raced up four flights of stairs, but in all likelihood he has just moved from the lounge to the kitchen to answer the phone.

"She's gone," says Manuel. He sounds angry.

"Gone?"

Silence flows down the line.

"Dead," says Manuel, and with that the phone goes dead, as though his last word was a command.

Angelo stands with the phone to his ear, looking out at the stars over the city. He has never felt so lonely, even the stars feel further away tonight.

He dials Blanca's number again, then again, and again. He needs a voice, and even Manuel's will suffice.

Finally he answers. "What do you want?" he shouts down the phone.

"Manuel, Manuel, don't hang up, not yet, please, I'm so sorry about Blanca. I really am. But just tell me something, something about Maria, and then I'll leave you in peace, I promise."

"Maria? Who the fuck is Maria?" His anger is building, and Angelo realizes this man has bigger issues to be dealing with than a tenant that died last year.

"Please Manuel, please. We both lost someone, I lost Maria. She lived above you, in number 12. I just wanted to, well, talk to someone about her."

Manuel murmurs something that doesn't quite make it down the line.

"Manuel?"

"Who the hell is Maria?" he growls. This call to reaffirm Maria's existence is not going well.

"Blanca dealt with her I guess, but she left you with a package to send to me, remember?"

"Oh," he huffs down the phone. "The pregnant one?"

"No, no, the woman with long hair, almost to her waist, she lived above you."

"I know who the hell lived above me," he shouts, "and it was the pregnant one! She was constantly sick for two weeks, we could hear it all night long."

Angelo is still sure Manuel has the wrong person, or at least the wrong situation. He takes a few seconds and remembers something, Maria was sick the last time he saw her.

"I think she was just sick," he says.

"No," says Manuel. "Blanca was worried there was something really wrong with her, wanted to take her to hospital with her, she was always in that goddamn hospital. But it was just a baby."

Angelo has nothing else to ask and Manuel is happy to be hung up on. Angelo's head is filled with more questions jostling for supremacy, like a bar brawl getting out of hand. Was Maria pregnant with his baby? Was that why she was planning on moving in with him? But why hadn't she told him? Could it have been another man's baby she was pregnant with? Is that why she didn't tell him?

The moon is full and, in it's light, Maria seems to come to life again. Her eyes shine at him with all the love the lonely moon has to offer, and he finds it hard to believe she would do anything to hurt him. Angelo spends the whole night sitting on the window sill, gazing at Maria with the moon. Occasionally, he feels one of his other portraits looking at him so intensely that he looks in their direction. In real life, staring eyes always look away when caught, but in his studio that is never the case, and time after time he is met with the knowing look of the dead. It is as though they all know Maria's secret, they know everyone who died on that flight, including his unborn child.

20:12, Thursday February 20th, 2014
7 The Stables, South Kensington, London

Tom feels a strange buzz during the day; a layer of excitement that lies in his belly and keeps him from sitting still. It's a silly feeling to have, it is only Steph coming round for dinner to commiserate about their lonely lives, but still... Between the school runs and emails, he prepares a moussaka with extra care and takes great lengths to pick a special bottle of red from his collection. The moussaka looks so good that he decides against his original plan of giving portions to the kids for their dinner, the idea of serving it up to Steph, in it's purple Le Creuset casserole dish, to have half of it missing troubles him. Instead the kids are thrilled with a midweek treat of pizza.

"Can we stay up to see Auntie Steph?" asks Miles as he crams a floppy slice of pizza into his mouth as quickly as possible.

"Not tonight buddy." Luckily Miles doesn't pursue his line of questioning. He's more intent on getting all the pizza he can fit into his mouth, before his dad realizes it isn't a weekend or a special occasion.

Steph arrives ten minutes later than agreed, and stupidly Tom finds himself pacing around the lounge, only stopping to gulp some cheap wine he won't be serving. The bell rings and he races to open the door but slows his pace in the hallway, in case Steph can hear him. He glances in the mirror, undoes the second button of his grey shirt, does it up again and opens the door.

"Hey Steph," he says, trying to sound casual.

"Hey, how you doing sad loser?"

He laughs immediately feeling more relaxed. "Well you know, sad, lonely, desperate."

"That makes two of us then, let's celebrate."

She walks past him into the hallway and takes off her winter layers; slouchy grey hat and matching scarf, long black puffer coat and high heel boots. She becomes smaller and shorter, and he prefers her this way, she seems easier to handle, more manageable. Under her outdoor apparel she is wearing a green wool dress and grey tights. It's difficult to tell if Steph has made an extra effort tonight, she always looks pristine. She smiles at him and the colour of her dress changes the blue of her eyes into a pretty turquoise.

"Hey, I forgot to ask the other day – are you growing your hair?" she asks, reaching up and giving it a ruffle.

"Oh, well." He looks into the mirror. "Maybe I am. Not intentionally but…"

"It looks good Tom. You look younger, like when I first met you."

Tom has been thinking a lot about his younger self over the last few days, and he's not expecting to be slung back there by Steph. He has a sudden desire to talk to her about the old days, to connect with the boy he hardly recognizes now, but she brings him back to the here and now.

"So what's for dinner? I could eat a scabby horse." She walks in to the lounge and he follows her.

"Moussaka. Sorry, no scabby horse, that was last night. Let me pour you some wine."

As he opens the bottle he glances at Steph. She is standing on the rug by the roaring fire and looking tentatively at the dinner table. Shit, he realizes. Too much effort. There are fresh flowers at one end of the table, a big fat church candle in the middle and the plates and cutlery are already out. Normally, Steph would lay the table with Katy, while Miles bangs it with his toys. Everything on the table tonight is spelling out the word date and everything in the room they so commonly share is making them feel a little awkward; the dimmed lighting, the roaring hearth, the lack of noise, the dinner table dressed with romance rather than family mess.

"So, I thought, it's not just the smug couples that deserve a treat," he suddenly takes a U-turn. "As well as sticking our fingers up at all the blissful lovers out there, I wanted to say thank you Steph, for all you've done for us since, well, since we lost Beth." This is a completely impromptu gesture, but it seems to fit, is probably long overdue, and will hopefully diffuse the romance that hangs in the air trying to get a hook into someone.

"You know you don't have to thank me Tom. Beth was my best friend, I would have done anything for her, living or dead." This is a pretty strong statement and Tom knows it to be true. It makes him feel bad about his original intentions for the evening, not that they were clear in his head, but they definitely weren't completely innocent. It also makes him question whether Steph *would* give up the secrets of her best friend, would her loyalty to these secrets endure after death?

"Well, I just want you to know that we appreciate it. We wouldn't have got this far without you."

Phew. So now the dinner, the candle, the fire and the kids in bed early, are all part of a gesture of thanks. Tom and Steph are comfortable once again in each other's company, and neither notices the spark of excitement that disappears from the other's eyes.

Tom hands a glass of very good wine to Steph and they raise their eyes and their glasses to one another.

"Cheers to you Steph, for everything."

"And you Tom. For everything." They take a sip of wine. "Fuck, that's good!" says Steph. "Now let's get shitfaced."

*

For the first time in a very long time, Tom and Steph don't talk about the kids or Beth all night, and they realize how light their lives can be without the weight of death and responsibility bearing down on them. They speak of Steph's failed love life and the amusing dates she has endured over the last few years, they speak of Steph's sister and her unruly kids, and they speak of Steph's plans to see the world. Tom finds himself circling between laughter, complete fixation on Steph's stories and curiosity for the next. Towards the end of their second bottle of wine, they move from the table to the sofa, and Steph curls her long legs up beneath her.

"Steph, I don't think we have ever talked so much about you," says Tom.

"Oh Shit, I'm so sorry! Have I turned into one of *those* women? I hate those women whose favourite subject is themselves."

"No, no. Not at all. You hardly ever speak about yourself and it's really nice to hear. I had no idea you were so passionate about seeing the world."

"Some people keep their passions hidden," she says. The pink make-up on her cheeks intensifies for a moment. "Do you remember how passionate you were about music?"

Tom shrugs. "Not really. It's like looking at a different man back then. I completely left him behind."

"Why? What made you do that?"

Tom takes a big slurp from his glass. "Beth," he says it without thinking, a consequence of the too-many glasses of wine.

Steph shakes her head, confused. "But she loved that about you. It was one of the things that drove her crazy about you; she said you were never more alive than when you were playing. She adored your passion for music, your focus. The fact you didn't care what anyone else thought."

"But I did care." Tom hasn't told anyone this before, in fact he's never said it out loud, but the honesty of the evening together with two bottles of Bordeaux have loosened his secrets.

"I couldn't have both."

"Couldn't have both what?"

He takes a deep breath. "I couldn't have Beth and my music."

Steph can see a story teetering on the edge of Tom's lips, and she rearranges herself to face him straight on.

"Tell me."

"It's no big deal Steph, just the way things had to be for me to get to... well, to here," he gestures around the lounge.

"You gave up music to pursue this? This kind of life?"

He nods.

"Bollocks! Tom at twenty would never have considered that."

He shrugs. "Well, someone helped me consider it."

"What happened?" Steph sees that Tom is reflecting on whether this sleeping dog should be left alone or kicked awake. "Tom I'm not going to judge you, and I'm not going to tell anyone what you tell me, but I'd like to know."

Tom knows that the woman in front of him can be trusted, and he has always wondered how people would react to his story. It has been kept captive in his own mind for so long that the story has become completely tamed and docile, he has no idea how it will be treated out in the open. And so he tells the story that has never been told, and that he has managed to forget for the most part.

"So, when Beth and I got together, we were from different worlds. You remember?"

She nods. "Different worlds, but almost the same person."

"Well anyway. She did well in my world, coming to gigs, staying at the bedsit, meeting my folks. She really encouraged my life and my music." He laughs. "She was my biggest fan. I had never met someone so interested in me, and the fact that she was beautiful and kind and intelligent, just blew me away. I couldn't believe my luck Steph. I was in love with the greatest girl in the world and she felt the same way about me, things couldn't have been any better."

Steph smiles, but with a little sadness, maybe because Beth is no longer, or maybe because she's never had a relationship like the one Tom describes.

"She kept me away from her world for a while but we knew our future was together and so she let me in. God, I remember that first visit to Willowman Grange. I was shitting myself, and so was she, but Jim and Veronica couldn't have been nicer to me. It was like I was family already, on my first visit."

Steph smiles and nods. "They were a lovely couple."

"I even got a mention in Jim's new year speech. He made me feel very special and very included back then." Tom goes to open a new bottle of wine and returns to the sofa with it. "But then things changed."

Steph's eyes cloud over with suspicion. She only ever knew Veronica and Jim to be the kindest and most genuine people.

"I know what you're thinking Steph. Jim and Veronica were always faultless, they never did anything unjust or unkind, and now with hindsight, I know that what Jim did *was* the right thing."

"What did he do?"

"Beth and I had been together for over a year. My music was going pretty well, Beth had been helping me get in touch with promoters and I had some good gigs lined up, and was getting a loyal following. Obviously, I wasn't making much money from it, but I was bringing in decent money from the bar jobs, so I was happy enough. I had a weekend without gigs and we decided to go and see Jim and Veronica. He was persevering in teaching me golf. God knows why, I hadn't shown a speck of talent. Veronica and Beth had gone shopping, and Jim and I were out on the golf course. He was his usual charming self and was asking me about my music and what I had planned for my musical career, while I thrashed around in a bunker. And then he suddenly looked at me and said 'and what do you have planned with my daughter?'"

Steph raises her eyebrows. "And what did you say?"

"I told him the truth, that Beth and I planned on spending our futures together. And that's when he told me."

"Told you what?"

"That he had different plans for her."

"What? He said what?" Steph's voice rises with each question.

"Well, not in so many words, he was his usual diplomatic self; started by telling me how much he liked me, that I was a nice guy and a talented musician. But then he told me how he'd hoped the relationship between Beth and I would have fizzled out by that point."

Tom has Steph's full attention and she is shaking her head in disbelief.

"Then he said something about how much Beth liked me, and that I obviously cared very much for her, but that my future wasn't with her. He said it just like that 'your future isn't with my daughter.' It's the harshest thing I ever heard him say."

"And what did you say to him?" Steph's mouth hangs open and is ringed in red wine just to make her shock more obvious.

"I wanted to tell him to fuck off, that Beth's life was her own and that she could make her own decisions. But then he went from defiant father to successful diplomat. 'I'm looking out for her best interests,' he said, 'and a struggling musician working part-time in a pub is not in her best interests.' He asked me to think ahead into my own future. He said, 'One day, perhaps you'll have children, a girl, and you'll understand where I'm coming from. You'll want to secure your daughter's future, as I do for Beth, and you won't want her committing her life to someone like you.'"

Steph is breathing fast, her shock transformed into anger.

"Fucking hell Tom, he really said that?"

"Yes."

"Fucking hell Tom." Steph doesn't seem able to form any other words. She shakes her head, first with slow precision, then quickly, like she is trying to shake something out of it.

"He told me he could make life very difficult for me, said that he had been nice until that point, was waiting for the relationship to end naturally, but felt that now he had to intervene. He made it clear that Beth's future husband would be a successful and accomplished man, like he was. He even told me about a few candidates he had lined up. I was gobsmacked."

"As am I," says Steph. She grips her shaking head by the ears and looks down at her knees. "He really wanted you out of her life?"

"Completely. He even offered me money to leave her and to leave London, suggested I head back up north and pursue my music there."

"No fucking way!"

Tom nods his head. A tiny fire inside of him that was long ago extinguished is being rekindled by Steph's anger. "The last thing he said to me before we walked back to the house was 'Tom, my daughter will *not* be marrying an struggling musician.' And the way he looked at me Steph when he said it, I knew it to be true, he wouldn't let it happen."

"So what did you do?" asks Steph.

"I thought about it a long time, a really long time. I became distant with Beth for a few months, you might not remember but she became convinced I was having an affair."

Steph nods frantically. "I remember, I remember. She was beside herself."

"So was I." He takes a glug of wine. "I had no idea what to do."

197

Steph is tipping forwards toward Tom in a bid to get to his words faster by sitting closer. "So what did you do?"

He shrugs. "I became the successful self-made man that Jim wanted her to marry."

Steph sits back, confused. "I don't understand."

"I enrolled on a maths and computer course at Birkbeck."

She laughs. "No you didn't! You took a music technology course," says Steph, a big smile on her face as though Miles has just tried to convince her the sky is green. "To help with recording your music."

He shakes his head. "No, I didn't. That was a lie. I was never going to pick up a decent job without qualifications, so I did my diploma in maths and computing."

"A diploma? In maths and computing? But you were a musician working in a bar." Steph is muddled and the tangle of questions in her mind is trying to come loose. "What? How on earth did you pay for a diploma? From your bar work? Or did Jim pay?"

"God no! I wouldn't have given him the satisfaction. For all he knew I was making my exit plan from Beth. And I gave up most of the bar work, it took up too much time, what with studying."

"But you seemed to work every night at the bar."

"Birkbeck is evening classes, and when I wasn't there I was at the library."

"Fuck Tom!" Steph can't find the words strong enough to show how she feels, and so she reverts to the word most versatile. "Fuck." She stands up and begins to pace. "And Beth had no idea?"

He shakes his head. "Never did, and never will."

Steph is pacing fast and scratching her neat blonde hair into a mess. She stops.

"So how did you pay for it then?" Steph remembers Tom as one of those young men forever strapped for cash.

"Well, at my parents house I had this pot..."

Steph gasps loudly. "No!"

Tom smiles. "I didn't realize you knew about it."

The red wine glaze that had covered Steph's eyes has completely disappeared, and she is alert and focused.

"Beth always hated your dad for accepting that money." Her voice begins to rise in volume. "You told her he needed it to buy a new car."

"I spent it on the computer course," says Tom.

Steph spreads her feet, as if to gain some balance. Her breathing becomes loud and slow, as if she is trying to control it after a long run. "Let me get this straight. You used the guitar money you had been saving for years to pay for the course that would get you a job worthy of Beth's father."

Tom looks at Steph strangely. Her tone of voice is like she is talking to Miles and trying to make him understand that he's made a big mistake. "And what about your music?"

He shrugs. "Beth was more important than my music."

Steph's eyebrows are dipped in either anger or confusion. She keeps looking at Tom, as though checking he is still there, and his story still exists. She kneels in front of him and takes a long sip of wine.

"You gave up your music, for Beth?" The question is clear but the look on her face is not.

"Yes, I did."

Now the look becomes clear. She is furious. She glugs down the wine and stands again.

"You fucking gave it up for *her*? Because of some fucking pretentious thing that Jim once said? You gave up the one thing you were most passionate about for *her*?"

Tom doesn't like the way Steph keeps emphasizing the word 'her', as though Beth doesn't deserve a name. He stands up.

"The thing I was most passionate about was Beth," he shouts at Steph.

"Fuck Beth!" shouts Steph at the top of her voice. "And fuck Jim!" she shouts even louder. She holds her glass like she wants to throw it and her eyes are gleaming with fury. Her next words are slow and deliberate again. "You have no idea Tom." She shakes her head. "No fucking idea."

She's right, Tom really has no idea. He has no idea how such a nice evening turned into a shouting match. He has no idea why Steph is so upset and he has no idea why Steph is storming into the hallway. He goes after her and finds her in the hallway zipping up her boots.

"Steph, what's wrong? I don't understand what just happened."

She pulls her hat over her blonde bob with a force that could take off her ears. "Exactly Tom," she says with no sign of her anger dissipating. "You don't fucking understand." She closes the front door behind her and he hears her bellow into the winter air "You understand fucking nothing!"

16:21, Friday February 28th, 2014
14 Carrer Lleo, Al Raval, Barcelona

Teresa looks around the apartment in disdain. She is used to the squalor in which some artists choose to engulf themselves, but Angelo's apartment seems to have taken this to a new level. Ominous dead faces cover all four walls now, and two of his newest paintings stare down from the ceiling. This leaves nowhere for Teresa to comfortably settle her eyes, other than on the dirt and disorder which litter the floor.

Angelo has been living on a diet of whiskey and caffeine since his conversation with Manuel. He uses the caffeine to jumpstart his heart and mind, and the whiskey to dull them. In this way he is able to control his level of consciousness, putting himself to sleep and waking himself up as needed. His recent portraits are characterized by more careless brushstrokes, less precision in the face, but still the same knowing look behind the eyes. It's not that the eyes are a formula he's mastered, it is not simply the application of paint in the same pattern to the canvas, it's just that he only truly connects with the person, and is able to bring the dead back to life, when he reaches their eyes. Only one portrait from his recent set has been completed slowly, in meticulous detail throughout.

There was only one baby on AS636, at least one outside of the womb. It would be impossible to tell whether the dark fuzz of hair and vacant staring eyes were male or female, if it were not for the pink outfit in the photograph. Angelo decided to paint the baby androgenous, neither male nor female, like the secret baby inside Maria. He took great pains to give the face more knowledge than its years, or indeed months, would give it. Now the baby stares down from the ceiling at the top of Teresa's French pleat.

"So, *mi tresor*," she says, looking into the dark pits of Angelo's tired eyes. "We have our venue, we have great sponsors, and I think we're going to have quite an audience."

Angelo says nothing, but gulps down a cup of cold coffee. It is the nearest thing he can get his hands on, and he isn't bothered whether it's whiskey or caffeine, anything to distract from what Teresa is saying.

"Not only have I got interest from many portrait collectors, but AirStar are sending out an invitation to the families of all the victims."

He is trying to ignore her words, but he can't ignore these last five 'families of all the victims.'

"What? What did you just say?"

She sighs. "Why do I feel like you are never listening to me Angelo? I said that I have interest from many portrait collectors…"

"No, no, not that bit. The last thing you said."

She ponders this, "I can't for the life of me remember…"

"Fuck Teresa! About the families, about the families, what did you say?"

"Oh yes, AirStar have invited them all to the exhibition, it's great news, your paintings are so, well, so realistic, I'm sure most of them will sell to family members."

"No!" He clutches his head. "No!" He holds his head and walks in a few tight circles. Teresa looks at him with caution, as though she is witnessing a man walking from sane to insane.

"What's wrong Angelo?" Teresa feels a sense of doom that is more often than not warranted when talking with Angelo.

"Why? Why?" He continues walking in circles, cradling his head in his hands. 142 pairs of eyes shine at him with sympathy from the edges of the room, and one pair looks at him in astonishment.

"Well, for goodness sake Angelo, what's wrong with you? I thought you'd be pleased about the interest in your exhibition. None of your other work has attracted so much attention."

"That's the entire fucking problem," he says under his breath at first, but then shouting it across the room at her. "That's the entire fucking problem!"

He clears the few metres between them in a split second, amazing considering the amount of debris that litters the gap. He grabs her by the shoulders and looks down into her wide, frightened eyes.

"I - do - not - want - to - sell - any - of - these - paintings." He annunciates each word separately and clearly, like stepping stones in a stream, it's important that she doesn't miss a single one. "In fact, I don't want any of them leaving my apartment."

Angelo feels as though all the faces around the room are behind him, united in this opinion.

"But, but, *mi tresor*, we discussed this months ago." She treads carefully. "I have already paid you ample amounts in advance, not that that's a problem, because, well, in terms of money, you are set to do very well from…"

"I don't care about fucking money!" he yells into her face. If she weren't so scared by the look in his eye, she would be repulsed by the acrid smell accompanying his words.

"But, *mi tresor*," she tries a different tack, aiming for his ego rather than his wallet. "Your work here is fantastic, we have to share it with the world."

He grips her so tightly that she gasps in pain. "Listen to me. For the first time in your fucking life, listen to me. I am not selling one of these paintings, do you hear me? Not one."

16:11, Tuesday March 4th, 2014
7 The Stables, South Kensington, London

"Why doesn't Auntie Steph come in for tea anymore daddy?" asks Katy. She is sitting at the dining table working neatly on a colouring-in book while Miles thwarts her efforts by scribbling all over the page.

"She has a busy life sweetie, she has lots of things to do after she picks you up from school."

Katy concentrates for a while on the neat green hat of a bunny wearing a scribbled jacket, courtesy of her brother. She keeps her eyes down when she speaks.

"Is it because of the argument you had with her?"

Tom looks up from the chopping board where he is slicing carrots. "What argument?"

Miles also looks up from Mr. Rabbit's jacket. "What argument?"

Katy bites her lip. "The one you had about mummy."

Tom sighs. He has no idea what Katy heard, probably just the noisy tail end of their row. "Katy, Steph still misses your mummy very much, they were very close friends for a long time. Sometimes she gets angry about it."

"You were angry too," she mumbles.

"I was," he says. And in truth he still is. He's not sure what he was expecting from sharing his story with Steph, it's not as though he wanted sympathy from her, but he definitely wasn't expecting anger.

"Daddy. I don't want Auntie Steph to go," says Katy. Now *she* is biting her lip.

"What do you mean sweetie?"

Her face crumbles. "I don't want Auntie Steph to leave us, like mummy did."

Tom leaves the kitchen and sits down opposite his two children. Miles is looking with concern at his sister. "Where is Auntie Steph going?" he asks.

"Auntie Steph is going nowhere," says Tom.

"But we only see her on Tuesdays and Fridays when she picks us up," says Katy. "And she never comes to the house anymore. I don't want her to leave us like mummy did."

"Me neither," says Miles, his eyes wide at the possibility of Steph disappearing.

"That's not going to happen," says Tom. "She loves you both very much."

"Mummy loved us very much," says Katy.

There is a sharp edge of annoyance in Tom's voice. "Auntie Steph is very different from mummy. She is very loyal and she won't leave you, she won't leave this family." As he says the words he realizes how much he wants them to be true.

Katy looks her father straight in the eye. It's a habit she has adopted for when she wants to see how truthful her father is being. Like her mother, Katy is very perceptive.

"Will Auntie Steph come to my spring ballet performance?"

Tom nods and tries to keep his eyes on Katy's. "I'm sure she'd love to."

"And can we go for pizza afterwards like last time?"

Tom swallows. "Of course honey, if that's what you'd like to do."

She nods carefully still staring into her father's eyes.

"Yay! Pizza! Pizza!" Miles interrupts the conversation and jumps up from the table to do his pizza dance. It is a ridiculous set of jumps and twists that has nothing to do with pizza, but is basically a celebration of something that makes him very happy. Tom and Katy both laugh and when their eyes next meet, they are not full of suspicion, but full of joy, even if just for a few moments.

*

Later that evening Tom thinks over Katy's words from that afternoon. "I don't want Auntie Steph to leave us like mummy did." There is probably nothing deeper in them than a young child's desire for a mother-figure, but he can't help but wonder whether Katy is referring to her mother's disappearance long before she died.

22:57, Friday March 28th, 2014
14 Carrer Lleo, Al Raval, Barcelona

It's a relief to be talking about someone else's life for a change. Angelo feels as though the past eight months have been a concentrated period of himself, and himself alone. It was like getting to the end of a bottle of juice. Everything is fine and balanced and life tastes OK but then you get to a point where life isn't mixed up so well, it's not distributed evenly, and you get a big gulp of reality, the intense taste of being. The last eight months have been a concentrated lump of life, but tonight he feels more balanced.

Xavier is strumming the guitar and talking absent-mindedly about the girl he is trying to woo.

"I mean seriously, I thought girls from Latin America were supposed to be easy to get into bed, but this girl is making me jump through fucking hoops." He plays some angry chords. "And the amount of money I've spent on her! All for one lousy kiss so far."

Angelo smiles. "Then save the money and head to *La Casita*. It's impossible to leave that place without taking someone home with you."

Xavier shrugs. "Yeah, but I don't want any of those skanks, I want this girl. Fuck, you should see the ass on her!" He picks up the empty bottle of wine. "You could rest this bottle and two glasses on it, and still have space for your ashtray, and then you could stick…"

"Alright man! I get it. She's the one you want."

"Yeah, but I have no idea how long it's gonna take, and how much it's gonna cost."

They both take a couple of glugs of wine.

"Hey, you got me thinking," says Xavier. "You wanna go find Green Shoes?"

Green Shoes is the notorious prostitute who marks her location around El Gotico, El Born and Al Raval by hanging a pair of lurid high heels from the window. She is said to be the best fuck in Barcelona, and can do things with her internal muscles that make men cry. She increases her demand and popularity by moving location every few weeks, causing horny men to roam the streets searching for the green shoes that will mark the end of their loneliness for a night.

Angelo cocks his head to the side. "You just told me you don't want any skanks. Change your mind so quickly?"

"Not for me man! For you! Your dick must hate you right now. By my calculations, it's had no action for… well… for a long time." He stands up and puts the guitar down. "Let's get you laid."

Angelo downs his wine. "Fuck off," he says, looking into the base of the glass.

"No man, I mean it. It'll fall off if you don't use it, and it'll be good for you, well, mentally too. You know, kind of cleansing, for your mind, and your dick."

Angelo stands and Xavier claps his hands together in glee, but his face falls when he sees that Angelo is just heading to the kitchen. He comes back with a full bottle of red and fills Xavier's glass.

"This is cleansing," says Angelo. "And I'm happy to live my sex life, vicariously, through you."

"Then both our dicks are going to fall off," says Xavier with a sigh.

21:14, Tuesday April 1st, 2014
7 The Stables, South Kensington, London

Tom watches Steph at she tidies away Miles' train set, searching beneath the sofa for a runaway train. Tom has missed her, there's no denying it. The last four weeks have only offered him courteous hellos and polite smiles from her as she drops the kids off. Tonight has been lovely, they have laughed, chatted and celebrated Katy's performance together, but now, after a very late bedtime for Katy and Miles, they are alone for the first time since their bizarre row. He doesn't want to start another argument, though he is still intrigued by what caused their last, their first in fact.

He is watching her behind wiggling as she reaches under the sofa. "Got you!" she exclaims.

For a moment Tom thinks she is referring to having caught him staring at her and he gulps down his guilt, but then she emerges from under the furniture brandishing a green engine. "Henry's back," she says, smiling at Tom. He watches her put the train back into the box with Thomas and friends, and wonders how it is that a childless woman knows the names of the toys in his house better than him. The toys are packed away, the pizza remnants are cleared and now there is nothing to tidy up apart from their argument. Tom takes a deep breath and walks over to her.

"I'm sorry Steph," he says. He looks into her blue eyes, they are back to their natural shade.

She smiles. "Me too. I've really missed you guys."

They are standing a few feet from each other, with nothing between them, not even an apology anymore.

"I've missed you too," he says. He meant to say 'we', but a selfish 'I' escapes.

Tom opens his arms in a gesture of forgiveness and Steph walks into them. The embrace begins as a matey squeeze and Tom is about to pat her on the back when something changes. Maybe it is the smell of her perfume, maybe it is the far from 'matey' shape of her body against his, maybe it is the way she buries her head into his woollen jumper and breathes it in slowly. Whatever it is, the way their bodies are touching each other is no longer the momentary grasp of two mates, it is far more significant. Tom bows his head into Steph's hair and closes his eyes. Her silky hair is freshly washed and the scent of shampoo is dangerously familiar, the same brand Beth used to use. Her shoulders are broad but he is still able to encircle them in his arms, and he holds her tightly. Her body rises and falls in slow movements like this is the most relaxed she has felt in a long time. Too many moments have passed for Steph and Tom to separate and pretend nothing has happened, and anyway neither of them wants to.

Tom's hands move down the long slopes of her back and rest at the base of her spine. He loves the feeling of this woman in his arms, the only woman he has felt for nine months. He pulls his head away from the crown of her head and kisses her forehead. This is the starter gun, the sign that something more is about to happen, and he wants it to. Steph lifts her head to kiss the man she has loved for so long. As her lips touch his, Tom feels a rush of something that starts in his lips and races to his skin. The delightful kiss of a woman, the sensation of a soft mouth against his, moist skin on skin. He immediately gives in to the feeling and kisses her back, urgently, a man starved of kisses. He grabs her face, his eyes still closed, and runs his hands through her hair, but... his fingers are lost. They have emerged from the hair too soon, where are the long waves? He pulls back and remembers who he is, and who she is not. He pulls away further from Steph and his hands drop to his sides. He wants her, he knows he wants her, but his kiss has been reserved for one woman for so long that, despite the fact that woman is dead, he feels full of deceit.

He stares at Steph in bewilderment, not knowing what to say or do. But Steph, constantly enduring Steph, knows what to say as always.

"It's OK Tom. I can wait."

He looks sheepish. "I'm sorry," he stammers.

She takes a deep breath. "Tom, I have waited long enough, I can wait longer. Just tell me one thing."

He nods.

"That I won't have to wait fucking forever."

Her swearing breaks the tension, and he smiles. "I promise."

19:28, Friday April 4th, 2014
14 Carrer Lleo, Al Raval, Barcelona

Angelo buzzes Xavier in. He's not really in the mood for company, let alone meeting someone new, but he owes his friend a mountain of favours and this can be the first. He hears the tap-tap of heels on the stairs, a sound that normally fills him with dread, but today it's not Teresa, and he tries to force a smile as the heels reach the front door.

"Hey man!" says Xavier, clapping him on the back. "I'd like you to meet Aurora."

Angelo doesn't know which new person to look at first. Every inch of Xavier looks different today, from his greased-back hair to his shining shoes, it is a much refined version of his friend that Angelo sees, and he wants to laugh. But Xavier shoots him a look that begs him not to, and Angelo swallows his amusement.

"Hi," says Aurora. "Nice to meet you." She touches Angelo gently on the shoulder and sweeps her face against either side of his, her greeting is more like a gentle breeze than solid contact, and Angelo can understand the difficulty Xavier is having getting close to her.

"And you," he says. "Come in." He watches her enter the room with her cautious heels picking a path towards the far corner. She has long perfectly straight hair that tapers down to her round behind, like an arrow pointing at her best feature. She wears a patterned dress with a high collar and yellow heels, and seems to dress older than her years.

"Aurora loves art," says Xavier. "She was very excited to meet you, a real life artist."

"And a prolific one!" she says, turning from a portrait in the far corner to look at Angelo.

"Well, it's something of a project I'm working on, it's…"

"Yes, Xavier explained," she says giving him a gentle smile. Her features are set slightly wide apart, probably only a few millimetres wider than the Spanish norm, but together with her fine hair and her quick, sing-song voice, it's enough to suggest an exotic background. She begins a slow parade of the paintings, scrutinizing each.

"Can I get you a drink?" he offers.

"Coffee please. Black."

Angelo wanders into the kitchen and Xavier follows. "She's very particular about her coffee," he whispers.

"Me too," says Angelo, shrugging. "I only drink this particular type... the cheapest." He smiles.

Xavier paces in the tiny kitchen. "Well at least give her the cup with the handle," he whispers.

Angelo takes his friend by the arms to stop him pacing. "Calm down man. She's just a chick. And it's just a coffee."

"*Neither* of those is true," says Xavier shaking his head, "not for her."

When they emerge from the kitchen, Aurora is standing in front of Maria's picture.

"Here's your coffee," says Angelo. She doesn't turn around.

"I know this woman," she says.

Xavier interrupts. "No, *mi amor*, that's the woman I was telling you about, you remember? The one who..."

"Of course I remember," she says bluntly. "But I still know her."

Angelo approaches Aurora and stands by her side.

"How do you know her?" he asks, full of wonder.

A few moments pass and Aurora squints in concentration at the portrait. "I don't know," she shakes her head. "But I have met her before. Maybe a long time ago. Was she ever in Chile?"

He shakes his head. "Have you spent time in Madrid?"

She looks at him confused. "No, not much."

"And how long have you been in Barcelona?"

"Six months."

"Maybe you have her confused with someone else?"

"I don't think so." She shakes her head slowly.

Now it is Angelo's turn to scrutinize Aurora. They stand locked in each other's stare until Xavier interrupts. He places his hand on her back and tries to steer her away from Angelo and Maria.

"Well, anyway, don't miss out the other paintings *mi amor*, they are all excellent."

She stands her ground. "They are, but this one is clearly the best. Did she sit for you Angelo?" She looks back at the painting now.

"Yes, she did."

"I can see she was very much in love with you."

"Really?" says Angelo.

"Of course, it's clear."

"This is one of my favourites," says Xavier from the other side of the room. He is standing next to the black man with the folds of skin hanging from his face like dark meringue. "Aurora, Aurora come take a look." His raised voice catches her attention and she goes over to check out the black man.

The three of them make small talk as she wanders around the remaining portraits, but every now and again she looks in Maria's direction, with the hope that a fresh look will identify the woman for her.

When Xavier and Aurora leave, her cheek makes contact with Angelo's and once again she gives him a gentle sad smile.

"I can't remember where or when I met Maria, but once upon a time I think I liked her very much. I'm sorry for your loss."

Xavier slaps him on the back. "See you later." He leans in close. "And thanks man, I think you've put her in a lovin' kind of mood."

Angelo smiles. "*Hasta luego.*"

He shuts the door and, as Aurora's heels carefully tap down the dark staircase, he hears her voice.

"I know that woman, I'm sure I know that woman."

19:46, Tuesday April 8th, 2014
7 The Stables, South Kensington, London

"You seemed to be in a real rush to get the kids to sleep," says Steph, touching Tom's back lightly as they descend the stairs. Their first kiss has not been repeated, but both are creeping towards a second with seemingly careless caresses that have a lot of care behind them.

"There's something I want to show you. I've been wanting to show you all night." He races down the stairs and she skips along after him. He opens his laptop and sets it on the kitchen island. Steph notices that his password is still Beth1999, the year he met his wife.

"Look at this email. I was sent it this morning."

Steph rests her head on Tom's shoulder and reads the message aloud. It is from AirStar Airlines.

"Dear Mr Turner and family. As I am sure you are all aware, July 12th 2014 will mark the first anniversary of the AS636 tragedy that shattered the lives of so many. To pay tribute to those lost on this flight, we invite you to celebrate their lives at the anniversary memorial. A Catholic service of remembrance will be held at the memorial garden on July 12th, and a series of accompanying events will be happening across Madrid in the weeks to follow. These events are listed below.

"AirStar Airlines will of course offer all family members (up to a maximum of four) complimentary return flights from any European airport within our network.

"Events celebrating the lives of those lost in the AS636 tragedy include: a classical musical tribute at *Teatro Real*, a contemporary dance recital representing the flight of souls." Steph rolls her eyes. "*167 Fallen Hearts*, a portrait exhibition of all victims by Angelo Octavez, services of remembrance at the following churches…"

Steph reads the entire email and detailed list of events out loud, not because she is interested or feels that Tom needs to hear it, but so that she can think about the appropriate response. It feels as though she has been making great progress with Tom these last few weeks, and he is mentioning Beth less and less. In the race to secure Tom as her own, Steph has been inching ahead of Beth and had a clear lead up until about two minutes ago.

"Wow," she says, after finally reaching the end of the lengthy email. "That's a lot to think about."

Tom nods. He doesn't look at Steph. In truth, this email has been a much-needed reminder that his wife died less than a year ago, and he can't ignore the fact that he is still grieving for her. Steph has been a useful distraction, an anaesthetic for the pain, but he can't be sure whether she represents more than that.

He nods, and for some reason, from nowhere, he feels a hard lump forming in his throat. He concentrates on the AirStar logo at the top of the email and swallows once, then twice, but the lump keeps rising, keen to free itself. The more he stares at the yellow and red of the airline logo, the more the colours seems to represent life and death, the loss of his wife. He turns from the computer and busies himself with the sink, running a sponge over its already sparkling surface.

Steph approaches him and he can feel how close she stands, although she decides not to touch him. Tom really hopes she says something mundane, about the tiles maybe, or the dinner, anything that might help dislodge the lump.

"It's OK to still be sad Tom. You lost your wife."

And instantly those kind words break up the lump in his throat, and the pieces emerge as tears. He cries into the pristine sink and continues to wipe it cleaner than clean, trying to mop up his sadness.

Steph takes the sponge from him and replaces it with her own hand. It is not a gesture of romance, more one of solidarity. "I still miss her too Tom."

He is unable to show Steph his miserable face, and so buries it into her shoulder. She turns him round to face her and he cries into her silk blouse. He stands awkwardly, leaning into a shorter woman and trying to gather strength from her. The embrace could not be more different than their last but somehow, for Tom, this is a more natural arrangement. Steph has always been the stronger one.

12:14, Saturday April 12th, 2014
Willowman Grange

The kids' birthdays have always been celebrated at home, but in a concerted effort to make a positive memory out of this first motherless birthday, and also as distraction for Veronica who is alone with her ghosts, the party happens at Willowman Grange. Four of Miles' best friends from school are chasing him around one of Veronica's most treasured sculptures, and four sets of parents are trying not to comment on the phallic nature of the eight-foot sculpture.

"Little Miles is doing so well," says Rosie's mum to anyone who might be listening. She is sipping Champagne, and a bracelet laden with silver charms jangles around her wrist.

"Isn't he? You would never guess what a difficult year he's had," says another mother. "He's a very resilient little boy."

Tom is talking to one of the dads, trying not to listen to his son's character assessment. The man he talks to is Kristoff, a Polish builder whose son was accepted into the school due to his unearthly intelligence.

Kristoff looks completely uncomfortable at Willowman Grange, and his shuffling feet and fidgeting hands remind Tom of his own first visit.

"How much you think a place like this is worth?" Kristoff asks Tom.

Tom smiles, it is a question his twenty-year-old self asked Beth, and he repeats her answer.

"More than we will ever be able to afford."

Kristoff seems happy with this response. It places him in the same aspiring boat as Tom.

Just then Veronica enters the marquee that has been erected on the veranda, with a Thomas the Tank Engine cake teetering in her outstretched arms. In a bid to appear casual for the day's antics, she wears her long black hair loose and a pair of ballet pumps. She looks tiny behind the impressive cake and her image is so similar to Beth's that, for a moment Tom's wife hasn't died, she is glowing with happiness behind five candles ready to celebrate another year of motherhood.

"Okay, cheeldren. Ees time for cake," shouts Beth's' image in a strongly accented voice. Tom is back in real life immediately and he could punch Thomas' smug creamy face. The children make no sign of hearing Veronica.

"Miles! It's time for cake," shouts Steph in a voice that could have come from all of the fathers put together.

The word cake makes for an immediate response and, within seconds, Miles, Katy and four other sweaty faces circle Thomas.

"Okay, *mi amor*," says Veronica. "Are you ready to make a weesh?"

Miles nods frantically.

"You 'ave to blow 'em all out for a wish," says Kristoff's boy.

"I will," says Miles with full confidence.

Veronica nods at Steph and Tom, and they begin the chorus. On past birthdays Miles has hopped around during the song, but today he stands still and licks his lips in preparation for making his wish. As the song comes to an end he looks at his father, who gives him the nod. He takes a huge breath, seems to double in size and blows out all five candles. His resulting smile stretches wide and stays that way, even while he is stuffing it with cake.

*

That night after Tom has said a proud goodnight to his five year old, he stands outside the door as Veronica talks to her grandson.

"Deed you 'ave a lovely day *mi amor*?" she asks.

"Yes grandma."

"And you weeshed very 'ard when you blew out your candles, deedn't you?"

"Uh-huh."

"What deed you weesh for?" she asks gently.

There is silence and Tom leans closer in to the door.

"You can tell me, ees our little secret," she says.

Tom holds his breath. All day long he has been trying not to dwell on the missing person at the party. Was she also in Miles' thoughts?

"Well, I know that maybe I should have wished for mummy," says Miles. There is hesitation in his voice. "But Katy told me mummy is never coming back, and no wishing and praying will help."

Tom bites his lip.

"So what did you weesh for?" asks Veronica, her voice waivers slightly.

"I wished for Auntie Steph."

This sentence has the same effect on both Tom and Veronica, although a wall separates them. In the glow of the bedside light, Veronica's eyebrows rise.

"What did you weesh for Auntie Steph?" asks Veronica.

"Katy says we will have a new mummy one day. She said it is invettable. So I wished that it could be Auntie Steph."

Now Veronica is hushed for a few moments and when she speaks it is with a rattle in her words. "You like Steph very much?"

"Yes. And daddy is happier when she's around."

Shit. Tom wishes Miles hadn't just said that. He doesn't want his mother-in-law thinking that her daughter has been replaced so quickly.

"Well, in that case *mi amor*. I weesh for the same thing," says Veronica. Her voice is stronger now.

Tom hears the gentle rustle of sheets and he turns to creep away, but Miles speaks again and he stops to listen.

"Your hair looks really pretty Grandma."

"Thank you *mi amor*."

"Can I play with your hair Grandma? While I fall asleep."

"Of course," says Veronica.

Tom smiles and tiptoes down the hall. The corridors of Willowman Grange are long, offering plenty of thinking time between rooms. He has been given the all-clear by his mother-in-law and his children, and his heart seems to be in agreement with them. It's only his conscience that appears to be putting up a fight. Is it his conscience, or is it his dead wife? Would Beth approve of Tom and Steph, or would she hate the idea? Obviously if Beth were still alive, her husband forming a relationship with her best friend would be unthinkable, but what about now? What happens after death? Is it unthinkable? He certainly seems to be thinking about it.

17:31, Monday May 5th, 2014
14 Carrer Lleo, Al Raval, Barcelona

Angelo's small studio apartment has more angelic faces than the Sistine chapel. Today he finished the last of his 167 portraits and now Maria is accompanied by all of her fellow AS636 passengers. He expects her to look different somehow; proud, or maybe relieved, but she continues to stare at him with those secretive, knowing eyes. Aurora said they were eyes filled with love and he used to think the same thing, but now he can't help but wonder whether they are full of secrets instead. Perhaps deceit and love are easily confused. Are loving eyes so different from lying eyes? When he looks at Maria now he sees a woman he hardly knew, but that he loved very much, that he still loves very much.

He goes to sit on the window sill and looks out, ignoring the faces behind him. He feels let down by them. He thought they would give him answers, make him feel comforted, but now he knows it was the process rather than the outputs that offered him the catharsis, and now that process is over. Still, he won't part with them. They may not offer answers, but they are intrinsically linked with Maria, and he will not betray her by selling any of them.

There is a knock on the door and he takes a deep breath and repeats his mantra, *I'm not selling any of them.*

He lets Teresa in and neither of them says a word. She looks tired, and for once is wearing flat shoes, perhaps for a hasty getaway. She walks to the far end of the room and surveys the final eight portraits that are suspended from the ceiling. She nods slightly, sweeps her eyes around the full collection and takes a deep breath, puffing herself up for battle.

"Hear me out Angelo," she says. He opens his mouth to speak but she raises her hand to silence him. "Just listen, no interruptions."

He sighs and collapses onto the sofa.

"Nearly six months ago you agreed to this exhibition, and I have since paid you five thousand euros, of my own money, in the good faith that we would deduct this from your profits. I have booked a venue, secured three high-profile sponsors, and invited a host of reputable portrait collectors from all over Europe. Curators from the Gugenheim, MAPFRE and Reina Sofia have promised to be there. The exhibition has been advertised in *El Pais* and all the art press. This is the highest-profile exhibition of new art in Madrid for years and, more than that, many families of victims have expressed their desire to attend."

Angelo shakes his head in anger. "I don't…"

"Shut up Angelo! I asked you to listen and I haven't yet finished." Her voice trembles. "This is by far, *by far*, the most interest any of your work has ever generated and, if you ask me, your future work will never generate this interest again. Your talent for painting was amplified by what happened to Maria, something in the anguish and hurt that you have been feeling has generated, well, has generated this." She waves her pink talons round the room. "And now it is the anniversary of that dreadful tragedy. Everyone is interested again, hearts are saddened, emotions are running high, it's time to remember! To remember all these people. And what better way to remember than by honouring the dead with these beautiful portraits!"

"I *have* honoured them!" he shouts, no longer able to stay silent. "I have honoured them, that is exactly what I've done. And putting a price on each of their heads does nothing more for them. It cheapens my work, it cheapens their lives. I will not sell a single painting."

She puts her hands on her hips.

"And so you will live in this chapel of death forever? Is that the plan? Is that what you want? Because I tell you, if you don't have this exhibition, your future as an artist is dead! It will be the end of you Angelo. No one will ever take you seriously again. But if you go ahead with this exhibition, you will be famous! You will be talked about, written about, your work will fetch huge prices, isn't that what you want? Isn't that what Maria always wanted? To see you succeed? To be a successful artist?"

"Leave Maria out of this," says Angelo. "She'd agree with me." Although his voice would suggest he is not completely sure of this.

"What? She'd want you to hole yourself up in this fleapit with 167 portraits of the people who died with her? You really think that's what she'd want?"

"I have no idea what she'd fucking want!" he shouts at Teresa. "I thought I knew her, but I have no idea what she fucking wanted."

Teresa marches over to where Maria stares out, and stands in front of her image.

"She wanted you to be happy Angelo. She loved you and wanted you to be happy. If she was here now she would be *begging* you to have this exhibition, to sell as many paintings as possible to the grieving families, to offer them a beautiful memory of the person they loved. She wouldn't want you to deny them that. She cared, she always cared about other people, don't you remember?" Teresa sees she is making some headway with this approach and is talking quickly with no gaps that he can pry open. "She'd hate to see you surrounded by these morbid images every day, she'd want the families of these people, these very special people, to share this art, to see these beautiful faces. Don't you think? Don't you think *mi tresor*?"

Angelo looks at Teresa, his eyes full of confusion. Maybe that is what Maria would have wanted, but he can't part with these paintings, his heart is too attached to them now.

"Don't you think that the lovers, fathers, mothers, children of these people should be able to see these final, timeless images of them? Don't you think they deserve that?"

Angelo bites his lip and sighs. "Yes they do." A victorious aura fills the space around Teresa. "But I'm not selling any of them."

15:13, Sunday May 25th, 2014
Hampstead Heath

Steph lies on the picnic blanket next to Tom and times her breathing with his gentle snore. She leans her head against his shoulder and he continues to snore. She turns so that her face touches his arm. His skin is hot from the sun and smells, deliciously, of sweat and sun cream. She loves his smell, loves his snore, loves him so much, but she knows that, when his slumber lifts, she will raise her face from his skin and the connection will be lost. This is the closest they have been in a long time. She smiles into his arm and hopes he will snooze all afternoon.

She could kick the dog that runs past barking madly at nothing. Tom coughs into life and Steph removes her face from his skin, missing its touch immediately.

"How long was I asleep for?" he asks with a yawn.

Not long enough, thinks Steph. "About twenty minutes," she says, staring up at the sky.

"Sorry."

"Don't be silly. I'm having a lovely time here, even with you asleep."

He laughs. "Maybe more so when I'm asleep?"

"No, not exactly. But it's nice to see you so relaxed Tom."

"It doesn't happen often," he says. "This is going to sound bad, but I'm already having a great weekend without the kids. It's so peaceful."

They both laugh. Tom rolls onto his side and props his head up with his hand. It's time to ask Steph. He thinks she'll agree, she's always so amenable, but there is a tiny doubt that seems to be resonating at the back of his head. But why would she say no?

"Steph, I wanted to ask you something."

She is looking at a fluffy cloud that is floating alone across the sky. She can't see any particular shape in it, but for some reason it seems a very happy, lonely cloud. She turns her head to Tom and is surprised by how close his face is.

"Sure, what?"

"Well, you remember the email I received from AirStar?"

"Yes. Of course."

"Well." The doubt at the back of his head seems to be more insistent now, trying to get his attention. He ignores it. "I've decided to go. I want to go to the site again, and I'd like to attend some of the events. It's important for me. This will sound stupid I know, but I want to go and talk to Beth."

"That's not stupid at all," says Steph, smiling sadly at him.

"So anyway, I wanted to ask you a favour. It will only be for a few days."

"Of course," says Steph, her smile growing. "Of course I will."

Tom knew that niggle of a doubt was misplaced. "You will?" he laughs. "But I haven't even asked you yet!"

"Yes, but I know what you're going to ask. And of course I'll come with you."

Tom's smile runs off after the barking dog. Oh. He really hadn't anticipated that response.

"That is what you were going to ask me isn't it? To go with you?"

He bites his lip. "Well, no." He can't find any sugar to sprinkle on his response.

She looks confused. "Then what did you want to ask me?"

He wishes he could backtrack now. He wishes he was still dozing, with the hot sun on his face and Steph's face against his arm. He takes a deep breath for strength.

"To look after the kids while I'm away."

A cloud passes across the sun, and her eyes darken.

"You want me to look after the kids?"

He nods.

"While you go to talk to Beth?" There is an edge of sarcasm in her voice.

"It's only for a few days Steph. I asked Veronica but she has a fundraising event that weekend and…"

"Oh, so I wasn't even first choice?" Steph sits up.

Tom can't say anything right and he has no idea what words might take them back five minutes.

"Well no. I didn't want to bother you, erm, you know, you've got your own life to lead, so I asked Veronica first, but she couldn't help, and so… I don't want to burden you."

Steph's pretty face is full of anger. "For fuck's sake Tom. Don't you understand? I want to be bothered by this family, I *want* to be part of this family." She stands up, and starts walking this way and that. Her white summer dress is crinkled and covered in grass but she doesn't notice.

"For fuck's sake Tom. Let me in. Let me in properly, let me into your family, not just as some second-rate babysitter you might just fuck one day."

"Steph!" Her name emerges from his mouth like his kids' names emerge when they have done something really naughty. But he's beginning to realize it is himself who has done something really naughty. He has been taking Steph for granted. He knows now that she loves him, he has known for a while now, but he has kept her at a safe distance. She is the sweet little kitten and he is dangling his love in front of her like a ball of wool, which he snatches away as soon as she gets close. The kitten is on the prowl, Steph is walking back and forth and, rather than calming down, she seems to be getting angrier. Her pace is quickening, her turns are sharper, and she is flexing and squeezing her hands into tight fists like she is preparing to do something with them. For a split second a thought flits through his head, is she going to hit me?

"Steph, please. I'm so sorry if I seem ungrateful. I don't see you as a babysitter at all."

Her head swings to face him. "Then what do you see me as?"

Tom is, once again, stumped for the right words. "I, I don't know," he falters.

Her eyes narrow and her face flushes. "Beth is dead Tom, and I'm more part of this family than she was for a long time. Can't you see that?" She grabs two chunks of her hair as though she wants to pull them out. "Fuck!" she screams. "She didn't even... she didn't even..." her voice dwindles into nothing.

"Didn't even what?" Tom stands now. "What were you going to say?"

She swallows. "When was the last time you and Beth made love? Before she died."

Tom is stumped. "I don't see what that has to do with anything. Why the hell are you asking that?" He is unnerved now, Steph obviously knows something, perhaps Beth talked to her.

"You know why they call it making love Tom?"

What the hell is she getting it? He looks at her open mouthed. She picks up her handbag and slings it over her shoulder.

"Because it's what two people do when they're in love." And with that she sets off down Parliament Hill, her elegant figure marching in an angry straight line.

20:22, Thursday July 10th, 2014
La Carcel gallery, Madrid

"I knew no one would come," says Angelo. "I don't know why I let you talk me into this, and into this ridiculous suit." He fiddles with his shirt collar, the top three buttons are undone, but he still feels as though he's wearing a straitjacket.

Teresa smiles at him. She is radiant with jewels and excitement. "Don't worry *mi tresor*, this room will be full."

Angelo looks around. He doubts it. His exhibition fills three floors of this converted jail building and at the moment, other than the catering staff, only three people have arrived: the artist, the agent and the curator. It is hardly the full house Teresa predicted, not that he wants a full-house, that would mean meeting people, small talk, and pretending he is happy with the event. He takes a deep breath and heads to the door, motioning to Teresa that he needs a cigarette.

Outside he takes a walk. As he chain-smokes four cigarettes, he ambles past the Reina Sofia, the Prado, MAPFRE, and the Thyssen, all advertising their dead man's art on billboards bigger than Angelo's studio. Perhaps Angelo will gain some recognition when he dies? That's not such a bad thing, he would be in good company. He starts listing all the artists he knows that led humble lives, only to make millions when dead, El Greco, Van Gogh, Vermeer, Gauguin. By the time he gets back to the gallery, he has counted 23 artists who only made an impact on the art world when dead. The numbers are reassuring. He knows he is a good artist, even if no one else does, he can wait for recognition, he's happy to die first. What would he do with a heap of money anyway?

As he climbs the steps to the gallery he hears a gentle murmur. At first he thinks it must be coming from the building next door but, as he opens the double door of the building, the murmur erupts into a fusion of voices. He stops, startled by the noise and not sure what to do about it. He stands to the side to let a smartly dressed couple past. He loiters in the entrance hall, and three more people pass him by. One of them, a short man with long hair and thick glasses, says to his partner, "I've never heard of him before but supposedly his work is very unique." Angelo stares after them as they round the corner. He bites his lip, nervous that they will be disappointed. Just then, Teresa emerges from the room.

"There you are Angelo. For goodness sake, what are you doing out here? Everyone is looking for you!" She grabs him by the arm and drags him into the gallery. As soon as they enter the room, her claw-like grip loosens and she threads her arm through his. The gallery is full, so much so that Angelo can't even see his paintings that cover the walls. Twenty minutes ago the room was full of painted people but now real, talking, walking people fill the gallery.

"The artist has arrived!" shouts Teresa.

Everyone turns to see Angelo and, before his eyes take up residence on the floor, he can't help but notice a look of approval on the faces of those in the gallery. Maybe he won't have to die first?

*

"It is an audacious, some might say arrogant, move to have made," says the woman whose name Angelo has forgotten. "But I think it's the right thing to do, it's a statement of belief in your own talent. At such an early stage in your career, exhibiting without selling is as much an exhibition of your talent as it is of your conviction."

Inside, Angelo is rolling his eyes and swearing, but outwardly he smiles and tries to look engaged. Teresa made him promise to be polite to everyone he meets tonight. "You don't know who you might end up insulting my dear, a future buyer, an art critic or, worse still, a journalist. And please, please," she had begged, "try not to punch Pedrosa this time." Angelo eyes the little bespectacled man who is keeping a safe distance at the far end of the gallery. He tries not to think about their last encounter.

"You must be very confident in your future success," states the woman. He looks past her frizzy hair, scattered with plastic butterflies, and tries to find someone to save him, but only unknown eyes meet his, and they all look keen to talk to him.

He sighs. "Sorry, what did you say you did again?" He's keen to move the conversation away from him and his assured future success, of which he has no idea.

"I'm a journalist."

Shit, thinks Angelo, she's going to write about this dire conversation.

"Who do you write for?"

"*Vamos Madrid.*"

"Oh really?" His eyes widen. Now he actually is interested in her. "I'm sorry, what was your name again? I've met so many people tonight that I can't keep track."

She smiles, but not in a very sincere way. "Maria. Maria Fernandez."

At first Angelo laughs, a nervous chuckle as though he doesn't know what to make of this bad-taste joke, but then he looks at her in all seriousness, and she sees nothing amusing in her own name.

07:56, Friday July 11th, 2014
7 The Stables, South Kensington, London

"So, you guys are going to be good for Auntie Steph right?" says Tom. He is kneeling in the hallway, his two children in front of him and his small suitcase to his side. Steph stands behind Miles and Katy, a hand on each of their shoulders, as though they need the support.

"Daddy," says Miles. "The plane you are flying in… it's a good plane isn't it? There's nothing wrong with it is there?"

Tom strokes Miles' flyaway hair, trying to smooth it into some kind of order. He did the same thing with his own earlier that morning,

"Buddy. Don't you worry. I'm being flown to Spain in the best and safest plane in the sky."

"Aren't all planes supposed to be safe daddy?" asks Katy.

"Yes, they are," says Steph. "But there is also an extra-safe plane, and that's the one your daddy's taking."

Tom smiles at Steph and she offers him a smaller version in return.

"I'll phone you guys from the airport when I arrive," he says. "You'll be back from swimming by then. And I'll be seeing you very soon."

He opens his arms and both his children cling to him, like little monkeys.

"Daddy, I have something for mummy's tree," whispers Katy. She slips something small into his jeans pocket.

Tom kisses both of them, and stands to leave.

"Remember Steph, you can call me whenever you need to." He kisses her on the cheek, a dainty little touch that is just more than a breath.

"I'm sure I won't need to," she says. He picks up his suitcase and looks at her, a little bashful. "But I might want to." She smiles at him and he is happy to be leaving with that expression. He walks out the door with suitcase in hand and her pretty smile in his head.

21:52, Friday July 11th, 2014
Hotel Accordia, Madrid

He would never admit it to Teresa, because he is still hell bent on hating the idea of this exhibition, but it has been a great distraction for him. The mind can be a sharp inward weapon when it has time to think, and the anniversary of Maria's death would have been a dangerous time for Angelo, alone with his mind and his death shrine. Still, there is no forgetting that a year ago today he and the world had Maria, and a year ago tomorrow she was gone. Xavier has taken the bus from Barcelona to join Angelo in his anonymous beige hotel room. He is giving some life to the beige space and helping his friend forget what tomorrow brings. If Xavier can get his friend drunk enough, the next day will float past in the mist of a hangover, like a mammoth ship sneaking past unnoticed in the fog.

"Man, you must be seriously over the moon with the exhibition opening. The sign of news that is newsworthy is if it makes it to Monserrat's, and this morning when I ordered my *espresso* before heading to the bus station, miserable Monserrat herself was telling a customer about the exhibition while her grandson stuck up your poster. 'Dead people,' she says, 'what is the world coming to when people queue to see pictures of dead people.' Then, with every coffee she served, she shook her head and repeated 'Dead people, *deu meu*, dead people.'"

Angelo laughs and moves further up the double bed to make space for Xavier. They are surrounded by roll-up papers, empty mini-bar miniatures, and the remnants of take-out pizza. Angelo feels a little more at home now he is surrounded by disorder.

"And the press! They've gone *loco* for it man, I've been online this morning and you've been rated five stars in every review, except for one dumb *bagassa* called Maria who writes for *Vamos Madrid*, she gave you two stars and claimed your art was…" He squints to remember her words, "vulgar and base."

Angelo considers telling his friend about the journalist he met last night, the journalist Maria claimed to be, but Xavier is on a happy roll.

"Listen to this, listen to this," he says, scrolling through something on his smart phone. "OK, here we are. Vidal Figueras, art correspondent for *Hola Barcelona* says 'The art of Catalan newcomer Angelo Octavez is no less than a marvel.' Blah, blah, blah," Xavier scans the article with his eyes and finger. "Here we are, 'Octavez thrusts his 167 portraits on us with no mercy for our sensibilities or fears around death, and he makes these fears irrational in the light of the beauty he has brought to life. These are pictures of the victims we could all have been, and all will be one day, I only wish to be remembered in such a beautiful way as has been afforded the victims of AS636. Do not miss your chance to see the debut exhibition of an artist who promises to be our newest Catalan master.'"

Angelo drinks the Champagne that Xavier bought from the bottle shop across the road. He drinks it straight from the bottle. He dislikes Champagne, but its bubbles of excessive gas combine well with the words Xavier is reading.

"And here's another," says Xavier, animated. "This one's from *El Pais*. Man, you've gone national! Five Stars. 'In just one year, Angelo Octavez has taken his own loss and converted it into the most precious and original of collections. A tribute to those departed that will stay in your mind long after you leave the gallery. A rough yet delicate style with amazing use of space and light that would not seem out of place next to Goya and Velasquez in the Prado. Could Octavez be our newest national treasure?' National treasure! Bollocks!" exclaims Xavier. "You're a Catalan treasure, and I always knew it, that's why I'm still friends with you." He winks at Angelo. "I knew you'd strike gold if you kept digging."

Angelo shakes his head. "No gold for me. Remember, they're not for sale."

Xavier sighs. "And that tactic is making them even more desirable. Come on man, you've got to at least consider the option of selling. What the hell are you going to do with 167 portraits?"

"Redecorate the apartment," he says with a smile. "Just the way it was." He is already missing the company of his portraits, and Maria's eyes, despite the fact they only lied and deceived him in real life. His head drops as he remembers all the questions about Maria that will remain unanswered, and the life together that will remain unfulfilled.

"Well, to sell or not to sell. You're still going to make a fortune from exhibiting," says Xavier.

Angelo shrugs, "50% goes to charity, that was the deal with the sponsors, at least 20% on costs and 10% to Teresa. Doesn't leave much."

Xavier frowns. He can't believe that, with all the publicity surrounding the artist in front of him, he is going to return to the struggles in his studio surrounded by his dead pictures. It seems he would still rather wallow in death than relish in life.

Xavier picks up a glass from the floor, downs the remaining vodka in it and holds it out to Angelo who fills it with Champagne. The fizz overflows onto the beige carpet, but neither man notices, or cares.

"A toast," says Xavier. "To fame and…" he hesitates, "misfortune."

Angelo lifts the Champagne bottle to Xavier's glass. "Fame and misfortune," he says, before downing the rest of the bottle.

19:37, Saturday July 12th, 2014
Garden of Remembrance, Madrid

Tom decided to miss the ceremony. He isn't really interested in systemized grieving, and he isn't Catholic so group prayers just feel like standing around at a party he wants to get out of, trying to participate in conversations he knows nothing about. But he does want to honour the date and Beth's memory, so he heads for the memorial garden at a time when he hopes that all the grievers will have left. His rental car meets a few others going in the opposite direction along the dusty field lane and they pull in, or reverse for each other, exchanging solemn nods.

At the field, which is still field rather than forest, only a few stragglers are left behind. They stand like dark shadows next to their respective trees. Every tree seems to be rooted in a mound of fresh flowers.

From the car Tom walks past the poles and slats of a stage half dismantled. No workmen remain. They must be returning tomorrow. He remembers roughly where they planted Beth's tree and heads in that direction, but soon finds himself lost among spindly trees and floral tributes. He scans the landscape, trying to find the yellow field with a ruined hut that he remembers seeing from Beth's spot, but all of the surrounding fields are yellow and they all seem to be scattered with ruined huts. He's in no hurry, so wanders the avenues of young trees reading the names of the dead. He hasn't thought much about all the other lives lost a year ago, the loss of Beth was consuming enough. But now, as he ambles past all these new lives, these young shoots, each marking an individual death, he begins to think about them too. About Pedro, Sandra and Miguel, about Stuart, Heather and Denise. Names and trees, they hardly seem enough to honour the entire life of one person, but that's what is left. Some people don't even get that.

He comes across Beth's tree in a corner of the sprouting forest. It hasn't grown as much as he thought it would, it only stands about seven feet tall, but its trunk has widened visibly. He holds the trunk in his hand, like a shepherd with his trusty staff. The trunk is warm from the day's sun and strangely, if he closes his eyes, it feels like the warmth of skin. He likes that idea and sits on the grass with his eyes closed, holding the tree.

"Hey Beth," he says to the warmth beneath his fingers. He wants to ask how she's doing, but realizes that's a stupid thing to say. "It's a nice spot here, to be remembered. You always loved the sun didn't you? Well now you can have it all day long. Not like back home." He glances over at the eternal flame that is burning beneath a metal pagoda in the centre of the field. He knows that Beth's actual ashes are somewhere beneath the fire with Denise, Sandra, Miguel and all the others.

"Oh, Katy asked me to bring you this." Tom pulls a tiny doll out of his pocket and dangles it between himself and the tree. "She made it for the Christmas tree but she says she wants it here instead." He holds it up in the fading light. "She made a ballerina, it's really good actually, if you look carefully you can see she has long brown hair like Katy and is wearing a pink tutu and matching slippers. You should have seen Katy dance at her last show sweetheart, she was fantastic! The best dancer in her age group by a long way. I was so proud." He takes a deep breath. "You'd have been so proud." He swallows down some tears and distracts himself by tying the little doll to one of the highest branches. The doll sways gently in the breeze. "Now, you can watch Katy dancing all day," he says.

Tom takes his eyes away from the doll and looks around him at all the other saplings, framed by flowers.

"Shit," he says. "Shit. I forgot flowers." He shakes his head, berating himself for forgetting such a simple thing. He could come back tomorrow with some, or maybe… He looks around the field. He is the only living person there now. He thinks it over, and he thinks it would be OK.

He stands and walks to Heather's tree. She was clearly very popular and won't miss a single stem. He takes a white rose from the bunch and moves on to Denise, where he plucks a bright orange gerbera. He moves from tree to tree, collecting flowers until both hands are full. He then takes them back to Beth's tree and arranges them around the base. But he needs more, and now that he has stolen a memorial token from twenty or thirty of her grave mates, he feels he should do the same for everyone.

An hour and a half later and Maria's tree is surrounded by flowers of every kind and colour. As Tom made his procession around the trees he found others that were bare and couldn't stand to walk past them, so did some further flower arranging to ensure that everyone was remembered with flowers today.

Now he sits a further distance from the tree, due to all the flowers, and holds the warm trunk once again.

"So sweetheart. Now you have flowers." He laughs to himself, and then looks at the heap of muddled flowers and laughs louder. These are not the actions of a stable family man in his mid-thirties. Suddenly he realizes this is the type of thing he would have done at twenty, when he was broke and Beth first fell in love with him. He was reckless, and creative, and didn't really think about the world around him and how it might react to his actions. And then, right there, holding onto a warm branch that seems to symbolize the life he has lost, he wants to sing. He wants to sing *Love Light* to the woman who inspired it. But he can't remember the words and he can't remember that woman. He can't remember the woman whose eyes shone with love and passion for him. And instead of singing he cries.

17:23, Sunday July 13th, 2014
Madrid

Tom is not impressed by the matinee performance of *Out of the Blue*. He has never been a fan of contemporary dance and this performance has reminded him why. In the interval he creeps out. His smartphone tells him that the portrait exhibition is not far away and so he walks about twenty minutes, passes the *Porta del Sol*, stops for a fantastic coffee in a shitty café, and then finds the building. It is an old jailhouse with a tiled mosaic of San Isidro above the double doors, and heavy iron gratings over the windows. It is a very quiet, unassuming building for an exhibition and he wonders whether he has the right address. He climbs the stairs and finds the door ajar, he pushes it open, walks two paces and stops dead in the threshold, as though he has walked into a pane of glass.

His mouth is open, his eyes are wide, and his heart is racing. At the end of the short corridor, mounted on the wall, sits a portrait of Beth. A portrait so vivid that Tom feels he is face to face with the wife he lost. The portrait is not lifelike in the way a photograph might be, but it is lifelike in the way it has captured all the rich life from Beth, and swept it across a canvas. And it is not the Beth who died; it is the Beth who lived. It is the Beth of fifteen years ago, and her eyes are shining at Tom, they are shining with love and passion.

"It's beautiful isn't it?" says a female voice.

Tom's eyes don't budge from Beth's.

"It's the artist's girlfriend. She died in the plane crash."

And with these words, Tom's eyes depart the painting and see the dreadlocked girl who can't be much more than twenty.

He shakes his head. "No, that's my wife, Beth. She died in the crash."

Now the dreadlocked girl shakes her head at him. "No sir. Believe me, your wife's painting will be inside." She gestures to the doors she just emerged from. "This is Angelo Octavez's girlfriend. She was the inspiration for this whole collection."

21:54, Sunday July 13th, 2014
Room 515, The Sheraton, Madrid

Tom paces back and forth in his room. It's a tiny room and he is a tall man, so he does more turning than he does pacing. He's still trying to piece together what happened that afternoon. The painting is undoubtedly Beth, but the girl, and indeed the curator of the exhibition, insisted it is was someone else entirely. He sits down on the edge of his bed and shakes his head. What the fuck do they know? They must have confused the paintings. Yes, that makes sense. But still, a little atom of doubt is vibrating at the back of his head and it won't rest. These atoms of doubt keep pestering him. He picks up his phone and dials Steph.

She answers after less than one ring. "Hey Tom! How are you? How was it?"

It sounds as though she has been longing for his call.

"Hey Steph." Among all the foreign sights and sounds, it's nice to hear her familiar voice. "How's everything there?" As soon as he asks this question, he realizes how much he wants to be there to see for himself.

"Fine, great. We had a lovely day just playing in the garden. We got the paddling pool out."

"I thought it was covered in punctures," says Tom.

"It was. And now the kids know how to find and fix punctures."

Tom laughs. Steph has always been so practical, maybe it comes from having no other choice. Without a father or husband in her life, she's learnt how to deal with lots of things that other women would simply pass to the men in their lives.

"And how was your day? Did you get to many of the events?"

He pauses. Now he wonders whether what he is about to say is going to sound ridiculous. "Actually, it was kind of strange."

"How so?"

He takes a deep breath. "Well, I went to the portrait exhibition, and, I, erm." He takes a deep breath. "I saw Beth."

Steph laughs. "Tom, you sound surprised! Weren't you expecting to see her picture? It's an exhibition of everyone from the flight."

"Yes, I know. But this painting was amazing, truly amazing. It was as though the artist knew Beth, and captured a moment from years ago, decades maybe. And the strange thing was that the curator told me the portrait of Beth was of someone else, the artist's girlfriend."

Tom is calling from Spain, thousands of miles separate him from Steph and the line is not great, but Tom can still hear a gasp. It is not a gasp of complete surprise, it is a gasp of guilt, the noise you emit when you've been found out, when someone is onto you, knows your secret. It is the kind of gasp that accompanies your brain working as quickly as it can to come up with something to say, something reasonable, believable, something that will keep your secret concealed.

"Steph?"

"Sorry Tom, I didn't quite catch that last sentence, it's a bad phone line. What did you say?"

Tom's heart is beating so fast, he is sure Steph can hear it.

"You heard me Steph. Tell me what you know."

09:45, Monday July 14th, 2014
La Carcel gallery, Madrid

Teresa has no idea why she has been summoned to the gallery, especially at such an ungodly hour in the morning, but the voicemail from Sandra sounded urgent. Perhaps Angelo had turned up in a fit of rage to take back the pictures he never wanted to exhibit in the first place. That ungrateful bastard, couldn't he see she was doing all this in his best interests? He had never produced work to this standard before. This was his one big chance. She wondered why she even bothered with him, he wasn't worth the hassle. She could find another artist, an artist who might even be willing to sell a few paintings now and again. Fancy that! By the time she has jostled her Mercedes through the traffic of Madrid, and arrives at the gallery, she is wound up as tight as the Chanel belt around her waist, and is ready to shout at someone, anyone.

The door of the gallery slams against the wall as she thrusts it open, and her Prada heels have enough momentum for her to walk through the opposite wall, but they slow down when she realizes neither of the two people standing in front of Maria's painting is the artist himself. One is Sandra, wearing a dreadful purple ensemble and a pair of pink pumps, will that woman ever learn? The other is a strapping man with blonde curls and piercing blue eyes. He is dressed in a smart shirt, with dark jeans and deck shoes. Her anger immediately dissipates, to be replaced by charm.

"Hello my dear," she says to Sandra, kissing her on both over-rouged cheeks. "You look lovely as ever."

"Morning Teresa," says Sandra, in English. "I'd like to introduce you to Tom. He's from London. How's your English?"

Teresa's face crumples into a sweet smile, she loves a British gentleman. "My English is super, okey dokey in fact." She giggles, but alone. "It is lovely to meet you Tom." She waits for a kiss but instead gets a firm handshake.

"Tom is interested in this painting," says Sandra in English, then in Spanish she whispers. "I told him it's not for sale, but I think he might pay a great deal for it."

A phone rings somewhere and Sandra wanders off to answer it.

"Can you tell me about this painting?" asks Tom. His blue eyes are very bright in the gallery lights and Teresa has trouble focusing on his words.

"Sorry?"

"Can you tell me about the painting?"

"Yes, yes of course. But there's not much to tell. This is the artist's girlfriend. They were very much in love, very happy together, but she was on the AS636, and since then Angelo has dedicated himself and his painting to her memory and the other victims of the crash."

"Did you meet her?"

"Yes, I did. And this is a fantastic likeness, really, it's uncanny. The sparkle in her eyes is captured perfectly. Maria was a very beautiful woman."

Tom nods his head, looking at Maria rather than Teresa. "She was." A few moments pass before Tom speaks again. "The relationship between the artist and this woman? It had been going on a while?"

Teresa has no idea why this man is so interested in Angelo's love life, but she can't refuse his eyes. She can see straight through them.

"Not a huge amount of time, six months or so. But it was very intense and they were very happy together. She lived and worked here in Madrid but spent about half her time with Angelo in Barcelona."

"And the artist. What's he like?"

Teresa takes a deep breath and raises her eyebrows. "Well, what can I tell you? He's a true artist; stubborn, passionate, somewhat alcoholic, but as you can see, very talented."

Tom's heart is heavy, but at the same time strangely quiet, as though it has found some peace in what this woman is saying. The artist's girlfriend was deeply in love with him, they were happy together. Before she died, this woman in the painting, was happy.

"How much?" he asks.

Teresa cocks her head to the side and shakes it. "I'm sorry dear. It's not for sale. He is very passionate about this portrait."

"So am I," says Tom and his eyes lock on hers.

10:32, Tuesday July 15th, 2014
Hotel Accordia, Madrid

"No fucking way Teresa," he shouts down the phone. "Why the fuck are you even asking me that? What the hell goes through that head of yours. Don't you ever fucking listen to me?"

He kicks the sofa with his foot, some of its wooden frame has started to splinter, probably from too many suitcases knocking past it. He likes the feeling of the wood giving way, at least he has some control over this cheap piece of wood, even if he has no control over anything else, least of all his own agent.

"I told him no, of course I did *mi tresor*, but he insisted I ask you."

"Well you can tell him to fuck off. I'm not selling. Not for any price."

"You know Angelo, I believe this man is very wealthy and…"

"I'm not selling it." He has a sudden panic about the picture, he sees an image of his apartment, bare with no traces of Maria. He sees Teresa selling the picture without his approval, or this unknown man stealing it.

"In fact, in fact, I'm going to go and get it. I want it back."

"But Angelo! Don't be so silly. The exhibition is scheduled for another four weeks, you can't take it back."

"Yes I can." He slams down the phone and leaves the room. He knows Teresa will be on her way to the gallery and for once he's pleased with the central location of his crumbling hotel. He walks the six streets to the gallery quickly, sidestepping tourists and jumping on and off the kerb. The capital always makes him need a cigarette but he doesn't even stop to light up. He throws open the door of the gallery and, instead of being greeted by Maria, the first thing he sees is the back of a man. He stands close to the picture and has a nest of blonde curls. His shirt is neatly tucked into dark jeans and his brown belt matches his shoes. Other than his wayward hair, he looks well maintained, probably dressed by his wife.

Angelo walks around the man and lifts the painting from its hook. He wants no interruptions, he just wants to leave quietly with Maria, but the other man grabs him by the shoulder and says something in English. Angelo looks into the strangers' blue eyes. They are exactly the same height as his own and they are full of distress. He probably thinks Angelo is stealing the picture.

"It's mine. It's my painting," he shouts in Catalan. "I'm Angelo Octavez." He points at himself and then to the name that is emblazoned in red against the side wall. He shifts the frame to a comfortable position under his arm and heads for the door, but the blonde man races around him and stands in front of the exit.

Tom looks at the man and he knows, he knows that he is face to face with the man his wife was in love with, the man who made Beth's eyes shine like they once had for him. This man made Beth happy when Tom had lost the ability, or perhaps the desire to. He doesn't know whether to thank him or punch him. The man looks like he is more accustomed to punches than thanks. His long hair falls either side of his deep dark eyes and makes his face look gaunt and long. His face is fatigued and the lines etched into his forehead suggest more frowns than smiles. A grey shirt hangs from broad shoulders and seems to merge with equally baggy trousers of no particular colour. He looks disheveled and chaotic, and, other than their equal height, couldn't appear more different from Tom.

"I want the picture," says Tom slowly, his eyes not moving from Angelo's gaze.

Angelo shakes his head. He has no idea what this man is saying, and is about to push him out the way when the door behind opens and Teresa emerges. She is out of breath and out of make-up, two states Angelo has never seen her in before.

"Oh, Tom, hello my dear." She flushes slightly. "I see you have met Angelo." She tries to regain her composure and runs a hand through her hair.

"Not really," says Tom.

"Oh, well. Please allow me." She takes a few breaths and introduces the artist to the interested buyer, in English and Spanish. Neither of them smiles as they shake hands.

"Please translate for me," says Tom in a voice that has more demand than request about it. "I want to buy this picture. Ask him how much he wants."

Angelo remains expressionless. "It's not for sale."

"Tell him I'll pay any price."

"It's not for sale."

Angelo heads for the door one more time, but this time it is himself that delays his exit. He turns around slowly and looks at Tom through narrowed eyes. "Why do you want it?" he asks.

Tom sees two slivers of suspicion in Angelo's face. Does he have any idea who Tom might be? Does Angelo know that his girlfriend was two-timing him with a husband and kids? Tom's heart beats faster. Should he preserve this man's memories of Maria, whatever they are, or should he tell him the truth? They stare at each other for a few more moments.

"It reminds me of someone I used to know. A long time ago."

Angelo nods slowly. "Someone that you loved?"

"Yes. Very much."

"Then you will understand why this is not for sale," says Angelo. He walks out the door. Tom shouts after him, "Everyone has a price!" But Angelo doesn't understand and keeps walking the six streets back to his hotel. There, he locks and chains the door and props Maria up against the sofa. The mini-bar has been restocked and he drinks four miniature bottles of wine; two red and two white, and six miniature bottles of spirits; two vodka, two whiskey and two gin. That night he sleeps soundly for the first time in four nights. It has nothing to do with all the alcohol he consumed, and everything to do with the lady he consumed it with. Maria watches him sleeping.

21:34, Tuesday July 15th, 2014
7 The Stables, South Kensington, London

"Tell me everything Steph. And I mean *everything*. No more lies."

Steph looks a mess. They are sitting at the dining table across from each other under the harsh light of the pendant lamp, the scene is set for honesty. She wears no make-up, her face is grey with worry and her eyes are red.

"I'm so sorry Tom, I'm so sorry. She was working things out in her head, and I'm sure she'd have come to the right decision, I'm sure of it."

"Don't tell me what you're sure of. Tell me what you know. Now."

Steph rubs her hand across her face in a gesture of complete exhaustion.

"I always thought Beth wasn't right after Jim died. It was strange but she really closed herself off to me. She had never done that before. And she stayed that way. I thought it was grief, that she would get over it in time." Steph bites her thumbnail. "But the truth was, rather than her getting back to her old self, I got used to the new Beth, and with time I pretty much forgot how light and cheery she had once been."

Steph sighs and takes a long swig of wine. She can't look at Tom. "About two months before she died, I had a work event to go to. I bought a new dress but didn't have any jewellery to match it, so Beth suggested I borrow something." Steph lifts her eyes from the table. The scene is one of interrogation. "She was downstairs choosing a wine and she told me to look through her jewellery box and take whatever I liked. I found a necklace and earrings that matched perfectly, but at the same time I found this strange silver necklace." She pauses. "Actually I don't even think it was silver. It was just this basic little metal thing with a pendant M, the letter M. I didn't think much of it, I assumed it was an M for Miles, but I asked her anyway when I went downstairs. The look on her face when I asked about it was complete shock, like I had just found a dead body upstairs." Steph hesitates, and takes a deep breath. "She stammered and stuttered and had nothing to say. Then she looked me in the eye, and said 'Maria'. Then she burst into tears. And that's when she told me." Steph pauses. "That she was Maria."

"Why? I don't understand, why on earth did she invent this new person?"

"Because she wasn't happy with the one she had become." Steph's eyes fall to the table. "And she fell in love with someone else because, well because she didn't like the man you'd become."

"What? What does that mean?" asks Tom. "I was the same man she met fifteen years ago." But even as the words emerge he knows they aren't true and he walks round the table to try and get away from them.

"Tom," says Steph quietly. "She fell in love with you because you were different from any man she'd ever met. Beth grew up in a world ruled by expectancy, she was expected to say the right things at the right times, wear the right things, do the right things. Everything in her world was about creating the perfect perception, and then she met you."

Tom sits down, a heaviness has settled on him. He looks up at Steph and she gives a gentle smile.

"You didn't care about perceptions or possessions, you grew up without expectation and you were true to yourself and what you loved.

You loved music and you didn't care how you lived, as long as you had music."

"But then I started to care," says Tom. "When I met Beth, and saw her family and lifestyle, I started to care."

Steph takes his hand that rests on the table. "But she never wanted you to. You turned into all the other men she had encountered in her life."

Tom shakes his head. "But it was the only way to keep her, the only way to have her as my wife, and I thought she wanted all this."

He looks around his open plan living area and a little ball of anger gains energy inside him. He wants to spit it out and send it ricocheting round the room, destroying all the stupid souvenirs of their fake life together, the Rene Herbst armchair, the Liberty lighting, the reclaimed fireplace that ended up costing more than any modern alternative.

He releases his hand from Steph's and beats the table with his fist.

"Fuck!" He beats his hand again. "Fuck!" he shouts. He wants to beat the table so hard that it splinters, but he and Beth spent thousands on this thick walnut and it's not going anywhere. He stands and reaches for the Lalique vase he and Beth bought from a Parisian antique fayre. It is full of white lilies, which he has bought every week for longer than he remembers. When did Tom become the kind of man who buys white lilies every week? He stares into the yellow stamens of the lilies, trying to find an answer. The vase flies at the fireplace, smashes like a firework and lands in a modern art arrangement of water, leaves, petals and glass crystals.

He looks for his next victim but something is restricting him like a straitjacket. He pushes Steph away with a force that puts her on the floor. He picks up the plates from dinner that sit neatly piled above the dishwasher. He hurls them like Frisbees in no particular direction and they smash loudly into the French doors. Amazingly one of the plates doesn't break. This frustrates him beyond belief and he heads towards it, ready to pummel it, crush it, bite it, anything to get it into pieces. But Steph jumps in front of him.

"The kids! The kids!" she shouts. She grabs him by the arms. "You'll scare them Tom." She lifts her eyes to indicate upstairs. "You'll scare them."

Tom stands confused. For a moment he is split behind 20-year-old Tom and 35-year-old Tom, he is split between showing his feelings and hiding them, between screaming obscenities and imprisoning his words. He is confused, which Tom is he?

"Tom sweetheart," says Steph looking into his confusion. "You're being true to your feelings, you're angry and you're showing that. But you have to remember, Katy and Miles are asleep upstairs."

Of course he's not young and erratic anymore, he's a responsible father of two. He sighs, and once again feels the heaviness of everything that has fallen on him this last year. He takes Steph by the hand and leads her to the sofa.

"Sorry. I'm so sorry. What happened? More." Tom's ability to put words together has left him, he feels empty and weak. "More."

Steph strokes Tom's hand as she speaks.

"Jim talked to Beth last, out of everyone in the family, he spoke his last words to her, and she said it was the most honest thing he'd ever said to her."

Tom nods. "What?"

"He told her to be true to herself. He said he was never true to himself, was always trying to be something he wasn't and now it was too late for him. He told her to be true to whatever makes her genuinely happy."

"I didn't make her genuinely happy?"

"You did, really you did, but after Jim died she started reassessing everything, I mean *everything*. Started looking backwards, analyzing her life. She was down, really down on herself. The first thing to go was her career."

"Why, I thought she loved advertising?"

"She decided it was false and manipulative. Her first love was art, but she forgot about it all when Jim fixed her up with that first job at *Broad and Devaney*. From then, she got further and further away from her love of art."

Tom swallows. "Was art the reason she fell for the artist?"

"Not entirely," says Steph. "I think it helped. But mostly she was just trying to find someone genuine."

"Like I once was?" asks Tom.

She squeezes his hand. "Tom, I know that everything you've ever done has been for Beth. I can see that, but she couldn't. Jim's death messed with her thinking and she started this search for truth, and she thought she'd found it in Spain."

Tom takes a few deep breaths. "Was she coming back to me?"

Steph frowns. She could lie, but she's pretty sure he would see through it.

"I really don't know. She wouldn't talk to me. She avoided being alone with me. She knew how I felt about you guys. You're the family I lost, the perfect happy unit, and I didn't want anything to destroy that. I was so fucking angry when she told me, but at the same time I wanted to help her, help her get back to you. Grief does crazy things to people. I was planning how I could get her to see sense, how I could help her. And then, she was gone."

Tom's head is still brimful with questions. As soon as Steph answers one, another steps forward from the queue behind, impatient to be served. He scratches his curls. They have grown long in the last few months but he hasn't noticed.

"How? How did this happen?"

How Maria began

Autumn 2012
El Infinito, Madrid

Maria loved watching people. She loved to see how one person interacts with another, how smiles radiate from one person to the next, how rich people stiffen at the approach of the poor, how adult eyes are averted from the sight of the unfortunate whilst child eyes stare at everything without fear of reproach. She had found a perfect spot for watching all the life forms supported by the city. El Infinito offered a bohemian and dusty space inside and a sheltered yet sunny terrace outside. It sat on the corner of Calle San Isabel and the Plaza de la Reina, and may once have been grand enough to live up to its address. The *café con leche* was smooth and sweet, the red walls were lined with shelves of tattered books interspersed with unknown artists' work, and the double doors were devoted to flyers, cards and posters telling everyone what everyone else was up to.

The café was where she christened herself, where she became Maria out loud. Beth had spent many hours there, gazing out the window and trying to puzzle her way through what she should be doing with her father's last words. The dust and disarray of El Infinito were so far from the polish and pretence of her life in London that it was easier to forget herself there. Work and Angie, campaigns and conference calls, emails and etiquette, were all fast becoming a distant memory. They were things that belonged to another woman in another life. The other things that belonged to that other woman in that other life were much harder to dissociate from, but on her fifth trip to Madrid when orange leaves were falling from the trees on Calle San Isabelle, she was able to shed her own dead leaves and make way for a new life.

11:48, Wednesday October 3rd, 2012
El Infinito, Madrid

"Which is your favourite?" she asked the scruffy boy behind the counter, nodding to his dog-eared book as he fumbled with the coffee machine.

"Huh?" he said, looking at Beth through his smudged glasses.

"Which story? Of Chekhov's." She clarified.

His eyes lit up, an excitement visible even through his grubby lenses. He left the coffee machine languishing and came to face Beth. He was the world's slowest barista.

"You like Chekhov?" he asked, eyes wide.

She nodded. "Especially *The lady with the little dog*. I'm a sucker for a forbidden love story."

"I prefer those with an emphasis on disillusionment and failed ideals."

"Well, there are plenty of those!"

They discussed literature for a few minutes before he paused and cocked his head, squinting at her through the steam of the coffee machine.

"You originally from Madrid?" he asked.

Beth laughed. She knew her accent was pretty close to that of a *madrileña*, having been raised more closely by Lolli than by her Columbian mother, but it was ridiculous to think it was close enough for her to be mistaken as one. Or was it? The steam that separated her from the boy's enquiry made it somehow easier to attempt the lie. A veil of haze that made it easier to step into.

"Yes," she replied. "Well just outside Madrid."

He nodded, needing no further explanation.

He came out from behind the coffee machine and presented Beth with her *café con leche*. Her heart was racing at the lie she had just told and the possibilities that were beginning to take shape in her head.

"I'm Carlos," the boy said.

Now was the time to find a name. She smiled and cast her eyes down momentarily at her own book. Mary Shelley's Frankenstein.

"I'm Mar-ia," she said.

"Well it's good to meet someone who doesn't just come in to read flyers," he said, gesturing with his head to a straggle of students studying the cards and notices by the door.

"I love reading," she said.

He nodded again. "Escapism."

And as if remembering how much he himself loved reading, he perched back on his high chair and lifted his book, indicating the conversation was over.

Beth reached for her purse.

"That one's on the house Maria," said Carlos, not lifting his specs from his disillusionment and failed ideals.

She smiled to no one and took her coffee and book to her favourite spot in the window. She watched the orange and red leaves drifting down before performing their jolly dance along the pavement. She read a few chapters of Frankenstein and became swept up in the new life created.

*

She visited the café as often as possible when she was in Madrid, it was the only place in the entire world that she was officially Maria. However, as the weeks passed the persona grew confidence outside of El Infinito and there was less Beth and more Maria in the woman who ambled around the city and its galleries. She had always dressed more casually when in Madrid but, once her character had been given a name, she took great care to dress her. Maria was bohemian and carefree. She wore her hair long and flowing or tied in a loose plait over one shoulder. She never wore heels or make-up. Maria, like other Spaniards, covered herself in colour and pattern. Maria's fingers were covered in rings, her wrists in leather bangles, her feet in tatty boots and her toes in chipped paint. Maria loved walking without destination, she loved ambling around Parque del Retiro, spending time with each of its magnificent sculptures, she loved drinking acidic wine alone in dark bars, eating oily tapas in grotty cafes, smiling as life happened around and within her. Maria, Maria, Maria, she loved being this woman. It was almost like having a job again, something to busy herself with. A routine; someone else's routine, but one in which she felt completely happy.

At El Infinito, Maria always stopped to look at the notices, taking note of how many people had stripped a tab from Anna's Yoga class, or what new English lessons were being offered by enthusiastic Americans. She then greeted Carlos, who needed to be pulled from his latest novel every time someone wanted a coffee, and would pick one of her favourite spots. Many days she chose the wonky table by the window that allowed her a good view of the entrance and a hidden peek at the life of Calle Santa Isabel. On days when the autumn sun shone strong enough, she chose the outdoor chair almost next to her favourite indoor spot, but with a pane of glass separating them. On a sunny day, Maria's reflection in the window was an exact picture of where she sat on a grey day and, whether inside or out, she took comfort from the pretty, carefree woman that smiled at her in the glass.

21:32, Tuesday November 6th, 2012
Hostel Havana, Madrid

She was drinking cheap wine in her cheap hostel when a man in the building opposite caught her attention. He emerged onto one of the ramshackle balconies in a once-white vest and lit a cigarette from a match. He was overweight and balding. Like his off-white vest, his face and body appeared to have greyed through over-use. One hand held the cigarette to his lips, and the other tapped out a tune on the rusty rail. Once he had sucked the cigarette down to his fingertips, he dropped the stub without a care and used both hands to drum out a rhythm on the rail. His hands were agile and fast, and he used his fingers, palms and backs of hands to change the sound. The beat got faster and faster, and soon he was separating the rhythm of his hands with a kick to a sand bucket next to him. He had made an entire drum kit of his balcony and looked full of joy. Maria looked on in awe.

    This happy scene, played out live in front of her, made Maria think of truth and authenticity and it triggered something in her memory, something her father had said to her during their last conversation. She closed her window and sat on the floor cross-legged, she had to indulge the memory so it wouldn't run away before she had understood its meaning. She thought back to that day.

20:34, Wednesday June 13th, 2012
Willowman Grange

The doctor had told them all this was likely to be his last day. Last day on top of this earth and under this blue sky.

    As Beth approached along the corridor she saw Michael emerge from the room, and stop to take a few deep breaths outside, his hand still on the doorknob. She paused in the darkness and allowed him his recovery time. Her brother looked scarily like her father had done in his prime, and she gulped back a tear, thinking about the wrecked man lying in bed behind that door. Michael took his hand from the door and put both to his head. Beth couldn't stand the thought of him crying and so stamped down the hallway to announce her approach. He immediately pulled himself together and stepped out of the light into the safety of the darkened hallway. He raised a hand and a smile and they high-fived as they crossed in the corridor. As kids they went through phases of liking and disliking each other and, dependent on how they felt, would either high-five or punch each other as they passed in the many corridors of Willowman Grange.

Beth gave a soft knock on the door and entered her father's room. He had been put into the guest suite, since the space and bathroom were most fitting for the 24/7 nurse to basically live there and to care for him. That morning, the nurse had emptied his catheter, cleaned him with a warm soapy flannel, changed his pyjamas, brushed his teeth and done the amazing trick of changing his bedclothes by only moving him the slightest degree. It was like when a magician sweeps away the tablecloth from a heavily laden table, while everything stays happily in place. She had then brushed his hair, adjusted the syringe drive that pushed morphine into his veins and given him a light kiss on the head. She had cared for countless people nearing death, and she knew he wouldn't last another night.

Beth tiptoed into the room, sat on the dining chair next to Jim's bed and looked at her father.

His skin was like tissue stretched over a jagged stone. He had grown so thin it looked as though his bones might just tear through his grey skin if they tried to move. His teeth looked huge in his shrunken face and his eyes were dull and matt. Despite the sweet efforts the nurse had gone to, he looked more dead than alive.

She held his hand. It felt like stone.

Jim turned his head to Beth and held her stare for a long time. A tear slowly built up and emerged from the outside of his right eye. It began a slow decent down his paper skin. Everything he did in the last few weeks was slow, and now even gravity seemed to have adhered to this slowness.

Beth looked down at the bright white quilt that made his gloom even more apparent. She couldn't look at her father. She had never seen him cry. He had always been the strongest man in her life, full of power, control and charm, and she couldn't bear to see him with none of these, and crying. The tear dropped onto the white quilt where her eyes lay, and immediately turned the bright white to grey. His greyness was spreading.

Another teardrop joined the first on the Egyptian cotton, and then a noise forced Beth to look up. It was like a gurgling cough. It was her father weeping. His tissue face had crumpled in on itself and his eyes were creased and streaming with tears. Possibly a lifetime's worth of tears, all coming out at once.

Beth's lip quivered and she shook her head, trying to deny what was happening but then the tears came. There was too much emotion lodged in her neck for her to talk, but she managed one word, and it spilled out over and over with her tears.

"Daddy," she said. "Daddy, Daddy, Daddy."

She buried her head in the cotton where her tears could join his, and she felt his hand on the back of her head. It clumsily stroked her hair. Minutes passed and the frantic weeping of father and daughter slowed to a sob and then a sniffle. Beth raised her head from the duvet and a long line of snot stretched between herself and the bed, like stringy cheese.

"Charming," said Jim, and they both gave a chuckle. Jim's chuckle caught him off guard, he'd clearly had few reasons to laugh recently, and he began to cough. It was a deep sound that seemed to emerge from his stomach, and the grimace on his face showed how painful it was. Beth put her arm around his bony shoulders and lifted him into a sitting position. He managed to gesture to the table next to him and she grabbed a tissue and held it in front of his mouth. He coughed into the tissue, and Beth felt the stringy muscles around his shoulders and neck tense. Finally the cough subsided and he collapsed back against the pillow. He closed his eyes and took deep troubled breaths, which were accompanied by a rattle.

Beth went to put the tissue in the bin and noticed that it was full of something thick and black. She threw it away.

Back in the chair, she gave him some water. It took a while for Jim to recover, but she stroked his stone hand and his breathing became shallow and regular. At last, he spoke. His words were slow, almost every one emerging on it's own with no connection to the last or next.

"Sweet girl," he said. "I have lied to you. To everyone. My life. A lie."

Beth had no idea what he was talking about. "Daddy, don't be silly, you're no liar, you're the most honest person I know."

A just-perceptible shake of his head. "I am the least."

He gestured for more water, and Beth held the straw to his mouth. His lips were coming apart in large cracks.

"I have been diplomatic. All my life," he said. "No longer." One side of his mouth turned up into a tiny smile.

"Beth, be true." He continued. His glassy eyes narrowed in focus and he took a few moments to pump himself full of air.

"Be true to what makes you happy. Whatever it is. Do not worry. About expectation. About money."

Jim stopped talking and a strange noise emerged from deep inside him, from somewhere between his stomach and chest. He winced as the deep rattling groan came to an end, and Beth clutched his hand. The syringe drive that sat on the ornate headboard buzzed another pulse of morphine into him. It didn't have much left in it, but Jim didn't have much left in him either. They were both almost empty.

Jim's head lolled back into the pillow and he gasped for breath that didn't seem to come. He looked at his only daughter with eyes that were full of fear. He had never shown anything but complete control, authority over every situation, but here he had none, and he was full of fear. His mouth moved and Beth leant close to him.

"What is it daddy? What is it?"

"Remember. How you once were." The words emerged without any hint of movement or breath, as though he were dead already. "Be true," he said.

When Beth pulled away from him, his eyes were closed and his head had fallen deep into the pillow. His forehead was creased as though concentrating and his mouth was pursed into the shape of the last word that had emerged.

21:54, Tuesday November 6th, 2012
Hostel Havana, Madrid

Be true to what makes you happy.
 Beth stood, looked out the window and saw the man again, now silhouetted in front of the light of his apartment, still tapping and kicking his own little rhythm out of his crumbling balcony. He was doing what made him happy, doing what his heart desired. He was true. He didn't need a drum kit, didn't need an audience, didn't need anyone else. Truth did not need to be momentous, it did not need to be world-changing, it just needed to be genuine.
 She had only ever known her father to be articulate, charming, planned and thoughtful, so she had never any reason to think he might be otherwise. It had been this truth that she had always tried to live up to, always tried to emulate, and now she realized that that truth was not his. He was acting, emulating the person he thought he should be. Not only was her father now gone, but in his last words to her, he had obliterated just about everything she thought she knew about him. Every memory she had was now in doubt. But despite this she knew two things; he was her father and he was wise. And if the final words he spoke urged her to live in the moment and to be true to what she felt, then that was what she must do.
 And right now she didn't feel like being a wife, didn't feel like being a mum and didn't feel like leading the life she had built for herself in London.
 She opened the window and sat on the single dining chair in her room looking down the noisy street illuminated by neon and brought to life by the noisy *madrileños*. Here in Madrid she felt happy, she felt free with herself and from herself. She was alone to do what inspired her, what fired her, what intrigued her. Maria's truth was sitting in sunny cafes reading great literature, wandering around galleries, walking barefoot through Retiro, drinking cheap wine.
 She closed her eyes. She smelt oily cooking from the restaurant below. She felt a humid breeze on her face from an air conditioning unit somewhere. She felt the hard wooden chair beneath her, and the floor beneath her bare feet. She felt true.

10:38, Thursday December 13th, 2012
El Infinito, Madrid

It was a winter's day. She dragged Carlos from Victor Hugo's French Revolution to order her *café con leche,* and as he reluctantly worked the old coffee machine she noticed a new painting behind him. It was a simple portrait; a man's face, multicoloured, with a background of deep red. The brushstrokes were wide, so much so you would doubt any detail could be achieved, but the effect was almost exactly the opposite. All the colours and brushstrokes condensed into a focus, with a fantastic level of detail in the man's eyes. They looked sad, downright miserable, and there was nothing but despair in the painting. The intensity of the man's expression made Maria's heart beat faster. She sidestepped the counter, and Carlos, to take a closer look.

"Wow, this painting is amazing."

Carlos grunted an acknowledgement.

"Who is it by?"

Carlos grunted again.

"Carlos! I asked who is the artist?"

"Oh, some guy from Barcelona."

"That's all you know?"

Carlos sighed, he liked Maria but he preferred Marius and Cosette and would rather get back to them.

"His name is Angelo Octavez. I think he has an exhibition coming up. Check the door."

Maria took her coffee and a new position where she could gaze at the portrait. Carlos was right, the door told her that Angelo Octavez had an exhibition in Galleria Ubik on Calle de San Isidro. The road sounded familiar, she must have walked it on one of her meanders around the city. Maria stared at the portrait as her coffee cooled. There were real people, real faces, interacting within metres of her, but she couldn't tear herself away from the painted face, not even to navigate her hands to her coffee cup. She had studied the great portrait artists at university, she had re-enlivened her appreciation of art these last few months in both London and Madrid, but this picture struck her in a way no other ever had. There was something about the man in the portrait that Beth could relate to, not Maria, but Beth.

Her reverie was only broken when a bunch of students interrupted her line of sight. She looked down at her coffee in surprise, as though forgetting she had ordered it. She looked at her watch and dashed out, leaving her coffee cold, and the eyes of the painting watching her go. She had a flight back to Beth to catch.

13:51, Wednesday December 19th, 2012
Galleria Ubik, Madrid

A week later and Maria was back in Madrid, while Beth was supposedly at a new client meeting in Paris. Almost as soon as she arrived, after she had peeled away and replaced the smart layers of business dress with layers of cotton colour, she found herself at the exhibition. It was in a small gallery, on a road round the back of the Reina Sofia gallery. A few roads behind the Reina Sofia is as close as most artists' work will ever get to it. The little gallery had whitewashed walls, a Spanish tiled floor and a bitch of a proprietress stalking Maria.

The pictures were all portraits in which dark, brooding colours were swept around the canvas with thick brush strokes. Maria couldn't help but feel disappointed by what was on show. The painting in the café had such feeling, such emotion in the eyes, as though the sitter and the artist had an understanding, something not spoken of, but shared between the two. The paintings in the gallery were good, very good, but had little meaning behind them. The eyes and the faces were just colours, oil on canvas in an arrangement, nothing more.

"They are beautiful, aren't they?" said the curator.

"Mmm, hmm." Maria changed direction, trying to avoid the woman.

"I especially love the self-portrait." The woman came to stand in front of one of the pictures.

Maria was curious and found herself walking towards, rather than away, from the woman.

The painting was small, one of the smallest in the gallery, only about ten inches square. In it, a man with long dark hair, gypsy-dark skin, and deep-set eyes stared out at her. It was perfect. All of the rough thick strokes of paint came to a clear focus in each of the eyes that had the tiniest glint of white, so tiny that you wondered whether it was there at all. The eyes were like those in the cafe painting, turned down at the sides in a sad way, but with creases of faded smiles surrounding them, and the mouth seemed to toy with happiness. Once again Maria was captivated.

"Is it for sale?" she asked.

"Yes," said the woman, she looked from Maria's tatty boots up past her cheap bracelets to her fake nose ring. "But it's very expensive."

"How much?"

The woman raised her eyebrows and went to retrieve a price list.

"*Autoretrato*… that has a price of…" she scanned the list. "Twelve hundred euros." She looked at Maria with smugness.

"I'll take it," said Maria.

16:34, Thursday December 20th, 2012
El Infinito, Madrid

Angelo's exhibition had not quite been the financial success he'd hoped for. He'd sold *La Anciana Fumando*, *El Niño Travieso*, and *La Catalana* each for 400 euros, and amazingly his *autoretrato* had gone for 1200. He wondered whose wall his face was staring out from. He hoped it wasn't some smug middle class banker with a shiny apartment of glass and granite, but at twelve hundred euros it probably was. He sat on a graffitied wall on the way back from the gallery and did some mental arithmetic with the crumpled cash that filled his pockets.

His landlady, Señora Carmen, had reached the end of her patience with Angelo and had demanded the next three months' rent up front. He couldn't blame her, he had only just paid the last six months with a loan from Xavier. So he had to pay Señora Carmen and Xavier, the gallery, Teresa, his hotel, and the bus back to Barcelona. Even with the most optimistic arithmetic, the euros in his pocket didn't stretch that far.

He headed for the café to pick up his father's picture and concentrated on ways of making fast money. It seemed impossible, his bus was booked for the next day and Señora Carmen would most likely be waiting on the doorstep when he got home, cigarillo in one hand and the other waiting to be filled with his cash.

Maria was sitting inside El Infinito watching a young boy outside getting tied up in knots by the lead of his yapping puppy. Every time the boy turned one way to release himself from the lead, the eager puppy ran in the opposite direction. She was smiling at the scene, and smiled even wider when another pair of legs got caught up in the tangle. A tall man with a mess of dark hair was leaning down to unwind the puppy. She couldn't see his face, but could tell from his shaking body that he was laughing. A few moments of pantomime continued, and finally the little puppy was in the boy's arms and the man was petting it as it licked his hands. The man ruffled the young boy's head and turned towards the café. Maria's heart skipped a beat as she recognized the deep-set eyes and angular features from the self-portrait. She swallowed and forced her eyes back into her book. She suddenly felt warm and her hands were clammy.

At El Infinito Angelo pushed the door and it opened with unusual force, banging against the wall of notices. Juan's room to let and Annabelle's offer of unbelievably cheap English classes fell to the ground, and Angelo noticed a pretty woman sitting by the window jump. He lifted his hand in apology and smiled at her. In return she blushed slightly and smiled back.

"Hey man," he said to the gormless nerd behind the counter. He stole another glance at the pretty brunette by the window.

"Hey," he repeated, waiting for the stringy boy to lift his eyes from his book. "Can I take my picture back?" he asked, gesturing to the portrait behind the boy's head.

"Sure, it gives me the creeps," said the boy before dropping his head back into his book.

"Good," said Angelo. He lifted the portrait from the wall and put it under his arm before turning to leave. At the door he stopped, waited a moment, head bowed in thought, and turned back.

"I don't suppose anyone showed any interest in this portrait?" he asked.

Carlos lifted his head and screwed up his eyes in thought. "A couple of people commented on how creepy it was."

"Yeah man, you said that already. I mean, did anyone actually *like* it?"

Carlos squinted in concentration, it was far more difficult to recall real life events than those he read about. Angelo drummed his dirty fingernails on the counter.

Maria watched Carlos and the painter talk from the outskirts of page 144 but could not hear their words. She had spent the previous evening opposite the portrait of Angelo, as though he were her dinner date, but it was only now, looking at the real man that she realized how incredibly attractive he was. Not in a traditional Prince Charming way, but in a rugged way. Like a classical statue that is only more beautiful as age and weather ravage it. He was tall, a good few inches above six foot she guessed, and his features were strong and straight, like a Picasso portrait. Then the Picasso turned.

"That's her," said Carlos loudly, pointing at Maria. "*She* liked it."

Maria gulped and took a deep breath, as Angelo covered the distance between them.

He drew out the chair opposite her and made himself comfortable. His face was only the distance of a small table away from hers, just like his image last night. His eyes were the shape of almonds and his hair hung around his face, creating a messy heart-shaped frame. His mouth was curled in a delicious grin that crinkled his eyes into a hundred smiles.

"Hello," he said.

"Hello."

He looked her up and down and she felt herself flush. "You look like a woman of exquisite taste."

She giggled, immediately feeling more at ease. He smiled wider and his eyes became thousands of smiles.

"And how can you tell that?"

"You're reading Marquez and you liked my portrait." He put the portrait up on the table next to him, as though a third person had joined them. "You obviously have an appreciation of great art."

Again she giggled. She knew she was acting like a schoolgirl but she couldn't help herself. She considered telling him that she bought his self-portrait yesterday, but it seemed somehow creepy now that he was sat in front of her.

"It's great," she said, nodding at the framed picture and its stern eyes. "It's really, really fantastic."

Angelo's eyes glowed with the praise.

"Yeah, speccy up there said you liked it."

"I do."

Angelo nodded. "Enough to buy it?"

Maria looked from Angelo to the portrait. She didn't know why she hadn't spotted it before, but it was clearly a relative of Angelo's. The painted lines and the contours of Angelo's face followed the same angles.

"Is it your father?" she asked.

He thought about this question a moment, with his eyes examining the table. The late afternoon sun was shining on him and flyaway hairs caught the light and looked like little electrical charges moving in and out of his head. "You could say that." He spoke without lifting his eyes.

"You really want to sell it?"

He looked up at her and his face in the pink light was glorious. "I need to sell it."

The mood had changed and his face was all seriousness, making him even more similar to the portrait by his side. She longed to see his smile again, in fact at that precise moment in El Infinito, she felt that she would give anything to make him smile. There was nothing more important than seeing that smile.

"How much?" she asked.

He bent his head in thought, and his hair created a dark veil behind which he thought for a few moments. It was clear he hadn't thought this far ahead. His fingers and lips moved, as though calculating. He looked up at her shabby clothes and then up to her face. He was trying to work out how much she could afford but he got distracted. Her eyes were so dark he couldn't see the pupils, he leant forward to locate them but they remained hidden. The rest of her face blurred out of focus as he looked into them. She'd make a great painting. She blushed again and he found himself analysing the colour in her cheeks.

"So, how much?" she repeated.

"Fifteen hundred," he said. It was supposed to sound definitive, but it emerged tentative.

She wanted the picture, more to make Angelo happy than anything else, but she had already parted with 1200 euros the day before and, when in Spain, she had to keep a close eye on her spending. "Can I think about it?"

255

There was another pause, in which he stared and she blushed. He was studying her face, trying to commit the lines to memory that would emerge on canvas later. He shook himself from his scrutiny and sat further back in his chair.

"Not for long. I'm leaving tomorrow morning."

A sharp little arrow of disappointment hit her.

He grabbed her book, which she had opened at a random page to appear engrossed, pulled a pen from his shirt and scribbled a number next to his name at the bottom of page 144. He turned the book over, laid it face down on the table and tapped the front cover with his pen.

"There aren't any others," he said to her. Then he stood, winked and left.

She watched him go, puzzled, then she turned the book over and remembered what she was supposed to be reading; *Love and other Demons*.

19:02, Thursday December 20th, 2012
Hostel Havana, Madrid

Maria went back to the Havana and started a cheap bottle of Rioja with the painting of Angelo. Now that she had some personality to put behind the colours, she felt even more entranced by the image. Angelo in person was unkempt, he was unstructured and unplanned. He was un-a lot of things.

She stared into Angelo's eyes and thought back to the way he'd stared at her that afternoon. She thought about his actions: the way he sat down without asking, the way he grabbed her book (which wasn't even *her* book) and scribbled his details in it, and the way he left as promptly as he arrived.

She sat a few more moments, biting her nails before she got down on the floor and retrieved her suitcase from under the bed. Inside she found her laptop case, which held her long-abandoned computer and her stash of euros. She began counting. Of course, she had enough to buy the painting but it would mean taking a hefty amount from the account she shared with Tom. Despite their wealth, Tom monitored every pound in and out of their bank account, this was one of the few traits remaining of the broke musician she first met. She would need a good excuse. Or maybe she could just pass it off as an investment? It was only last week that her brother had been telling the family the only sure investments were art and wine. For all Tom knew, Angelo Octavez could be an up and coming artist she saw at an exhibition with a client. She spoke it over in her head and it sounded plausible, believable even, and anyway she liked the picture. She really did.

She looked at the self-portrait again. It was a poor replica of the face that had sat opposite her today, but it still captured some of the life that shone out from him, and it was enchanting. She found herself smiling at him, and something in the painted eyes seemed to glimmer as though smiling back at her. She lowered her eyes, embarrassed. Wait, what the hell was she doing? Flirting with an oil painting.

She stood up and went to the window, lifted the blind and perched on the ledge. She looked down the busy street and tried to concentrate on other people down below, giving them lives and dreams beyond this street, but her mind wouldn't let her. It kept returning to Angelo. A part of her head had filled with him and it was seeping by osmosis into the rest of her body, making him impossible to ignore.

Her heart was beating fast and her skin felt warm despite the draught from the old window frame. She felt full of adrenalin, full of Angelo and full of possibility. Before she could change her mind, she downed the glass of wine and dialed his number.

"Hello."

She took a deep breath.

"Hi Angelo, it's Maria. We met at the café this afternoon."

"We did," he stated the fact. "Have you thought about the painting?"

"Yes."

"And will you buy it?"

Maria adored his directness. She stared into the oil on canvas eyes in front of her. "Yes, I'd like to buy it."

"You would?" Angelo sounded incredulous.

"Yes," she laughed. "You sound surprised."

"No, well, maybe a little. But like I said, you have great taste." He was over the moon and Maria brimmed at the thought she had sent him there.

"You want me to drop it to yours?" he asked.

Maria looked around the room. "No, I'll come to you. Where shall we meet?"

"I'm at the Hostel Girasol on Gran Via. I'll get the picture ready for you, room 26. Make sure you sneak past the *bruja* in reception, she doesn't like visitors."

"OK, I'll sneak past and see you soon."

He hung up. Maria bit her lip. So that was decided then. She was an investor in art.

She looked at the floor. From inside her suitcase she retrieved her designer purse, and from inside a photo of Miles and Katy. Had she really hidden them so far away? She smiled at their beautiful beaming faces for a few moments but once again Angelo's face came into stark view. A massive wave of guilt pushed Miles and Katy back into the purse and back into hiding. She quickly packed everything away and hid her other life under the bed, the wave of guilt crashed somewhere beneath the mattress and she took a deep breath. She'd see the kids soon enough, be Beth again soon enough, and right now she was concentrating on herself, Maria. Be true to what makes you happy. And right now it was Angelo.

20:43, Thursday December 20th, 2012
Hostel Girasol, Madrid

Maria was sure he could hear her heart beating through the door, but she knocked anyway. Angelo opened the door and stared intensely at her. She really would make a great painting. Angelo was more handsome than she remembered, and his dark eyes chased hers down to the floor.

"Hey," he said, after a long gap. "Come on in."

He stood to one side and gestured into the small room. She walked past him, smelling cigarettes and noticing how tall he was, about Tom's height. The room was basic and crumbling, a small holdall and a wheeled crate sat in the corner. On the bed, the portrait lay in the middle of some brown paper. He pointed towards it and at the same time placed his hand on the base of her spine to guide her. She almost yelped at the heat of his touch. She took a deep breath and approached the picture. When she turned to him she realized he had been inspecting her once more. She felt self-conscious and fiddled with the end of her plait.

"Does he like it?" she asked.

"Who?"

"Your father. Does he like the portrait?"

Angelo stepped forward and looked at the painting, his hair was pulled into a ponytail and she stared at his face. It was beautiful. It was angular and lined, heavy beneath the eyes, aged like a handsome piece of mahogany. She wondered if he was ignoring her question.

"I don't know," he said at last. Suddenly Maria realized that Angelo's father was dead, and that she was buying the memory of a dead man.

"Have you many pictures of your father?" She asked.

He didn't answer her, but started to wrap the painting in the brown paper. He had beautiful careful hands, they were the darkest part of him and were contoured with defined veins and muscles, all of which were spattered with specks of forgotten paint. The last fold of wrapping covered the eyes of the portrait, and Angelo took one last look into them before he made the fold and taped it over. Maria looked at him. His eyes were sad like his father's. She wanted to put her arms around him, to tell him to keep the painting and that she would still give him the money, but that was just stupid, she was a stranger, and strangers don't go around giving fifteen hundred euros to each other with a hug.

"You can come visit it when you're in Madrid," she said hurriedly.

He looked at her strangely with his head cocked and then laughed, showing eyes immediately lifted from their gloomy contemplation.

"You're funny," he said. "A girl like you could be very good for me." He stared at her intensely, and once again she looked to the floor and fiddled with the end of her plait.

"So, fifteen hundred," she mumbled.

Angelo shook his head vigorously, as though waking himself from a daydream.

"I'll write you a receipt." He turned away and began rummaging through his bag. She watched his form, his bones and muscles shifting beneath his shirt, and a sliver of brown skin emerging at his waistline.

She gulped. She needed more time with him, she longed to know more, and to give him time to want her like she wanted him. Adrenalin coursed through her veins when he was near, and she couldn't bear the thought of that never happening again. She made an immediate decision, she had to see him again. While his back was turned, she reached into her satchel, took out the envelope of money and removed five hundred euros, which she stuffed into the bag again.

"Angelo," she said. "I need to talk to you about the payment."

He was still rummaging through his bag. "What do you mean?"

"Well, it's just that the bank wouldn't let me draw out the full amount today. I only have a thousand."

He turned around slowly with narrowed eyes that almost scared her. "But you agreed fifteen hundred." He approached and stood over her. "You can't negotiate now." At that moment, his directness was intimidating rather than inspiring.

"No, no! I don't want to negotiate," said Maria, gulping down the fear in her voice. "I am still going to pay fifteen hundred, I give you my word, but it needs to be in two instalments. One today, one... another day." She removed the notes from the envelope and fanned them in front of Angelo, the sight of the money slightly calmed him. He looked from the colour of the banknotes into the blackness of her eyes. She was stunningly beautiful, even more so with a fan of euros spread beneath her face like a ruffled collar. He thought about painting her in this position of supplication.

"I'm regularly in Barcelona," she lied. "For work. Next time I'm there, which will be soon, I can bring the money, which will be soon." She knew she was babbling. Lies are often accompanied by an abundance of words that do nothing to strengthen them. His suspicious eyes continued to gaze at her. He was trying to work out whether a thousand euros would cover his debts. They wouldn't.

"Listen Maria, the truth is I really need that money. All of it."

"And you'll get it, really. I just can't draw it all today. I promise you, the next time I'm in Barcelona, I will bring the remaining five hundred." She looked up into his brown eyes. She wanted to make them smile again.

"You have my word," she said.

"Unfortunately *guapa*, your word means nothing to me." He shrugged his shoulders. The sentence struck her but of course he was right, she was nothing to him, yet.

"Well, well, take something of mine, until I see you next." She looked down at herself, at her tattered boots, her layers of cotton and wool, the countless plastic beads that hung from her neck. Beth would have had a vintage Omega watch, a set of diamond earrings, a Tiffany charm bracelet, any number of expensive trinkets to choose from, but Maria had none.

"I'll take the ring," he said, nodding at her hand.

She followed his stare to her right hand where Lolli's emerald ring sat. She swallowed. The ring was worth a lot more than five hundred euros, in both money and memories. Maybe at this point, she should just rustle around in the base of her bag and miraculously come up with the remaining five hundred – Ta-dah! But then she would never see this man again, she would part with the money and with Angelo, and take her old life back with just the painting as a souvenir of what could have been.

"That's worth a lot to me."

"And you'll have it back when you pay the rest for my painting." He said it so simply that Maria knew it to be true.

They held each other's stare a moment, before she wrestled the ring from her finger and passed it to him. He slipped it onto his little finger and admired it a moment.

"Very pretty," he said. Then he looked back at her. "Very pretty," he repeated.

She bit her lip and looked from his face to the ring and back again.

"Don't worry, I'll take care of it," he said as he scribbled her out a receipt. She looked at the scrawl, it had his name and address in Barcelona, followed by a functional description of the portrait and its size. Beneath that it said 'Received: one thousand euros and an old ring. Yet to receive: five hundred euros.'

"You haven't mentioned me getting the ring back," she said quickly.

He took back the paper with the tiniest of smiles and added 'Old ring to be returned on receipt of further 500.' He signed the paper with an enormous A, and handed it to her.

She slipped the receipt into her satchel, picked up the package and looked at Angelo.

"Thank you," she said.

He winked at her. "*Hasta pronto.*"

His gesture and words seemed to completely empty her lungs of air. She took a deep breath. "See you soon," she replied.

12:15, Friday December 21st, 2012
Hilton Madrid

Beth had a Skype call the next afternoon and, although she was sure Tom would not spot her empty ring finger, she had scoured the shops of Gran Via that morning. Eventually she found a cheap imitation ring that was passable, if she squinted at it. It made her feel a little better, but the cheap metal weighed heavily on her conscience as she settled into the leather couch of an anonymous hotel bar, and dialled into Skype.

"Hello darling," said the image of a perfect husband.

"Hi," she said, spreading her freshly painted lips into a curve.

"How's Berlin?"

"*Gut danke*," she said. This was her standard response from Germany, and it was replicated into any number of languages, dependent on where she had told Tom she was going. She kept a note of the destinations in her diary, along with any notes of what she was supposed to be doing. Today the diary had accompanied her to concept testing for a new ad campaign in Berlin, although in reality it had only ever seen London and Madrid.

"Good meetings?"

"Fine," she said. "The new concepts are going down well in research, so it looks like we have a favourite for this market."

"Great, so where's the next testing?"

Beth gulped and tried to sound as casual as her heart would allow. "Barcelona," she said. "In the new year. So what's happening back home?"

He thought for a minute. "Oh yes, I was talking to Trish, Ella's mum, at school yesterday and she said she's found a great tutor to help Ella with her SAT tests. I called the tutor and she's got space for Katy so I've booked her in for sessions Mondays and Wednesdays."

"OK," said Beth. The grips she had used to pin her hair into place were too tight, and beginning to give her a headache, she tried to loosen them.

"And the wine delivery arrived this morning," he said, smiling like a child in a sweet shop. "We'll *definitely* be taking the best bottles to Hugh and Tess' new year bash, we've got a *Pol Roger Cuvee Sir Winston Churchill*, I've half a mind to leave the price tag on."

Beth smiled, although inside she was cringing. She had forgotten about the godawful gathering of snobs at Tom's boss' penthouse for new year. She began to formulate an excuse in her head as Tom rambled on about the rare wine he'd managed to source.

"So Beth, you looking forward to your Christmas break?" he asked. He leant closer toward the camera and one of his carefully coiffed curls fell out of place and onto his forehead.

She looked at it and felt like it had the power to make her cry. The occasional messy little blonde curl was all that was left of the man she had fallen in love with. She forgot where she was and where she was supposed to be, and focused on the ringlet that seemed to hold all the passion and happiness she had once felt for this man. In the blonde spiral she saw a talented musician, a messy bedsit, a scruffy pair of Converse All Stars, reckless sex, a dingy pub, fingers dancing around guitar strings, fierce kisses and an empty fridge. It all came back to her with such force that she gasped at the love she felt for that once-boy.

Tom looked closer into the screen and must have seen the image of himself. He pushed back the curl and smoothed it into place.

"You looking forward to your Christmas break?" he repeated.

"Yes," she said. "It will be a lovely break, really looking forward to it, will be great to spend some time together, as a family." She was babbling.

14:52, Saturday December 22nd, 2012
14 Carrer Lleo, Al Raval, Barcelona

Angelo took his bag of clothes, crate of pictures and full wallet back to Barcelona. On the bus he watched towns and cities enter and exit the frame of the window and tried not to think about the sacrifice he had made to fill his wallet. It was just a picture. He was in the business of pictures and so it was just business.

He arrived back at his attic apartment on Carrer Lleo, hot and flustered from carrying the crate up the four flights of stairs. Many of the buildings in Al Raval were constructed before the luxury of lifts became commonplace and, without this ease of access, the top floors had remained as run-down cheap attic spaces. Angelo's place reeked of caffeine and tobacco and he inhaled the smell of home with a big grin, happy to be back in his crumbling garret. He opened the large bay window to cool himself, and immediately the noise of traffic and shouting mixed with the stagnant air. His grin grew.

He wheeled his paintings into a corner, where they were destined to stay, sat on the window ledge and thought about his trip to Madrid. It wasn't quite the success he had hoped for, but he had sold a few portraits and two had gone for prices he normally wouldn't dare associate with his own work. Maybe this was the start of something. Maybe his work was finally being recognized. He poured away the red dregs of wine in a glass and filled it with whiskey.

"To Angelo Octavez," he said, lifting his glass. The ring on his little finger glinted in the sunlight and he looked at it properly for the first time. It was dotted with tiny green and clear sparkling stones and, although no expert, he thought it looked old, very old. Who did this ring belong to? Who was Maria? She was a woman who sat reading tattered copies of Marquez, whose shirt was oversized and torn, whose dark plait fell across her shoulder and down almost to her waist, whose eyes were dark holes of obscurity, and who agreed to part with fifteen hundred euros for a painting she knew nothing about. She was a mystery, one that he would enjoy thinking about.

He took a slow walk around the living space of his apartment, which was his bedroom, his studio, his everything. He took a long glug from the glass and chose a blank canvas from his pile. It was the largest he had. He put it onto an easel, placed it into the sunshine from the window and closed his eyes. She sat smiling behind his eyelids and he smiled back.

11:14, Saturday January 5th, 2014
14 Carrer Lleo, Al Raval, Barcelona

Angelo painted with a drive he had not experienced in a long time. All he could think about was Maria, her dark secretive eyes that contained everything; defiance, uncertainty, nerves and joy, and at the same time; nothing. He ached to commit her to canvas, not her beauty but her mystery, her eyes. She had secrets, things running around and around behind those closed windows, things that left shadows, but nothing he could make out clearly. Angelo painted from the moment he woke till the moment the sun deserted him. He attempted to paint at night, but a mystery needs light, not darkness, and even with all the bulbs of his apartment pointed at his canvas, she still kept her distance. Only with sunlight was he able to approach her, to get close. When he wasn't painting her, he was thinking or dreaming about her. Maria was on his mind and on his canvas.

After two weeks of frenzied work, he had six paintings of Maria, of her long brown plait, of her full mouth, of her petite frame immersed in a man's shirt, of her delicate hands, of the antique ring on one of them, but every picture remained incomplete. He had painted, repainted and given up on her eyes. He was sitting on the window sill smoking and looking into the six chasms of Maria, when someone knocked on the door.

He hadn't left his apartment in four days and the existence of the outside world suddenly surprised him. He smoked the last of his roll-up and sauntered to the door. It was Xavier.

"Man! Where've you been? You weren't at the concert last night?" He walked past Angelo into the apartment.

"What concert?"

"You know, *Volcania*, the Balkan gypsy band? The one you agreed to come see if I stopped talking about them?"

"Well, you obviously stopped talking about them. I forgot."

Angelo slapped his friend on the shoulder, headed for the kitchen and stuck his head back round the door, holding a bottle of red in one hand and the coffee pot in the other.

"Red or black?" he asked.

Xavier looked at his watch, it was past eleven in the morning. "Red," he said.

Once Angelo had located two cleanish glasses and opened the bottle he returned to the studio. Xavier was scrutinizing the six canvases that were arranged in a semi-circle around the window.

"New exhibition?" he said. "Woman without eyes."

Angelo smiled. "Something like that."

He returned to the window sill and gulped some wine. He looked at Maria in the largest canvas.

"I'll finish them when she comes."

"What? Who is she? You found a new girl? What about Ceci?"

Angelo shook his head, still staring at the canvas.

"She bought a painting from me."

"Oh man, I forgot. How was the exhibition? Your first exhibition in the capital hey! Let's drink to that."

He raised his glass to Angelo's and Angelo turned from the painting.

"*Salut.*"

Their glasses touched in the light from the window, revealing just how dirty and smeared they both were.

"So?" Xavier prompted. "How was it?"

Angelo answered by wandering over to the crate in the corner and rummaging around inside it. He turned with a big smile, flourishing a fan of money, like a magician with a white rabbit. Xavier would have been less surprised by a white rabbit.

"Wow! How much did you make?"

"Enough to pay you back Xavi," said Angelo.

He scrunched the euros into a pile and handed them over.

"Thanks for the loan."

"It was an investment," said Xavier, patting his friend on the shoulder. "Into art. You know me, I like to make high-brow investments. So what sold?"

"A couple of smaller portraits, the self-portrait and ..." He nodded towards an empty hook on the opposite wall. The hook was surrounded by a small white square where the wall had been shielded from the resident grime and smoke.

Xavier turned to him, eyes full of surprise.

"You sold it?"

"Yes. To her." He looked at the canvas in front of him.

"To a woman with no eyes? Maybe that should be your target customer. How much?"

"Fifteen hundred."

"Wow man, that's a serious price, a professional price. This could be the start for you, the start of something big. That's a successful trip." He patted Angelo on the back. "Let's celebrate." He topped up both their glasses and started to roll a joint.

Two bottles of red, and a couple of joints later, Xavier was strumming an un-tuned guitar, blues-style, in front of the canvases. He made up the words as Angelo looked on with a wry smile.

'Fell in love with a woman, la la la la.
But she had no eyes, la la la la
Said she liked my art, la la la la
But it was all lies, ooohhhh"

Angelo's phone rang. He considered letting it ring so he could enjoy Xavier's next drunken verse, but he noticed that it was a Madrid number. He leapt for it.

"Hello," he said into the receiver.

"Hello." It was her.

"Maria?"

"Yes."

Angelo gestured for Xavier to shut up.

"I'm coming to Barcelona this week," she said. "I was hoping I could come and pay you the rest of the money."

"Yes, yes of course. You have my address?"

"Yes, you wrote it on the receipt." There was a pause. It was a pause in which Maria was supposed to suggest they meet elsewhere, a café, a plaza, somewhere for a quick functional transaction. She had thought it over and Beth helped her realize how stupid she was being, infatuated by a stranger. She would make a quick trip to Barcelona, a perfunctory transaction of money to get Lolli's ring back, and be on her way back to her tranquil Madrid existence, drinking coffees, ambling the streets and engaging in no love affairs outside of books. But now the moment had arrived to cement this plan, and she couldn't find the words she had rehearsed.

"Come any time. I'm always here. If the buzzer doesn't work, call my phone."

"OK." Last chance to say something. "I'll see you soon."

"See you soon." She hung up and bit her lip, attempting to stop the smile that was growing.

He hung up and looked at his friend with a big grin. "She's coming."

Xavier started up again.

"Fell in love with a woman, la la la la
She had no eyes, la la la la
I painted her new ones
And I got between her thighs, ohhhhhh"

14:37, Tuesday January 8th, 2013
Barcelona

Maria did the Beth thing and took a taxi from the airport to Al Raval. She hadn't been to Barcelona in years and the only recollections she had were of pointed Picasso faces and Gaudi architecture that melted off the brickwork. She sat in the middle of the backseat and looked out of both windows eagerly. Her eyes and mind were filling with the imagery of Angelo's city. The taxista mistook her excitement for impatience to arrive. Being an obstinate man, who liked nothing more than to infuriate others, he drove slowly and unusually graciously, allowing traffic to cut in front of him with a polite wave of the hand. And so, both taxista and passenger took great joy from the extended journey.

As the outskirts of the city converged into tighter roads and older buildings, the pavements filled with people; their feet making their routine paths through their Tuesdays. And here was Maria taking a very different path through hers.

"Stop, stop here please. I'll walk the rest." She had a sudden urge to join everyone else and to feel the city alive beneath her feet.

The taxista smiled, she really was desperate to get out of his taxi. He took further pleasure in telling this Spanish-speaking woman the inflated price in Catalan.

Maria carried her satchel and an old leather holdall along Las Ramblas. Although it was winter, the walkway was filled with tourists and with persistent people trying to enrich the tourists' holidays with offers of walking tours, set lunches and tourist buses. Men painted in gold and silver attracted small change by standing still or posing with reluctant children. A pug dog sat on a skateboard staring forlornly at a pile of money in front of him while a loud and large American tourist asked the dreadlocked owner if the dog could actually ride the skateboard. The dreadlocks moved from side to side like an extension of his head as he said 'No, he just sits there, spare some change?' Maria followed the excited movements of a blonde girl in a pink polyester flamenco dress. The child skipped from stall to busker to portrait artist and back to her family, where two other little girls, one in a pram, wore the same flamenco outfits. Maria found herself thinking about how quickly those dresses would catch alight, but she shook her head empty of these motherly concerns. She walked past thousands of Picasso fridge magnets, hundreds of chocolate-covered churros, countless buskers, and collected six flyers before she turned down Carrer Pintor Fortuny. It was immediately quieter, like taking the exit from a blocked motorway. She had memorized the route to her hostel, not wanting to look like a tourist by consulting a map, and now she traced the roads in her head with her boots.

She wandered down leafy roads dotted with ecological clothing shops and organic restaurants. This was really not what she was expecting from Angelo's territory and for some reason she felt disappointed, by the middle class trimmings that could easily be relocated to Brixton Village, to Greenwich village, in fact any prosperous village springing up within a city. She wandered deeper into Al Raval, down streets named after unknown Catalans.

The buildings got taller and the streets and people darker. Chinese faces abounded and the smell of fried cooking hit the air randomly with no signs of its origin. Every building started with a foundation of graffiti and then rose past a jumble of electrical cables to finish with drapes of washing; the layers of life. Maria puzzled at a pair of bright green high heels that hung from an electrical wire. Further on a woman sat staring at Maria with a cigarette drooping from her mouth and a line of greying knickers drying beside her. A short man in impeccable overalls pushed an empty shopping trolley past her with purpose, as though he were strolling down the aisles of a supermarket with one item in mind. Around the next corner, a young boy used a screwdriver to remove the bronze from a pile of old doors in a skip. He sat inside the skip and dropped the metal fixtures into a clinking pile on the street. A bronze screw rolled past Maria's feet and he eyed her with suspicion when she picked it up and put it alongside his others. Past the skip, a group of three women with noses and shoulders from South America sorted through a pile of rubbish, mining for gold. And then she was at Angelo's road. She couldn't bear the thought of bumping into him yet and so she hurried past, casting a quick look down Carrer Lleo. It was crumbling, loaded with washing, and noisy with the shouts of young boys kicking a football around.

She walked on in haste and in a few minutes she arrived at Hostal Radio, her home for three nights. The reception had been converted into a launderette and an inordinately short Chinese woman led her up two flights of stairs. She was so short that she grunted with the effort of pulling her legs up each step. The woman radiated the heat and smell of washed clothes, and was as communicative as a wet sock. Maria was shown to a yellowing room and the little woman departed with a grunt. At last alone, she sat on the single bed and listened to the shouts of the boys playing football. It gave her a thrill to think of how close she was to Angelo. She longed to see him again. Just to see him would be enough.

She took a shower, shaved her legs (convincing herself they needed doing anyway), unpacked a few things and took a walk.

The area was strewn with artists and poverty, its poverty being both the result and inspiration of the artists. It appeared as though no one had had a haircut, a shower or a decent meal in years. Sun-bleached dreadlocks attracted flies, and dirty bare feet padded over the litter-strewn pavements. White faces turned black by the sun ignored Maria as she strolled past. A man with ribs protruding from a torn T-shirt played guitar on a corner, while three stoned women made slow pirouettes in front of him. Maria felt like a tourist here, with her clean hair, moisturized skin and painted nails. She bought a tiny metal pendant that was bent into an 'M' with pliers by an insistent and stringy Frenchman.

It felt good to have the slight weight of an M tied around her neck, further proof of her new being.

She found a bar and supped wine in a dark corner while she thought about why she was in Barcelona. She was here to pay her debt, get her ring back and leave, but every time an opportunity arose to carry out this plan, she backed away from it. When she booked her flight she was meant to book her return for the following day, but found herself clicking on a return date three days later. When she looked for a hotel she was meant to book a room in Gracia, a nice neighbourhood some distance from Angelo, but now she found herself in a room barely two corners from him. She was meant to do a lot of things, she was meant to be a doting mother of two children, but Spain and Angelo made an exciting new world she preferred to be in. It was a world she was creeping into, rather than retreating from. And the adrenaline flowing through her body in that dark little bar was enough to have her sprinting and throwing herself further in. She couldn't remember the last time she had felt so excited about a man, it had happened but it was such a distant recollection that it was barely there, it was like someone else's memory.

She drank two more glasses of wine in the darkness, ran her fingers through her hair, and applied some lip gloss, then she headed to Angelo's. He lived in a tall crumbling building covered in the faded stripes and stars that wave in the breeze for Catalan independence. She walked past it twice before she had the courage to ring the buzzer. She waited. Like he predicted, the buzzer didn't work. Maybe this was her chance, her chance to scribble his name on the envelope of cash, post it through his door and donate her ring to a worthy artist. She put her hand into her bag, but it wasn't looking for the envelope, it was searching for her phone. She dialed his number quickly, and he said he would come down to let her in.

Angelo had already prepared the studio for her arrival. He had hidden five of her portraits in the shower, leaving only the largest by the window. He had cleared a space on the sofa and cleaned as best as possible two glasses and two coffee mugs. His frenetic hands had dropped the second mug as he washed it, so he was down to one intact and one without a handle. When she called him, he took a large swig from the bottle of whiskey, ran his hands through his hair and took a deep breath, before dashing down the four flights.

"Hi," he said as he opened the door.

"Hi."

His eyes and smile shone wide.

"Come up."

Maria followed him up the creaky stairs. The staircase was dimly lit, but at every floor a dusty window thrust light into the hallway, and she used each of these opportunities to study Angelo. He was slim but had broad shoulders that tapered into a slim waist. His grey shirt was spattered with paint, and was half tucked, half un-tucked into jeans too large. A brown leather belt almost circled him twice and she could see the curve of his rear with every step. Her heart beat much faster than the four flights warranted. Eventually they got to his apartment, and he turned to look at her in the sunlight. Her hair was loose and beautiful, but it shaded her face and didn't match his portraits of her.

Maria smiled. "You still have my ring," she said looking at his right hand.

He nodded. "Of, course. It hasn't left my hand. It's worth five hundred euros."

She reached into her bag, but suddenly panicked. She was going to give him the money, he was going to give her the ring and then she would have no reason to stay. As she fumbled in her bag he spoke.

"Actually, on second thoughts, it's worth more than five hundred euros."

"What do you mean?"

"Would you do me a favour?"

"What?" she asked, relieved to have postponed the transaction.

Angelo beckoned her around the easel that stood by the window. She followed him and looked at the canvas that was tacked to the wood. It took her a moment to comprehend who it was, and when she did it made her nervous. Propped up on the easel was proof of two things. Firstly there was painted proof that Maria existed and secondly that something more than an innocent purchase had occurred between them. She had his image in her head and on her wall, and now he had hers on canvas in his studio, and clearly in his head. The brushstrokes were thick and textured, the style she had become so familiar with, but the focus that they built towards was lost in a black space where her eyes should be.

"Would you sit for me?" he asked.

She was feeling light-headed and giddy, again a feeling she knew she must have experienced before. She nodded.

Angelo's whole countenance changed into one of animation. He leapt into action, grabbing a stool and moving it around into the light from the window until he was happy. He then turned his attention to Maria, taking her satchel from her shoulder and placing it on the sofa, gripping her by the shoulders and shifting her onto the stool. All the while, he didn't take his focus from her eyes. He scrutinized her as she sat in place, and then pulled her hair from her face and shook it to fall down her back. He was choreographing her like a bowl of fruit. He stood back by the window and squinted at her to assess the picture he had arranged. He shook his head. He looked around, picked up an elastic band and gave it to her.

"Plait you hair. The way you had it in Madrid." He gestured to a door in the far corner. "There's a mirror in there."

Maria obeyed like a little girl. In the bathroom she saw a pale version of herself in the cracked mirror. She shouldn't be doing this, she shouldn't be spending thousands of euros on a handsome pair of eyes, and she shouldn't be sharing her own. Being infatuated with someone, someone unobtainable, was one thing, but a glimpse of their shared feelings, the possibility of what could be, was plain scary. Of course, this is what she wanted, to be free with her feelings, but now that the prospect presented itself she felt like running away, running back to Beth. She plaited her hair over her right shoulder as she always wore it in Madrid.

Angelo called through, "coffee or wine?"

"Wine," she shouted back a little too quickly.

When she returned to the studio Angelo was sitting on the window sill. He guided her into place, so that her face looked directly into the window, and her body was turned at a slight angle. A high three-legged stool was placed next to her with a tumbler of red wine. He walked back to the window and looked at her, she cast her eyes down, away from his.

"No, no. You have to look at me, right at me."

She took a big slug of wine, got back into position and fixed her eyes on his.

"Good. Now don't look away." Maria liked the way he told her what to do, there were no manners to distract from what he wanted.

Angelo started mixing paints on a plank of wood, taking long, concentrated looks at Maria, always at her eyes. She was beautiful, truly beautiful, and he would have her, he knew that. But he had to complete the picture, already it was the best thing he had ever produced and it wasn't even finished. Something dawned on him and he walked around his easel to Maria. He bent down in front of her, removed the ring from his little finger and slipped it onto the ring finger of her left hand. Maria giggled, and he looked up at her in confusion, before laughing also. It was good to see him laugh again, to see his eyes crinkle in happiness.

"Wrong hand?" he asked.

"Wrong hand," she stated with a smile.

"I'm a quick worker but not that quick," he said with a wink.

He switched the ring to her right hand. His large hands were coarse, like tree bark. He returned to the window sill and seemed to take hours to mix a colour that looked black. He smudged teardrops of ultramarine, crimson and cadmium along the outer edge of the plank and took up a thick brush. He then looked straight at Maria.

When someone stares at you without words, without noise even, the seconds feel like minutes, and the minutes hours. To look into someone's eyes without smiling, without playing, is a rare intimacy. Mothers and daughters, brothers and sisters, priests and their parishioners, even lovers will not look at one another without the help of some distraction, some words, some giggles, some kisses. To look too deeply is to expose yourself, and this is exactly what Angelo was looking for in Maria, to know what was happening in her head.

Maria felt strained and anxious sitting in front of him, but time relaxes the strangest situations, and soon her pulse slowed and the sun loosened her shoulders and posture. As much as he was studying her, she began to study him. With the sun behind him he was mostly a silhouette, but his body and the way it moved captivated her. Here in his studio he was vibrant, agile and fluid. He leant on the window sill, with one bare foot on the floor and one on the crate. The short plank of colours balanced along his thigh and he held the paintbrush with his right hand, leaving his left hand to rub at his stubble, to push his hair from his face, or pick up his glass of wine. She could just make out the glint of his eyes in the blackness of his silhouette, and they didn't leave her alone, unless to mix a new colour or to assess his work. Otherwise, the wine glass was picked up, a paintbrush was dipped into a jam jar, dried on a hardened rag, and used to pick up a new colour without his eyes leaving hers. It was as though he had robotic limbs, until of course his paintbrush stroked the canvas, and then it moved as fluidly as the wind.

At times it looked as though Angelo was conducting an orchestra. He would lift his right arm high into the air and use his left to navigate himself around Maria's face, moments would pass before he made a few determined brushstrokes. At other times, his brush seemed to wander around the canvas aimlessly. As his arms danced gracefully behind the easel, the edges of his long hair were highlighted in gold by the sun. He didn't utter a word to Maria, only to himself, and nothing that made much sense.

"Here, no, no, here." "Maybe, yes." "What if it were just a little more…" "Too much, too much."

Maria loved the way he painted and she loved the way all she had to do was sit there. Nothing was expected of her, she didn't have to be Beth or Maria, she just had to be a body and a face. She breathed long and deep, and took in her surroundings. The whole environment was art; canvases and paints, jam jars of colour, rags everywhere, even a guitar that sat in the far corner by the bathroom was covered in green, as though an animal with painted paws had tried to get comfortable on it. Everything here in front of her contributed to his art and happiness. She admired this kind of single-minded passion for something, this something that was so deep inside Angelo that all of life's responsibilities sat a distance away. It was clear that money, technology, vanity, status, all meant nothing to him, they were just words he probably never used. Angelo was true to himself. He lived honestly and simply, and did things to make himself happy. She wanted that, and she wanted him.

She wanted his coarse, coloured hands to touch her. She wanted to be one of the simple things in life that Angelo could enjoy. She wanted his artist's hands, his artists's body to enjoy her, nothing more, nothing complicated. Just to indulge in the simplest form of human nature. Something honest and true. It was while she was thinking this that he spoke to her, for the first time in over an hour.

"Your eyes have changed since Madrid," he said.

"Have they?"

"Yes. In Madrid they were a mystery to me, but here sat in the sunshine, I can see right into them."

She blushed, and felt nervous about what her eyes were saying.

Angelo stepped closer and studied the tiny golden threads that radiated from her pupils into the dark brown of her irises. He stood so close that she could smell his musty mix of smoke and coffee and she could feel the warmth of his skin.

"Perfect," he said. She felt the same way.

He retreated back to the other side of the canvas and she felt like crying out for him to come back.

His brush moved around the canvas for another few minutes until the light in the room dimmed into greyness. It was as though the sun itself had decided it was time for the painting to finish and the romance to start.

"Finished for today," he said.

She stood up and stretched her back out. Although he was cleaning his brushes, he was watching her petite body as it took form beneath her oversized clothes.

He put the plank of colour down and went to the bathroom. Inside he ran the tap that only ran cold, and splashed the icy water onto his face. He then sat on the toilet seat and took some deep breaths. His desire for Maria was building but he had to keep it in his head and his pants until he'd finished the painting. He knew what he saw in her now would be changed once they'd given in to each other. He stood to take a pee.

While Angelo was in the bathroom, Maria gazed out of the window, at real life. Opposite, a string of children's clothes hung from a tatty terrace, little boy's clothes the same size as Miles'. She gulped and turned away from the view.

When he came out he picked up both of their glasses and went into the kitchen. She thought he'd emerge with two more glasses of wine, but he emerged empty-handed. She looked at him with eyes incapable of lying.

"Why so sad?" he asked.

"I'm not sad," she said with a forced cheer.

He walked to the door and held it open for her. "I'll make you smile tomorrow," he said with a wink. "But only once I've finished your painting."

Maria's face burst into a smile and she went to the door and stood in front of him.

"That's more like it," he said and touched her face. The touch from this man she'd spent minutes with felt more genuine than the touch of the man she'd spent years with, and she blushed at the intimacy.

"So I'll come back tomorrow?" she asked.

"Yes, at about the same time, for the light," he explained.

"Erm, OK." She paused. "I guess I could change things round and come back again."

"You do that." He didn't ask what she had to change around, he didn't want to know about what she did. The impression we have of colourful people at first glance is often greyed as soon as the reality of their life presents itself. He opened the door wider for her but she had trouble stepping out.

"It needs to be in daylight, OK? About the same time again."

"OK, sure. Can I just use your bathroom?" She was stalling. She couldn't leave just yet. She wanted to smell, feel and see the truth of Angelo's life for as long as possible.

He gestured to the door.

Once in the bathroom, she looked at herself, cracked in two in the broken mirror. There was Beth in her regular life a flight away, and there was an image of a different life here in Maria. Maria was the woman a young Beth had visions of becoming, the free-spirited woman who didn't need money, didn't need the responsibilities of being a mother, a wife nor a Willowman. Maria was the woman who got more joy from the simple and free things in life than she did from the most valuable objects in the world. Maria smiled at herself.

In the reflection in the mirror she noticed that the shower curtain was stretched at an odd angle. She turned and pulled it back. Behind it was a loose roll of canvases. It made her smile to think that even his shower was a place for art. It was most likely used more often for art than for showering. She took the roll and gingerly opened it out, making as little noise as possible. She immediately recognized her plait and ringed finger. Her heart sped in anticipation as she looked beneath the image at the other canvases. They were all of her, slightly different angles of her, one with her chin resting on her hand, one with fragile fingers resting over her mouth, one with her body in profile and her face turned, and all with one thing in common; a dark abyss where her eyes should be. Her heart sped. She rolled the canvases back up, flushed the toilet and took a few deep breaths, trying to quench the thrill that was growing inside her.

Outside she picked up her satchel, and gave Angelo the envelope of money.

"Thank you," he said. "But you will come back tomorrow right?" There was an edge of concern in his voice.

She smiled at him, trying to keep her feelings in check. "Yes. *Hasta mañana.*"

"*Adios*," he said as the door clicked behind her.

03:37, Wednesday January 9th, 2013
14 Carrer Lleo, Al Raval, Barcelona

Angelo couldn't sleep that night. In the lights of the moon and street that drenched his studio, he got up from his mattress on the floor, padded over to the window and turned the canvas around to face him. The freshly painted lines glinted at him, and he realized that he had painted a tiny smile on her lips, only just perceptible. Had it been there that afternoon or had he painted what he wanted to see? Did he care if she was happy or not? She had paid him what she owed, and now she was just a *madrileña* he intended to sleep with. He thought about Maria's happiness as the sunlight took over from the moon.

A few roads away, Maria also watched the day sneak into her room having not slept. She was so close to Angelo but so far away, even when she sat a few feet away from him it felt the same way, like the easel between them was an abyss. She couldn't help herself, she wanted to be closer to him, to feel the glow from him when he painted, to feel his conductor's hands on her. And he wanted to be close to her, perhaps more than just physically, her heart raced again when she thought of the canvases hidden in the bathroom, the secret stash of his interest in her, a concealed obsession, to match hers. That whole night she was Maria thinking about Angelo. The husband and children in London belonged to someone else. Angelo made it easy for her to focus and at the same time forget.

12:03, Wednesday January 9th, 2013
14 Carrer Lleo, Al Raval, Barcelona

She found herself heading to his studio at midday. He didn't question the fact she was early, he was just glad she was. That morning he had been hit by a fear that she might not turn up, that his painting would go unfulfilled, and that he would never see her again. But here she was with her eyes shining at him. They were ringed with sleepy circles, but all Angelo saw was their radiance, their white glow around their black centres. Perhaps it was the midday sun gleaming on her in the street but, as she followed him up the stairs and he turned to look at her, the sparkle from her eyes continued.

Maria felt like overtaking him on the stairs to get to his studio first, to see the chaos, to smell the coffee and cigarettes, to be his model, to feel his eyes on her and to see his brush whipping across the canvas - creating her. Documenting in paint the existence of this new person - Maria. Inside the room at last and she felt a warmth inside her. He poured her a glass of wine without asking if she wanted it, and gestured for her to take her position. She sat in place and smiled at him.

He stood behind his easel, assessing her with a critical eye. He then approached her and adjusted her shoulders, hands, and hair. The firmness of his touch excited her, and the throbbing of her heart spread out through her body and to her skin. Back behind his easel he squinted at her.

Maria looked squarely at him, her eyes full and sparkling, a tiny smile sat on her lips. He breathed slowly and looked at her, first with knotted brows and then with an open intensity. She held his stare, almost defiantly. He wanted her, and he was trying to decide what action to take; to finish the picture or to do something about his desire, to do something about the woman whose eyes dared him to come closer.

Angelo felt his pulse throbbing in his neck, it was like his head was trying to remind him to keep focused, to make him paint, it was telling him to finish the picture, his best picture yet.

He pulled his eyes away from her and reached for his tubes of paints. He let his hair fall over his face, it helped him hide from her as he methodically prepared his collection of colours, matching them to the dried stains on the plank from yesterday. He took a lot longer to arrange himself and his tools than he normally would, wanting to give himself time to cool down and collect his thoughts. Finally he took a medium brush, a deep breath and a clear look at his model.

Her eyes were still glowing and her cheeks were flushed. Before he could get too involved in her expression, he threw his brush into the paint and swept it across the canvas in quick twitching movements, it returned to the palette along with his eyes that were nervous to look at her too long, and this process continued for a few minutes. The intensity of her stare deserved urgency, quick and fat strokes of paint. His heart raced as fast as his brush, and in no time at all the painting was complete. He looked at it. It was perfect.

"I'm finished," he said. The first two words he had spoken that day.

She stood up and walked to the easel. There, staring back at her, was a woman in love, a woman filled with want. She blushed and swallowed. She didn't know what to say. She felt embarrassed, ashamed by what she had communicated to him. This was all a big mistake, a huge lie, she shouldn't have come.

She turned to say something to him, maybe a 'goodbye' but as her mouth opened to fill the space, his mouth closed on hers and she forgot that she had anything to say. The *'adios'* she had meant to speak turned into something different altogether, and their mouths told each other all that they wanted without a word.

08:43, Thursday January 10th, 2013
14 Carrer Lleo, Al Raval, Barcelona

The next morning, Angelo stood naked sipping a sweet black coffee from a cup with no handle. Over the cracked rim, he watched Maria run her fingers through her long dark hair, straightening out the knots he had made in it during the night. She wore his once-white shirt that was spattered with all the colours of her portrait. Below the crumpled hem of the shirt her brown legs also had specks of paint, and he remembered how his hands had wandered up beneath her dress. They'd had a great night together and normally by his first black coffee of the day he would ensure he was alone, requesting that Celia or any other woman in his bed leave quickly, but this time he wanted to talk, wanted to know about her. In a role-reversal Maria wanted the opposite.

"You sure you don't want a coffee?" he asked.

"Sure," she said. "I need to go."

"Why? Where are you going?"

Maria looked around the studio in search of her clothes.

"Back to Madrid."

"You done everything you needed to do in Barcelona?"

"Mmm-hmm," she nodded. She turned away and padded around the apartment.

"So what brought you to Barcelona anyway?"

She couldn't tell him what brought her to Barcelona. "Work," she said.

Her dress was peeping out from behind the crate, and her bra was on the floor nearby, she picked up both and scanned the studio further. She picked up her white knickers from the plank of paints where they had been dropped. She couldn't help but laugh. Maria turned to look at Angelo, a big smile on her face and her underwear in hand. Before he could ask her any more questions, she had to bring the conversation back to the here and now.

"Where's your bin?" she said, brandishing the paint-stained fabric.

"No way," he said, shaking his head. "They're as good as new, a bit of colour in your pants."

She laughed. "You certainly gave me that."

He took her underwear, turned it around and bent to the floor, placing it so that she could step into it. Her toes with chipped varnish stepped in and he pulled the painted knickers up her legs slowly, his thumbs hooked inside the elastic and his fingers tracing the contours of her legs. He pulled her knickers into place and lifted his shirt to admire her body speckled in paint.

"A masterpiece," he said. "My best work yet." He ran his fingers up the sides of her waist, his coarse hands tickling her skin, like old bark on a fresh petal. The sun, the caffeine and Maria were all fuel to Angelo's body and she watched the excitement build in him.

Maria took a last look at Angelo and a deep breath, before removing his hands and heading to the bathroom.

"Can I take a shower?" she called over her shoulder.

"Er, sure." He sighed and watched her dark hair swing as she approached the bathroom. "Wait!" he called. "I just need to…." He dodged in front of her, picked up the roll of canvases from the shower and walked out with them in his arms, six eyeless Marias rolled up against his bare chest. His excitement over the real Maria had turned to panic.

"Just needed to clear the shower," he muttered as he walked past her.

Behind the closed door, Maria looked down at the paint-spattered shirt that hung open across her breasts, she assessed her legs that were dotted with colour, the souvenirs of Angelo's creeping fingers. She eyed herself in the cracked mirror and bit her lip. She saw a guilty Beth, not a liberated Maria. She looked at herself for a few moments before getting into the shower. There was no hot water but that suited her just fine, she scrubbed her skin until the paint came away and she began to feel a little cleaner. She dried herself with the only towel available and then stood dripping on the tile floor, deep in thought. She put on her bra and dress, and then her paint-stained knickers – the last souvenir. She looked at herself resolutely in the mirror and left the bathroom.

Angelo was tidying the studio when she emerged. From Maria's point of view it looked like he was rearranging the mess. He had thrown the sheets in a corner, the same corner from which he had grabbed them in the night, and the mattress was leaning up against the wall. His naked figure was now pulling the sofa to the position where the mattress had lain. He looked up and smiled at Maria. Her wet hair hung over her shoulders and was making dark rivers in her dress, that almost appeared to become her legs, like some kind of mythical creature. Thetis emerging from the sea. He would probably draw it later. He pulled the crate in front of the sofa and the transition was complete, his night studio had become his day studio.

Angelo placed his hands on his hips, satisfied with his environment and clearly happier without clothes than with them. "Coffee now?" he asked.

"No," she said, looking at the paint-soiled floorboards. Then she looked up with a smile. "Well, actually yes, that would be good."

Angelo beamed, happy to have her happy in front of him again. Even her short spell in the shower had felt too long. He studied her pretty face a moment and then went into the kitchen to prepare some coffee. As it brewed in the pot he washed up the only cup with a handle. He poured two coffees. Did she take sugar?

"You want sugar?"

When there was no response he poked his head around the doorframe. "You want sugar?" he asked of the empty room. His heart jumped. He put the two cups down and raced to the only other room in the apartment. She wasn't there.

"Maria?" he said into the silence. He ran to the window, pulled it up and hung his naked torso out, scanning the street below. "Maria!" he shouted.

There was not one person on the street.

Angelo was at a loss. He pulled on some trousers, sprinted down the stairs and began wandering around Al Raval looking for traces of Maria. The area was a maze of streets, parks and alleys, perfect for getting lost and never found. He asked a few of the regular hippies and vagrants if they had seen her, but she had left no answers behind her. He plodded back to his studio, his hair hanging over his face and swinging from side to side as he shook his head. Would he see her again? Why did she vanish? A dart of optimism struck him as he turned the corner back to his road, maybe she had just popped out to get something; a croissant, a toothbrush, anything. He ran to his building and raced up the stairs hoping to see her at every turn of the stairwell, but every turn was empty. He burst through the open door back into his space, shouting her name "Maria!" But the word just flew from his mouth and out the open window.

A few streets away Maria leant her back against the cool wall of an unknown alleyway, letting her breathing slowly return to normal. Her eyes were filled with tears as she looked around her and took note of where she was; the side street was dark, empty and filled with litter. She looked around again furtively, before dropping her satchel, lifting her dress and wiggling out of her underwear. She kicked them into the darkness and left the alley to wonder about its newest gift left by a stranger; a pair of white cotton knickers patterned in blue, green and black acrylics.

13:51, Thursday January 10th, 2013
Hostel Havana, Madrid

Back in Madrid, Maria didn't want to go out, she didn't want to sit in El Infinito stroking a coffee cup and watching other people's lives. She didn't want to go to exhibitions, didn't want to read books, didn't want to see anybody. She wasn't interested in any of it. Those things had no impact on her or her happiness any more, they made no difference to her life.

She sat on her cardboard sofa and pondered; was she more miserable as Maria or as Beth? She wasn't sure anymore. As Beth, she had completely betrayed her family and the morals she had once prided herself on. As Maria she had been reckless and stupid and had fallen for a man she must never see again.

She sent Tom a text so she could delay facing him, *'client wants more meetings next week, have to stay this weekend to prepare – sorry! Love to kids x'*. She then spent most of the next week in her room with Angelo's portrait, feeling as sad as his image looked. She replayed her time in Barcelona over and over in her head; how Angelo had looked at her as she sat for him, how scared she was by the image he had captured of her, but how her fear had transformed into something stronger when his lips touched hers. She had felt so light and carefree with him. In his ramshackle studio, nothing mattered but painting and feeling. The trivialities of life had melted away in his apartment and in his arms. But as those things melted into oblivion, they had taken with them other pieces of her life, more important pieces.

She tried to force herself back into living. She left the painted eyes of Angelo in her room and went to the café. Carlos was absorbed in Dostoyevsky, and didn't look up until he had reached the end of his paragraph - When he did, his eyes opened in alarm.

"God Maria, are you ok?" he asked.

"I'm fine," she said. *"Un café con leche."*

She felt awkward taking her favourite seat by the window, with Carlos' eyes following her. He delivered her drink.

"Have you been sick?" he asked.

"No." She grabbed the nearest book from the shelf behind her and buried her head somewhere in the middle of it. Carlos had never shown any interest in her well-being before, and if he asked any more questions she was certain she would shout at him, or possibly cry.

"Well, you look like death," he mumbled as he returned to his own book.

When she was safely alone, she put the book down and looked out of the café window. Life was happening around her, a couple walked along locked in each other's arms and eyes, a new mother sat on one of the outside chairs jiggling and giggling with her baby, a businessman walked past embroiled in an angry telephone exchange. Everyone living their own full lives, not like her fragile two halves. Maria refocused to look at the woman staring back at her in the glass. Beth stared back. She was gaunt and miserable, dark lines hung beneath her eyes and frown lines were etched on her brow. She tried to iron them out with a smile at herself, but even this didn't remove them. The fingers of her left hand automatically moved to touch the ring on her right, the ring that had spent a week with Angelo, on his skin, feeling his blood race past. Maria knew the only way to feel full again, to smile again, and to lose the lines of sorrow on her face, was to see him. But how could Beth feel full again?

17:22, Sunday January 10th, 2013
14 Carrer Lleo, Al Raval, Barcelona

Angelo tried to throw himself into his painting but, since another light had entered his studio, the glow from his original passion had dimmed. It was stupid, he knew, to be so affected by a woman but he couldn't help himself. He felt none of the magic when he picked up a paintbrush, he got no buzz from mixing the perfect hue, and his attempts at new paintings were lifeless. He had tickets to an exhibition of his favourite

Catalan artist, but even the prospect of meeting Pedrosa himself at the opening was not enough to tempt him outside. He was consumed with the memory of Maria, and so he sat and fermented in his little garret, drinking wine, then whiskey, then rum, and staring at his picture of Maria.

One evening as the sun was dipping behind the buildings, and Angelo was watching Maria's eyes darkening, there was a knock at the door. He sat still, hoping the knocker would leave.

"Angelo, man! It's me." Xavier's voice filled the room. "Open up!"

Angelo kept silent. Xavier didn't know he was there.

"I know you're there. Your landlady just told me. Said you've hardly been out in weeks. Told me if I find a corpse to search the pockets for this months rent."

Angelo sighed, opened the door and retreated to his safe place in front of Maria. Xavier entered the room, his arms raised to the ceiling like an actor returning to the stage for his encore.

"He's alive, praise the lord! He looks like a corpse, but the fact he opened the door means he still has a pulse!" He lifted two empty bottles. "A pulse made of whiskey by the looks of it. Man, what's happening?" He gave Angelo two slaps on the back, the force of which made Angelo topple from the window ledge, and move his focus to his friend.

"*Nada*. Nothing's happening."

"You look like shit," said Xavier.

Angelo smiled. "You know all the right things to say, is that how you charm the ladies?" He slapped his friend on the shoulder. "It's good to see you Xavi, want a drink?"

Xavier couldn't remember saying no to a drink before, but looking at the state of Angelo and his studio, he thought it best to make an exception.

"No. I'm taking you out."

"No, Xavi. Let's just stay here. I've got plenty to drink. You can tell me what's been happening with you, there's always a story to tell."

"There's always a story, you're right, but I'm telling it over dinner. And at this exact moment there's no one else to accompany me, except perhaps your miserable old landlady but, between her misery and yours, I pick yours, so get yourself together." He opened the big bay window and took a whiff of Angelo at the same time. "Treat yourself and me to a shower hey?"

Angelo lifted his shirt and took a sniff. "That bad?"

Xavier nodded.

"Fine, I'll take a shower, but I really don't want to go out."

"Well, I do. It was bonus week this week, and my bonus was keeping my job, so we're going to celebrate, with a big meal. My treat."

He stood behind Angelo, picked him up from under his arms and pushed him in the direction of the shower.

When Xavier could hear the water running, and was sure his friend was in the shower, he started to clean up the apartment. He picked up every receptacle that had been Angelo's drinking buddies and placed them in the sink, he cleared away the makeshift ashtrays that dotted every surface, and threw away any stinking remnants of food. He picked up the clothes that were strewn across the apartment and heaped them in a corner, perhaps he could convince his friend to visit the launderette, or maybe he would do it for him. Once again he noticed the empty hook on the wall from where Angelo's father had surveyed the room, was that the reason for Angelo's downturn? Just as he was considering this, Angelo came out of the bathroom with a towel around his waist, his wet hair hanging sadly into his boney clavicles. He traipsed around the apartment in search of clothes.

"In the corner man, not sure how fresh they are."

As Angelo picked through the pile of grubby clothes Xavier went to sit by the open window in front of the painting. His eyes widened.

"Man! This painting! This painting is fucking fantastic." Having just taken a seat on the window ledge, he immediately left it to look more carefully at the portrait. "Wow, Angelo. Seriously, this is the best I've seen. The face, the eyes, the expression. This is amazing."

Angelo came to stand next to his friend, doing up his shirt buttons whilst looking at the painting.

"It was all in the model," he said quietly.

Xavier immediately understood.

"Well, let's go for dinner. You can tell me all about her."

*

The last few weeks, Angelo's feelings had triumphed over his body. Every stagnating moment had been spent thinking, dwelling, pondering, and despairing over Maria to the detriment of his physical state.

However, his body was now reviving itself, as though it had been held under water to the point of pain, and was now released into the fresh air. Angelo and Xavier sat in the triangular space outside Café Babel in the unseasonal warmth. Behind them, a Roman wall was surrounded by a moat of rubbish and cigarette butts and an iron fence (as though the defences of trash were not enough). To the left, three stoned guitarists strummed out Catalan classics on a low wall where fellow stoners rolled joints and wobbled their heads. To the right, a collection of cobbled streets converged, and tourists and locals alike strolled past trying to avoid each other. The tattooed waiter brought out *cañas* and cutlery, olives and bread and Angelo launched into the food like a beggar at a banquet. Xavier watched the bread and olives disappear, waiting for Angelo's mouth to free up.

"So, the woman with no eyes… now has eyes."

Angelo sighed into his beer, back to reality.

"Her name is Maria."

"And?" Xavier prodded.

"That's about all I know." He smiled. "She came, she settled her bill, she sat for me and she vanished."

Xavier's mouth widened into a grin. "And when you say 'she sat for you', you mean she sat on you?"

Angelo's face cracked into a smile, he couldn't help it with Xavi's schoolboy humour. "She stayed over, then grabbed her things and ran, not even a goodbye."

"Reminds me of someone else," said Xavier, lifting an eyebrow at his friend. "I'd have thought that would be the perfect situation for you."

"Normally, it would." Angelo paused. "But there was something different about her. The way she looked at me, the way she touched me, this mystery about her, all of it made me want her, and not just for the night. It was the start of something."

"Que romantica!"

The two men ate and watched as two policemen on bikes dismounted and moved the guitarists on. It was a shame.

Angelo repeated himself, as though truth came about from repetition. "It was definitely the start of something. And she knew it too. I think that's why she disappeared."

"Can you find her?"

"No, I know nothing about her. Just that her name is Maria and she lives in Madrid."

"Well that narrows it down!"

Angelo sighed. "Even if I knew more about her, I don't think she wants to be found."

"Well man, if nothing else, you got a fantastic fuck and a fantastic face out of it. I'm telling you, that painting in your apartment's going to make your fortune."

"I'm not selling it," said Angelo.

"Come on man, don't get sentimental on a one-nighter. That picture is a masterpiece I tell you, get that agent of yours to take a look, she'll tell …"

The waiter arrived with their *tortilla*, *estofado* and *pimientos de padron*.

"I'm not selling it," said Angelo loudly. He wasn't sure why the idea made him angry. The waiter raised his eyebrows and left them to change the subject.

10:03, Monday January 28th, 2013
Barcelona

The following day, remembering his promise to Xavier, Angelo headed to the launderette with a dustbin bag of clothes. He sat watching the clothes and soapy water churn in circles. The old Chinese woman who ran the launderette mopped the floor around him, but his eyes didn't budge from the machine. When her mop reached his boots, she spat out of the door, tutted and pushed his feet out of the way to complete her job. He walked slowly home, the rhythm of a forgotten belt in the washing machine echoed in his head. His eyes watched the concrete. As he passed familiar graffiti and approached his building, he mechanically reached into his pocket for the key.

"Angelo," a voice said.

The monotony of his morning and the mornings of the past few weeks was broken at once. He looked up and there she was. Beautiful, mysterious, Maria. For a moment he could do nothing but look at her, his mouth agape. Then he dropped his washing and grabbed her. He held her in his arms, breathed in the sun's heat and freshness from her hair, and felt her heart pumping against his belly. He didn't want to let her go.

Maria loved being in his arms, feeling his artist hands gripping her, smelling his familiar mix of smoke, coffee and grime. He felt thinner than last time, but his broad shoulders and strong arms still gave her a thrill, and she found herself moving her hands around his body to feel him, to remind herself of all the contours she had been thinking about, all the lines she had been missing. Her hands wandered beneath his shirt and moved across the bones and muscles of his back, not wanting to leave an inch untouched.

Angelo's skin prickled at her touch like her fingers were ice. He pulled her slightly away from him, but only so far that he could kiss her, otherwise their bodies remained tightly entwined. They kissed forcefully, with all the weeks of missed kisses catching up with each other. He couldn't get close enough to her with his hands and mouth.

He got the key from his pocket and fumbled for the lock, wanting to be inside with her but not wanting to lose his grip on her. He pushed the heavy metal door open, grabbed the bag of washing and threw it up the stairs. The couple stumbled into the building and took a few steps up the stairwell before the same thought dawned on them both. They couldn't wait four flights of stairs. They ripped at each other's clothes and nestled onto the bag of still-warm washing until, with a gasp from Maria, their bodies were as close as two bodies can be. They made love on the first few steps of the stairwell and were so lost in each other that they didn't notice Señora Carmen open her door to see what the racket was. The landlady twisted and turned her head to try and identify the couple and what they were doing on her staircase. Her eyebrows shot to the ceiling when she recognized the act, it had been a long time, almost 40 years, since she had witnessed anything like that in real life. She was about to shout at them to stop what they were doing, when she noticed the paint-spattered shirt, and realized it was Angelo. She breathed a sigh of relief in the knowledge her tenant was still very much alive, before she retreated to her apartment and turned up the volume on her midday *telenovela*.

*

Angelo and Maria made love once more without interruption on the third set of stairs in the building, before finally arriving in his studio, with bodies matched in sweat and dust, and faces matched in smiles. The weeks of decline that had etched their suffering on Maria's face lifted at the first sight of Angelo and she was radiant and young again. Angelo's body, although still emaciated, had begun to respond to the nourishment of food and friendship from the night before, and the two lovers looked with hunger at each other's glowing bodies. From the ripped laundry bag, Maria flung a pair of jeans to Angelo and chose a green shirt for herself. They settled either side of the large window with their legs touching in the middle, their bodies bordered the sides and base of the window in a lovers' frame. A cold draught from the dilapidated window cooled the heat from their bodies, and both of them felt perfectly happy.

Angelo wanted to know so much about the woman in front of him, but he knew he had to be careful. The very last thing he wanted was to scare her away, she was like a beautiful but vulnerable bird that could fly out the window at any moment. She had come back to him, and that was the important thing. He could find out about her in time, for now he was just happy to be sitting here, his feet touching hers in the winter sunshine.

"I'm glad you came back," he said.

"So am I," she said and her eyes told him it was true.

*

Maria stayed with Angelo for four days before returning to Madrid. They filled their time with each other, with sunshine, with walks in the park and with planning her next visit. At first Maria was hesitant in conversation, afraid she would give something of her other life away. But as the hours, days and words passed, her immersion into Maria deepened and Beth became a distant memory. Beth was a long-ago friend she had grown apart from. Despite her growing ease around him,

Angelo remained careful in what he asked. Among the hundreds of questions that itched for release, he asked very few.

"So, had you won the lottery? The day you bought an overpriced painting from a stranger in a café?"

"Overpriced? I thought it was a bargain!"

They were lying in bed, naked and eye-to-eye. The perfect environment for seeing through a lie. Maria laughed but it was a perfectly valid question. How had someone like Maria afforded a painting on a whim? There was a pause before she answered. "Not quite the lottery." She lifted her right hand displaying the ring. "My grandmother died not long back, I was her only grandchild."

"Well, I'm sorry for her, but happy that it meant you bought my work."

Maria sat up and sipped her wine.

"So you're living off the family jewels?" He looked at her intently but with the curl of a smile.

She answered quickly this time. "I only use that money when I need to." She softened and tried out her next lie for size. "Or when there is something I really want. Otherwise I write for a couple of different magazines in Madrid, upcoming events, gigs, exhibitions, that kind of thing."

"You wrote about my exhibition?" he asked.

"No." She looked out the window. "But I will next time."

"I doubt there'll be a next time." He shrugged. "I made next to no money and sold the two pictures I wanted to keep. I mean, they were my favourites. Of course, I'm happy that you have one of them, that it has a good home." He smiled and pinched her cheek. "I'm sure my dad would be happier looking at you all day than looking at me." He motioned towards the empty hook where the portrait had hung.

"I'm sure your dad would be happiest looking at you," she said looking at the sad useless hook.

And so Maria and Angelo continued to throw themselves at each other physically, and to creep into each other's histories on tiptoes. Over the four days they became as comfortable in conversation with each other, as they were in bed with each other. Maria learnt that Angelo was a prolific but poor artist, who made money any way he could and spent it all on good brushes and paints first, and bad coffee and dreadful wine second. Together with the paintings strewn around his apartment, his artwork was displayed in several cafes in Al Raval, El Gotico and El Born, which guaranteed free coffees when they wandered locally. Other pieces were stored in friends' houses and, without Señora Carmen knowing, in the dusty cupboard beneath the communal stairs. His paintings were eclectic in subject but consistent in style; fat brushstrokes of colour that achieved amazing detail at a certain focal point. He had a special way of perceiving people and objects. Even the most mundane subject matter seemed to contain hidden feeling and depth when Angelo painted it. It made Maria slightly nervous, if he could reveal the hidden depths of an old teacup by painting it, would he see her secrets?

"You have a great style," Maria told him one day, as she rifled through a roll of still-lifes under the sink.

He shrugged. "Café paintings. I can churn them out in a few hours, and they'll give me 100 euros tops, but they're not going to change anyone's lives. They'll make someone smile as they sit on the toilet and they'll keep my landlady happy."

Maria laughed. "And you? What makes you happy?"

"A real painting. A painting that connects. That reveals more than…" he looked at the picture Maria was scrutinizing, "a couple of oranges and a vase of flowers."

Maria thought the picture he referred to was immensely sad. The flowers were on the edge of losing their beauty, some brighter and more upright than others, but all doubtless fading from life. A fresh and vibrant orange sat on the edge of the image, as though trying to distance itself from the dying beauty in the centre. She looked up from where she was crouching. "And how about the picture I bought from you? Does that one connect?"

"Yes."

"Was it difficult to paint?"

Angelo busied himself with the plates and glasses in the sink, something he never did.

"Yes."

Maria pried no further. In return for keeping his secrets close, Angelo respected Maria's. He discovered she was free, fluent and happy when talking about Madrid, art, music; anything in the here and now, but she became quiet and stumbling talking of her past. The most he extracted from her about her history was that her family came from a small suburb of Madrid and that she had spent most of her childhood with her grandmother. Her eyes twinkled with affection, not tears, when she spoke of her.

"She was ferocious with boys, *hated* men, she always told me she didn't know what she'd have done if I'd turned out to be a boy. She said she would have had to sell me to the circus or tie rocks to my feet and teach me to swim. Luckily I was a girl, and she lavished everything on me. She dressed like a pauper, all in black though she'd never married, wasn't a widow, but she dressed me like a princess and she loved to take me out walking and to see all the looks I'd get. With all the ribbons and laces she put on me I was the prettiest girl in town. When I got older she actively hated every boyfriend I brought home, in fact she hated them before I'd even brought them back." Maria laughed. Her memories were all sincere, real memories of Lolli, and in this make-believe world with Angelo it was nice to relax and share a speck of truth.

"You still are the prettiest girl in town," said Angelo, taking her hand and making her twirl. "Even without the lace and ribbons."

Maria smiled and took her hand from Angelo.

"The only pretty thing she owned was this ring, I have no idea how long it was in her family." Maria held it up, transfixed. "And now she's given that to me, even in death she gave everything to me."

19:43, Wednesday January 30th, 2013
14 Carrer Lleo, Al Raval, Barcelona

The evening before Maria had to leave, Xavier came round. Angelo and Maria were lying entwined on the mattress listening to Brazilian jazz.

"Shit," said Angelo. "That's Xavi."

"Who?" asked Maria. The last few days had been so intensely shared between the two of them that it seemed strange to have the outside world interrupting.

"Xavier, my friend."

"I know you're in there!" came a shout from outside, "I can hear that shitty music. Turn that *mierda* off before you start getting complaints from neighbours."

Angelo sighed and stood up.

"Do you need to let him in?" whispered Maria. Her eyes looked in alarm from Angelo to the door.

"I'll get rid of him quickly," said Angelo, clearing a path from the mattress towards the incessant knocking.

Maria arranged her hair and self and went to sit by the window.

"About time!" said Xavier as the door opened before him. He went to walk in, but then hesitated, stuck his nose in the air like a hound on a scent and smiled. "Smells like sex in here," he said with a wink. Angelo opened his mouth to speak, but Xavier continued with a pat on his friend's arm. "Good on you man, that's what you needed, to wet your dick, was it Ceci? You're looking better al…" He stopped mid-sentence as Maria came into view behind the easel. His manner changed immediately, a dirty chameleon walking into a bed of flowers.

"Aah, I see you have a new masterpiece, what a pretty picture," he approached Maria looking through his hands to form a frame. She watched him with suspicion. "She looks so real, but she is too beautiful to exist in real life." He stood close to Maria, then suddenly jumped to the left and then to the right. "And hey! Her eyes follow me round the room, a true Mona Lisa!"

At this, she couldn't help but laugh.

"Xavi, this is Maria," said Angelo.

Xavier beamed and kissed Maria on both cheeks.

"Nice to meet you," said Maria, although her voice suggested she wasn't sure.

"And you. You are just the medicine my friend needed."

"Coffee?" Angelo asked Xavier.

"Wine," said Xavier. Angelo sighed, wine was a much longer drink for his friend than coffee, it normally involved a few bottles.

"Don't worry," said Xavier, noticing his friend's reluctance. "This is just my aperitif, I'm meeting Enriq and the others soon. Just wanted to come and check on you man."

Maria relaxed, she would be alone again soon with Angelo. Xavier went to turn the music down while Angelo went to the kitchen, but he quickly thought better of it and used the quiet corner created by the jazz to talk to Maria in private.

"Maria, I don't know you, I'd like to know you and I hope I have that chance, because you have made a difference to Angelo, and Angelo's important to me. When you ran out on him it really hurt him, I hadn't seen him that way for years, since his father. But now I see, he is restored, a new man."

She opened her mouth to speak but was silenced by the appearance of Angelo.

"Let's keep him that way," whispered Xavier as he passed her to turn off the music.

"Aah, the sound of silence," he continued aloud. "Best appreciated after…" he picked up the CD case. "Jazz fusion."

Angelo laughed. "Xavier and I differ in many ways, music taste being one of them."

"Yes," said Xavier sipping his wine. "The difference is that I like music, and he doesn't."

Angelo and Xavier entered into a well-rehearsed discussion of what constitutes music, and Maria looked on. Although most of the discussion points were voiced by Xavier, her eyes hardly left Angelo, and Xavier's theatrical performance was lost on her. As a result, Xavier soon lost interest.

"OK, well I should leave you two. My evening continues elsewhere, and yours here." He kissed Maria and hugged Angelo, patting him with force. "She's your medicine, take her regularly," he whispered.

"*Adios!*" said Angelo and Maria, their shared voice chasing him out the door.

Angelo pulled Maria back to the mattress. The time spent with Xavier already felt like time lost with her. She lay down next to him, her chin on his chest. She couldn't let it be the first thing she said, although it was burning to get out of her.

"He's a nice guy."

"He's a good friend," said Angelo.

They fell into silence; his contented and hers not.

"Who's Ceci?" she asked.

Angelo looked down at Maria's face. She was trying but failing to keep her jealousy hidden, the tense little envy muscles around her jaw wouldn't relax. Angelo held on to her tightly and looked straight at her.

"She's a girl I'll never see again."

06:52, Thursday January 31st, 2013
14 Carrer Lleo, Al Raval, Barcelona

Maria woke up hours before Angelo and an hour ahead of the sun. She moved alongside him and felt the gentle rise and fall of his sleeping body until the sun allowed her the view, and then she watched. His mouth was slightly ajar and making the beginnings of a snore which never emerged. His fingers twitched constantly and she wondered whether he was painting in his sleep. She adored him as much asleep as she did awake. Here she could appreciate him quietly. She touched his arm, it was warm and dark against her skin and she kept her hand there, relishing the difference between them. She wanted the natural heat of Angelo to warm her, to bring some energy to her life, to bring some fire. She had done the right thing, coming here, it was good for her and it was good for him.

*

The next two weeks apart felt like a prison sentence for them both; isolated, lonely and desperate for the freedom they felt with each other. At Maria's request, they didn't talk on the phone, "it would make it too difficult," she said. "It'll be difficult enough as it is."

During their time apart, Angelo painted many nudes and many bowls of fruit that strangely resembled nudes. With the proceeds from two phallic fruit creations, he bought new bed linen, stocked the fridge and got a spare set of keys cut. Xavier claimed this was close to marriage and that the next investment would be a ring. Angelo shook his head with a smile, but couldn't find the words to disagree.

Maria spent ten days in Beth's life and three back in Madrid. The ten days felt like a huge lie, even though they were actually her truth. Being in London, speaking English, sleeping in a huge bed with layers of lavender-scented cotton, dressing and making her face look like Beth, receiving a dry kiss from her husband every morning - it all felt like a pretence, as though she were acting out the life of someone else. Her three days in Madrid were real life. They were filled with building a base for her Maria there. She trawled café flyers, newspapers and websites for rental apartments. After seventeen phone calls, miles of walking around

Google Earth on her laptop and almost as many miles trudging around the real streets, she visited a rundown apartment block in Lavapies. She liked it. Only four streets away was a large anonymous hotel with free wifi, frequented by business travellers. The neutral lobby, scattered with watercolours and briefcases, was a perfect setting for Skype calls to the family from any European destination. The prospects for both Maria and Beth were good.

The first words spoken by the landlady, Blanca, were "It's nothing special," even before hello kisses.

Maria smiled. Little did Blanca know 'nothing special' was exactly what Maria was looking for. Maria looked at her future landlady. She was mouse-like in size and features, with her hair as wispy as a baby's. Her tiny body was made smaller still by the huge doorframe of rotten wood that surrounded her. The hallway beyond her was dark and foreboding. Maria had a good feeling about the place before she set foot inside, and as she followed Blanca up the staircase she felt more sure with every step. Conversely, Blanca seemed intent on putting Maria off the idea of moving in.

"I've cleaned the place up as best I can, but to be honest with you dear, the last tenant lived like a dog, and some of the strange stains he left behind have been impossible to shift. Also, the boiler is something of an antique and the radiator leaks." She stopped on a stair and turned to look at Maria in the gloom. Her eyes twinkled faintly in the darkness. "You realize it is a shared bathroom dear?"

Maria nodded. "Yes, it was in the advert."

As they reached the second floor a single light bulb lit up in welcome, and Blanca fumbled with a large bunch of keys.

"This is it dear, number 12."

She tried a few different keys before finally opening the door to Maria's new life in Madrid. The cheap door of cardboard wood swung open and showed both women a small room with yellowing walls, basic and worn furniture and a couple of antiquated appliances.

Blanca looked at the room with her head to one side, in the same way you might look at an unfortunate child.

"As I said…" she started.

"I'll take it," said Maria.

That very same day, Maria checked out of Hostel Havana and took her few belongings to Apartamentos Buenavista. Once installed, she did her hair and make-up and raced to the nondescript hotel to make her Skype date.

"Hello sweetheart," said Tom.

The man looked far away and foreign to Maria. His white collar, clean-shaven face and piercing blue eyes struck her as strange, and it took a moment or two for Maria to remember who she was supposed to be. She looked quizzically into the screen.

"Beth, are you ok?"

"Of course, of course. I'm fine." She concentrated on being Beth. "How are the kids?"

His face glowed, even from thousands of miles away. "They're great. Miles got a prize at school today for maths, he can count up to fifty in twos and then backwards again,"

Beth knew she should feel a glow of pride in this, but instead she found herself wondering what use counting backwards from fifty would ever be.

"And Katy drew this for you."

He held up a crayon picture and angled it to fill Beth's screen. It showed a lopsided tower, and a woman stood next to it, seemingly holding it up with a waving hand. The woman had long black hair and a smile that extended past both cheeks.

Beth cocked her head to one side. "Is that me?"

"Yes darling, with the Eiffel tower."

A sudden ache of guilt rose from her stomach and she gulped it back down.

"How's Paris?"

"Oh you know," she said looking down. "It's, well, it's French."

She heard him laugh. "Thanks for the insight sweetheart. But I guess you haven't seen much more than your hotel and a meeting room?"

She nodded her head. Just then the woman at the table next to her beckoned over a waiter loudly in Spanish. Before he was even within earshot she started shouting out an elaborate food order.

"I've got to go Tom," said Beth hurriedly. "I've erm, just seen one of my colleagues." She smiled and waved a hasty hand in the direction of nobody and then turned to her laptop, continuing the wave to Tom.

"Oh, OK. Au revoir," said Tom. "Maybe we can speak again…"

"*Au revoir, au revoir,*" said Beth loudly over the Spanish voices next to her. She closed her laptop and glared at the mouthy woman next to her. The woman glared back and as Beth stood to leave she heard the woman mutter "Damn French."

Outside the hotel, Beth let down her hair and shook it loose. Despite the bitter chill, she undid a few buttons on her shirt and breathed deeply. Being Beth was stressful and stifling, and she decided to walk it off. She ambled the long way from the anonymous hotel to her new apartment. She stopped to read the billposters dripping off the gaudy walls of the *Cine D'Ore*, she ambled around the *mercado* checking out prices and smiles to decide where might become a local favourite of hers, she bought a kilo of oranges and kilo of tomatoes, and drank a euro espresso. She mooched around a dusty dark bookshop and headed in the direction of home. As she turned into her street she smiled at the pink neon of *'Buenavista'*. "Indeed," she said to herself. As she approached her new home, and searched in her bag for the key, she felt as light and free as air, and the life of Beth in London could not have been further away.

That night, while Blanca lay awake worrying about her sweet new tenant upstairs, Maria slept soundly.

16:35, Tuesday February 19th, 2013
14 Carrer Lleo, Al Raval, Barcelona

"God I missed you," she said to him, as they lay naked and sweating in the new sheets, half an hour after she arrived. She stroked his hair.

"I started talking to your portrait," he said, his mouth breaking into a wide smile. "It helped me choose the bed linen."

"It should have told you not to bother," said Maria.

"What? You don't like it?" Angelo moved onto his elbows to look at her.

"No, I do. But you didn't need to. Your old sheets were fine." Maria liked the old mattress just as it was, with torn, threadbare sheets that had absorbed Angelo's scent and bore witness to his life in the studio. She liked him and his apartment just the way they were; in creative squalor, existing through need and passion alone.

"With you here with me I think these sheets will be old in no time," he said with a wink.

He was right. With a full fridge, coffee to make them awake when sleepy, and wine to make them sleepy when awake, they spent three days between the kitchen, the mattress, the sunny window and occasional moments apart for the bathroom. On the morning of their fourth day, Maria made Angelo paint.

"You must paint," she said, putting a brush into his hand. "This isn't a holiday you know."

"Why must I paint? You don't have to write."

She paused. "If I had an article to write I would do. But I finished it on the bus, so now I am free to model!" She grabbed the sheet, draped it over her and struck a Roman pose.

He laughed and his eyes crinkled into a thousand smiles, then they widened to absorb the light and composition around her. He scrutinized her from head to toe.

"Too much sheet, not enough skin," he said.

"I bet that's what all the great masters said, just before they screwed their models."

He laughed. "So there's hope for me yet. No honestly," he said. "Your skin is more interesting than the sheet. Sit down on the ledge and cover your toes with the sheet."

"Just my toes?" she giggled.

"Yes." He started gathering paintbrushes. "They're the only bit I don't like, the only unnatural bit."

Maria stared down at her purple painted toenails and cocked her head. "You don't …"

"And take off all your jewellery."

Maria didn't object. She could tell by his tone that his creativity was fired and she loved it. Forget the world, forget being broke, forget her, he was entering into his tiny world of line and colour. She removed the little M necklace, her bracelets, her many rings, even the plastic stars in her ears, although they couldn't be seen behind her hair. She sat down on the window ledge, her naked body greeting the sun and anyone else watching from the opposite apartments. She swung her legs onto the ledge and wound the sheet around her toes. It was strange to be so naked with the exception of her toes. She wrapped her arms around her knees and looked at Angelo.

"Too tense," he said. "Relax. Enjoy."

She leant back against the wall, her body making a lazy *N* shape against the window. She moved her long hair so it hung down over her shoulder and past the ledge. Although she spent most of her time with Angelo dressed in little or nothing, she felt self-conscious and found herself holding her stomach in and her chest out.

"Now breathe," he said. "Show me the bulge of your tummy and the fall of your tits."

Maria laughed. He knew her body so well already, she couldn't hide it from him.

"That's better he said. Now look out the window, feel the sun, feel loved."

"Feel loved?" She looked at Angelo. He was eyeing her form and adjusting his easel so that he could stand and paint. It took a few moments until he was happy with the easel, with his paints and with brush in hand.

"Yes," he said. "I love you." It was a statement of fact, like the sky is blue and the grass is green and it was no more difficult for him to say than either of those.

She felt a burst inside her. To hear those words from this man made a light burn bright inside Maria, her own internal sunshine. She bathed in the light of both; the sun streaming through the window and that which Angelo had just lit inside her. She lay her head back and looked at the blue sky. No matter what was going on beneath it, in other people's lives in other countries, everything was fine, as long as there was blue sky and there was Angelo.

22:44, Wednesday March 20th, 2013
14 Carrer Lleo, Al Raval, Barcelona

"Angelo, why is your father so sad in the painting I bought of him?" she asked.

They were eating *tortilla, jamon* and *pimientos de padron* in a little bar within the labyrinth of Al Raval. Unlike the first month of their relationship, they were now willing to share each other with the outside world, and to have some space between their skin. Tonight, a small metal table, lit by a bottle made fat by candle wax, separated them.

"Tell me, why was he so sad?"

Angelo looked at the food he had piled onto his plate and suddenly wasn't so hungry.

"Because he was dying."

"Oh." She didn't know what she was expecting, but it wasn't that.

"I made him sit for it, well, he didn't have much choice, by that time he could only sit." He forced a laugh.

Maria choked on a hot pepper, it felt like it was fighting against her. Suddenly an image of Jim appeared in her head, grey and dying. She tried to put the image somewhere else, somewhere it wouldn't make her cry.

"You'd never painted him before?"

Angelo took a few swigs of wine.

"No."

"Why not?"

He put his fork down. "You really want to know?"

She nodded.

"I'd never known him before."

Her eyes bulged and another pepper made her cough. It was as though the tapas were working with Angelo to avoid these questions. "Why? What happened?"

Angelo took a deep breath and filled his glass.

"He left my mother when she was pregnant with me. He had a wife and kids, my mother was just a bit of fun for him, and the fun ended when I came along."

Maria was beginning to wish she hadn't asked. The truth was too sad. Lies can be much easier to hear, and your own assumptions much easier to bear. But now she was curious.

"Will you tell me about him?"

Angelo hadn't talked about his father for a long time, for years, and even then only vaguely with Xavier. The only memory he had of his father was in death and those memories are best kept buried, or they'll bury you too. But the other stuff, the early stuff that formed an angry ball inside of him, had been rolling around gathering heat too long.

"He was a businessman, full of ideas, full of money, full of himself."

"And your mother?" asked Maria.

"She was a singer." He paused. "The opposite to him; no ideas, no money and no idea of her talent. The guitar in the apartment?"

Maria nodded.

"That was hers."

"You play?" asked Maria.

"Not like her, no. I didn't inherit her talent, just her lifestyle." He laughed in a sad way. Angelo paused and lifted his eyes momentarily to Maria's.

"They met at the *Sant Agusti* hotel. He was in town for business and heard her singing there, and that night, well, she got to stay in the fanciest hotel in Barcelona. The first of many nights. Whenever he returned to Barcelona he sought out my mother. The way she used to talk about him was crazy, like he was the love of her life." He shook his head. "She was a romantic, a hopeless one, truly hopeless. She thought a baby was great news, she even named me after him; Angelo fucking Junior. She thought I would bring him to her, but it did the opposite. She still had this ridiculous idea that he would leave his family, that he would come to her, but he never came. All that ever came was the occasional cheque. Not that she knew what to do with it, she'd spend it all on flashy dresses and jewellery. She always thought he'd come back. That he would see her, in all her sparkle, and he would come back to her."

He looked at the wax that was welling up in the little dish made by the heat of the candle, it spilt over and slowly ran down the bottle.

"Even when she died, she hoped he would come, you know, after. She asked to be dressed in her best dress, with her hair how she used to wear it for him, in all her jewellery. She wanted him to see her." He shook his head and sighed. "Even dead. She wanted to see him again, wanted to show him she still loved him, that she was still beautiful for him. She waited her whole fucking life for him, she even fucking waited in the coffin."

Maria took Angelo's hand away from the hot wax that he was playing with, and held it still.

"And did he come?"

He shook his head. "No. And he knew, knew she was dead, Tia Mona made sure of it. But still he didn't come."

They ate in silence for a few moments. Maria knew the rest would come. He didn't need questions, just a little fuel.

"He only came when *he* was dying. Selfish fucking bastard. I'd never met the man and he turns up at my door, says 'I'm your father,' and expects a welcome. I closed the door on him. But he kept coming, week after week. Firstly on his own, then with a nurse, and finally the nurse came alone."

"You talked to her?"

He nodded. "She was sweet, and beautiful. He liked pretty things. He liked my art, or at least he said he did. When she finally persuaded me to visit him, his home was full of it. He'd been buying it for years. I hated that. But I liked seeing him, and you know why?"

She shook her head.

"Because he was suffering. He was in a lot of pain, and he was miserable. His wife had left him. She found out about my mother, and all the others. The way my mother talked about him, he was vibrant, full of life. When I saw him he was a sad old man, crumbling, and that's how I wanted to remember him. So I visited him again, and I painted him."

"What did he say to you? About your mother, about all the years?"

"He told me a load of shit. That he really loved my mother, that she was the most beautiful woman he had ever seen, with the most beautiful voice, but that he had a family, kids to think of, responsibility. If he really loved her, he'd have left them."

Now Maria played with the hot wax of the candle. She had a strange urge to stick her fingers right into the flame. "Sometimes it's not that easy," she said. She couldn't look him in the eye.

"It's fucking easy," said Angelo, almost blowing out the candle. She had never seen him angry. "Love is the easiest thing. Responsibility was just a fucking excuse, to make himself feel better. My mother waited her whole fucking life for him, waiting for him to return, to sweep her off her expensive heels and love her again, like she *thought* he had loved her to start. But it was all *mierda*. He made a joke of her, a joke of her life. So I was happy, happy at his sadness, and the painting was my memory."

Maria's eyes were filled with tears and she could hardly speak. This little peek into Angelo had opened up holes in herself. It had prised open all the little gaps she had managed to seal over while being Maria - her dishonesty, her bereavement, her betrayal. She was playing with Angelo the exact same way his mother had been played, and if Angelo knew he'd hate her in the same way he hated his father. She was failing Angelo in the same way his father had, and she knew she had more in common with his deceitful father than any of the good souls in his past. In a whisper she repeated her first question. "Why is your father so sad in the painting?"

Angelo looked at Maria and studied her a moment. It was a good question. "Perhaps because he was dying; he had enjoyed life and it was coming to an end. Perhaps because he was alone."

Maria thought about all the holes in herself. "Perhaps because of his mistakes," she said, biting her lip.

Angelo shrugged. "I'll never know."

She gripped his hand and tried to smile at him, but she couldn't. She was too full of her own deceits.

*

They didn't make love that night, but she held him close until he fell asleep. She felt his soft breath on her skin and, more than anything now, she wanted to make Maria the truth for Angelo. She wanted him to feel full, full of genuine love. If she could make him feel full, and loved, and faithful, then perhaps those feelings would be reflected back onto her. She could help this fantastic man, she could do something good.

In the morning she shared some of her articles with him. She had discovered a prolific journalist who wrote about culture and travel, she liked the way Maria Fernandez wrote – it was light but informative, and if Maria was to be a journalist she'd like to be this one. Angelo was excited to read her words, her opinions, her craft, and his eyes shone wide.

"Wow, your name in print. I didn't even know your surname! Maria Fernandez explores the hidden histories of immigrant *madrileños*... A night at the museum by Maria Fernandez... A weekend in Toledo – what not to miss by Maria Fernandez." His eyes lit up and he made himself comfortable on the mattress. "*Mi amor*, you're famous!"

She smiled. "You don't need to read them all. I'll make some coffee."

"I don't need to, but I want to."

Maria fussed around the apartment as Angelo read. He noticed her nervous movement out of the corner of his eye.

"These are great," he said. "I never would have guessed they were you. Really professional and interesting. You are opening my eyes to the world of our capital city! Next time I'll have to visit you."

She smiled, but shook her head. "I prefer coming here. You can see from the articles, far too much of my time is spent in Madrid, my head's full of it. I like coming here, to escape."

"Oh, so that's why you come here? Your escape from the city."

She crept into bed alongside him. "You're my escape. And not just from the city. From everything." This was the truest thing she had said to him. Her hands slid under the sheets and over his stomach, pushing her magazines out the way.

"Hey, I'm trying to read this very informative article by a woman called Maria Fernandez!" he said.

"You can read her later." She rolled on top of him. "You can have her now."

11:21, Friday March 22nd, 2013
Apartamentos Buenavista, Calle de los tres peces, Madrid

Back in Madrid, and before her flight back to Beth, Maria spent the morning not staring at the portrait of Angelo, but staring at the portrait of his father. Within his sunken, grey face, his eyes were pure sadness. She could recognize regret in them, and they looked at hers as if begging for forgiveness. She felt for this man in the image, not because he was dying, but because of the decision he'd had to make.

13:32, Wednesday April 3rd, 2013
14 Carrer Lleo, Al Raval, Barcelona

"Hey, I've got some great news. After years of annoying her, the gallery owner of El Quadre has agreed to include me in a new exhibition."

Maria had just arrived at the apartment, letting herself in with her own key. She could tell he was excited about something as soon as she opened the door. Despite the silence of the studio, he hadn't heard the key turn in the old lock, and he stood surrounded by his own canvases, engrossed. Angelo only looked up when Maria walked across the sea of pictures and entered his little island of empty floor space.

"That's fantastic," said Maria, hugging him. "Well done *mi amor*. So what's the exhibition?"

"It's called 'A local perspective' and it's all artists from Barcelona. My paintings will be in great company; Franco and Pedrosa are both exhibiting."

"Wow," said Maria, not having a clue who Franco and Pedrosa were. "How many do you need?" She surveyed the collection.

"She wants six, but I'm going to push for eight." He moved his focus to Maria. "Hey, I was thinking. Maybe you could write an article on it, for one of your magazines?"

Maria moved her focus from Angelo to a nearby landscape and took a few moments in the field of sunflowers to consider her response. "I'd love to. But you know, I only cover Madrid. The magazines I write for only have a circulation in the capital."

"Yes, but you guys still write about things outside of Madrid. There was an article on Salamanca in *Nos Capital* and a review of an exhibition in Toledo in *Vamos Madrid*."

"Was there?" Maria was surprised at his memory. She moved to the next picture and wished she could be sat on that wooden chair in that dark room, wherever the hell it was. "Oh yes, I remember now. But the Catalan articles are nearly always written by freelancers from this area."

Angelo was looking straight at her now. "But you spend lots of time here, you're as good as Catalan."

She came out of the dark room with the wooden chair and reflected his stare. "But I'm not. I'm a *madrileña*."

"So you keep reminding me," he said. He put his hands on his hips and cocked his head. It was a tiny sign of displeasure, and it was the first one he had ever shown towards Maria. She felt a physical pain in her chest at having upset him. "I thought you might be interested in supporting the exhibition, supporting me, your boyfriend."

Maria didn't mean to, but her face twitched and her eyes swelled at the word he had just used. Until that point, their relationship was free and easy, spontaneous and flowing. Now Angelo had given himself a title and it felt like all the fluidity between them had just been bottled. He lifted his eyebrows.

"I am your boyfriend right?" he asked. When she didn't respond, he raised his voice. "Well? Am I your boyfriend or am I just some guy you come to Barcelona to fuck when you get bored with Madrid?"

Maria reached out to him but he moved away, so all she got was shirt. "Yes, yes of course you are. We've just never... used those words before."

"So what word *would* you use for me?" He looked at her, fully angry now. "I'm curious. I'm fucking curious. Because from my point of view, this whole thing, this whole 'Maria and Angelo' whatever the fuck it is, is all on your terms. You come here when you want, you stay as long as you want, then you go back to Madrid. You're treating me like my bastard father treated mama. What am I to you? A fucking gigolo?"

She reached out for him and he backed away again, knocking over a line of canvases.

"No Angelo, please. Don't be angry with me. You are everything to me, you're not a boyfriend, you're not a lover, you are *everything*." She hated to see him upset with her, and she reached for him in desperation like he was falling away from her. "And I'm sorry we live in different cities, different worlds, but I love being in your world, I love it more than my own. You have no idea, *no* idea, how much I love it here." Maria was speaking the truth and it was making her chest ache to have the words out of her mind and into the open. "And that's why I come here, as often as I possibly can, because I love it. You... and this," she gestured around the studio, "are everything to me."

Angelo's anger soon turned to something else, the fire behind his eyes converged into a controlled flame, and he grabbed Maria by the shoulders. "Then come here for good. Move here. Move in with me."

Maria held his stare and felt his grip on her shoulders, this was the first and last place she wanted to be. She wanted to be in his arms, in his eyes, in his heart, in his studio, in his paintings, but she knew it was impossible to be always in his life.

"I would love to move here with you," she said, meaning it.

Angelo took her desire for consent and pulled her into him, kissing the top of her head. She remained that way a few moments before she pulled away, enough of a distance that she could look at him.

"But that doesn't mean that I can," she continued.

Angelo wanted to push her away, to tell her to stop playing with him, but now that she was in his arms he had trouble parting with her.

"Why not?" he said softly.

"What about my work? It's important to me. I've built up a good reputation, a good network in Madrid."

"Then you know how to do it. Do the same in Barcelona."

Maria hesitated.

"And what about my family, they live near Madrid."

"*Mi amor*," he said, pushing some hair away from her face. "You hardly ever talk about your family, other than your grandmother, and now she's gone. I can be your family, we can be each other's. We don't need anyone else. I love you and I don't want to be apart from you. Do you feel the same way?"

"You know I do."

"Then the answer is simple."

She paused several long seconds, looking at Angelo and realizing how strongly she wanted to be with him. All the time. Beth disappeared into the dark corners of her mind, and a smile spread across her face.

"You need to give me time to sort some things out," she said. "There are some assignments for work I need to do, make some contacts here, and organize my apartment." At her words, everything about Angelo seemed to get bigger, she had pumped new life into him. She couldn't remember seeing him happier.

"You've made me so happy. We will be so happy together. I can't wait, *mi cariño*, I can't wait." His broad shoulders and arms seemed to wrap around her a few times and in those few moments, in the warmth of his love, she couldn't remember being happier, or being anyone else.

15:21, Friday April 12th, 2013
14 Carrer Lleo, Al Raval, Barcelona

When Maria returned to Madrid, Angelo's happy high continued with the organization of the exhibition. His agent, Teresa, got wind of the arrangement and turned up, all smiles and Chanel, at his door.

"Angelo!" She exclaimed at the doorway, holding her arms wide. "My second favourite artist!" This was a long-standing joke of Teresa's, who claimed to have a tenuous familial link to Salvador Dali. Angelo didn't approach Teresa, and so for a moment she stood in her flowing kaftan and scarf, arms out, a crucifixion in silk.

"How have you been?" she asked, covering Angelo in kisses and perfume.

"Fine," said Angelo, returning to the safety of his canvases. He still hadn't decided on the final three of the seven images he had negotiated with Silvia at El Quadre, and his apartment remained a sea of paintings.

Teresa picked her way carefully through the pictures, and planned her verbal approach with similar care.

"So," she said. "I've been talking with Silvia." She kept her eyes down. "She's the gallery owner at El Quadre, you might not know her, but she's very excited about our little exhibition."

Angelo stood, hands on hips, looking at Teresa. A tiny smile emerged on one side of his mouth. She saw it, but decided to ignore it.

"So, I thought you and I had better discuss final arrangements." One of her painted nails flicked through a stack of paintings.

"Teresa," said Angelo. "Teresa!" He repeated himself until she looked at him. "I know exactly who Silvia is, she is the woman I first approached two years ago at the *Tapies* retrospective. She is the woman I have been pestering for a chance, a shot at an exhibition for two years. She is the woman who finally agreed, and she is also the woman who has never heard of Teresa Puy Lopez."

Teresa opened her mouth to speak, but Angelo stole her space. "You're not getting a cut Teresa. You've done no work on this one, in fact you've done no work for me for months."

"But, *mi tresor*, I'm your agent. We have a professional arrangement, a work arrangement."

Angelo nodded. "Yes, we do, so it's about time you did some fucking work."

Teresa opened her mouth, closed it and pouted. She considered her options and their likely outcomes, then sighed.

"Well, what if I get some collectors along to the opening?" Hope hung in her voice.

Angelo scrutinized her. "If one of your imaginary collectors turns up and buys one of my paintings, you can have an imaginary 20% of that sale, but I think we both know that's not going to happen."

Teresa rearranged her scarf and surveyed the room. "You seem to have lost all your confidence in me Angelo. I have no idea why, all I ever do is try."

He rolled his eyes and went to the kitchen to make some coffee. When he came out Teresa was holding the portrait of Maria, tilting it into the light.

"I assume this is going to the exhibition," she said.

He shook his head. "It's going nowhere."

"But, *mi tresor*, this is fantastic." She walked to the empty hook on the wall, hung the picture and walked to the far side of the studio to look at it again. "Seriously Angelo, that painting is *incredible*." She prowled around the apartment, her eyes sticking to the picture, examining Maria from every angle. "Incredible."

Angelo offered her a cup of coffee. She took it as though it were full of sewage, and took a tentative sip, before screwing up her nose and looking around for a clear surface to dispense with it.

"You really need to include that portrait Angelo. I'm telling you this as your friend and as your agent, I really think…"

"It's going nowhere," he said with force. "Now if you want to be of any use to me at all, you can help me choose which of these to include." He nodded to the pictures around him.

"I don't know why I bother," she muttered, coming to join him. "A measly 20% if I can get a sale, I don't know why I bother, I must have a soft heart."

Angelo and Teresa spent a few hours rifling through Angelo's collection and arguing over what would sell versus what best showed his talent. Teresa found herself distracted by the portrait of Maria, and kept glancing at it, as though a handsome stranger stood against the wall. When Teresa left she promised to call all her contacts and get them to the exhibition opening.

"It will be a splendid exhibition, *mi tresor*," she said, kissing Angelo goodbye. "I can see big things ahead for you."

"*Adios* Teresa," he said, holding the door. She cast one last glance at the portrait of Maria and left the apartment. Outside, before she negotiated the rickety stairs, she sighed. "Oh, to be so in love."

07:12, Friday April 26th, 2013
7 The Stables, South Kensington, London

Beth was awake before the alarm. She always was. She stared at the grey sky, and took a few deep breaths before she had to begin another day as this strange woman. Tom lifted his eye mask and fumbled with the alarm, before turning to his wife and kissing her shoulder. She never slept facing him anymore.

"Morning sweetheart," he said.

"Good morning."

"I'll get the kids ready," he said sleepily. He left the bed and room and she felt marginally better.

After one final look at the dark clouds gathering, Beth pulled herself out of bed and ambled into the en-suite. Life in London was slow and steady, her pulse and feet moved at a dawdling plod and her senses felt dulled. She tried to wake them by splashing cold water on her face. In the pristine mirror she saw the tired and drained face of an unfulfilled mother of two.

She showered and dressed, her robotic fingers following the buttons and zips of a work outfit that hadn't worked in half a year. Downstairs she shrugged off breakfast and slouched on the kitchen island staring at their old railway clock. She was certain that its skinniest arm moved a second, then waited several before acknowledging another.

When the clock finally got to eight she kissed the blonde curls and dark silk of her children's heads, as they tucked into bowls of Cheerios.

"Have a good day at school kids," she said.

"We will," said Katy with confidence. "What are we doing this weekend daddy?"

Beth didn't even notice the ease with which this question was aimed at Tom, as though mummy never made decisions like this anymore.

"Well, Auntie Steph's coming round for dinner tonight and…"

"Is she?" Beth's and Katy's words were synchronized, a little and large version of the same person.

"Yup," said Tom. "I'm cooking lasagne."

"Yes!" yelled Katy, clenching a fist next to her Cheerios. "I love your lasagne daddy."

"Can I have mine without…" Miles looked with wide eyes at his father.

"Yes buddy. I'm cooking yours separately without mushrooms."

"Good coz they're like…"

"Snails without homes," said Katy rolling her eyes.

Miles sighed. It was tiresome to always have someone finish his sentences. Beth watched as Tom ruffled his son's blonde curls and kissed his forehead. She felt like an outsider watching through a window.

She grabbed her Mulberry handbag and laptop case.

"I'm off," she said.

"Have a good day sweetheart," said Tom. He held her by the shoulders and kissed her on the lips. Her body rose and tensed and then she was out the door, along the hallway, out of the house and immediately happier. Not happy, but happier.

She wandered in the direction of South Kensington tube station. Sometimes she would actually take the tube, but more often than not she did what she was doing today and perched on a bench on Exhibition Road. Here she watched the hunched suits and stern faces that marched past to begin their workdays. She changed her Gucci heels for the running shoes stuffed into her handbag, and wandered up to Hyde Park. She had an eight-hour workday to fill, and she'd start it with a wander around the Serpentine and a coffee by the water. Wandering and caffeine made her feel more like Maria.

After a few hours spent in the fresh air, she walked to the National Gallery. The Tate, the Courthauld and the National were her favourite places to chase away hours, and despite their distance from Hyde Park she had time on her hands and rubber under foot, so always plodded across the Capital. The little lady in the smart business suit and Nike trainers was dressed like a person in a rush, but walked as though she had all the time in the world.

Beth went immediately to see Velasquez' *Rokeby Venus* and felt an immediate warmth, the only warmth she ever felt in London now. Art, particularly Spanish, both fired and calmed her. The fire was sparked by feeling immediately closer to the excitement of Maria's life. The calm came about from feeling small and insignificant in front of masterpieces that had inspired centuries of reverence. There were bigger things than her and the mess she was in, there was art, there was history, there was beauty.

She sat down on the polished bench in the empty gallery. She had sat on this very same spot numerous times as a student. Back then she could appreciate the simple and timeless beauty of paint on canvas, and could spend hours gazing into centuries-old images. And now she could appreciate it once more. It felt good to connect with the younger Beth, she was much happier with her student self. Her younger self loved simple pleasures: art and music, the feel of the sun and the smell of the sea.

She looked into the mirror that Cupid held for Venus and saw, not Venus but her own younger self, a girl infatuated with the ideas of love and beauty. And what was wrong with that? Of course, the issue had been her family; rich, pretentious and materialistic. She had a role to play: that of diplomat's daughter. But then Tom had appeared and, like Venus' Cupid, he had held up a mirror and shown Beth who she really was. And Tom was love, and Tom was beauty, and Tom was true. Beth's eyes filled with tears and, when someone entered the gallery, she put her head into her hands to hide them. She breathed slowly. What had happened to Tom? The love of her life. Tom had morphed into Jim, it had been a slow process, so slow that Beth hadn't realized it was happening until it was too late and her role had become one of pretention and diplomacy once more.

The footsteps departed and she stood, stepped closer to the painting and gazed into the oil brushstrokes that made up Venus' skin. She focused on an individual streak of paint, as fine as a split hair. She then stepped back from the painting and the brushstroke was lost. She stood on the other side of the hall and smiled at the painting. Her life was as fine and anonymous as that brushstroke and, as long as no one looked closely, her love could endure.

Outside the National she checked her watch and happily acknowledged that over two hours had passed in the gallery. She walked to the expensive gym where she and Tom shared a couple's membership. It was always dead in the afternoons so she could relax in the knowledge that no familiar faces would question her daytime workout. She exercised and gave her mind a holiday by watching daytime quiz shows. She then showered and took her time to prepare her face and hair in the same style that she had that morning.

She walked home from the gym, averting her eyes from a bus shelter than made her feel uncomfortable. A few months back when her heart was still full of guilt, she stood weeping here, at the sight of an advertisement for toothpaste. An elderly lady selling the Big Issue asked if she was OK, but Beth couldn't get any words out, and ran away from the lady and the white smiles of the beautiful family in the ad. The family was still sparkling at the bus stop and despite their attempts she managed to ignore them.

She walked slowly to ensure she would miss Miles' and Katy's bedtime. Bathing, reading stories to, and tucking up her children, were too difficult. The less time she spent with them, the less guilt she felt.

When she turned her key in the lock she heard gleeful shouts from beyond.

"Mummy's home! Mummy's home!"

There was a nostalgic swelling in her chest as she heard the joy in her children's voices, but her overarching feeling was one of dread. She had hoped they'd be in bed already.

She put her shoes in the shoe cupboard and hung up her jacket. The shouting continued.

"Can we eat now daddy. Please can we eat?"

Damn, Beth remembered. Steph was coming round for dinner that night. She hadn't seen her best friend for months and wasn't mentally prepared for it. At least the kids were staying up, that would act as some distraction and she could always feign a headache and aim for an early night. She took a mighty breath outside the lounge door.

"Steph!" she screamed in the way a best friend should scream after a long absence.

"Beth! So good to see you."

They hugged tightly then parted to get a look at each other. Beth tried to hold her friend's stare with a smile.

"Wow, you look great," said Steph, scanning every inch of her face. "Really, you look fantastic. You have some real colour." Steph caressed Beth's face fondly and Beth's colour deepened.

"What colour Auntie Steph?" asked Miles. "What colour does mummy have? Is it green? Coz that's my favourite."

Everybody looked at Miles and laughed.

"No, sweetie. I just mean... she looks healthy and tanned."

"Mummy's always tanned," said Katy. "It's because grandma's Columbian, and mummy's half Columbian and I'm a quarter Columbian."

Steph nodded, impressed at Katy's knowledge.

"And what am I?" asked Miles.

Katy looked at her brother, pulled one of his blonde ringlets to its full length and said in all seriousness, "adopted?"

The adults muffled their laughs and, although Miles had no idea what adopted meant, he didn't like the sound of it and so started an argument with his sister.

"Try a glass of this sweetheart," said Tom. "It's a 2002 Burgundy, very special." Beth took the glass and a few sips. It was good wine, but she preferred the bad stuff now.

"Very special," she repeated.

Katy and Miles continued to argue until dinner was served and Miles' mouth was filled with Lasagne.

"Mummy," Katy said turning to Beth. "Auntie Steph's got a boyfriend." Katy's eyes were wide with scandal and Beth couldn't help but laugh, especially when Miles started chanting "Auntie Steph's got a boyfriend, Auntie Steph's got a boyfriend," while banging his cutlery on the table.

Tom laughed too. "It certainly seems that way, from what I can gather she normally only uses men for DIY or plumbing." He turned to his wife. "But this one gets to take her away for the weekend."

Steph shrugged. "Well, at least I don't have to DIY my own plumbing anymore."

Beth and Tom sniggered and the kids looked confused. It dawned on Beth that she was actually enjoying herself.

"So where's he taking you?" asked Beth, as she separated the layers of lasagne on her plate, a childhood habit that she had recently taken up again.

"Barcelona," said Steph.

Beth looked up immediately. "Why?" she said loudly. Tom and Steph looked at her in surprise.

"Why not?"

"Well, I mean." Beth gulped and returned to the architecture on her plate. "Why particularly Barcelona? Why did he choose that city?"

Steph took a huge mouthful of food, and nodded until she finished it. For someone as glamorous as she looks, it was always a shock to see that she ate like a trucker.

"Sebastian used to work in Barcelona, he has lots of friends there, knows some cool places. And there's some kind of art festival going on, lots of exhibitions, local artists, that kind of shit." Both kids looked at their father wide-eyed. Steph pulled an apologetic expression and shrugged. "Should be fun."

Beth and Katy both started talking at the same time, but Katy's voice drowned out her mother's.

"Sebastian! Yuck. There's a boy in my class called Sebastian, he has freckles and smells like poo."

"Well, I'm pretty sure it's a different Sebastian," said Tom. "Unless..." he turned to Steph with a mischievous smile. "Does yours have freckles and smell like poo?"

Miles and Katy looked to Steph, awaiting her answer, and Steph put on a thinking face. "Well, he might have a few freckles." She drummed her perfectly painted red fingernails on the table. "But what does he smell of..."

318

Katy leant in closer.

Beth wasn't in the mood for friends, games, or waiting to ask her question a second time.

"When are you going?" Her question had some force to it, and Steph stopped drumming the table and turned to her friend.

"Thursday till Sunday." She cocked her head quizzically and Beth retreated to her dinner, she forced herself to eat a few forkfuls, so her mouth couldn't say anything that might incriminate her. Her heart was pounding and she was glad of Miles who diverted the attention of the table.

"Auntie Steph, what *does* your boyfriend smell like?"

Beth abandoned the conversation and focused on what Steph's last words meant for her. Her best friend would be in the same city as Maria next Thursday and Friday, with a man who had friends there and intended to take her to see some local art. Was it a big enough city for Steph and Sebastian and Maria and Angelo not to meet? Could she take that risk?

She looked at Steph. She had shared so much with this woman over nearly twenty years of friendship, but she couldn't share this. She wasn't ready to let Maria go, leave her to die, and she knew that was exactly what Steph would force her to do. Steph was immensely loyal, and with only one sister remaining of her own family she had made Beth's family her own. She wouldn't understand what Beth had done, was still doing, and just the thought of bumping into Steph in Barcelona was making it difficult for Beth to breathe. What would she say to Steph, what would she say to Angelo? She knew how important the exhibition was to him and she'd promised she'd be there. He wouldn't forgive her. Her breathing became even more unsteady. Is this where it ended?

"You OK sweetheart?" asked Tom, touching her arm lightly. His touch made her feel sick and she pushed her chair back.

"Sorry, must have been something I had for lunch," she shouted over her shoulder as she ran from the room. She raced to the upstairs bathroom, trying to get as much space between herself and her family as possible. Sat in front of them at the dining table, her lies weighed heavily on her, but up here, sat on the floor with her eyes shut and her head against the cold tiles, the weight began to lift. She tried to immerse herself entirely in the darkness behind her eyes. She wished it would swallow her up.

17:55, Monday April 29th, 2013
14 Carrer Lleo, Al Raval, Barcelona

Angelo was on a high for the whole of April, but highs only exist in contrast to lows, and Angelo's contrast soon emerged.
"I can't come to the exhibition," her voice said down the line.
"What? Why not?" Angelo was confused.
"I'm not coming to Barcelona."
Angelo and his empty studio waited for more, but she said nothing.
"What are you talking about?"
"Angelo, I can't come to Barcelona this week. The magazine - *Vamos Madrid*, they've asked me to work on a special article. A late article."
Angelo stared at his phone, not believing what it was saying to him. "Well, tell them that you can't."
"I did, I did *mi amor*. But they said I was their only option, and that if I didn't help them out on this occasion, then they wouldn't hire me again." Maria's voice was quiet, whilst Angelo's was loud.
"Then tell them to fuck off."
"Angelo, I can't. They're my main magazine. I need to do this for them."
He couldn't believe what he was hearing. "No, no you don't. You need to do this for *me*. You need to get on that fucking bus tomorrow, and you need to come here." His voice rose. "You need to show me that I'm more important than some fucking arse-end magazine in Madrid, that treats you like *mierda*. You need to do this, you need to love me, show me that you love me. You need to do things for me, be here for me, be at the exhibition on Friday."
He waited a long time for her response, his heart pounding.
"I can't," is all she said.
"If you can't come to Barcelona Friday, don't bother coming again." He couldn't believe the words coming from his own mouth now. They

were slow and calm, a complete contrast to how he really felt. "I mean it Maria. If I don't see you Friday, I don't want to see you again."

He hung up the phone and took a couple of deep breaths, his mobile hanging limply by his side. Then he looked at it in disbelief and threw it as hard as he could against the window, like a grenade he needed distance from. The single layer of glass smashed and his phone dropped four floors to the road.

21:17, Thursday May 2nd, 2013
El Quadre, Barcelona

Angelo was the only artist present during the hanging of the exhibition. All the others had considered themselves too important for such a menial task and had left their agents to bicker and fight for the best positions. Angelo, in contrast, remained passive, and as a result most of his pieces were relegated to a far corner. When, finally, the curator herded out the agents, turned off the lights and was about to lock up, Angelo swatted at his pockets and gasped.

"My wallet, I left my wallet inside," he told Silvia.

She sighed and held the door open.

"Be quick."

The crowd dispersed and Angelo ducked into the darkness. He raced down the corridor, past the painted list of artists, with his name at the bottom, and into the gallery. He switched on the light and set about rearranging some of the pieces. His name may be bottom of the list but he would make sure his art was top of mind. He replaced a café scene by Pedrosa with an empty theatre by Angelo Octavez, and a seascape by Franco with a starved male nude by Angelo Octavez. He moved the corresponding plaques and stood back to admire his placements. Now his two favourite paintings hung in pride of place under skylights that would flood the theatre and naked man with natural light come tomorrow.

He turned out the light and raced back to Silvia, who stood hand on hip and eyebrow raised in the entrance.

"Found it?" she asked.

"Yes, " he smiled, patting his empty pocket.

18:23, Friday May 3rd, 2013
El Quadre, Barcelona

Angelo arrived on time for the opening and drank four beers, pacing the floorboards, before anyone else arrived. God, he wished Maria was there with him. Had he really meant what he screamed at her? Was it really over? He sincerely hoped not, she was the best thing that had happened to him in a long time. In fact, she was the best thing that had ever happened to him. But she couldn't keep letting him down, if she really loved him she'd commit. If she really loved him, she'd be there tonight. Did she really love him? He distracted himself from this question by counting floorboards.

The flow of afternoon guests was slow, and Angelo had shuffled around and counted 376 floorboards before anyone asked him a question.

"You're Angelo Octavez?" asked a white-haired man with horn-rimmed glasses.

"Yes," said Angelo.

The little eyes behind the spectacles looked him up and down and offered his hand with a smile. "I'm Hernan Pedrosa."

"Pedrosa!" Angelo's raised voice prompted stares from the other visitors and a wider smile from the man in front of him. Angelo shook the man's hand with energy.

"It's a real pleasure, a real pleasure," he said. "I've followed your work for years. The series of *La dansa* is one of my favourites and the simplicity of your lines in *El Pastor* inspired me hugely in the 90's." Angelo continued to talk, without pausing for air, about the influence this man has had on him. He then led Pedrosa a few steps to his own art, which showed a sad empty theatre. "I'd love your thoughts on my own work. This was inspired by a trip to the Teatre Romea to see the matinee of a classic Catalan play, I can't remember the name, but the actors were as bored as the audience…" Angelo cast a glance from the empty theatre to the man he was addressing and immediately stopped talking. Pedrosa held an expression of complete absorption but he was looking at the artist, not the art.

"You have the eyes of your mother," he said.

Angelo took a breath. "You knew my mother?"

He nodded. "I knew her very well. *Very* well."

Angelo didn't like the tone of Pedrosa's voice or the direction he was taking the conversation.

"What do you think of my painting?" he asked.

Pedrosa kept his eyes on Angelo. "Fine," he said. He continued to stare at Angelo, through his round little lenses as though examining an insect through a microscope. Then he glanced quickly at Angelo's painting. "Though you'll need to cheer up the colours if anyone's going to buy it."

Just then Silvia's voice rang out through the gallery.

"Hernan, Hernan! Come tell us the story behind this painting, Señor Pinyol may just reach for his wallet!"

Pedrosa took one last look at Angelo before shuffling off, on the scent of a sale. Angelo looked after him and watched as the little man took on a new walk and a new life as he approached Silvia's circle of investors. At the same time Angelo also took on a new walk and a new life. Rather than shuffling in circles and counting floorboards, he strode up and down the gallery with clenched fists. What a sellout Pedrosa turned out to be! He didn't care about art, he just cared about making sales. For years, Angelo had followed and revered his work, and now in person, he turned out to be a money-hungry, rude asshole. Angelo dug his fingernails into his palms, if there had been brushes to hand they would have been snapped in two. As Angelo marched past the group of suits, silk and scent that surrounded Pedrosa he heard the artist's voice.

"No, I don't see any new talent in Barcelona." Angelo came to a halt outside the circle to listen further. "The era of Catalan creativity has faded fast, and is all but over."

"What about Angelo Octavez?" Angelo recognized the voice of Teresa and, for once, was glad to hear it.

"Who?" said Pedrosa. There were titters from the group.

"Angelo Octavez," said Teresa. "The man you were just talking to."

"Oh, him." There was a pause. "I used to know his mother. She was *something* to look at, but completely devoid of talent." There was another pause in which Angelo grew a few inches taller and a few degrees hotter. "Much like Octavez's paintings," said Pedrosa. His mouth was just opening, to join the chuckles of those around him, when

Angelo's fist struck the side of his face. Everyone who had formed a tight and clamourous circle around the artist took a few steps back.

"Don't you fucking dare talk about me or my mother like that," shouted Angelo.

Pedrosa had his hand on his cheek, and his mouth and eyes were wide in disbelief.

"Who the hell do you think you are?" he said in a low voice.

"I'm Angelo Octavez!" shouted Angelo. "Angelo Octavez!"

Angelo felt two sets of hands gripping his shoulders, leading him backwards and away from the little man with the white hair and red cheek.

"You're nobody," said Pedrosa. Angelo went to launch himself at the man again and Pedrosa cowered beneath his hands.

"Keep him away from me!" he begged in a child's voice.

The strong arms holding Angelo submitted to the request and Angelo could only squirm futilely. "You piece of shit! You fucking piece of shit," he screamed. "My mother wouldn't have wasted her time on you, and neither will I."

"Hold him," instructed Pedrosa. He then took a few steps closer and his mouth stretched into a smile. "You're nothing Angelo Octavez, and you never will be."

Angelo launched a ball of spit at the insult and it hit the left shoulder of Pedrosa's linen suit.

"Take him outside," demanded Silvia. "And when you come back in take down all of Angelo's work and remove his name from the list, he will *not* be exhibiting."

"But Silvia, please. He's just a passionate artist who deserves…" Angelo heard Teresa's pleas as he was led towards the exit. As the two sets of arms pushed the dejected body of Angelo out the door, Pedrosa's words rang out in the gallery space once more, "You're nothing Angelo Octavez, nothing!"

He dusted himself off and took deep breaths. He should have been overjoyed when Maria raced up to him, her arms outstretched.

"I'm here *mi amor*. I made it! I'm here."

But he walked on with no direction and, rather than her voice, all he could hear were those words.

"You're nothing Angelo Octavez, nothing!"

And into the future...

12:52, Saturday March 22nd, 2014
Apartamentos el Diamont, Barcelona

So it turns out everyone does have a price. And Angelo's was 10 million euros. He'd said it in jest; a figure so remote he had no idea how to even write it down. It was a number beyond his comprehension and beyond his wildest dreams, but now he was living within it. Angelo Octavez is not nothing anymore.

He stands at the window and looks at the view. The green sea sparkles as its waves are caught by the sun. There is a balcony beyond the window but for some reason Angelo prefers to look at the view through glass. Perhaps it adds a dimension of fiction to the seascape, as though he is looking at a picture in a frame. Perhaps it reminds him of his trusty old window back in Al Raval. He feels hands on his back and he turns to face Aurora.

"Day-dreaming again *mi amor*?" She smiles up at him. "I thought we could go for lunch at *Vidal's*, that new restaurant on the harbour?"

"Sure."

"Then perhaps we could go shopping? Buy some things to liven this place up?" She looks around at the white walls, so imposing and brilliant that they hurt your eyes in the midday sun.

Angelo likes the walls as they are. Stark and empty except for one picture.

"Do we need to make a reservation for lunch?" he asks.

She smiles at him, it's an expression that hides a giggle. He still doesn't understand how renowned he is in the city now.

"Of course not. You don't need to make a reservation *anywhere*."

Angelo watches Aurora trot off to the dressing room where she will spend the next hour beautifying her perfect self, and choosing clothes for Angelo.

Aurora left Xavier for Angelo about four months ago. He took her with open arms and hasn't seen Xavier since. He misses him sometimes but his friend reminds him too much of his past, and he was happy to trade the company of old Xavier for new Aurora. He doesn't love her, but she fits perfectly into his new lifestyle. She helps cement his new status and helps him forget the old.

Of course, Aurora did remember where she recognized Maria from. She was Beth, the young girl she spent a summer with when Aurora's father was posted to the Chilean embassy in Columbia. The two ten year olds had bonded instantly, and taken advantage of the embassy's soft-hearted chauffeur to ferry them all over Bogota and the local shopping malls. With their long sleek hair and ballerina-like elegance, they were often mistaken for sisters, twins even. They had parted with heavy hearts and promises of life-long friendship, both of which faded within months.

Once Aurora had connected Beth from the embassy with Angelo's dead lover she did some investigation. She discovered that Beth had been living in London and had indeed died in the AS636 disaster, but she also discovered that Angelo was completely unaware of any of this and so kept the news to herself. Angelo was just the type of man she had been looking for, at least he was since the big sale, and she didn't want to risk losing him to this dead woman all over again.

The tiny portrait of his father is all the art that Angelo has left. After the picture of Maria was sold, it was easy to part with the others. Their faces meant nothing to him on their own. Almost half of them went to families of the victims, others went to collectors for higher prices and the remaining 30 or so sit in a permanent collection at the Thyssen in Madrid.

Maria wasn't who she said she was, he knows that now. She told him more lies than truths, and he doesn't even know if her love was a lie or a truth. One thing he will always wonder is whether she was leaving him or joining him. A flight to London, a secret baby and a vacated apartment all point to the same miserable conclusion, but there is still a spark of optimism inside him, and that spark lights up a different possibility.

He walks over to the tiny image of his father. The sad look in his father's eyes reminds Angelo of Maria. Of course, there was the gorgeous glow about her that he captured in his portrait, but since he has been reunited with his father's picture, he realizes that the last few weeks with Maria were with a different woman, a sadder one. Angelo likes to indulge his own sadness by looking at the portrait. One day, like his father, he will be a miserable old man who never knew his child.

Angelo still has more questions than he does answers about Maria, but money, fame and Aurora are great distractions. He was never ambitious, it was just his passion that drove him to paint, he couldn't imagine a day without a brush in hand, and when love and art collided he created a masterpiece. A ten million euro masterpiece.

He doesn't paint anymore, he doesn't feel like it.

16:51, Sunday March 23rd, 2015
32 Stanley Road, Crouch End, London

He promised himself a treat when he finished painting the lounge and so he rolls the green paint over the walls in a hurry. He leaves until last the white space where four pairs of green handprints look to be climbing the wall. He smiles at the memory of the fun afternoon they all had picking the colour and then smearing it all over the wall and each other. He can't bring himself to paint over the family graffiti and so paints a haphazard circle around it and leaves it. He washes the green from his hands, climbs the stairs and then wrestles with the attic ladder. He likes the house, of course the size has taken some getting used to, and there's a lot of work to be done, but it already feels like a happy place. And the attic is an especially happy place for him.

He picks up his guitar and hammers out some familiar riffs, tapping his paint-spattered Converse All Stars on the cheap MDF flooring. He restrung and tuned the guitar last night and it sounds great. He looks out of the dusty attic window and sees the piercing blue of a spring afternoon. A thought enters his mind, and he stops playing so that he can indulge it, not lose it to his guitar. He feels happy; truly happy. He gave up his highly-paid job, sold his central London home, spent most of his savings, and is a widower, but despite all this he is happier than he has been in a long time. He laughs and turns his head to look at Beth. Her eyes shine at him, and he thinks she might be laughing also.

He turns to face her and gets comfortable on the old dining chair left by the previous owners. Five months ago when he packed up everything he owned, he opened his guitar case for the first time in fifteen years, and from that moment on the case has remained empty.

He has sung the song to her a few times since then. Always when they are alone.

"I gave this up for you Beth, I thought it was the only way to be with you, but I should have had more faith in you. I should have known you'd stick with me, with the old Tom no matter what. I'm sorry I changed, I'm sorry I became the cardboard cutout of everything that meant nothing. I took your love for granted. I didn't even notice when you were unhappy." He swallows. "Not until you'd gone. I won't lose myself again Beth, I promise. And I'm saving up again." He smiles. "To buy the Gibson." He gestures into the corner where the bottle sits. "But for now, I just have my old Fender Strat and all my old songs."

His fingers flitter along the strings of his guitar and he plays a couple of comfortable classics.

He hears the front door open then slam, and the frantic chattering of his two children.

"We're home!" shouts Steph, as if Tom could have missed their noisy entrance.

"I'm up here," he shouts back. He thinks of climbing down from the attic, he doesn't want Steph to think he has been up here all afternoon with his guitar and dead wife. But then he changes his mind, he has nothing to feel guilty about.

The ladder creaks as Steph climbs it, he sees her perfect blonde bob and wide smile emerge from the floor. She stops with half her body in and half out of the attic.

"Penny for your thoughts?" she asks.

He shakes his head. "All pennies go towards my new guitar, remember?" He nods towards the bottle in the far corner.

"Fine," she says. She enters the attic, fishes a coin from her jeans and ducks her head in the beamed corner to make her donation. "Your thoughts generally aren't worth a penny anyway."

"They're not?"

She approaches him and sits on his knee. He moves his guitar to the floor and puts his arms around her.

"No, they're normally full of smut."

He laughs and tips his head onto her shoulder.

"What can I say? You bring out the worst in me."

They look into each other's eyes for a few moments.

"And the best," she says. They kiss and Steph runs her hands through his curls. He begins to manoeuvre her into a straddle position when there is a little call from below.

"Can we come up daddy?"

Tom and Steph smile at each other. Their kisses will save.

"Of course!" Tom goes over to the hole in the floor, squats and lowers his arms. He grips hands with Katy's and pulls her up into the attic.

"One monkey," he says.

He repeats the same manoeuvre for Miles. "Two monkey."

"Sing us a song daddy?" pleads Miles, picking up the guitar and giving it to his father. He is beginning to get tall now, his dumpy little figure is lengthening and his chubby cheeks narrowing, but his halo of curls keep him looking cherubic.

"What do you want to hear buddy?" asks Tom, knowing full well that Miles will dance to anything.

"Something mummy liked," says Katy. Steph and Tom look at her in surprise, she has never asked this before.

"OK sweetie," says Tom. "Well, mummy liked lots of great music."

"Something special," says Katy. "Something she *really* liked."

Tom looks to the floor. There is only one song going through his head right now, the song he first sang to Beth when he fell in love with her and the song he should have sung every night to her since. It feels like a guilty secret.

Steph squeezes his shoulder. "Sing it," she says.

"Sing what?" he asks, turning to her.

"The song you hum to yourself when you've been up here." She smiles at him, a gentle smile that has more love than sadness inside of it. He stammers to say something, but he doesn't quite know what. She leans down to his ear.

"It's alright Tom. You can play it. We all loved her."

"I don't think I can, erm, remember it," he says, not able to look at Steph.

"Sure you do." She rests her hand on his shoulder.

"Come on daddy!" shouts Miles. He is standing on one foot, ready to dance.

Tom takes a deep breath and closes his eyes. He hums the chorus to himself a few times, concentrating on the melody and where it takes his hands. His left hand finds the chords and moves over them silently as he hums. Then, after a few tentative moments, he looks at Steph, smiles and plays *Love Light*. Only a few chords in and his fingers feel at home, they know exactly where they are and it's nice to be back. When he begins to sing, Miles jumps from foot to foot and twirls around; his movements have absolutely no connection with the song and Steph laughs. She takes Katy by the hands and the two of them spin and shuffle around the attic. By the third chorus, both kids and Steph join Tom in singing.

"Love Light
A sparkle and glow
Never believed in first sight
Now I know"

By the last chord Miles has spun himself into exhaustion and throws himself onto the torn leather sofa beneath the skylight. Katy and Steph perform a curtsy, as all great ballerinas know how, and join Miles on the sofa. The attic is silent now, except for heavy breathing.

"Daddy, I really like that song," says Katy. "Is it by one of those old bands you like? The Rolling Stones?"

Tom beams at her. "No sweetie, it's by me, I wrote it for your mummy."

She gasps. "Really daddy? Did you really write it and make it all by yourself?"

He smiles.

"You could be a pop star!" shouts Miles. Katy nods in agreement. "Like Justin Bieber."

They all laugh. "I don't want to be a pop star," says Tom. He looks at his family assembled under the pink light of the setting sun. He casts a glance at the portrait.

"I'm happy just the way I am."

Everyone does have a price, and Tom is glad that Angelo's was so high.